The Ivory Child

The Ivory Child
H. Rider Haggard

MINT EDITIONS

The Ivory Child was first published in 1916.

This edition published by Mint Editions 2021.

ISBN 9781513277677 | E-ISBN 9781513278087

Published by Mint Editions®

MINT
EDITIONS
minteditionbooks.com

Publishing Director: Jennifer Newens
Design & Production: Rachel Lopez Metzger
Project Manager: Micaela Clark
Typesetting: Westchester Publishing Services

Contents

I

ALLAN GIVES A SHOOTING LESSON

Now I, Allan Quatermain, come to the story of what was, perhaps, one of the strangest of all the adventures which have befallen me in the course of a life that so far can scarcely be called tame or humdrum.

Amongst many other things it tells of the war against the Black Kendah people and the dead of Jana, their elephant god. Often since then I have wondered if this creature was or was not anything more than a mere gigantic beast of the forest. It seems improbable, even impossible, but the reader of future days may judge of this matter for himself.

Also he can form his opinion as to the religion of the White Kendah and their pretensions to a certain degree of magical skill. Of this magic I will make only one remark: If it existed at all, it was by no means infallible. To take a single instance, Harût and Marût were convinced by divination that I, and I only, could kill Jana, which was why they invited me to Kendahland. Yet in the end it was Hans who killed him. Jana nearly killed me!

Now to my tale.

In another history, called "The Holy Flower," I have told how I came to England with a young gentleman of the name of Scroope, partly to see him safely home after a hunting accident, and partly to try to dispose of a unique orchid for a friend of mine called Brother John by the white people, and Dogeetah by the natives, who was popularly supposed to be mad, but, in fact, was very sane indeed. So sane was he that he pursued what seemed to be an absolutely desperate quest for over twenty years, until, with some humble assistance on my part, he brought it to a curiously successful issue. But all this tale is told in "The Holy Flower," and I only allude to it here, that is at present, to explain how I came to be in England.

While in this country I stayed for a few days with Scroope, or, rather, with his fiancée and her people, at a fine house in Essex. (I called it Essex to avoid the place being identified, but really it was one of the neighbouring counties.) During my visit I was taken to see a much finer place, a splendid old castle with brick gateway towers, that had been wonderfully well restored and turned into a most luxurious modern dwelling. Let us call it "Ragnall," the seat of a baron of that name.

I had heard a good deal about Lord Ragnall, who, according to all accounts, seemed a kind of Admirable Crichton. He was said to be wonderfully handsome, a great scholar—he had taken a double first at college; a great athlete—he had been captain of the Oxford boat at the University race; a very promising speaker who had already made his mark in the House of Lords; a sportsman who had shot tigers and other large game in India; a poet who had published a successful volume of verse under a pseudonym; a good solider until he left the Service; and lastly, a man of enormous wealth, owning, in addition to his estates, several coal mines and an entire town in the north of England.

"Dear me!" I said when the list was finished, "he seems to have been born with a whole case of gold spoons in his mouth. I hope one of them will not choke him," adding: "Perhaps he will be unlucky in love."

"That's just where he is most lucky of all," answered the young lady to whom I was talking—it was Scroope's fiancée, Miss Manners—"for he is engaged to a lady that, I am told, is the loveliest, sweetest, cleverest girl in all England, and they absolutely adore each other."

"Dear me!" I repeated. "I wonder what Fate *has* got up its sleeve for Lord Ragnall and his perfect lady-love?"

I was doomed to find out one day.

So it came about that when, on the following morning, I was asked if I would like to see the wonders of Ragnall Castle, I answered "Yes." Really, however, I wanted to have a look at Lord Ragnall himself, if possible, for the account of his many perfections had impressed the imagination of a poor colonist like myself, who had never found an opportunity of setting his eyes upon a kind of human angel. Human devils I had met in plenty, but never a single angel—at least, of the male sex. Also there was always the possibility that I might get a glimpse of the still more angelic lady to whom he was engaged, whose name, I understood, was the Hon. Miss Holmes. So I said that nothing would please me more than to see this castle.

Thither we drove accordingly through the fine, frosty air, for the month was December. On reaching the castle, Mr. Scroope was told that Lord Ragnall, whom he knew well, was out shooting somewhere in the park, but that, of course, he could show his friend over the place. So we went in, the three of us, for Miss Manners, to whom Scroope was to be married very shortly, had driven us over in her pony carriage. The porter at the gateway towers took us to the main door of the castle and handed us over to another man, whom he addressed as Mr. Savage, whispering to me that he was his lordship's personal attendant.

I remember the name, because it seemed to me that I had never seen anyone who looked much less savage. In truth, his appearance was that of a duke in disguise, as I imagine dukes to be, for I never set eyes on one. His dress—he wore a black morning cut-away coat—was faultless. His manners were exquisite, polite to the verge of irony, but with a hint of haughty pride in the background. He was handsome also, with a fine nose and a hawk-like eye, while a touch of baldness added to the general effect. His age may have been anything between thirty-five and forty, and the way he deprived me of my hat and stick, to which I strove to cling, showed, I thought, resolution of character. Probably, I reflected to myself, he considers me an unusual sort of person who might damage the pictures and other objects of art with the stick, and not seeing his way how to ask me to give it up without suggesting suspicion, has hit upon the expedient of taking my hat also.

In after days Mr. Samuel Savage informed me that I was quite right in this surmise. He said he thought that, judging from my somewhat unconventional appearance, I might be one of the dangerous class of whom he had been reading in the papers, namely, a "hanarchist." I write the word as he pronounced it, for here comes the curious thing. This man, so flawless, so well instructed in some respects, had a fault which gave everything away. His h's were uncertain. Three of them would come quite right, but the fourth, let us say, would be conspicuous either by its utter absence or by its unwanted appearance. He could speak, when describing the Ragnall pictures, in rotund and flowing periods that would scarcely have disgraced the pen of Gibbon. Then suddenly that "h" would appear or disappear, and the illusion was over. It was like a sudden shock of cold water down the back. I never discovered the origin of his family; it was a matter of which he did not speak, perhaps because he was vague about it himself; but if an earl of Norman blood had married a handsome Cockney kitchenmaid of native ability, I can quite imagine that Samuel Savage might have been a child of the union. For the rest he was a good man and a faithful one, for whom I have a high respect.

On this occasion he conducted us round the castle, or, rather, its more public rooms, showing us many treasures and, I should think, at least two hundred pictures by eminent and departed artists, which gave him an opportunity of exhibiting a peculiar, if somewhat erratic, knowledge of history. To tell the truth, I began to wish that it were a little less full in detail, since on a December day those large apartments felt uncommonly cold. Scroope and Miss Manners seemed to keep warm, perhaps with the inward fires of mutual admiration, but as I had no one to admire except Mr. Savage, a temperature of about 35 degrees produced its natural effect upon me.

At length we took a short cut from the large to the little gallery through a warmed and comfortable room, which I understood was Lord Ragnall's study. Halting for a moment by one of the fires, I observed a picture on the wall, over which a curtain was drawn, and asked Mr. Savage what it might be.

"That, sir," he replied with a kind of haughty reserve, "is the portrait of her future ladyship, which his lordship keeps for his private heye."

Miss Manners sniggered, and I said:

"Oh, thank you. What an ill-omened kind of thing to do!"

Then, observing through an open door the hall in which my hat had been taken from me, I lingered and as the others vanished in the little gallery, slipped into it, recovered my belongings, and passed out to the garden, purposing to walk there till I was warm again and Scroope reappeared. While I marched up and down a terrace, on which, I remember, several very cold-looking peacocks were seated, like conscientious birds that knew it was their duty to be ornamental, however low the temperature, I heard some shots fired, apparently in a clump of ilex oaks which grew about five hundred yards away, and reflected to myself that they seemed to be those of a small rifle, not of a shotgun.

My curiosity being excited as to what was to be an almost professional matter, I walked towards the grove, making a circuit through a shrubbery. At length I found myself near to the edge of a glade, and perceived, standing behind the shelter of a magnificent ilex, two men. One of these was a young keeper, and the other, from his appearance, I felt sure must be Lord Ragnall himself. Certainly he was a splendid-looking man, very tall, very broad, very handsome, with a peaked beard, a kind and charming face, and large dark eyes. He wore a cloak upon his shoulders, which was thrown back from over a velvet coat, and, except for the light double-barrelled rifle in his hand, looked exactly like a picture by Van Dyck which Mr. Savage had just informed me was that of one of his lordship's ancestors of the time of Charles I.

Standing behind another oak, I observed that he was trying to shoot wood-pigeons as they descended to feed upon the acorns, for which the hard weather had made them greedy. From time to time these beautiful blue birds appeared and hovered a moment before they settled, whereon the sportsman fired and—they flew away. *Bang! Bang!* went the double-barrelled rifle, and off fled the pigeon.

"Damn!" said the sportsman in a pleasant, laughing voice; "that's the twelfth I have missed, Charles."

"You hit his tail, my lord. I saw a feather come out. But, my lord, as I told you, there ain't no man living what can kill pigeons on the wing with a bullet, even when they seem to sit still in the air."

"I have heard of one, Charles. Mr. Scroope has a friend from Africa staying with him who, he swears, could knock over four out of six."

"Then, my lord, Mr. Scroope has a friend what lies," replied Charles as he handed him the second rifle.

This was too much for me. I stepped forward, raising my hat politely, and said:

"Sir, forgive me for interrupting you, but you are not shooting at those wood-pigeons in the right way. Although they seem to hover just before they settle, they are dropping much faster than you think. Your keeper was mistaken when he said that you knocked a feather out of the tail of that last bird at which you fired two barrels. In both cases you shot at least a foot above it, and what fell was a leaf from the ilex tree."

There was a moment's silence, which was broken by Charles, who exclaimed in a thick voice:

"Well, of all the cheek!"

Lord Ragnall, however, for it was he, looked first angry and then amused.

"Sir," he said, "I thank you for your advice, which no doubt is excellent, for it is certainly true that I have missed every pigeon which I tried to shoot with these confounded little rifles. But if you could demonstrate in practice what you so kindly set out in precept, the value of your counsel would be enhanced."

Thus he spoke, mimicking, I have no doubt (for he had a sense of humour), the manner of my address, which nervousness had made somewhat pompous.

"Give me the rifle," I answered, taking off my greatcoat.

He handed it me with a bow.

"Mind what you are about," growled Charles. "That there thing is full cocked and 'air-triggered."

I withered, or, rather, tried to wither him with a glance, but this unbelieving keeper only stared back at me with insolence in his round and bird-like eyes. Never before had I felt quite so angry with a menial. Then a horrible doubt struck me. Supposing I should miss! I knew very little of the manner of flight of English wood-pigeons, which are not difficult to miss with a bullet, and nothing at all of these particular rifles, though a glance at them showed me that they were exquisite weapons of their sort and by a great maker. If I muffed the thing now, how should I bear the scorn of Charles and the polite amusement of his noble master? Almost I prayed that no more pigeons would put in an appearance, and thus that the issue of my supposed skill might be left in doubt.

But this was not to be. These birds came from far in ones or twos to search for their favourite food, and the fact that others had been scared away did not cause them to cease from coming. Presently I heard Charles mutter:

"Now, then, look out, guv'nor. Here's your chance of teaching his lordship how to do it, though he does happen to be the best shot in these counties."

While he spoke two pigeons appeared, one a little behind the other, coming down very straight. As they reached the opening in the ilex grove they hovered, preparing to alight, for of us they could see nothing, one at a distance of about fifty and the other of, say, seventy yards away. I took the nearest, got on to it, allowing for the drop and the angle, and touched the trigger of the rifle, which fell to my shoulder very sweetly. The bullet struck that pigeon on the crop, out of which fell a shower of acorns that it had been eating, as it sank to the ground stone dead. Number two pigeon, realizing danger, began to mount upwards almost straight. I fired the second barrel, and by good luck shot its head off. Then I snatched the other rifle, which Charles had been loading automatically, from his outstretched hand, for at that moment I saw two more pigeons coming. At the first I risked a difficult shot and hit it far back, knocking out its tail, but bringing it, still fluttering, to the ground. The other, too, I covered, but when I touched the trigger there was a click, no more.

This was my opportunity of coming even with Charles, and I availed myself of it.

"Young man," I said, while he gaped at me open-mouthed, "you should learn to be careful with rifles, which are dangerous weapons. If you give one to a shooter that is not loaded, it shows that you are capable of anything."

Then I turned, and addressing Lord Ragnall, added:

"I must apologize for that third shot of mine, which was infamous, for I committed a similar fault to that against which I warned you, sir, and did not fire far enough ahead. However, it may serve to show your attendant the difference between the tail of a pigeon and an oak leaf," and I pointed to one of the feathers of the poor bird, which was still drifting to the ground.

"Well, if this here snipe of a chap ain't the devil in boots!" exclaimed Charles to himself.

But his master cut him short with a look, then lifted his hat to me and said:

"Sir, the practice much surpasses the precept, which is unusual. I congratulate you upon a skill that almost partakes of the marvellous, unless, indeed, chance—" And he stopped.

"It is natural that you should think so," I replied; "but if more pigeons come, and Mr. Charles will make sure that he loads the rifle, I hope to undeceive you."

At this moment, however, a loud shout from Scroope, who was looking for me, reinforced by a shrill cry uttered by Miss Manners, banished every pigeon within half a mile, a fact of which I was not sorry, since who knows whether I should have it all, or any, of the next three birds?

"I think my friends are calling me, so I will bid you good morning," I said awkwardly.

"One moment, sir," he exclaimed. "Might I first ask you your name? Mine is Ragnall—Lord Ragnall."

"And mine is Allan Quatermain," I said.

"Oh!" he answered, "that explains matters. Charles, this is Mr. Scroope's friend, the gentleman that you said—exaggerated. I think you had better apologize."

But Charles was gone, to pick up the pigeons, I suppose.

At this moment Scroope and the young lady appeared, having heard our voices, and a general explanation ensued.

"Mr. Quatermain has been giving me a lesson in shooting pigeons on the wing with a small-bore rifle," said Lord Ragnall, pointing to the dead birds that still lay upon the ground.

"He is competent to do that," said Scroope.

"Painfully competent," replied his lordship. "If you don't believe me, ask the under-keeper."

"It is the only thing I can do," I explained modestly. "Rifle-shooting is my trade, and I have made a habit of practising at birds on the wing with ball. I have no doubt that with a shot-gun your lordship would leave me nowhere, for that is a game at which I have had little practice, except when shooting for the pot in Africa."

"Yes," interrupted Scroope, "you wouldn't have any chance at that, Allan, against one of the finest shots in England."

"I'm not so sure," said Lord Ragnall, laughing pleasantly. "I have an idea that Mr. Quatermain is full of surprises. However, with his leave, we'll see. If you have a day to spare, Mr. Quatermain, we are going to shoot through the home coverts to-morrow, which haven't been touched till now, and I hope you will join us."

"It is most kind of you, but that is impossible," I answered with firmness. "I have no gun here."

"Oh, never mind that, Mr. Quatermain. I have a pair of breech-loaders"—these were new things at that date—"which have been sent down to me to try. I am going to return them, because they are much too short in the stock for me. I think they would just suit you, and you are quite welcome to the use of them."

Again I excused myself, guessing that the discomfited Charles would put all sorts of stories about concerning me, and not wishing to look foolish before a party of grand strangers, no doubt chosen for their skill at this particular form of sport.

"Well, Allan," exclaimed Scroope, who always had a talent for saying the wrong thing, "you are quite right not to go into a competition with Lord Ragnall over high pheasants."

I flushed, for there was some truth in his blundering remark, whereon Lord Ragnall said with ready tact:

"I asked Mr. Quatermain to shoot, not to a shooting match, Scroope, and I hope he'll come."

This left me no option, and with a sinking heart I had to accept.

"Sorry I can't ask you too, Scroope," said his lordship, when details had been arranged, "but we can only manage seven guns at this shoot. But will you and Miss Manners come to dine and sleep to-morrow evening? I should like to introduce your future wife to my future wife," he added, colouring a little.

Miss Manners being devoured with curiosity as to the wonderful Miss Holmes, of whom she had heard so much but never actually seen, accepted at once, before her lover could get out a word, whereon Scroope volunteered to bring me over in the morning and load for me. Being possessed by a terror that I should be handed over to the care of the unsympathetic Charles, I replied that I should be very grateful, and so the thing was settled.

On our way home we passed through a country town, of which I forget the name, and the sight of a gunsmith's shop there reminded me that I had no cartridges. So I stopped to order some, as, fortunately, Lord Ragnall had mentioned that the guns he was going to lend me were twelve-bores. The tradesman asked me how many cartridges I wanted, and when I replied "a hundred," stared at me and said:

"If, as I understood, sir, you are going to the big winter shoot at Ragnall to-morrow, you had better make it three hundred and fifty at least. I shall be there to watch, like lots of others, and I expect to see nearly two hundred fired by each gun at the last Lake stand."

"Very well," I answered, fearing to show more ignorance by further discussion. "I will call for the cartridges on my way to-morrow morning. Please load them with three drachms of powder."

"Yes, sir, and an ounce and an eighth of No. 5 shot, sir? That's what all the gentlemen use."

"No," I answered, "No. 3; please be sure as to that. Good evening."

The gunsmith stared at me, and as I left the shop I heard him remark to his assistant:

"That African gent must think he's going out to shoot ostriches with buck shot. I expect he ain't no good, whatever they may say about him."

II

ALLAN MAKES A BET

On the following morning Scroope and I arrived at Castle Ragnall at or about a quarter to ten. On our way we stopped to pick up my three hundred and fifty cartridges. I had to pay something over three solid sovereigns for them, as in those days such things were dear, which showed me that I was not going to get my lesson in English pheasant shooting for nothing. The gunsmith, however, to whom Scroope gave a lift in his cart to the castle, impressed upon me that they were dirt cheap, since he and his assistant had sat up most of the night loading them with my special No. 3 shot.

As I climbed out of the vehicle a splendid-looking and portly person, arrayed in a velvet coat and a scarlet waistcoat, approached with the air of an emperor, followed by an individual in whom I recognized Charles, carrying a gun under each arm.

"That's the head-keeper," whispered Scroope; "mind you treat him respectfully."

Much alarmed, I took off my hat and waited.

"Do I speak to Mr. Allan Quatermain?" said his majesty in a deep and rumbling voice, surveying me the while with a cold and disapproving eye.

I intimated that he did.

"Then, sir," he went on, pausing a little at the "sir," as though he suspected me of being no more an African colleague of his own, "I have been ordered by his lordship to bring you these guns, and I hope, sir, that you will be careful of them, as they are here on sale or return. Charles, explain the working of them there guns to this foreign gentleman, and in doing so keep the muzzles up *or* down. They ain't loaded, it's true, but the example is always useful."

"Thank you, Mr. Keeper," I replied, growing somewhat nettled, "but I think that I am already acquainted with most that there is to learn about guns."

"I am glad to hear it, sir," said his majesty with evident disbelief. "Charles, I understand that Squire Scroope is going to load for the gentleman, which I hope he knows how to do with safety. His lordship's orders are that you accompany them and carry the cartridges. And, Charles, you will please keep count of the number fired and what is killed dead, not reckoning runners. I'm sick of them stories of runners."

These directions were given in a portentous stage aside which we were not supposed to hear. They caused Scroope to snigger and Charles to grin, but in me they raised a feeling of indignation.

I took one of the guns and looked at it. It was a costly and beautifully made weapon of the period, with an under-lever action.

"There's nothing wrong with the gun, sir," rumbled Red Waistcoat. "If you hold it straight it will do the rest. But keep the muzzle up, sir, keep it up, for I know what the bore is without studying the same with my eye. Also perhaps you won't take it amiss if I tell you that here at Ragnall we hates a low pheasant. I mention it because the last gentleman who came from foreign parts—he was French, he was—shot nothing all day but one hen bird sitting just on the top of the brush, two beaters, his lordship's hat, and a starling."

At this point Scroope broke into a roar of idiotic laughter. Charles, from whom Fortune decreed that I was not to escape, after all, turned his back and doubled up as though seized with sudden pain in the stomach, and I grew absolutely furious.

"Confound it, Mr. Keeper," I explained, "what do you mean by lecturing me? Attend to your business, and I'll attend to mine."

At this moment who should appear from behind the angle of some building—we were talking in the stableyard, near the gun-room—but Lord Ragnall himself. I could see that he had overheard the conversation, for he looked angry.

"Jenkins," he said, addressing the keeper, "do what Mr. Quatermain has said and attend to your own business. Perhaps you are not aware that he has shot more lions, elephants, and other big game than you have cats. But, however that may be, it is not your place to try to instruct him or any of my guests. Now go and see to the beaters."

"Beg pardon, my lord," exclaimed Jenkins, his face, that was as florid as his waistcoat, turning quite pale; "no offence meant, my lord, but elephants and lions don't fly, my lord, and those accustomed to such ground varmin are apt to shoot low, my lord. Beaters all ready at the Hunt Copse, my lord."

Thus speaking he backed himself out of sight. Lord Ragnall watched him go, then said with a laugh:

"I apologize to you, Mr. Quatermain. That silly old fool was part of my inheritance, so to speak; and the joke of it is that he is himself the worst and most dangerous shot I ever saw. However, on the other hand, he is the best rearer of pheasants in the county, so I put up with him. Come in, now, won't you? Charles will look after your guns and cartridges."

So Scroope and I were taken through a side entrance into the big hall and there introduced to the other members of the shooting party, most of whom were staying at the castle. They were famous shots. Indeed, I had read of the prowess of some of them in *The Field*, a paper that I always took in Africa, although often enough, when I was on my distant expeditions, I did not see a copy of it for a year at a time.

To my astonishment I found that I knew one of these gentlemen. We had not, it is true, met for a dozen years; but I seldom forget a face, and I was sure that I could not be mistaken in this instance. That mean appearance, those small, shifty grey eyes, that red, pointed nose could belong to nobody except Van Koop, so famous in his day in South Africa in connexion with certain gigantic and most successful frauds that the law seemed quite unable to touch, of which frauds I had been one of the many victims to the extent of £250, a large sum for me.

The last time we met there had been a stormy scene between us, which ended in my declaring in my wrath that if I came across him on the veld I should shoot him at sight. Perhaps that was one of the reasons why Mr. van Koop vanished from South Africa, for I may add that he was a cur of the first water. I believe that he had only just entered the room, having driven over from wherever he lived at some distance from Ragnall. At any rate, he knew nothing of my presence at this shoot. Had he known I am quite sure that he would have been absent. He turned, and seeing me, exclaimed: "Allan Quatermain, by heaven!" beneath his breath, but in such a tone of astonishment that it attracted the attention of Lord Ragnall, who was standing near.

"Yes, Mr. van Koop," I answered in a cheerful voice, "Allan Quatermain, no other, and I hope you are as glad to see me as I am to see you."

"I think there is some mistake," said Lord Ragnall, staring at us. "This is Sir Junius Fortescue, who used to be Mr. Fortescue."

"Indeed," I replied. "I don't know that I ever remember his being called by that particular name, but I do know that we are old—friends."

Lord Ragnall moved away as though he did not wish to continue the conversation, which no one else had overheard, and Van Koop sidled up to me.

"Mr. Quatermain," he said in a low voice, "circumstances have changed with me since last we met."

"So I gather," I replied; "but mine have remained much the same, and if it is convenient to you to repay me that £250 you owe me, with interest, I shall be much obliged. If not, I think I have a good story to tell about you."

"Oh, Mr. Quatermain," he answered with a sort of smile which made me feel inclined to kick him, "you know I dispute that debt."

"Do you?" I exclaimed. "Well, perhaps you will dispute the story also. But the question is, will you be believed when I give the proofs?"

"Ever heard of the Statute of Limitations, Mr. Quatermain?" he asked with a sneer.

"Not where character is concerned," I replied stoutly. "Now, what are you going to do?"

He reflected for a moment, and answered:

"Look here, Mr. Quatermain, you were always a bit of a sportsman, and I'll make you an offer. If I kill more birds than you do to-day, you shall promise to hold your tongue about my affairs in South Africa; and if you kill more than I do, you shall still hold your tongue, but I will pay you that £250 and interest for six years."

I also reflected for a moment, knowing that the man had something up his sleeve. Of course, I could refuse and make a scandal. But that was not in my line, and would not bring me nearer my £250, which, if I chanced to win, might find its way back to me.

"All right, done!" I said.

"What is your bet, Sir Junius?" asked Lord Ragnall, who was approaching again.

"It is rather a long story," he answered, "but, to put it shortly, years ago, when I was travelling in Africa, Mr. Quatermain and I had a dispute as to a sum of £5 which he thought I owed him, and to save argument about a trifle we have agreed that I should shoot against him for it to-day."

"Indeed," said Lord Ragnall rather seriously, for I could see that he did not believe Van Koop's statement as to the amount of the bet; perhaps he had heard more than we thought. "To be frank, Sir Junius, I don't much care for betting—for that's what it comes to—here. Also I think Mr. Quatermain said yesterday that he had never shot pheasants in England, so the match seems scarcely fair. However, you gentlemen know your own business best. Only I must tell you both that if money is concerned, I shall have to set someone whose decision will be final to count your birds and report the number to me."

"Agreed," said Van Koop, or, rather, Sir Junius; but I answered nothing, for, to tell the truth, already I felt ashamed of the whole affair.

As it happened, Lord Ragnall and I walked together ahead of the others, to the first covert, which was half a mile or more away.

"You have met Sir Junius before?" he said to me interrogatively.

"I have met Mr. van Koop before," I answered, "about twelve years since, shortly after which he vanished from South Africa, where he was a well-known and very successful—speculator."

"To reappear here. Ten years ago he bought a large property in this neighbourhood. Three years ago he became a baronet."

"How did a man like Van Koop become a baronet?" I inquired.

"By purchase, I believe."

"By purchase! Are honours in England purchased?"

"You are delightfully innocent, Mr. Quatermain, as a hunter from Africa should be," said Lord Ragnall, laughing. "Your friend—"

"Excuse me, Lord Ragnall, I am a very humble person, not so elevated, indeed, as that gamekeeper of yours; therefore I should not venture to call Sir Junius, late Mr. van Koop, my friend, at least in earnest."

He laughed again.

"Well, the individual with whom you make bets subscribed largely to the funds of his party. I am telling you what I know to be true, though the amount I do not know. It has been variously stated to be from fifteen to fifty thousand pounds, and, perhaps by coincidence, subsequently was somehow created a baronet."

I stared at him.

"That's all the story," he went on. "I don't like the man myself, but he is a wonderful pheasant shot, which passes him everywhere. Shooting has become a kind of fetish in these parts, Mr. Quatermain. For instance, it is a tradition on this estate that we must kill more pheasants than on any other in the country, and therefore I have to ask the best guns, who are not always the best fellows. It annoys me, but it seems that I must do what was done before me."

"Under those circumstances I should be inclined to give up the thing altogether, Lord Ragnall. Sport as sport is good, but when it becomes a business it grows hateful. I know, who have had to follow it as a trade for many years."

"That's an idea," he replied reflectively. "Meanwhile, I do hope that you will win back your—£5 from Sir Junius. He is so vain that I would gladly give £50 to see you do so."

"There is little chance of that," I said, "for, as I told you, I have never shot pheasants before. Still, I'll try, as you wish it."

"That's right. And look here, Mr. Quatermain, shoot well forward of them. You see, I am venturing to advise you now, as you advised me yesterday. Shot does not travel so fast as ball, and the pheasant is a bird that is generally going much quicker than you think. Now, here we are. Charles will show you your stand. Good luck to you."

Ten minutes later the game began outside of a long covert, all the seven guns being posted within sight of each other. So occupied was I in watching the preliminaries, which were quite new to me, that I allowed first a hare and then a hen pheasant to depart without firing at them, which hen pheasant, by the way, curved round and was beautifully killed by Van Koop, who stood two guns off upon my right.

"Look here, Allan," said Scroope, "if you are going to beat your African friend you had better wake up, for you won't do it by admiring the scenery or that squirrel on a tree."

So I woke up. Just at that moment there was a cry of "cock forward." I thought it meant a cock pheasant, and was astonished when I saw a beautiful brown bird with a long beak flitting towards me through the tops of the oak trees.

"Am I to shoot at that?" I asked.

"Of course. It is a woodcock," answered Scroope.

By this time the brown bird was rocking past me within ten yards. I fired and killed it, for where it had been appeared nothing but a cloud of feathers. It was a quick and clever shot, or so I thought. But when Charles stepped out and picked from the ground only a beak and a head, a titter of laughter went down the whole line of guns and loaders.

"I say, old chap," said Scroope, "if you will use No. 3 shot, let your birds get a little farther off you."

The incident upset me so much that immediately afterwards I missed three easy pheasants in succession, while Van Koop added two to his bag.

Scroope shook his head and Charles groaned audibly. Now that I was not in competition with his master he had become suddenly anxious that I should win, for in some mysterious way the news of that bet had spread, and my adversary was not popular amongst the keeper class.

"Here you come again," said Scroope, pointing to an advancing pheasant.

It was an extraordinarily high pheasant, flushed, I think, outside the covert by a stop, so high that, as it travelled down the line, although three guns fired at it, including Van Koop, none of them seemed to touch it. Then I fired, and remembering Lord Ragnall's advice, far in front. Its flight changed. Still it travelled through the air, but with the momentum of a stone to fall fifty yards to my right, dead.

"That's better!" said Scroope, while Charles grinned all over his round face, muttering:

"Wiped his eye that time."

This shot seemed to give me confidence, and I improved considerably, though, oddly enough, I found that it was the high and difficult pheasants which I killed and the easy ones that I was apt to muff. But Van Koop, who was certainly a finished artist, killed both.

At the next stand Lord Ragnall, who had been observing my somewhat indifferent performance, asked me to stand back with him behind the other guns.

"I see the tall ones are your line, Mr. Quatermain," he said, "and you will get some here."

On this occasion we were placed in a dip between two long coverts which lay about three hundred yards apart. That which was being beaten proved full of pheasants, and the shooting of those picked guns was really a thing to see. I did quite well here, nearly, but not altogether, as well as Lord Ragnall himself, though that is saying a great deal, for he was a lovely shot.

"Bravo!" he said at the end of the beat. "I believe you have got a chance of winning your £5, after all."

When, however, at luncheon, more than an hour later, I found that I was thirty pheasants behind my adversary, I shook my head, and so did everybody else. On the whole, that luncheon, of which we partook in a keeper's house, was a very pleasant meal, though Van Koop talked so continuously and in such a boastful strain that I saw it irritated our host and some of the other gentlemen, who were very pleasant people. At last he began to patronize me, asking me how I had been getting on with my "elephant-potting" of late years.

I replied, "Fairly well."

"Then you should tell our friends some of your famous stories, which I promise I won't contradict," he said, adding: "You see, they are different from us, and have no experience of big-game shooting."

"I did not know that you had any, either, Sir Junius," I answered, nettled. "Indeed, I thought I remembered your telling me in Africa that the only big game you had ever shot was an ox sick with the red-water. Anyway, shooting is a business with me, not an amusement, as it is to you, and I do not talk shop."

At this he collapsed amid some laughter, after which Scroope, the most loyal of friends, began to repeat exploits of mine till my ears tingled, and I rose and went outside to look at the weather.

It had changed very much during luncheon. The fair promise of the morning had departed, the sky was overcast, and a wind, blowing in strong gusts, was rising rapidly, driving before it occasional scurries of snow.

"My word," said Lord Ragnall, who had joined me, "the Lake covert—that's our great stand here, you know—will take some shooting this afternoon. We ought to kill seven hundred pheasants in it with this team, but I doubt if we shall get five. Now, Mr. Quatermain, I am going to stand Sir Junius Fortescue and you back in the covert, where you will have the best of it, as a lot of pheasants will never face the lake against this wind. What is more, I am coming with you, if I may, as six guns are enough for this beat, and I don't mean to shoot any more to-day."

"I fear that you will be disappointed," I said nervously.

"Oh, no, I sha'n't," he answered. "I tell you frankly that if only you could have a season's practice, in my opinion you would make the best pheasant shot of the lot of us. At present you don't quite understand the ways of the birds, that's all; also those guns are strange to you. Have a glass of cherry brandy; it will steady your nerves."

I drank the cherry brandy, and presently off we went. The covert we were going to shoot, into which we had been driving pheasants all the morning, must have been nearly a mile long. At the top end it was broad, narrowing at the bottom to a width of about two hundred yards. Here it ran into a horse-shoe shaped piece of water that was about fifty yards in breadth. Four of the guns were placed round the bow of this water, but on its farther side, in such a position that the pheasants should stream over them to yet another covert behind at the top of a slope, Van Koop and I, however, were ordered to take our places, he to the right and I to the left, about seventy yards up the tongue in little glades in the woodland, having the lake to our right and our left respectively. I noticed with dismay that we were so set that the guns below us on its farther side could note all that we did or did not do; also that a little band of watchers, among whom I recognized my friend the gunsmith, were gathered in a place where, without interfering with us, they could see the sport. On our way to the boat, however, which was to row us across the water, an incident happened that put me in very good spirits and earned some applause.

I was walking with Lord Ragnall, Scroope and Charles, about sixty yards clear of a belt of tall trees, when from far away on the other side of the trees came a cry of "Partridges over!" in the hoarse voice of the red-waistcoated Jenkins, who was engaged in superintending the driving in of some low scrub before he joined his army at the top of the covert.

"Look out, Mr. Quatermain, they are coming this way," said Lord Ragnall, while Charles thrust a loaded gun into my hand.

Another moment and they appeared over the tree-tops, a big covey of them in a long, straggling line, travelling at I know not what speed, for a fierce gust from the rising gale had caught them. I fired at the first bird, which fell at my feet. I fired again, and another fell behind me. I snatched up the second gun and killed a third as it passed over me high up. Then, wheeling round, I covered the last retreating bird, and lo! it too fell, a very long shot indeed.

"By George!" said Scroope, "I never saw that done before," while Ragnall stared and Charles whistled.

But now I will tell the truth and expose all my weakness. The second bird was not the one I aimed at. I was behind it and caught that which followed. And in my vanity I did not own up, at least not till that evening.

The four dead partridges—there was not a runner among them—having been collected amidst many congratulations, we went on and were punted across the lake to the covert. As we entered the boat I observed that, in addition to the great bags, Charles was carrying a box of cartridges under his arm, and asked him where he got it from.

He replied, from Mr. Popham—that was the gunsmith's name—who had brought it with him in case I should not have enough. I made no remark, but as I knew I had quite half of my cartridges left out of the three hundred and fifty that I had bought, I wondered to myself what kind of a shoot this was going to be.

Well, we took up our stands, and while we were doing so, suddenly the wind increased to a tearing gale, which seemed to me to blow from all points of the compass in turn. Rooks flying homewards, and pigeons disturbed by the beaters were swept over us like drifting leaves; wild duck, of which I got one, went by like arrows; the great bare oaks tossed their boughs and groaned; while not far off a fir tree was blown down, falling with a splash into the water.

"It's a wild afternoon," said Lord Ragnall, and as he spoke Van Koop came from his stand, looking rather scared, and suggested that the shoot should be given up.

Lord Ragnall asked me what I wished to do. I replied that I would rather go on, but that I was in his hands.

"I think we are fairly safe in these open places, Sir Junius," he said; "and as the pheasants have been so much disturbed already, it does not much matter if they are blown about a bit. But if you are of another opinion, perhaps you had better get out of it and stand with the others over the lake. I'll send for my guns and take your place."

On hearing this Van Koop changed his mind and said that he would go on.

So the beat began. At first the wind blew from behind us, and pheasants in increasing numbers passed over our heads, most of them rather low, to the guns on the farther side of the water, who, skilled though they were, did not make very good work with them. We had been instructed not to fire at birds going forward, so I let these be. Van Koop, however, did not interpret the order in the same spirit, for he loosed at several, killing one or two and missing others.

"That fellow is no sportsman," I heard Lord Ragnall remark. "I suppose it is the bet."

Then he sent Charles to ask him to desist.

Shortly after this the gale worked round to the north and settled there, blowing with ever-increasing violence. The pheasants, however, still flew forward in the shelter of the trees, for they were making for the covert on the hill, where they had been bred. But when they got into the open and felt the full force of the wind, quite four out of six of them turned and came back at a most fearful pace, many so high as to be almost out of shot.

For the next three-quarters of an hour or more—as I think I have explained, the beat was a very long one—I had such covert shooting as I suppose I shall never see again. High above those shrieking trees, or over the lake to my left, flashed the wind-driven pheasants in an endless procession. Oddly enough, I found that this wild work suited me, for as time went on and the pheasants grew more and more impossible, I shot better and better. One after another down they came far behind me with a crash in the brushwood or a splash in the lake, till the guns grew almost too hot to hold. There were so many of them that I discovered I could pick my shots; also that nine out of ten were caught by the wind and curved at a certain angle, and that the time to fire was just before they took the curve. The excitement was great and the sport splendid, as anyone will testify who has shot December pheasants breaking back over the covert and in a tearing gale. Van Koop also was doing very well, but the guns in front got comparatively little shooting. They were forced to stand there, poor fellows, and watch our performance from afar.

As the thing drew towards an end the birds came thicker and thicker, and I shot, as I have said, better and better. This may be judged from the fact that, notwithstanding their height and tremendous pace, I killed my last thirty pheasants with thirty-five cartridges. The final bird of all, a splendid cock, appeared by himself out of nothingness when we thought that all was done. I think it must have been flushed from the covert on the hill, or been turned back just as it reached it by the resistless strength of the storm. Over it came, so high above us that it looked quite small in the dark snow-scud.

"Too far—no use!" said Lord Ragnall, as I lifted the gun.

Still, I fired, holding I know not how much in front, and lo! that pheasant died in mid air, falling with a mighty splash near the bank of the lake, but at a great distance behind us. The shot was so remarkable that everyone who saw it, including most of the beaters, who had passed us by now, uttered a cheer, and the red-waistcoated old Jenkins, who had stopped by us, remarked: "Well, bust me if that bain't a master one!"

Scroope made me angry by slapping me so hard upon the back that it hurt, and nearly caused me to let off the other barrel of the gun. Charles seemed to become one great grin, and Lord Ragnall, with a brief congratulatory "Never enjoyed a shoot so much in my life," called to the men who were posted behind us to pick up all the dead pheasants, being careful to keep mine apart from those of Sir Junius Fortescue.

"You should have a hundred and forty-three at this stand," he said, "allowing for every possible runner. Charles and I make the same total."

I remarked that I did not think there were many runners, as the No. 3 shot had served me very well, and getting into the boat was rowed to the other side, where I received more congratulations. Then, as all further shooting was out of the question because of the weather, we walked back to the castle to tea.

As I emptied my cup Lord Ragnall, who had left the room, returned and asked us to come and see the game. So we went, to find it laid out in endless lines upon the snow-powdered grass in the quadrangle of the castle, arranged in one main and two separate lots.

"Those are yours and Sir Junius's," said Scroope. "I wonder which of you has won. I'll put a sovereign on you, old fellow."

"Then you're a donkey for your pains," I answered, feeling vexed, for at that moment I had forgotten all about the bet.

I do not remember how many pheasants were killed altogether, but the total was much smaller than had been hoped for, because of the gale.

"Jenkins," said Lord Ragnall presently to Red Waistcoat, "how many have you to the credit of Sir Junius Fortescue?"

"Two hundred and seventy-seven, my lord, twelve hares, two woodcocks, and three pigeons."

"And how many to that of Mr. Quatermain?" adding: "I must remind you both, gentlemen, that the birds have been picked as carefully as possible and kept unmixed, and therefore that the figures given by Jenkins must be considered as final."

"Quite so," I answered, but Van Koop said nothing. Then, while we all waited anxiously, came the amazing answer:

"Two hundred and seventy-seven pheasants, my lord, same number as those of Sir Junius, Bart., fifteen hares, three pigeons, four partridges, one duck, and a beak—I mean a woodcock."

"Then it seems you have won your £5, Mr. Quatermain, upon which I congratulate you," said Lord Ragnall.

"Stop a minute," broke in Van Koop. "The bet was as to pheasants; the other things don't count."

"I think the term used was 'birds,'" I remarked. "But to be frank, when I made it I was thinking of pheasants, as no doubt Sir Junius was also. Therefore, if the counting is correct, there is a dead heat and the wager falls through."

"I am sure we all appreciate the view you take of the matter," said Lord Ragnall, "for it might be argued another way. In these circumstances Sir Junius keeps his £5 in his pocket. It is unlucky for you, Quatermain," he added, dropping the "mister," "that the last high pheasant you shot can't be found. It fell into the lake, you remember, and, I suppose, swam ashore and ran."

"Yes," I replied, "especially as I could have sworn that it was quite dead."

"So could I, Quatermain; but the fact remains that it isn't there."

"If we had all the pheasants that we think fall dead our bags would be much bigger than they are," remarked Van Koop, with a look of great relief upon his face, adding in his horrid, patronizing way: "Still, you shot uncommonly well, Quatermain. I'd no idea you would run me so close."

I felt inclined to answer, but didn't. Only Lord Ragnall said:

"Mr. Quatermain shot more than well. His performance in the Lake covert was the most brilliant that I have ever seen. When you went in there together, Sir Junius, you were thirty ahead of him, and you fired seventeen more cartridges at the stand."

Then, just as we turned to go, something happened. The round-eyed Charles ran puffing into the quadrangle, followed by another man with a dog, who had been specially set to pick my birds, and carrying in his hand a much-bedraggled cock pheasant without a tail.

"I've got him, my lord," he gasped, for he had run very fast; "the little gent's—I mean that which he killed in the clouds with the last shot he fired. It had gone right down into the mud and stuck there. Tom and me fished him up with a pole."

Lord Ragnall took the bird and looked at it. It was almost cold, but evidently freshly killed, for the limbs were quite flexible.

"That turns the scale in favour of Mr. Quatermain," he said, "so, Sir Junius, you had better pay your money and congratulate him, as I do."

"I protest," exclaimed Van Koop, looking very angry and meaner than usual. "How am I to know that this was Mr. Quatermain's pheasant? The sum involved is more than £5 and I feel it is my duty to protest."

"Because my men say so, Sir Junius; moreover, seeing the height from which the bird fell, their story is obviously true."

Then he examined the pheasant further, pointing out that it appeared to have only one wound—a shot through the throat almost exactly at the root of the beak, of which shot there was no mark of exit. "What sized shot were you using, Sir Junius?" he asked.

"No. 4 at the last stand."

"And you were using No. 3, Mr. Quatermain. Now, was any other gun using No. 3?"

All shook their heads.

"Jenkins, open that bird's head. I think the shot that killed it will be found in the brain."

Jenkins obeyed, using a penknife cleverly enough. Pressed against the bone of the skull he found the shot.

"No. 3 it is, sure enough, my lord," he said.

"You will agree that settles the matter, Sir Junius," said Lord Ragnall. "And now, as a bet has been made here it had better be paid."

"I have not enough money on me," said Van Koop sulkily.

"I think your banker is mine," said Lord Ragnall quietly, "so you can write a cheque in the house. Come in, all of you, it is cold in this wind."

So we went into the smoking-room, and Lord Ragnall, who, I could see, was annoyed, instantly fetched a blank cheque from his study and handed it to Van Koop in rather a pointed manner.

He took it, and turning to me, said:

"I remember the capital sum, but how much is the interest? Sorry to trouble you, but I am not very good at figures."

"Then you must have changed a good deal during the last twelve years, Sir Junius," I could not help saying. "Still, never mind the interest, I shall be quite satisfied with the principal."

So he filled up the cheque for £250 and threw it down on the table before me, saying something about its being a bother to mix up business with pleasure.

I took the draft, saw that it was correct though rather illegible, and proceeded to dry it by waving it in the air. As I did so it came into my mind that I would not touch the money of this successful scamp, won back from him in such a way.

Yielding to a perhaps foolish impulse, I said:

"Lord Ragnall, this cheque is for a debt which years ago I wrote off as lost. At luncheon to-day you were talking of a Cottage Hospital for which you are trying to get up an endowment fund in this neighbourhood, and in answer to a question from you Sir Junius Fortescue said that he had not as yet made any subscription to its fund. Will you allow me to hand you Sir Junius's subscription—to be entered in his name, if you please?" And I passed him the cheque, which was drawn to myself or bearer.

He looked at the amount, and seeing that it was not £5, but £250, flushed, then asked:

"What do you say to this act of generosity on the part of Mr. Quatermain, Sir Junius?"

There was no answer, because Sir Junius had gone. I never saw him again, for years ago the poor man died quite disgraced. His passion for semi-fraudulent speculations reasserted itself, and he became a bankrupt in conditions which caused him to leave the country for

America, where he was killed in a railway accident while travelling as an immigrant. I have heard, however, that he was not asked to shoot at Ragnall any more.

The cheque was passed to the credit of the Cottage Hospital, but not, as I had requested, as a subscription from Sir Junius Fortescue. A couple of years later, indeed, I learned that this sum of money was used to build a little room in that institution to accommodate sick children, which room was named the Allan Quatermain ward.

Now, I have told this story of that December shoot because it was the beginning of my long and close friendship with Ragnall.

When he found that Van Koop had gone away without saying goodbye, Lord Ragnall made no remark. Only he took my hand and shook it.

I have only to add that, although, except for the element of competition which entered into it, I enjoyed this day's shooting very much indeed, when I came to count up its cost I felt glad that I had not been asked to any more such entertainments. Here it is, taken from an old note-book:

Cartridges, including those not used and given to Charles	£4	0	0
Game License	3	0	0
Tip to Red Waistcoat (keeper)	2	0	0
Tip to Charles	0	10	0
Tip to man who helped Charles to find pheasant	0	5	0
Tip to man who collected pheasants behind me	0	10	0
	£10	5	0

Truly pheasant shooting in England is, or was, a sport for the rich!

III

Miss Holmes

Two and a half hours passed by, most of which time I spent lying down to rest and get rid of a headache caused by the continual, rapid firing and the roar of the gale, or both; also in rubbing my shoulder with ointment, for it was sore from the recoil of the guns. Then Scroope appeared, as, being unable to find my way about the long passages of that great old castle, I had asked him to do, and we descended together to the large drawing-room.

It was a splendid apartment, only used upon state occasions, lighted, I should think, with at least two or three hundred wax candles, which threw a soft glow over the panelled and pictured walls, the priceless antique furniture, and the bejewelled ladies who were gathered there. To my mind there never was and never will be any artificial light to equal that of wax candles in sufficient quantity. The company was large; I think thirty sat down to dinner that night, which was given to introduce Lord Ragnall's future wife to the neighbourhood, whereof she was destined to be the leader.

Miss Manners, who was looking very happy and charming in her jewels and fine clothes, joined us at once, and informed Scroope that "she" was just coming; the maid in the cloakroom had told her so.

"Is she?" replied Scroope indifferently. "Well, so long as you have come I don't care about anyone else."

Then he told her she was looking beautiful, and stared at her with such affection that I fell back a step or two and contemplated a picture of Judith vigorously engaged in cutting off the head of Holofernes.

Presently the large door at the end of the room was thrown open and the immaculate Savage, who was acting as a kind of master of the ceremonies, announced in well-bred but penetrating tones, "Lady Longden and the Honourable Miss Holmes." I stared, like everybody else, but for a while her ladyship filled my eye. She was an ample and, to my mind, rather awful-looking person, clad in black satin—she was a widow—and very large diamonds. Her hair was white, her nose was hooked, her dark eyes were penetrating, and she had a bad cold in her head. That was all I found time to notice about her, for suddenly her daughter came into my line of vision.

Truly she was a lovely girl, or rather, young woman, for she must have been two or three-and-twenty. Not very tall, her proportions were rounded and exquisite, and her movements as graceful as those of a doe. Altogether she was doe-like, especially in the fineness of her lines and her large and liquid eyes. She was a dark beauty, with rich brown, waving hair, a clear olive complexion, a perfectly shaped mouth and very red lips. To me she looked more Italian or Spanish than Anglo-Saxon, and I believe that, as a matter of fact, she had some southern blood in her on her father's side. She wore a dress of soft rose colour, and her only ornaments were a string of pearls and a single red camellia. I could see but one blemish, if it were a blemish, in her perfect person, and that was a curious white mark upon her breast, which in its shape exactly resembled the crescent moon.

The face, however, impressed me with other than its physical qualities. It was bright, intelligent, sympathetic and, just now, happy. But I thought it more, I thought it mystical. Something that her mother said to her, probably about her dress, caused her smile to vanish for a moment, and then, from beneath it as it were, appeared this shadow of innate mysticism. In a second it was gone and she was laughing again; but I, who am accustomed to observe, had caught it, perhaps alone of all that company. Moreover, it reminded me of something.

What was it? Ah! I knew. A look that sometimes I had seen upon the face of a certain Zulu lady named Mameena, especially at the moment of her wonderful and tragic death. The thought made me shiver a little; I could not tell why, for certainly, I reflected, this high-placed and fortunate English girl had nothing in common with that fate-driven Child of Storm, whose dark and imperial spirit dwelt in the woman called Mameena. They were as far apart as Zululand is from Essex. Yet it was quite sure that both of them had touch with hidden things.

Lord Ragnall, looking more like a splendid Van Dyck than ever in his evening dress, stepped forward to greet his fiancée and her mother with a courtly bow, and I turned again to continue my contemplation of the stalwart Judith and the very ugly head of Holofernes. Presently I was aware of a soft voice—a very rich and thrilling voice—asking quite close to me:

"Which is he? Oh! you need not answer, dear. I know him from the description."

"Yes," replied Lord Ragnall to Miss Holmes—for it was she—"you are quite right. I will introduce you to him presently. But, love, whom do you wish to take you in to dinner? I can't—your mother, you know; and as there are no titles here to-night, you may make your choice. Would you like old Dr. Jeffreys, the clergyman?"

"No," she replied, with quiet firmness, "I know him; he took me in once before. I wish Mr. Allan Quatermain to take me in. He is interesting, and I want to hear about Africa."

"Very well," he answered, "and he *is* more interesting than all the rest put together. But, Luna, why are you always thinking and talking about Africa? One might imagine that you were going to live there."

"So I may one day," she answered dreamily. "Who knows where one has lived, or where one will live!" And again I saw that mystic look come into her face.

I heard no more of that conversation, which it is improbable that anyone whose ears had not been sharpened by a lifetime of listening in great silences would have caught at all. To tell the truth, I made myself scarce, slipping off to the other end of the big room in the hope of evading the kind intentions of Miss Holmes. I have a great dislike of being put out of my place, and I felt that among all these local celebrities it was not fitting that I should be selected to take in the future bride on an occasion of this sort. But it was of no use, for presently Lord Ragnall hunted me up, bringing the young lady with him.

"Let me introduce you to Miss Holmes, Quatermain," he said. "She is anxious that you should take her in to dinner, if you will be so kind. She is very interested in—in—"

"Africa," I suggested.

"In Mr. Quatermain, who, I am told, is one of the greatest hunters in Africa," she corrected me, with a dazzling smile.

I bowed, not knowing what to say. Lord Ragnall laughed and vanished, leaving us together. Dinner was announced. Presently we were wending in the centre of a long and glittering procession across the central hall to the banqueting chamber, a splendid room with a roof like a church that was said to have been built in the times of the Plantagenets. Here Mr. Savage, who evidently had been looking out for her future ladyship, conducted us to our places, which were upon the left of Lord Ragnall, who sat at the head of the broad table with Lady Longden on his right. Then the old clergyman, Dr. Jeffreys, a pompous and rather frowsy ecclesiastic, said grace, for grace was still in fashion at such feasts in those days, asking Heaven to make us truly thankful for the dinner we were about to consume.

Certainly there was a great deal to be thankful for in the eating and drinking line, but of all I remember little, except a general vision of silver dishes, champagne, splendour, and things I did not want to eat being constantly handed to me. What I do remember is Miss Holmes, and nothing but Miss Holmes; the charm of her conversation, the light of her beautiful eyes, the fragrance of her hair, her most flattering interest in my unworthy self. To tell the truth, we got on "like fire in the winter grass," as the Zulus say, and when that dinner was over the grass was still burning.

I don't think that Lord Ragnall quite liked it, but fortunately Lady Longden was a talkative person. First she conversed about her cold in the head, sneezing at intervals, poor soul, and being reduced to send for another handkerchief after the entrées. Then she got off upon business matters; to judge from the look of boredom on her host's face, I think it must have been of settlements. Three times did I hear him refer her to the lawyers—without avail. Lastly, when he thought he had escaped, she embarked upon a quite vigorous argument with Dr. Jeffreys about church matters—I gathered that she was "low" and he was "high"—in which she insisted upon his lordship acting as referee.

"Do try and keep your attention fixed, George," I heard her say severely. "To allow it to wander when high spiritual affairs are under discussion (sneeze) is scarcely reverent. Could you tell the man to shut that door? The draught is dreadful. It is quite impossible for you to agree with both of us, as you say you do, seeing that metaphorically Dr. Jeffreys is at one pole and I am at the other." (Sneeze.)

"Then I wish I were at the Tropic of Cancer," I heard him mutter with a groan.

In vain; he had to keep his "attention fixed" on this point for the next three-quarters of an hour. So as Miss Manners was at the other side of me, and Scroope, unhampered by the presence of any prospective mother-in-law, was at the other side of her, for all practical purposes Miss Holmes and I were left alone.

She began by saying:

"I hear you beat Sir Junius Fortescue out shooting to-day, and won a lot of money from him which you gave to the Cottage Hospital. I don't like shooting, and I don't like betting; and it's strange, because you don't look like a man who bets. But I detest Sir Junius Fortescue, and that is a bond of union between us."

"I never said I detested him."

"No, but I am sure you do. Your face changed when I mentioned his name."

"As it happens, you are right. But, Miss Holmes, I should like you to understand that you were also right when you said I did not look like a betting man." And I told her some of the story of Van Koop and the £250.

"Ah!" she said, when I had finished, "I always felt sure he was a horror. And my mother wanted me, just because he pretended to be low church—but that's a secret."

Then I congratulated her upon her approaching marriage, saying what a joyful thing it was now and again to see everything going in real, happy, storybook fashion: beauty, male and female, united by love, high rank, wealth, troops of friends, health of body, a lovely and an ancient home in a settled land where dangers do not come— at present—respect and affection of crowds of dependants, the prospect of a high and useful career of a sort whereof the door is shut to most people, everything in short that human beings who are not actually royalty could desire or deserve. Indeed after my second glass of champagne I grew quite eloquent on these and kindred points, being moved thereto by memories of the misery that is in the world which formed so great a contrast to the lot of this striking and brilliant pair.

She listened to me attentively and answered:

"Thank you for your kind thoughts and wishes. But does it not strike you, Mr. Quatermain, that there is something ill-omened in such talk? I believe that it does; that as you finished speaking it occurred to you that after all the future is as much veiled from all of us as—as the picture which hangs behind its curtain of rose-coloured silk in Lord Ragnall's study is from you."

"How did you know that?" I asked sharply in a low voice. For by the strangest of coincidences, as I concluded my somewhat old-fashioned little speech of compliments, this very reflection had entered my mind, and with it the memory of the veiled picture which Mr. Savage had pointed out to me on the previous morning.

"I can't say, Mr. Quatermain, but I did know it. You were thinking of the picture, were you not?"

"And if I was," I said, avoiding a direct reply, "what of it? Though it is hidden from everybody else, he has only to draw the curtain and see—you."

"Supposing he should draw the curtain one day and see nothing, Mr. Quatermain?"

"Then the picture would have been stolen, that is all, and he would have to search for it till he found it again, which doubtless sooner or later he would do."

"Yes, sooner or later. But where? Perhaps you have lost a picture or two in your time, Mr. Quatermain, and are better able to answer the question than I am."

There was silence for a few moments, for this talk of lost pictures brought back memories which choked me.

Then she began to speak again, low, quickly, and with suppressed passion, but acting wonderfully all the while. Knowing that eyes were on her, her gestures and the expression of her face were such as might have been those of any young lady of fashion who was talking of everyday affairs, such as dancing, or flowers, or jewels. She smiled and even laughed occasionally. She played with the golden salt-cellar in front of her and, upsetting a little of the salt, threw it over her left shoulder, appearing to ask me if I were a victim of that ancient habit, and so on.

But all the while she was talking deeply of deep things, such as I should never have thought would pass her mind. This was the substance of what she said, for I cannot set it all down verbatim; after so many years my memory fails me.

"I am not like other women. Something moves me to tell you so, something very real and powerful which pushes me as a strong man might. It is odd, because I have never spoken to anyone else like that, not to my mother for instance, or even to Lord Ragnall. They would neither of them understand, although they would misunderstand differently. My mother would think I ought to see a doctor—and if you knew that doctor! He," and she nodded towards Lord Ragnall, "would think that my engagement had upset me, or that I had grown rather more religious than I ought to be at my age, and been reflecting too much—well, on the end of all things. From a child I have understood that I am a mystery set in the midst of many other mysteries. It all came to me one night when I was about nine years old. I seemed to see the past and the future, although I could grasp neither. Such a long, long past and such an infinite future. I don't know what I saw, and still see sometimes. It comes in a flash, and is in a flash forgotten. My mind cannot hold it. It is too big for my mind; you might as well try to pack Dr. Jeffreys there into this wineglass. Only two facts remain written on my heart. The first is that there is trouble ahead of me, curious and unusual trouble; and the second, that permanently, continually, I, or a part of me, have something to do with Africa, a country of which I know nothing except from a few very dull books. Also, by the way—this is a new thought—that I have a great deal to do with *you*. That is why I am so interested in Africa and you. Tell me about Africa and yourself now, while we have the chance." And she ended rather abruptly, adding in a louder voice, "You have lived there all your life, have you not, Mr. Quatermain?"

"I rather think your mother would be right—about the doctor, I mean," I said.

"You *say* that, but you don't *believe* it. Oh! you are very transparent, Mr. Quatermain—at least, to me."

So, hurriedly enough, for these subjects seemed to be uncomfortable, even dangerous in a sense, I began to talk of the first thing about Africa that I remembered—namely, of the legend of the Holy Flower that was guarded by a huge ape, of which I had heard from a white man who was supposed to be rather mad, who went by the name of Brother John. Also I told her that there was something in it, as I had with me a specimen of the flower.

"Oh! show it me," she said.

I replied that I feared I could not, as it was locked away in a safe in London, whither I was returning on the morrow. I promised, however, to send her a life-sized water-colour drawing of which I had caused several to be made. She asked me if I were going to look for this flower, and I said that I hoped so if I could make the necessary arrangements. Next she asked me if there chanced to be any other African quests upon which I had set my mind. I replied that there were several. For instance, I had heard vaguely through Brother John, and indirectly from one or two other sources, of the existence of a certain tribe in East Central Africa—Arabs or semi-Arabs—who were reported to worship a child that always remained a child. This child, I took it, was a dwarf; but as I was interested in native religious customs which were infinite in their variety, I should much like to find out the truth of the matter.

"Talking of Arabs," she broke in, "I will tell you a curious story. Once when I was a little girl, eight or nine years of age—it was just before that kind of awakening of which I have spoken to you—I was playing in Kensington Gardens, for we lived in London at the time, in the charge of my nurse-governess. She was talking to some young man who she said was her cousin, and told me to run about with my hoop and not to bother. I drove the hoop across the grass to some elm trees. From behind one of the trees came out two tall men dressed in white robes and turbans, who looked to me like scriptural characters in a picture-book. One was an elderly man with flashing, black eyes, hooked nose, and a long grey beard. The other was much younger, but I do not remember him so well. They were both brown in colour, but otherwise almost like white men; not Negroes by any means. My hoop hit the elder man, and I stood still, not knowing what to say. He bowed politely and picked it up, but did not offer to return it to me. They talked together rapidly, and one of them pointed to the moon-shaped birthmark which you see I have upon my neck, for it was hot weather, and I was wearing a low-cut frock. It was because of this mark that my father named me Luna. The elder of the two said in broken English:

"'What is your name, pretty little girl?'

"I told him it was Luna Holmes. Then he drew from his robe a box made of scented wood and, opening it, took out some sweetmeat which looked as if it had been frozen, and gave me a piece that, being very fond of sweet, I put into my mouth. Next, he bowled the hoop along the ground into the shadow of the trees—it was evening time and beginning to grow dark—saying, 'Run, catch it, little girl!'

"I began to run, but something in the taste of that sweet caused me to drop it from my lips. Then all grew misty, and the next thing I remember was finding myself in the arms of the younger Eastern, with the nurse and her 'cousin,' a stalwart person like a soldier, standing in front of us.

"'Little girl go ill,' said the elder Arab. 'We seek policeman.'

"'You drop that child,' answered the 'cousin,' doubling his fists. Then I grew faint again, and when I came to myself the two white-robed men had gone. All the way home my governess scolded me for accepting sweets from strangers, saying that if my parents came to know of it, I should be whipped and sent to bed. Of course, I begged her not to tell them, and at last she consented. Do you know, I think you are the first to whom I have ever mentioned the matter, of which I am sure the governess never breathed a word, though after that, whenever we walked in the gardens, her 'cousin' always came to look after us. In the end I think she married him."

"You believe the sweet was drugged?" I asked.

She nodded. "There was something very strange in it. It was a night or two after I had tasted it that I had what just now I called my awakening, and began to think about Africa."

"Have you ever seen these men again, Miss Holmes?"

"No, never."

At this moment I heard Lady Longden say, in a severe voice:

"My dear Luna, I am sorry to interrupt your absorbing conversation, but we are all waiting for you."

So they were, for to my horror I saw that everyone was standing up except ourselves.

Miss Holmes departed in a hurry, while Scroope whispered in my ear with a snigger:

"I say, Allan, if you carry on like that with his young lady, his lordship will be growing jealous of you."

"Don't be a fool," I said sharply. But there was something in his remark, for as Lord Ragnall passed on his way to the other end of the table, he said in a low voice and with rather a forced smile:

"Well, Quatermain, I hope your dinner has not been as dull as mine, although your appetite seemed so poor."

Then I reflected that I could not remember having eaten a thing since the first entrée. So overcome was I that, rejecting all Scroope's attempts at conversation, I sat silent, drinking port and filling up with dates, until not long afterwards we went into the drawing-room, where I sat down as far from Miss Holmes as possible, and looked at a book of views of Jerusalem.

While I was thus engaged, Lord Ragnall, pitying my lonely condition, or being instigated thereto by Miss Holmes, I know not which, came up and began to chat with me about African big-game shooting. Also he asked me what was my permanent address in that country. I told him Durban, and in my turn asked why he wanted to know.

"Because Miss Holmes seems quite crazy about the place, and I expect I shall be dragged out there one day," he replied, quite gloomily. It was a prophetic remark.

At this moment our conversation was interrupted by Lady Longden, who came to bid her future son-in-law good night. She said that she must go to bed, and put her feet in mustard and water as her cold was so bad, which left me wondering whether she meant to carry out this operation in bed. I recommended her to take quinine, a suggestion she acknowledged rather inconsequently by remarking in somewhat icy tones that she supposed I sat up to all hours of the night in Africa. I replied that frequently I did, waiting for the sun to rise next day, for that member of the British aristocracy irritated me.

Thus we parted, and I never saw her again. She died many years ago, poor soul, and I suppose is now freezing her former acquaintances in the Shades, for I cannot imagine that she ever had a friend. They talk a great deal about the influences of heredity nowadays, but I don't believe very much in them myself. Who, for instance, could conceive that persons so utterly different in every way as Lady Longden and her daughter, Miss Holmes, could be mother and child? Our bodies, no doubt, we do inherit from our ancestors, but not our individualities. These come from far away.

A good many of the guests went at the same time, having long distances to drive on that cold frosty night, although it was only just ten o'clock. For as was usual at that period even in fashionable houses, we had dined at seven.

IV

HARÛT AND MARÛT

After Lord Ragnall had seen his guests to the door in the old-fashioned manner, he returned and asked me if I played cards, or whether I preferred music. I was assuring him that I hated the sight of a card when Mr. Savage appeared in his silent way and respectfully inquired of his lordship whether any gentleman was staying in the house whose Christian name was *Here-come-a-zany*. Lord Ragnall looked at him with a searching eye as though he suspected him of being drunk, and then asked what he meant by such a ridiculous question.

"I mean, my lord," replied Mr. Savage with a touch of offence in his tone, "that two foreign individuals in white clothes have arrived at the castle, stating that they wish to speak at once with a *Mr. Here-come-a-zany* who is staying here. I told them to go away as the butler said he could make nothing of their talk, but they only sat down in the snow and said they would wait for *Here-come-a-zany*."

"Then you had better put them in the old guardroom, lock them up with something to eat, and send the stable-boy for the policeman, who is a zany if ever anybody was. I expect they are after the pheasants."

"Stop a bit," I said, for an idea had occurred to me. "The message may be meant for me, though I can't conceive who sent it. My native name is Macumazana, which possibly Mr. Savage has not caught quite correctly. Shall I go to see these men?"

"I wouldn't do that in this cold, Quatermain," Lord Ragnall answered. "Did they say what they are, Savage?"

"I made out that they were conjurers, my lord. At least when I told them to go away one of them said, 'You will go first, gentleman.' Then, my lord, I heard a hissing sound in my coat-tail pocket and, putting my hand into it, I found a large snake which dropped on the ground and vanished. It quite paralysed me, my lord, and while I stood there wondering whether I was bitten, a mouse jumped out of the kitchenmaid's hair. She had been laughing at their dress, my lord, but *now* she's screaming in hysterics."

The solemn aspect of Mr. Savage as he narrated these unholy marvels was such that, like the kitchenmaid, we both burst into ill-timed merriment. Attracted by our laughter, Miss Holmes, Miss Manners, with whom she was talking, and some of the other guests, approached and asked what was the matter.

"Savage here declares that there are two conjurers in the kitchen premises, who have been producing snakes out of his pocket and mice from the hair of one of the maids, and who want to see Mr. Quatermain," Lord Ragnall answered.

"Conjurers! Oh, do have them in, George," exclaimed Miss Holmes; while Miss Manners and the others, who were getting a little tired of promiscuous conversation, echoed her request.

"By all means," he answered, "though we have enough mice here without their bringing any more. Savage, go and tell your two friends that *Mr. Here-come-a-zany* is waiting for them in the drawing-room, and that the company would like to see some of their tricks."

Savage bowed and departed, like a hero to execution, for by his pallor I could see that he was in a great fright. When he had gone we set to work and cleared a space in the middle of the room, in front of which we arranged chairs for the company to sit on.

"No doubt they are Indian jugglers," said Lord Ragnall, "and will want a place to grow their mango-tree, as I remember seeing them do in Kashmir."

As he spoke the door opened and Mr. Savage appeared through it, walking much faster than was his wont. I noted also that he gripped the pockets of his swallow-tail coat firmly in his hand.

"Mr. Hare-root and Mr. Mare-root," he announced.

"Hare-root and Mare-root!" repeated Lord Ragnall.

"Harût and Marût, I expect," I said. "I think I have read somewhere that they were great magicians, whose names these conjurers have taken." (Since then I have discovered that they are mentioned in the Koran as masters of the Black Art.)

A moment later two men followed him through the doorway. The first was a tall, Eastern-looking person with a grave countenance, a long, white beard, a hooked nose, and flashing, hawk-like eyes. The second was shorter and rather stout, also much younger. He had a genial, smiling face, small, beady-black eyes, and was clean-shaven. They were very light in colour; indeed I have seen Italians who are much darker; and there was about their whole aspect a certain air of power.

Instantly I remembered the story that Miss Holmes had told me at dinner and looked at her covertly, to see that she had turned quite pale and was trembling a little. I do not think that anyone else noticed this, however, as all were staring at the strangers. Moreover she recovered herself in a moment, and, catching my eye, laid her finger on her lips in token of silence.

The men were clothed in thick, fur-lined cloaks, which they took off and, folding them neatly, laid upon the floor, standing revealed in robes of a beautiful whiteness and in large plain turbans, also white.

"High-class Somali Arabs," thought I to myself, noting the while that as they arranged the robes they were taking in every one of us with their quick eyes. One of them shut the door, leaving Savage on this side of it as though they meant him to be present. Then they walked towards us, each of them carrying an ornamental basket made apparently of split reeds, that contained doubtless their conjuring outfit and probably the snake which Savage had found in his pocket. To my surprise they came straight to me, and, having set down the baskets, lifted their hands above their heads, as a person about to dive might do, and bowed till the points of their fingers touched the floor. Next they spoke, not in Arabic as I had expected that they would, but in Bantu, which of course I understood perfectly well.

"I, Harût, head priest and doctor of the White Kendah People, greet you, O Macumazana," said the elder man.

"I, Marût, a priest and doctor of the People of the White Kendah, greet you, O Watcher-by-night, whom we have travelled far to find," said the younger man. Then together,

"We both greet you, O Lord, who seem small but are great, O Chief with a troubled past and with a mighty future, O Beloved of Mameena who has 'gone down' but still speaks from beneath, Mameena who was and is of our company."

At this point it was my turn to shiver and become pale, as any may guess who may have chanced to read the history of Mameena, and the turn of Miss Holmes to watch *me* with animated interest.

"O Slayer of evil men and beasts!" they went on, in their rich-voiced, monotonous chant, "who, as our magic tells us, are destined to deliver our land from the terrible scourge, we greet you, we bow before you, we acknowledge you as our lord and brother, to whom we vow safety among us and in the desert, to whom we promise a great reward."

Again they bowed, once, twice, thrice; then stood silent before me with folded arms.

"What on earth are they saying?" asked Scroope. "I could catch a few words"—he knew a little kitchen Zulu—"but not much."

I told him briefly while the others listened.

"What does Mameena mean?" asked Miss Holmes, with a horrible acuteness. "Is it a woman's name?"

Hearing her, Harût and Marût bowed as though doing reverence to that name. I am sorry to say that at this point I grew confused, though really there was no reason why I should, and muttered something about a native girl who had made trouble in her day.

Miss Holmes and the other ladies looked at me with amused disbelief, and to my dismay the venerable Harût turned to Miss Holmes, and with his inevitable bow, said in broken English:

"Mameena very beautiful woman, perhaps more beautiful than you, lady. Mameena love the white lord Macumazana. She love him while she live, she love him now she dead. She tell me so again just now. You ask white lord tell you pretty story of how he kiss her before she kill herself."

Needless to say all this very misleading information was received by the audience with an attention that I can but call rapt, and in a kind of holy silence which was broken only by a sudden burst of sniggering on the part of Scroope. I favoured him with my fiercest frown. Then I fell upon that venerable villain Harût, and belaboured him in Bantu, while the audience listened as intently as though they understood.

I asked him what he meant by coming here to asperse my character. I asked him who the deuce he was. I asked him how he came to know anything about Mameena, and finally I told him that soon or late I would be even with him, and paused exhausted.

He stood there looking for all the world like a statue of the patriarch Job as I imagine him, and when I had done, replied without moving a muscle and in English:

"O Lord, Zikali, Zulu wizard, friend of mine! All great wizard friend just like all elephant and all snake. Zikali make me know Mameena, and she tell me story and send you much love, and say she wait for you always." (More sniggers from Scroope, and still intenser interest evinced by Miss Holmes and others.) "If you like, I show you Mameena 'fore I go." (Murmurs from Miss Holmes and Miss Manners of "Oh, *please* do!") "But that very little business, for what one long-ago lady out of so many?"

Then suddenly he broke into Bantu, and added: "A jest is a jest, Macumazana, though often there is meaning in a jest, and you shall see Mameena if you will. I come here to ask you to do my people a service for which you shall not lack reward. We, the White Kendah, the People of the Child, are at war with the Black Kendah, our subjects who outnumber us. The Black Kendah have an evil spirit for a god, which spirit from the beginning has dwelt in the largest elephant in all the world, a beast that none can kill, but which kills many and bewitches more. While that elephant, which is named Jana, lives we, the People of the Child, go in terror, for day by day it destroys us. We have learned—how it does not matter—that you alone can kill that elephant. If you will come and kill it, we will show you the place where all the elephants go to die, and you shall take their ivory, many wagon-loads, and grow rich. Soon you are going on a journey that has to do with a flower, and you will visit peoples named the Mazitu and the Pongo who live on an island in a lake. Far beyond the Pongo and across the desert dwell my people, the Kendah, in a secret land. When you wish to visit us, as you will do, journey to the north of that lake where the Pongo dwell, and stay there on the edge of the desert shooting till we come. Now mock me if you will, but do not forget, for these things shall befall in their season, though that time be far. If we meet no more for a while, still do not forget. When you have need of gold or of the ivory that is gold, then journey to the north of the lake where the Pongo dwell, and call on the names of Harût and Marût."

"And call on the names of Harût and Marût," repeated the younger man, who hitherto appeared to take no interest in our talk.

Next, before I could answer, before I could think the thing out indeed, for all this breath from savage and mystical Africa blowing on me suddenly here in an Essex drawing-room, seemed to overwhelm me, the ineffable Harût proceeded in his English conjurer's patter:

"Rich ladies and gentlemen want see trick by poor old wizard from centre Africa. Well, we show them, but please 'member no magic, all quite simple trick. Teach it you if you pay. Please not look too hard, no want you learn how it done. What you like see? Tree grow out of nothing, eh? Good! Please lend me that plate—what you call him—china."

Then the performance began. The tree grew admirably upon the china plate under the cover of an antimacassar. A number of bits of stick danced together on the said plate, apparently without being touched. At a whistle from Marût a second snake crawled out of the pocket of the horrified Mr. Savage, who stood observing these proceedings at a respectful distance, erected itself on its tail upon the plate and took fire till it was consumed to ashes, and so forth.

The show was very good, but to tell the truth I did not take much notice of it, for I had seen similar things before and was engaged in thoughts much excited by what Harût had said to me. At length the pair paused amidst the clapping of the audience, and Marût began to pack up the properties as though all were done. Then Harût observed casually:

"The Lord Macumazana think this poor business and he right. Very poor business, any conjurer do better. All common trick"—here his eye fell upon Mr. Savage who was wriggling uneasily in the background. "What matter with that gentleman? Brother Marût, go see."

Brother Marût went and freed Mr. Savage from two more snakes which seemed to have taken possession of various parts of his garments. Also, amidst shouts of laughter, from a large dead rat which he appeared to draw from his well-oiled hair.

"Ah!" said Harût, as his confederate returned with these prizes, leaving Savage collapsed in a chair, "snake love that gentleman much. He earn great money in Africa. Well, he keep rat in hair; hungry snake always want rat. But as I say, this poor business. Now you like to see some better, eh? Mameena, eh?"

"No," I replied firmly, whereat everyone laughed.

"Elephant Jana we want you kill, eh? Just as he look this minute."

"Yes," I said, "very much indeed, only how will you show it me?"

"That quite easy, Macumazana. You just smoke little Kendah 'bacco and see many things, if you have gift, as I *think* you got, and as I almost *sure* that lady got," and he pointed to Miss Holmes. "Sometimes they things people want see, and sometimes they things people not want see."

"Dakka," I said contemptuously, alluding to the Indian hemp on which natives make themselves drunk throughout great districts of Africa.

"Oh! no, not dakka, that common stuff; this 'bacco much better than dakka, only grow in Kendah-land. You think all nonsense? Well, you see. Give me match please."

Then while we watched he placed some tobacco, at least it looked like tobacco, in a little wooden bowl that he also produced from his basket. Next he said something to his companion, Marût, who drew a flute from his robe made out of a thick reed, and began to play on it a wild and melancholy music, the sound of which seemed to affect my backbone as standing on a great height often does. Presently too Harût broke into a low song whereof I could not understand a word, that rose and fell with the music of the flute. Now he struck a match, which seemed incongruous in the midst of this semi-magical ceremony, and taking a pinch of the tobacco, lit it and dropped it among the rest. A pale, blue smoke arose from the bowl and with it a very sweet odour not unlike that of the tuberoses gardeners grow in hot-houses, but more searching.

"Now you breath smoke, Macumazana," he said, "and tell us what you see. Oh! no fear, that not hurt you. Just like cigarette. Look," and he inhaled some of the vapour and blew it out through his nostrils, after which his face seemed to change to me, though what the change was I could not define.

I hesitated till Scroope said:

"Come, Allan, don't shirk this Central African adventure. I'll try if you like."

"No," said Harût brusquely, "*you* no good."

Then curiosity and perhaps the fear of being laughed at overcame me. I took the bowl and held it under my nose, while Harût threw over my head the antimacassar which he had used in the mango trick, to keep in the fumes I suppose.

At first these fumes were unpleasant, but just as I was about to drop the bowl they seemed to become agreeable and to penetrate to the inmost recesses of my being. The general affect of them was not unlike that of the laughing gas which dentists give, with this difference, that whereas the gas produces insensibility, these fumes seemed to set the mind on fire and to burn away all limitations of time and distance. Things shifted before me. It was as though I were no longer in that room but travelling with inconceivable rapidity.

Suddenly I appeared to stop before a curtain of mist. The mist rolled up in front of me and I saw a wild and wonderful scene. There lay a lake surrounded by dense African forest. The sky above was still red with the last lights of sunset and in it floated the full moon. On the eastern side of the lake was a great open space where nothing seemed to grow and all about this space were the skeletons of hundreds of dead elephants. There they lay, some of them almost covered with grey mosses hanging to their bones, through which their yellow tusks projected as though they had been dead for centuries; others with the rotting hide still on them. I knew that I was looking on a cemetery of elephants, the place where these great beasts went to die, as I have since been told the extinct moas did in New Zealand. All my life as a hunter had I heard rumours of these cemeteries, but never before did I see such a spot even in a dream.

See! There was one dying now, a huge gaunt bull that looked as though it were several hundred years old. It stood there swaying to and fro. Then it lifted its trunk, I suppose to trumpet, though of course I could hear nothing, and slowly sank upon its knees and so remained in the last relaxation of death.

Almost in the centre of this cemetery was a little mound of water-washed rock that had endured when the rest of the stony plain was denuded in past epochs. Suddenly upon that rock appeared the shape of the most gigantic elephant that ever I beheld in all my long experience. It had one enormous tusk, but the other was deformed and broken off short. Its sides were scarred as though with fighting and its eyes shone red and wickedly. Held in its trunk was the body of a woman whose hair hung down upon one side and whose feet hung down upon the other. Clasped in her arms was a child that seemed to be still living.

The rogue, as a brute of this sort is called, for evidently such it was, dropped the corpse to the ground and stood a while, flapping its ears. Then it felt for and picked up the child with its trunk, swung it to and fro and finally tossed it high into the air, hurling it far away. After this it walked to the elephant that I had just seen die, and charged the carcass, knocking it over. Then having lifted its trunk as though to trumpet in triumph, it shambled off towards the forest and vanished.

The curtain of mist fell again and in it, dimly, I thought I saw—well, never mind who or what I saw. Then I awoke.

"Well, did you see anything?" asked a chorus of voices.

I told them what I had seen, leaving out the last part.

"I say, old fellow," said Scroope, "you must have been pretty clever to get all that in, for your eyes weren't shut for more than ten seconds."

"Then I wonder what you would say if I repeated everything," I answered, for I still felt dreamy and not quite myself.

"You see elephant Jana?" asked Harût. "He kill woman and child, eh? Well, he do that every night. Well, that why people of White Kendah want you to kill *him* and take all that ivory which they no dare touch because it in holy place and Black Kendah not let them. So he live still. That what we wish know. Thank you much, Macumazana. You very good look through-distance man. Just what I think. Kendah 'bacco smoke work very well in you. Now, beautiful lady," he added turning to Miss Holmes, "you like look too? Better look. Who knows what you see?"

Miss Holmes hesitated a moment, studying me with an inquiring eye. But I made no sign, being in truth very curious to hear *her* experience.

"Yes," she said.

"I would prefer, Luna, that you left this business alone," remarked Lord Ragnall uneasily. "I think it is time that you ladies went to bed."

"Here is a match," said Miss Holmes to Harût who was engaged in putting more tobacco into the bowl, the suspicion of a smile upon his grave and statuesque countenance. Harût received the match with a low bow and fired the stuff as before. Then he handed the bowl, from which once again the blue smoke curled upwards, to Miss Holmes, and gently and gracefully let the antimacassar fall over it and her head, which it draped as a wedding veil might do. A few seconds later she threw off the antimacassar and cast the bowl, in which the fire was now out, on to the floor. Then she stood up with wide eyes, looking wondrous lovely and, notwithstanding her lack of height, majestic.

"I have been in another world," she said in a low voice as though she spoke to the air, "I have travelled a great way. I found myself in a small place made of stone. It was dark in the place, the fire in that bowl lit it up. There was nothing there except a beautiful statue of a naked baby which seemed to be carved in yellow ivory, and a chair made of ebony inlaid with ivory and seated with string. I stood in front of the statue of the Ivory Child. It seemed to come to life and smile at me. Round its neck was a string of red stones. It took them from its neck and set them upon mine. Then it pointed to the chair, and I sat down in the chair. That was all."

Harût followed her words with an interest that I could see was intense, although he attempted to hide it. Then he asked me to translate them, which I did.

As their full sense came home to him, although his face remained impassive, I saw his dark eyes shine with the light of triumph. Moreover I heard him whisper to Marût words that seemed to mean,

"The Sacred Child accepts the Guardian. The Spirit of the White Kendah finds a voice again."

Then as though involuntarily, but with the utmost reverence, both of them bowed deeply towards Miss Holmes.

A babel of conversation broke out.

"What a ridiculous dream," I heard Lord Ragnall say in a vexed voice. "An ivory child that seemed to come to life and to give you a necklace. Whoever heard such nonsense?"

"Whoever heard such nonsense?" repeated Miss Holmes after him, as though in polite acquiescence, but speaking as an automaton might speak.

"I say," interrupted Scroope, addressing Miss Manners, "this is a drawing-room entertainment and a half, isn't it, dear?"

"I don't know," answered Miss Manners, doubtfully, "it is rather too queer for my taste. Tricks are all very well, but when it comes to magic and visions I get frightened."

"Well, I suppose the show is over," said Lord Ragnall. "Quatermain, would you mind asking your conjurer friends what I owe them?"

Here Harût, who had understood, paused from packing up his properties and answered,

"Nothing, O great Lord, nothing. It is we owe you much. Here we learn what we want know long time. I mean if elephant Jana still kill people of Kendah. Kendah 'bacco no speak to us. Only speak to new spirit. You got great gift, lady, and you too, Macumazana. You not like smoke more Kendah 'bacco and look into past, eh? Better look! Very full, past, learn much there about all us; learn how things begin. Make you understand lot what seem odd to-day. No! Well, one day you look p'raps, 'cause past pull hard and call loud, only no one hear what it say. Good night, O great Lord. Good night, O beautiful lady. Good night, O Macumazana, till we meet again when you come kill elephant Jana. Blessing of the Heaven-Child, who give rain, who protect all danger, who give food, who give health, on you all."

Then making many obeisances they walked backwards to the door where they put on their long cloaks.

At a sign from Lord Ragnall I accompanied them, an office which, fearing more snakes, Mr. Savage was very glad to resign to me. Presently we stood outside the house amidst the moaning trees, and very cold it was there.

"What does all this mean, O men of Africa?" I asked.

"Answer the question yourself when you stand face to face with the great elephant Jana that has in it an evil spirit, O Macumazana," replied Harût. "Nay, listen. We are far from our home and we sought tidings through those who could give it to us, and we have won those tidings, that is all. We are worshippers of the Heavenly Child that is eternal youth and all good things, but of late the Child has lacked a tongue. Yet to-night it spoke again. Seek to know no more, you who in due season will know all things."

"Seek to know no more," echoed Marût, "who already, perhaps, know too much, lest harm should come to you, Macumazana."

"Where are you going to sleep to-night?" I asked.

"We do not sleep here," answered Harût, "we walk to the great city and thence find our way to Africa, where we shall meet you again. You know that we are no liars, common readers of thought and makers of tricks, for did not Dogeetah, the wandering white man, speak to you of the people of whom he had heard who worshipped the Child of Heaven? Go in, Macumazana, ere you take harm in this horrible cold, and take with you this as a marriage gift from the Child of Heaven whom she met to-night, to the beautiful lady stamped with the sign of the young moon who is about to marry the great lord she loves."

Then he thrust a little linen-wrapped parcel into my hand and with his companion vanished into the darkness.

I returned to the drawing-room where the others were still discussing the remarkable performance of the two native conjurers.

"They have gone," I said in answer to Lord Ragnall, "to walk to London as they said. But they have sent a wedding-present to Miss Holmes," and I showed the parcel.

"Open it, Quatermain," he said again.

"No, George," interrupted Miss Holmes, laughing, for by now she seemed to have quite recovered herself, "I like to open my own presents."

HE SHRUGGED HIS SHOULDERS AND I handed her the parcel, which was neatly sewn up. Somebody produced scissors and the stitches were cut. Within the linen was a necklace of beautiful red stones, oval-shaped like amber beads and of the size of a robin's egg. They were roughly polished and threaded on what I recognized at once to be hair from an elephant's tail. From certain indications I judged these stones, which might have been spinels or carbuncles, or even rubies, to be very ancient. Possibly they had once hung round the neck of some lady in old Egypt. Indeed a beautiful little statuette, also of red stone, which was suspended from the centre of the necklace, suggested that this was so, for it may well have been a likeness of one of the great gods of the Egyptians, the infant Horus, the son of Isis.

"That is the necklace I saw which the Ivory Child gave me in my dream," said Miss Holmes quietly.

Then with much deliberation she clasped it round her throat.

V

The Plot

The sequel to the events of this evening may be told very briefly and of it the reader can form his own judgment. I narrate it as it happened.

That night I did not sleep at all well. It may have been because of the excitement of the great shoot in which I found myself in competition with another man whom I disliked and who had defrauded me in the past, to say nothing of its physical strain in cold and heavy weather. Or it may have been that my imagination was stirred by the arrival of that strange pair, Harût and Marût, apparently in search of myself, seven thousand miles away from any place where they can have known aught of an insignificant individual with a purely local repute. Or it may have been that the pictures which they showed me when under the influence of the fumes of their "tobacco"—or of their hypnotism—took an undue possession of my brain.

Or lastly, the strange coincidence that the beautiful betrothed of my host should have related to me a tale of her childhood of which she declared she had never spoken before, and that within an hour the two principal actors in that tale should have appeared before my eyes and hers (for I may state that from the beginning I had no doubt that they were the same men), moved me and filled me with quite natural foreboding. Or all these things together may have tended to a concomitant effect. At any rate the issue was that I could not sleep.

For hour after hour I lay thinking and in an irritated way listening for the chimes of the Ragnall stable-clock which once had adorned the tower of the church and struck the quarters with a damnable reiteration. I concluded that Messrs. Harût and Marût were a couple of common Arab rogues such as I had seen performing at the African ports. Then a quarter struck and I concluded that the elephants' cemetery which I beheld in the smoke undoubtedly existed and that I meant to collar those thousands of pounds' worth of ivory before I died. Then after another quarter I concluded that there was no elephants' cemetery—although by the way my old friend, Dogeetah or Brother John, had mentioned such a thing to me—but that probably there was a tribe, as he had also mentioned, called the Kendah, who worshipped a baby, or rather its effigy.

Well now, as had already occurred to me, the old Egyptians, of whom I was always fond of reading when I got a chance, also worshipped a child, Horus the Saviour. And that child had a mother called Isis symbolized in the crescent moon, the great Nature goddess, the mistress of mysteries to whose cult ten thousand priests were sworn— do not Herodotus and others, especially Apuleius, tell us all about her? And by a queer coincidence Miss Holmes had the mark of a crescent moon upon her breast. And when she was a child those two men, or others very like them, had pointed out that mark to each other. And I had seen them staring hard at it that night. And in her vapour-invoked dream the "Heavenly Child," *alias* Horus, or the double of Horus, the *Ka*, I think the Egyptians called it, had awakened at the sight of her and kissed her and given her the necklace of the goddess, and—all the rest. What did it mean?

I went to sleep at last wondering what on earth it *could* mean, till presently that confounded clock woke me up again and I must go through the whole business once more.

By degrees, this was towards dawn, I became aware that all hope of rest had vanished from me utterly; that I was most painfully awake, and what is more, oppressed by a curious fear to the effect that something was going to happen to Miss Holmes. So vivid did this fear become that at length I arose, lit a candle and dressed myself. As it happened I knew where Miss Holmes slept. Her room, which I had seen her enter, was on the same corridor as mine though at the other end of it near the head of a stair that ran I knew not whither. In my portmanteau that had been sent over from Miss Manners's house, amongst other things was a small double-barrelled pistol which from long habit I always carried with me loaded, except for the caps that were in a little leather case with some spare ammunition attached to the pistol belt. I took it out, capped it and thrust it into my pocket. Then I slipped from the room and stood behind a tall clock in the corridor, watching Miss Holmes's door and reflecting what a fool I should look if anyone chanced to find me.

Half an hour or so later by the light of the setting moon which struggled through a window, I saw the door open and Miss Holmes emerge in a kind of dressing-gown and still wearing the necklace which Harût and Marût had given her. Of this I was sure for the light gleamed upon the red stones.

Also it shone upon her face and showed me without doubt that she was walking in her sleep.

Gliding as silently as a ghost she crossed the corridor and vanished. I followed and saw that she had descended an ancient, twisting stairway which I had noted in the castle wall. I went after her, my stockinged feet making no noise, feeling my way carefully in the darkness of the stair, for I did not dare to strike a match. Beneath me I heard a noise as of someone fumbling with bolts. Then a door creaked on its hinges and there was some light. When I reached the doorway I caught sight of the figure of Miss Holmes flitting across a hollow garden that was laid out in the bottom of the castle moat which had been drained. The garden, as I had observed when we walked through it on the previous day on our way to the first covert that we shot, was bordered by a shrubbery through which ran paths that led to the back drive of the castle.

Across the garden glided the figure of Miss Holmes and after it went I, crouching and taking cover behind every bush as though I were stalking big game, which indeed I was. She entered the shrubbery, moving much more swiftly now, for as she went she seemed to gather speed, like a stone which is rolled down a hill. It was as though whatever might be attracting her, for I felt sure that she was being drawn by something, acted more strongly upon her sleeping will as she drew nearer to it. For a while I lost sight of her in the shadow of the tall trees. Then suddenly I saw her again, standing quite still in an opening caused by the blowing down in the gale of one of the avenue of elms that bordered the back drive. But now she was no longer alone, for advancing towards her were two cloaked figures in whom I recognized Harût and Marût.

There she stood with outstretched arms, and towards her, stealthily as lions stalking a buck, came Harût and Marût. Moreover, between the naked boughs of the fallen elm I caught sight of what looked like the outline of a closed carriage standing upon the drive. Also I heard a horse stamp upon the frosty ground. Round the edge of the little glade I ran, keeping in the dark shadow, as I went cocking the pistol that was in my pocket. Then suddenly I darted out and stood between Harût and Marût and Miss Holmes.

Not a word passed between us. I think that all three of us subconsciously were anxious not to awake the sleeping woman, knowing that if we did so there would be a terrible scene. Only after motioning to me to stand aside, of course in vain, Harût and Marût drew from their robes curved and cruel-looking knives and bowed, for even now their politeness did not forsake them. I bowed back and when I straightened myself those enterprising Easterns found that I was covering the heart of Harût with my pistol. Then with that perception which is part of the mental outfit of the great, they saw that the game was up since I could have shot them both before a knife touched me.

"You have won this time, O Watcher-by-Night," whispered Harût softly, "but another time you will lose. That beautiful lady belongs to us and the People of the White Kendah, for she is marked with the holy mark of the young moon. The call of the Child of Heaven is heard in her heart, and will bring her home to the Child as it has brought her to us to-night. Now lead her hence still sleeping, O brave and clever one, so well named Watcher-by-Night."

Then they were gone and presently I heard the sound of horses being driven rapidly along the drive.

For a moment I hesitated as to whether I would or would not run in and shoot those horses. Two considerations stayed me. The first was that if I did so my pistol would be empty, or even if I shot one horse and retained a barrel loaded, with it I could only kill a single man, leaving myself defenceless against the knife of the other. The second consideration was that now as before I did not wish to wake up Miss Holmes.

I crept to her and not knowing what else to do, took hold of one of her outstretched hands. She turned and came with me at once as though she knew me, remaining all the while fast asleep. Thus we went back to the house, through the still open door, up the stairway straight to her own room, on the threshold of which I loosed her hand. The room was dark and I could see nothing, but I listened until I heard a sound as of a person throwing herself upon the bed and drawing up the blankets. Then knowing that she was safe for a while, I shut the door, which opened outwards as doors of ancient make sometimes do, and set against it a little table that stood in the passage.

Next, after reflecting for a minute, the circumstances being awkward in many ways, I went to my room and lit a candle. Obviously it was my duty to inform Lord Ragnall of what had happened and that as soon as possible. But I had no idea in what part of that huge building his sleeping place might be, nor, for patent reasons, was it desirable that I should disturb the house and so create talk. In this dilemma I remembered that Lord Ragnall's confidential servant, Mr. Savage, when he conducted me to my room on the previous night, which he made a point of doing perhaps because he wished to talk over the matter of the snakes that had found their way into his pockets, had shown me a bell in it which he said rang outside his door. He called it an "emergency bell." I remarked idly that it was improbable that I should have any occasion for its use.

"Who knows, sir?" said Mr. Savage prophetically. "There are folk who say that this old castle is haunted, which after what I have seen to-night I can well believe. If you should chance to meet a ghost looking, let us say, like those black villains, Harum and Scarum, or whatever they call themselves—well, sir, two's better company than one."

I considered that bell but was loath to ring it for the reasons I have given. Then I went outside the room and looked. As I had hoped might be the case, there ran the wire on the face of the wall connected along its length by other wires with the various rooms it passed.

I set to work and followed that wire. It was not an easy job; indeed once or twice it reminded me of that story of the old Greek hero who found his way through a labyrinth by means of a silken thread. I forget whether it were a bull or a lady he was looking for, but with care and perseverance he found one or the other, or it may have been both.

Down staircases and various passages I went with my eye glued upon the wire, which occasionally got mixed up with other wires, till at length it led me through a swing door covered with red baize into what appeared to be a modern annexe to the castle. Here at last it terminated on the spring of an alarming-looking and deep-throated bell that hung immediately over a certain door.

On this door I knocked, hoping that it might be that of Mr. Savage and praying earnestly that it did not enclose the chaste resting-place of the cook or any other female. Too late, I mean after I had knocked, it occurred to me that if so my position would be painful to a degree. However in this particular Fortune stood my friend, which does not always happen to the virtuous. For presently I heard a voice which I recognized as that of Mr. Savage, asking, not without a certain quaver in its tone,

"Who the devil is that?"

"Me," I replied, being flustered.

"'Me' won't do," said the voice. "'Me' might be Harum or it might be Scarum, or it might be someone worse. Who's 'Me'?"

"Allan Quatermain, you idiot," I whispered through the keyhole.

"Anna who? Well, never mind. Go away, Hanna. I'll talk to you in the morning."

Then I kicked the door, and at length, very cautiously, Mr. Savage opened it.

"Good heavens, sir," he said, "what are you doing here, sir? Dressed too, at this hour, and with the handle of a pistol sticking out of your pocket—or is it—the head of a snake?" and he jumped back, a strange and stately figure in a long white nightshirt which apparently he wore over his underclothing.

I entered the room and shut the door, whereon he politely handed me a chair, remarking,

"Is it ghosts, sir, or are you ill, or is it Harum and Scarum, of whom I have been thinking all night? Very cold too, sir, being afraid to pull up the bedclothes for fear lest there might be more reptiles in them." He pointed to his dress-coat hanging on the back of another chair with both the pockets turned inside out, adding tragically, "To think, sir, that this new coat has been a nest of snakes, which I have hated like poison from a child, and me almost a teetotaller!"

"Yes," I said impatiently, "it's Harum and Scarum as you call them. Take me to Lord Ragnall's bedroom at once."

"Ah! sir, burgling, I suppose, or mayhap worse," he exclaimed as he threw on some miscellaneous garments and seized a life-preserver which hung upon a hook. "Now I'm ready, only I hope they have left their snakes behind. I never could bear the sight of a snake, and they seem to know it—the brutes."

In due course we reached Lord Ragnall's room, which Mr. Savage entered, and in answer to a stifled inquiry exclaimed,

"Mr. Allan Quatermain to see you, my lord."

"What is it, Quatermain?" he asked, sitting up in bed and yawning. "Have you had a nightmare?"

"Yes," I answered, and Savage having left us and shut the door, I told him everything as it is written down.

"Great heavens!" he exclaimed when I had finished. "If it had not been for you and your intuition and courage—"

"Never mind me," I interrupted. "The question is—what should be done now? Are you going to try to arrest these men, or will you—hold your tongue and merely cause them to be watched?"

"Really I don't know. Even if we can catch them the whole story would sound so strange in a law-court, and all sorts of things might be suggested."

"Yes, Lord Ragnall, it would sound so strange that I beg you will come at once to see the evidences of what I tell you, before rain or snow obliterates them, bringing another witness with you. Lady Longden, perhaps."

"Lady Longden! Why one might as well write to *The Times*. I have it! There's Savage. He is faithful and can be silent."

So Savage was called in and, while Lord Ragnall dressed himself hurriedly, told the outline of his story under pain of instant dismissal if he breathed a word. Really to watch his face was as good as a play. So astonished was he that all he could ejaculate was—

"The black-hearted villains! Well, they ain't friendly with snakes for nothing."

Then having made sure that Miss Holmes was still in her room, we went down the twisting stair and through the side doorway, locking the door after us. By now the dawn was breaking and there was enough light to enable me in certain places where the snow that fell after the gale remained, to show Lord Ragnall and Savage the impress of the little bedroom slippers which Miss Holmes wore, and of my stockinged feet following after.

In the plantation things were still easier, for every detail of the movements of the four of us could be traced. Moreover, on the back drive was the spoor of the horses and the marks of the wheels of the carriage that had been brought for the purposes of the abduction. Also my great good fortune, for this seemed to prove my theory, we found a parcel wrapped in native linen that appeared to have fallen out of the carriage when Harût and Marût made their hurried escape, as one of the wheels had gone over it. It contained an Eastern woman's dress and veil, intended, I suppose, to be used in disguising Miss Holmes, who thence-forward would have appeared to be the wife or daughter of one of the abductors.

Savage discovered this parcel, which he lifted only to drop it with a yell, for underneath it lay a torpid snake, doubtless one of those that had been used in the performance.

Of these discoveries and many other details, on our return to the house, Lord Ragnall made full notes in a pocket-book, that when completed were signed by all three of us.

There is not much more to tell, that is of this part of the story. The matter was put into the hands of detectives who discovered that the Easterns had driven to London, where all traces of the carriage which conveyed them was lost. They, however, embarked upon a steamer called the *Antelope*, together with two native women, who probably had been provided to look after Miss Holmes, and sailed that very afternoon for Egypt. Thither, of course, it was useless to follow them in those days, even if it had been advisable to do so.

To return to Miss Holmes. She came down to breakfast looking very charming but rather pale. Again I sat next to her and took some opportunity to ask her how she had rested that night.

She replied, Very well and yet very ill, since, although she never remembered sleeping more soundly in her life, she had experienced all sorts of queer dreams of which she could remember nothing at all, a circumstance that annoyed her much, as she was sure that they were most interesting. Then she added,

"Do you know, Mr. Quatermain, I found a lot of mud on my dressing-gown this morning, and my bedroom slippers were also a mass of mud and wet through. How do you account for that? It is just as though I had been walking about outside in my sleep, which is absurd, as I never did such a thing in my life."

Not feeling equal to the invention of any convincing explanation of these phenomena, I upset the marmalade pot on to the table in such a way that some of it fell upon her dress, and then covered my retreat with profuse apologies. Understanding my dilemma, for he had heard something of this talk, Lord Ragnall came to my aid with a startling statement of which I forget the purport, and thus that crisis passed.

Shortly after breakfast Scroope announced to Miss Manners that her carriage was waiting, and we departed. Before I went, as it chanced, I had a few private words with my host, with Miss Holmes, and with the magnificent Mr. Savage. To the last, by the way, I offered a tip which he refused, saying that after all we had gone through together he could not allow "money to come between us," by which he meant, to pass from my pocket to his. Lord Ragnall asked me for both my English and my African addresses, which he noted in his pocket-book. Then he said,

"Really, Quatermain, I feel as though I had known you for years instead of three days; if you will allow me I will add that I should like to know a great deal more of you." (He was destined to do so, poor fellow, though neither of us knew it at the time.) "If ever you come to England again I hope you will make this house your headquarters."

"And if ever you come to South Africa, Lord Ragnall, I hope you will make my four-roomed shanty on the Berea at Durban your headquarters. You will get a hearty welcome there and something to eat, but little more."

"There is nothing I should like better, Quatermain. Circumstances have put me in a certain position in this country, still to tell you the truth there is a great deal about the life of which I grow very tired. But you see I am going to be married, and that I fear means an end of travelling, since naturally my wife will wish to take her place in society and the rest."

"Of course," I replied, "for it is not every young lady who has the luck to become an English peeress with all the etceteras, is it? Still I am not so sure but that Miss Holmes will take to travelling some day, although I *am* sure that she would do better to stay at home."

He looked at me curiously, then asked,

"You don't think there is anything really serious in all this business, do you?"

"I don't know what to think," I answered, "except that you will do well to keep a good eye upon your wife. What those Easterns tried to do last night and, I think, years ago, they may try again soon, or years hence, for evidently they are patient and determined men with much to win. Also it is a curious coincidence that she should have that mark upon her which appeals so strongly to Messrs. Harût and Marût, and, to be brief, she is in some ways different from most young women. As she said to me herself last night, Lord Ragnall, we are surrounded by mysteries; mysteries of blood, of inherited spirit, of this world generally in which it is probable that we all descended from quite a few common ancestors. And beyond these are other mysteries of the measureless universe to which we belong, that may already be exercising their strong and secret influences upon us, as perhaps, did we know it, they have done for millions of years in the Infinite whence we came and whither we go."

I suppose I spoke somewhat solemnly, for he said,

"Do you know you frighten me a little, though I don't quite understand what you mean." Then we parted.

With Miss Holmes my conversation was shorter. She remarked,

"It has been a great pleasure to me to meet you. I do not remember anybody with whom I have found myself in so much sympathy—except one of course. It is strange to think that when we meet again I shall be a married woman."

"I do not suppose we shall ever meet again, Miss Holmes. Your life is here, mine is in the wildest places of a wild land far away."

"Oh! yes, we shall," she answered. "I learned this and lots of other things when I held my head in that smoke last night."

Then we also parted.

Lastly Mr. Savage arrived with my coat. "Goodbye, Mr. Quatermain," he said. "If I forget everything else I shall never forget you and those villains, Harum and Scarum and their snakes. I hope it won't be my lot ever to clap eyes on them again, Mr. Quatermain, and yet somehow I don't feel so sure of that."

"Nor do I," I replied, with a kind of inspiration, after which followed the episode of the rejected tip.

VI

The Bona Fide Gold Mine

Fully two years had gone by since I bade farewell to Lord Ragnall and Miss Holmes, and when the curtain draws up again behold me seated on the stoep of my little house at Durban, plunged in reflection and very sad indeed. Why I was sad I will explain presently.

In that interval of time I had heard once or twice about Lord Ragnall. Thus I received from Scroope a letter telling of his lordship's marriage with Miss Holmes, which, it appeared, had been a very fine affair indeed, quite one of the events of the London season. Two Royalties attended the ceremony, a duke was the best man, and the presents according to all accounts were superb and of great value, including a priceless pearl necklace given by the bridegroom to the bride. A cutting from a society paper which Scroope enclosed dwelt at length upon the splendid appearance of the bridegroom and the sweet loveliness of the bride. Also it described her dress in language which was Greek to me. One sentence, however, interested me intensely.

It ran: "The bride occasioned some comment by wearing only one ornament, although the Ragnall family diamonds, which have not seen the light for many years, are known to be some of the finest in the country. It was a necklace of what appeared to be large but rather roughly polished rubies, to which hung a small effigy of an Egyptian god also fashioned from a ruby. It must be added that although of an unusual nature on such an occasion this jewel suited her dark beauty well. Lady Ragnall's selection of it, however, from the many she possesses was the cause of much speculation. When asked by a friend why she had chosen it, she is reported to have said that it was to bring her good fortune."

Now why did she wear the barbaric marriage gift of Harût and Marût in preference to all the other gems at her disposal, I wondered. The thing was so strange as to be almost uncanny.

The second piece of information concerning this pair reached me through the medium of an old *Times* newspaper which I received over a year later. It was to the effect that a son and heir had been born to Lord Ragnall and that both mother and child were doing well.

So there's the end to a very curious little story, thought I to myself.

WELL, DURING THOSE TWO YEARS many things befell me. First of all, in company with my old friend Sir Stephen Somers, I made the expedition to Pongoland in search of the wonderful orchid which he desired to add to his collection. I have already written of that journey and our extraordinary adventures, and need therefore allude to it no more here, except to say that during the course of it I was sorely tempted to travel to the territory north of the lake in which the Pongos dwelt. Much did I desire to see whether Messrs. Harût and Marût would in truth appear to conduct me to the land where the wonderful elephant which was supposed to be animated by an evil spirit was waiting to be killed by my rifle. However, I resisted the impulse, as indeed our circumstances obliged me to do. In the end we returned safely to Durban, and here I came to the conclusion that never again would I risk my life on such mad expeditions.

Owing to circumstances which I have detailed elsewhere I was now in possession of a considerable sum of cash, and this I determined to lay out in such a fashion as to make me independent of hunting and trading in the wilder regions of Africa. As usual when money is forthcoming, an opportunity soon presented itself in the shape of a gold mine which had been discovered on the borders of Zululand, one of the first that was ever found in those districts. A Jew trader named Jacob brought it to my notice and offered me a half share if I would put up the capital necessary to work the mine. I made a journey of inspection and convinced myself that it was indeed a wonderful proposition. I need not enter into the particulars nor, to tell the truth, have I any desire to do so, for the subject is still painful to me, further than to say that this Jew and some friends of his panned out visible gold before my eyes and then revealed to me the magnificent quartz reef from which, as they demonstrated, it had been washed in the bygone ages of the world. The news of our discovery spread like wildfire, and as, whatever else I might be, everyone knew that I was honest, in the end a small company was formed with Allan Quatermain, Esq., as the chairman of the Bona Fide Gold Mine, Limited.

Oh! that company! Often to this day I dream of it when I have indigestion.

Our capital was small, £10,000, of which the Jew, who was well named Jacob, and his friends, took half (for nothing of course) as the purchase price of their rights. I thought the proportion large and said so, especially after I had ascertained that these rights had cost them exactly three dozen of square-face gin, a broken-down wagon, four cows past the bearing age and £5 in cash. However, when it was pointed out to me that by their peculiar knowledge and genius they had located and provided the value of a property of enormous potential worth, moreover that this sum was to be paid to them in scrip which would only be realizable when success was assured and not in money, after a night of anxious consideration I gave way.

Personally, before I consented to accept the chairmanship, which carried with it a salary of £100 a year (which I never got), I bought and paid for in cash, shares to the value of £1,000 sterling. I remember that Jacob and his friends seemed surprised at this act of mine, as they had offered to give me five hundred of their shares for nothing "in consideration of the guarantee of my name." These I refused, saying that I would not ask others to invest in a venture in which I had no actual money stake; whereon they accepted my decision, not without enthusiasm. In the end the balance of £4,000 was subscribed and we got to work. Work is a good name for it so far as I was concerned, for never in all my days have I gone through so harrowing a time.

We began by washing a certain patch of gravel and obtained results which seemed really astonishing. So remarkable were they that on publication the shares rose to 10s. premium. Jacob and Co. took advantage of this opportunity to sell quite half of their bonus holding to eager applicants, explaining to me that they did so not for personal profit, which they scorned, but "to broaden the basis of the undertaking by admitting fresh blood."

It was shortly after this boom that the gravel surrounding the rich patch became very gravelly indeed, and it was determined that we should buy a small battery and begin to crush the quartz from which the gold was supposed to flow in a Pactolian stream. We negotiated for that battery through a Cape Town firm of engineers—but why follow the melancholy business in all its details? The shares began to decrease in value. They shrank to their original price of £1, then to 15s., then to 10s. Jacob, he was managing director, explained to me that it was necessary to "support the market," as he was already doing to an enormous extent, and that I as chairman ought to take a "lead in this good work" in order to show my faith in the concern.

I took a lead to the extent of another £500, which was all that I could afford. I admit that it was a shock to such trust in human nature as remained to me when I discovered subsequently that the 1,000 shares which I bought for my £500 had really been the property of Jacob, although they appeared to be sold to me in various other names.

The crisis came at last, for before that battery was delivered our available funds were exhausted, and no one would subscribe another halfpenny. Debentures, it is true, had been issued and taken up to the extent of about £1,000 out of the £5,000 offered, though who bought them remained at the time a mystery to me. Ultimately a meeting was called to consider the question of liquidating the company, and at this meeting, after three sleepless nights, I occupied the chair.

When I entered the room, to my amazement I found that of the five directors only one was present besides myself, an honest old retired sea captain who had bought and paid for 300 shares. Jacob and the two friends who represented his interests had, it appeared, taken ship that morning for Cape Town, whither they were summoned to attend various relatives who had been seized with illness.

It was a stormy meeting at first. I explained the position to the best of my ability, and when I had finished was assailed with a number of questions which I could not answer to the satisfaction of myself or of anybody else. Then a gentleman, the owner of ten shares, who had evidently been drinking, suggested in plain language that I had cheated the shareholders by issuing false reports.

I jumped up in a fury and, although he was twice my size, asked him to come and argue the question outside, whereon he promptly went away. This incident excited a laugh, and then the whole truth came out. A man with coloured blood in him stood up and told a story which was subsequently proved to be true. Jacob had employed him to "salt" the mine by mixing a heavy sprinkling of gold in the gravel we had first washed (which the coloured man swore he did in innocence), and subsequently had defrauded him of his wages. That was all. I sank back in my chair overcome. Then some good fellow in the audience, who had lost money himself in the affair and whom I scarcely knew, got up and made a noble speech which went far to restore my belief in human nature.

He said in effect that it was well known that I, Allan Quatermain, after working like a horse in the interests of the shareholders, had practically ruined myself over this enterprise, and that the real thief was Jacob, who had made tracks for the Cape, taking with him a large cash profit resulting from the sale of shares. Finally he concluded by calling for "three cheers for our honest friend and fellow sufferer, Mr. Allan Quatermain."

Strange to say the audience gave them very heartily indeed. I thanked them with tears in my eyes, saying that I was glad to leave the room as poor as I had ever been, but with a reputation which my conscience as well as their kindness assured me was quite unblemished.

Thus the winding-up resolution was passed and that meeting came to an end. After shaking hands with my deliverer from a most unpleasant situation, I walked homewards with the lightest heart in the world. My money was gone, it was true; also my over-confidence in others had led me to make a fool of myself by accepting as fact, on what I believed to be the evidence of my eyes, that which I had not sufficient expert knowledge to verify. But my honour was saved, and as I have again and again seen in the course of life, money is nothing when compared with honour, a remark which Shakespeare made long ago, though like many other truths this is one of which a full appreciation can only be gained by personal experience.

Not very far from the place where our meeting had been held I passed a side street then in embryo, for it had only one or two houses situated in their gardens and a rather large and muddy sluit of water running down one side at the edge of the footpath. Save for two people this street was empty, but that pair attracted my attention. They were a white man, in whom I recognized the stout and half-intoxicated individual who had accused me of cheating the company and then departed, and a withered old Hottentot who at that distance, nearly a hundred yards away, much reminded me of a certain Hans.

This Hans, I must explain, was originally a servant of my father, who was a missionary in the Cape Colony, and had been my companion in many adventures. Thus in my youth he and I alone escaped when Dingaan murdered Retief and his party of Boers,* and he had been one of my party in our quest for the wonderful orchid, the record of which I have written down in "The Holy Flower."

Hans had his weak points, among which must be counted his love of liquor, but he was a gallant and resourceful old fellow as indeed he had amply proved upon that orchid-seeking expedition. Moreover he loved me with a love passing the love of women. Now, having acquired some money in a way I need not stop to describe—for is it not written elsewhere?—he was settled as a kind of little chief on a farm not very

---

* See the book called "Marie."—Editor.

far from Durban, where he lived in great honour because of the fame of his deeds.

The white man and Hans, if Hans it was, were engaged in violent altercation whereof snatches floated to me on the breeze, spoken in the Dutch tongue.

"You dirty little Hottentot!" shouted the white man, waving a stick, "I'll cut the liver out of you. What do you mean by nosing about after me like a jackal?" And he struck at Hans, who jumped aside.

"Son of a fat white sow," screamed Hans in answer (for the moment I heard his voice I knew that it was Hans), "did you dare to call the Baas a thief? Yes, a thief, O Rooter in the mud, O Feeder on filth and worms, O Hog of the gutter—the Baas, the clipping of whose nail is worth more than you and all your family, he whose honour is as clear as the sunlight and whose heart is cleaner than the white sand of the sea."

"Yes, I did," roared the white man; "for he got my money in the gold mine."

"Then, hog, why did you run away. Why did you not wait to tell him so outside that house?"

"I'll teach you about running away, you little yellow dog," replied the other, catching Hans a cut across the ribs.

"Oh! you want to see me run, do you?" said Hans, skipping back a few yards with wonderful agility. "Then look!"

Thus speaking he lowered his head and charged like a buffalo. Fair in the middle he caught that white man, causing him to double up, fly backwards and land with a most resounding splash in the deepest part of the muddy sluit. Here I may remark that, as his shins are the weakest, a Hottentot's head is by far the hardest and most dangerous part of him. Indeed it seems to partake of the nature of a cannon ball, for, without more than temporary disturbance to its possessor, I have seen a half-loaded wagon go over one of them on a muddy road.

Having delivered this home thrust Hans bolted round a corner and disappeared, while I waited trembling to see what happened to his adversary. To my relief nearly a minute later he crept out of the sluit covered with mud and dripping with water and hobbled off slowly down the street, his head so near his feet that he looked as though he had been folded in two, and his hands pressed upon what I believe is medically known as the diaphragm. Then I also went upon my way roaring with laughter. Often I have heard Hottentots called the lowest of mankind, but, reflected I, they can at any rate be good friends to those who treat them well—a fact of which I was to have further proof ere long.

By the time I reached my house and had filled my pipe and sat myself down in the dilapidated cane chair on the veranda, that natural reaction set in which so often follows rejoicing at the escape from a great danger. It was true that no one believed I had cheated them over that thrice-accursed gold mine, but how about other matters?

I mused upon the Bible narrative of Jacob and Esau with a new and very poignant sympathy for Esau. I wondered what would become of my Jacob. Jacob, I mean the original, prospered exceedingly as a result of his deal in porridge, and, as thought I, probably would his artful descendant who so appropriately bore his name. As a matter of fact I do not know what became of him, but bearing his talents in mind I think it probable that, like Van Koop, under some other patronymic he has now been rewarded with a title by the British Government. At any rate I had eaten the porridge in the shape of worthless but dearly purchased shares, after labouring hard at the chase of the golden calf, while brother Jacob had got my inheritance, or rather my money. Probably he was now counting it over in sovereigns upon the ship and sniggering as he thought of the shareholders' meeting with me in the chair. Well, he was a thief and would run his road to whatever end is appointed for thieves, so why should I bother my head more about him? As I had kept my honour—let him take my savings.

But I had a son to support, and now what was I to do with scarcely three hundred pounds, a good stock of guns and this little Durban property left to me in the world? Commerce in all its shapes I renounced once and for ever. It was too high—or too low—for me; so it would seem that there remained to me only my old business of professional hunting. Once again I must seek those adventures which I had forsworn when my evil star shone so brightly over a gold mine. What was it to be? Elephants, I supposed, since these are the only creatures worth killing from a money point of view. But most of my old haunts had been more or less shot out. The competition of younger professionals, of wandering backveld Boers and even of poaching natives who had obtained guns, was growing severe. If I went at all I should have to travel farther afield.

Whilst I meditated thus, turning over the comparative advantages or disadvantages of various possible hunting grounds in my mind, my attention was caught by a kind of cough that seemed to proceed from the farther side of a large gardenia bush. It was not a human cough, but rather resembled that made by a certain small buck at night, probably to signal to its mate, which of course it could not be as there were no buck within several miles. Yet I knew it came from a human throat, for had I not heard it before in many an hour of difficulty and danger?

"Draw near, Hans," I said in Dutch, and instantly out of a clump of aloes that grew in front of the pomegranate hedge, crept the withered shape of the old Hottentot, as a big yellow snake might do. Why he should choose this method of advance instead of that offered by the garden path I did not know, but it was quite in accordance with his secretive nature, inherited from a hundred generations of ancestors who spent their lives avoiding the observation of murderous foes.

He squatted down in front of me, staring in a vacant way at the fierce ball of the westering sun without blinking an eyelid, just as a vulture does.

"You look to me as though you had been fighting, Hans," I said. "The crown of your hat is knocked out; you are splashed with mud and there is the mark of a stick upon your left side."

"Yes, Baas. You are right as usual, Baas. I had a quarrel with a man about sixpence that he owed me, and knocked him over with my head, forgetting to take my hat off first. Therefore it is spoiled, for which I am sorry, as it was quite a new hat, not two years old. The Baas gave it me. He bought it in a store at Utrecht when we were coming back from Pongoland."

"Why do you lie to me?" I asked "You have been fighting a white man and for more than sixpence. You knocked him into a sluit and the mud splashed up over you."

"Yes, Baas, that is so. Your spirit speaks truly to you of the matter. Yet it wanders a little from the path, since I fought the white man for less than sixpence. I fought him for love, which is nothing at all."

"Then you are even a bigger fool than I took you for, Hans. What do you want now?"

"I want to borrow a pound, Baas. The white man will take me before the magistrate, and I shall be fined a pound, or fourteen days in the *trunk* (i.e. jail). It is true that the white man struck me first, but the magistrate will not believe the word of a poor old Hottentot against his, and I have no witness. He will say, 'Hans, you were drunk again. Hans, you are a liar and deserve to be flogged, which you will be next time. Pay a pound and ten shillings more, which is the price of good white justice, or go to the *trunk* for fourteen days and make baskets there for the great Queen to use.' Baas, I have the price of the justice which is ten shillings, but I want to borrow the pound for the fine."

"Hans, I think that just now you are better able to lend me a pound than I am to lend one to you. My bag is empty, Hans."

"Is it so, Baas? Well, it does not matter. If necessary I can make baskets for the great white Queen to put her food in, for fourteen days, or mats on which she will wipe her feet. The *trunk* is not such a bad place, Baas. It gives time to think of the white man's justice and to thank the Great One in the Sky, because the little sins one did not do have been found out and punished, while the big sins one did do, such as—well, never mind, Baas—have not been found out at all. Your reverend father, the Predikant, always taught me to have a thankful heart, Baas, and when I remember that I have only been in the *trunk* for three months altogether who, if all were known, ought to have been there for years, I remember his words, Baas."

"Why should you go to the *trunk* at all, Hans, when you are rich and can pay a fine, even if it were a hundred pounds?"

"A month or two ago it is true I was rich, Baas, but now I am poor. I have nothing left except ten shillings."

"Hans," I said severely, "you have been gambling again; you have been drinking again. You have sold your property and your cattle to pay your gambling debts and to buy square-face gin."

"Yes, Baas, and for no good it seems; though it is not true that I have been drinking. I sold the land and the cattle for £650, Baas, and with the money I bought other things."

"What did you buy?" I said.

He fumbled first in one pocket of his coat and then in the other, and ultimately produced a crumpled and dirty-looking piece of paper that resembled a bank-note. I took and examined this document and next minute nearly fainted. It certified that Hans was the proprietor of I know not how many debentures or shares, I forget which they were, in the Bona Fide Gold Mine, Limited, that same company of which I was the unlucky chairman, in consideration for which he had paid a sum of over six hundred and fifty pounds.

"Hans," I said feebly, "from whom did you buy this?"

"From the baas with the hooked nose, Baas. He who was named Jacob, after the great man in the Bible of whom your father, the Predikant, used to tell us, that one who was so slim and dressed himself up in a goatskin and gave his brother mealie porridge when he was hungry, after he had come in from shooting buck, Baas, and got his farm and cattle, Baas, and then went to Heaven up a ladder, Baas."

"And who told you to buy them, Hans?"

"Sammy, Baas, he who was your cook when we went to Pongoland, he who hid in the mealie-pit when the slavers burned Beza-Town and came out half cooked like a fowl from the oven. The Baas Jacob stopped at Sammy's hotel, Baas, and told him that unless he bought bits of paper like this, of which he had plenty, you would be brought before the magistrate and sent to the *trunk*, Baas. So Sammy bought some, Baas, but not many for he had only a little money, and the Baas Jacob paid him for all he ate and drank with other bits of paper. Then Sammy came to me and showed me what it was my duty to do, reminding me that your reverend father, the Predikant, had left you in my charge till one of us dies, whether you were well or ill and whether you got better or got worse—just like a white wife, Baas. So I sold the farm and the cattle to a friend of the Baas Jacob's, at a very low price, Baas, and that is all the story."

I heard and, to tell the honest truth, almost I wept, since the thought of the sacrifice which this poor old Hottentot had made for my sake on the instigation of a rogue utterly overwhelmed me.

"Hans," I asked recovering myself, "tell me what was that new name which the Zulu captain Mavovo gave you before he died, I mean after you had fired Beza-Town and caught Hassan and his slavers in their own trap?"

Hans, who had suddenly found something that interested him extremely out at sea, perhaps because he did not wish to witness my grief, turned round slowly and answered:

"Mavovo named me Light-in-Darkness, and by that name the Kafirs know me now, Baas, though some of them call me Lord-of-the-Fire."

"Then Mavovo named you well, for indeed, Hans, you shine like a light in the darkness of my heart. I whom you think wise am but a fool, Hans, who has been tricked by a *vernuker*, a common cheat, and he has tricked you and Sammy as well. But as he has shown me that man can be very vile, you have shown me that he can be very noble; and, setting the one against the other, my spirit that was in the dust rises up once more like a withered flower after rain. Light-in-Darkness, although if I had ten thousand pounds I could never pay you back—since what you have given me is more than all the gold in the world and all the land and all the cattle—yet with honour and with love I will try to pay you," and I held out my hand to him.

He took it and pressed it against his wrinkled old forehead, then answered:

"Talk no more of that, Baas, for it makes me sad, who am so happy. How often have you forgiven me when I have done wrong? How often have you not flogged me when I should have been flogged for being drunk and other things—yes, even when once I stole some of your powder and sold it to buy square-face gin, though it is true I knew it was bad powder, not fit for you to use? Did I thank you then overmuch? Why therefore should you thank me who have done but a little thing, not really to help you but because, as you know, I love gambling, and was told that this bit of paper would soon be worth much more than I gave for it. If it had proved so, should I have given you that money? No, I should have kept it myself and bought a bigger farm and more cattle."

"Hans," I said sternly, "if you lie so hard, you will certainly go to hell, as the Predikant, my father, often told you."

"Not if I lie for you, Baas, or if I do it doesn't matter, except that then we should be separated by the big kloof written of in the Book, especially as there I should meet the Baas Jacob, as I very much want to do for a reason of my own."

Not wishing to pursue this somewhat unchristian line of thought, I inquired of him why he felt happy.

"Oh! Baas," he answered with a twinkle in his little black eyes, "can't you guess why? Now you have very little money left and I have none at all. Therefore it is plain that we must go somewhere to earn money, and I am glad of that, Baas, for I am tired of sitting on that farm out there and growing mealies and milking cows, especially as I am too old to marry, Baas, as you are tired of looking for gold where there isn't any and singing sad songs in that house of meeting yonder like you did this afternoon. Oh! the Great Father in the skies knew what He was about when He sent the Baas Jacob our way. He beat us for our good, Baas, as He does always if we could only understand."

I reflected to myself that I had not often heard the doctrine of the Church better or more concisely put, but I only said:

"That is true, Hans, and I thank you for the lesson, the second you have taught me to-day. But where are we to go to, Hans? Remember, it must be elephants."

He suggested some places; indeed he seemed to have come provided with a list of them, and I sat silent making no comment. At length he finished and squatted there before me, chewing a bit of tobacco I had given him, and looking up at me interrogatively with his head on one side, for all the world like a dilapidated and inquisitive bird.

"Hans," I said, "do you remember a story I told you when you came to see me a year or more ago, about a tribe called the Kendah in whose country there is said to be a great cemetery of elephants which travel there to die from all the land about? A country that lies somewhere to the north-east of the lake island on which the Pongo used to dwell?"

"Yes, Baas."

"And you said, I think, that you had never heard of such a people."

"No, Baas, I never said anything at all. I have heard a good deal about them."

"Then why did you not tell me so before, you little idiot?" I asked indignantly.

"What was the good, Baas? You were hunting gold then, not ivory. Why should I make you unhappy, and waste my own breath by talking about beautiful things which were far beyond the reach of either of us, far as that sky?"

"Don't ask fool's questions but tell me what you know, Hans. Tell me at once."

"This, Baas: When we were up at Beza-Town after we came back from killing the gorilla-god, and the Baas Stephen your friend lay sick, and there was nothing else to do, I talked with everyone I could find worth talking to, and they were not many, Baas. But there was one very old woman who was not of the Mazitu race and whose husband and children were all dead, but whom the people in the town looked up to and feared because she was wise and made medicines out of herbs, and told fortunes. I used to go to see her. She was quite blind, Baas, and fond of talking with me—which shows how wise she was. I told her all about the Pongo gorilla-god, of which already she knew something. When I had done she said that he was as nothing compared with a certain god that she had seen in her youth, seven tens of years ago, when she became marriageable. I asked her for that story, and she spoke it thus:

"Far away to the north and east live a people called the Kendah, who are ruled over by a sultan. They are a very great people and inhabit a most fertile country. But all round their country the land is desolate and manless, peopled only by game, for the reason that they will suffer none to dwell there. That is why nobody knows anything about them: he that comes across the wilderness into that land is killed and never returns to tell of it.

"She told me also that she was born of this people, but fled because their sultan wished to place her in his house of women, which she did not desire. For a long while she wandered southwards, living on roots and berries, till she came to desert land and at last, worn out, lay down to die. Then she was found by some of the Mazitu who were on an expedition seeking ostrich feathers for war-plumes. They gave her food and, seeing that she was fair, brought her back to their country, where one of them married her. But of her own land she uttered only lying words to them because she feared that if she told the truth the gods who guard its secrets would be avenged on her, though now when she was near to death she dreaded them no more, since even the Kendah gods cannot swim through the waters of death. That is all she said about her journey because she had forgotten the rest."

"Bother her journey, Hans. What did she say about her god and the Kendah people?"

"This, Baas: that the Kendah have not one god but two, and not one ruler but two. They have a good god who is a child-fetish" (here I started) "that speaks through the mouth of an oracle who is always a woman. If that woman dies the god does not speak until they find another woman bearing certain marks which show that she holds the spirit of the god. Before the woman dies she always tells the priests in what land they are to look for her who is to come after her; but sometimes they cannot find her and then trouble falls because 'the Child has lost its tongue,' and the people become the prey of the other god that never dies."

"And what is that god, Hans?"

"That god, Baas, is an elephant" (here I started again), "a very bad elephant to which human sacrifice is offered. I think, Baas, that it is the devil wearing the shape of an elephant, at least that is what she said. Now the sultan is a worshipper of the god that dwells in the elephant Jana" (here I positively whistled) "and so are most of the people, indeed all those among them who are black. For once far away in the beginning the Kendah were two peoples, but the lighter-coloured people who worshipped the Child came down from the north and conquered the black people, bringing the Child with them, or so I understood her, Baas, thousands and thousands of years ago when the world was young. Since then they have flowed on side by side like two streams in the same channel, never mixing, for each keeps its own colour. Only, she said, that stream which comes from the north grows weaker and that from the south more strong."

"Then why does not the strong swallow up the weak?"

"Because the weak are still the pure and the wise, Baas, or so the old vrouw declared. Because they worship the good while the others worship the devil, and as your father the Predikant used to say, Good is the cock which always wins the fight at the last, Baas. Yes, when he seems to be dead he gets up again and kicks the devil in the stomach and stands on him and crows, Baas. Also these northern folk are mighty magicians. Through their Child-fetish they give rain and fat seasons and keep away sickness, whereas Jana gives only evil gifts that have to do with cruelty and war and so forth. Lastly, the priests who rule through the Child have the secrets of wealth and ancient knowledge, whereas the sultan and his followers have only the might of the spear. This was the song which the old woman sang to me, Baas."

"Why did you not tell me of these matters when we were at Beza-Town and I could have talked with her myself, Hans?"

"For two reasons, Baas. The first was that I feared, if I told you, you would wish to go on to find these people, whereas I was tired of travelling and wanted to come to Natal to rest. The second was that on the night when the old woman finished telling me her story, she was taken sick and died, and therefore it would have been no use to bring you to see her. So I saved it up in my head until it was wanted. Moreover, Baas, all the Mazitu declared that old woman to be the greatest of liars."

"She was not altogether a liar, Hans. Hear what I have learned," and I told him of the magic of Harût and Marût and of the picture that I had seemed to see of the elephant Jana and of the prayer that Harût and Marût had made to me, to all of which he listened quite stolidly. It is not easy to astonish a Hottentot's brain, which often draws no accurate dividing-line between the possible and what the modern world holds to be impossible.

"Yes, Baas," he said when I had finished, "then it seems that the old woman was not such a liar after all. Baas, when shall we start after that hoard of dead ivory, and which way will you go? By Kilwa or through Zululand? It should be settled soon because of the seasons."

After this we talked together for a long while, for with pockets as empty as mine were then, the problem seemed difficult, if not insoluble.

VII

LORD RAGNALL'S STORY

That night Hans slept at my house, or rather outside of it in the garden, or upon the stoep, saying that he feared arrest if he went to the town, because of his quarrel with the white man. As it happened, however, the other party concerned never stirred further in the business, probably because he was too drunk to remember who had knocked him into the sluit or whether he had gravitated thither by accident.

On the following morning we renewed our discussion, debating in detail every possible method of reaching the Kendah people by help of such means as we could command. Like that of the previous night it proved somewhat abortive. Obviously such a long and hazardous expedition ought to be properly financed and—where was the money? At length I came to the conclusion that if we went at all it would be best, in the circumstances, for Hans and myself to start alone with a Scotch cart drawn by oxen and driven by a couple of Zulu hunters, which we could lade with ammunition and a few necessaries.

Thus lightly equipped we might work through Zululand and thence northward to Beza-Town, the capital of the Mazitu, where we were sure of a welcome. After that we must take our chance. It was probable that we should never reach the district where these Kendah were supposed to dwell, but at least I might be able to kill some elephants in the wild country beyond Zululand.

While we were talking I heard the gun fired which announced the arrival of the English mail, and stepping to the end of the garden, saw the steamer lying at anchor outside the bar. Then I went indoors to write a few business letters which, since I had become immersed in the affairs of that unlucky gold mine, had grown to be almost a daily task with me. I had got through several with many groanings, for none were agreeable in their tenor, when Hans poked his head through the window in a silent kind of a way as a big snake might do, and said: "Baas, I think there are two baases out on the road there who are looking for you. Very fine baases whom I don't know."

"Shareholders in the Bona Fide Gold Mine," thought I to myself, then added as I prepared to leave through the back door: "If they come here tell them I am not at home. Tell them I left early this morning for the Congo River to look for the sources of the Nile."

"Yes, Baas," said Hans, collapsing on to the stoep.

I went out through the back door, sorrowing that I, Allan Quatermain, should have reached a rung in the ladder of life whence I shrank from looking any stranger in the face, for fear of what he might have to say to me. Then suddenly my pride asserted itself. After all what was there of which I should be ashamed? I would face these irate shareholders as I had faced the others yesterday.

I walked round the little house to the front garden which was planted with orange trees, and up to a big moonflower bush, I believe *datura* is its right name, that grew near the pomegranate hedge which separated my domain from the road. There a conversation was in progress, if so it may be called.

"*Ikona*" (that is: "I don't know"), "*Inkoosi*" (i.e. "Chief"), said some Kafir in a stupid drawl.

Thereon a voice that instantly struck me as familiar, answered:

"We want to know where the great hunter lives."

"*Ikona*," said the Kafir.

"Can't you remember his native name?" asked another voice which was also familiar to me, for I never forget voices though I am unable to place them at once.

"The great hunter, Here-come-a-zany," said the first voice triumphantly, and instantly there flashed back upon my mind a vision of the splendid drawing-room at Ragnall Castle and of an imposing majordomo introducing into it two white-robed, Arab-looking men.

"Mr. Savage, by the Heavens!" I muttered. "What in the name of goodness is he doing here?"

"There," said the second voice, "your black friend has bolted, and no wonder, for who can be called by such a name? If you had done what I told you, Savage, and hired a white guide, it would have saved us a lot of trouble. Why will you always think that you know better than anyone else?"

"Seemed an unnecessary expense, my lord, considering we are travelling incog., my lord."

"How long shall we travel 'incog.' if you persist in calling me my lord at the top of your voice, Savage? There is a house beyond those trees; go in and ask where—"

By this time I had reached the gate which I opened, remarking quietly,

"How do you do, Lord Ragnall? How do you do, Mr. Savage? I thought that I recognized your voices on the road and came to see if I was right. Please walk in; that is, if it is I whom you wish to visit."

As I spoke I studied them both, and observed that while Savage looked much the same, although slightly out of place in these strange surroundings, the time that had passed since we met had changed Lord Ragnall a good deal. He was still a magnificent-looking man, one of those whom no one that had seen him would ever forget, but now his handsome face was stamped with some new seal of suffering. I felt at once that he had become acquainted with grief. The shadow in his dark eyes and a certain worn expression about the mouth told me that this was so.

"Yes, Quatermain," he said as he took my hand, "it is you whom I have travelled seven thousand miles to visit, and I thank God that I have been so fortunate as to find you. I feared lest you might be dead, or perhaps far away in the centre of Africa where I should never be able to track you down."

"A week later perhaps you would not have found me, Lord Ragnall," I answered, "but as it happens misfortune has kept me here."

"And misfortune has brought me here, Quatermain."

Then before I had time to answer Savage came up and we went into the house.

"You are just in time for lunch," I said, "and as luck will have it there is a good rock cod and a leg of oribé buck for you to eat. Boy, set two more places."

"One more place, if you please, sir," said Savage. "I should prefer to take my food afterwards."

"You will have to get over that in Africa," I muttered. Still I let him have his way, with the result that presently the strange sight was seen of the magnificent English majordomo standing behind my chair in the little room and handing round the square-face as though it were champagne. It was a spectacle that excited the greatest interest in my primitive establishment and caused Hans with some native hangers-on to gather at the window. However, Lord Ragnall took it as a matter of course and I thought it better not to interfere.

When we had finished we went on to the stoep to smoke, leaving Savage to eat his dinner, and I asked Lord Ragnall where his luggage was. He replied that he had left it at the Customs. "Then," I said, "I will send a native with Savage to arrange about getting it up here. If you do not mind my rough accommodation there is a room for you, and your man can pitch a tent in the garden."

After some demur he accepted with gratitude, and a little later Savage and the native were sent off with a note to a man who hired out a mule-cart.

"Now," I said when the gate had shut behind them, "will you tell me why you have come to Africa?"

"Disaster," he replied. "Disaster of the worst sort."

"Is your wife dead, Lord Ragnall?"

"I do not know. I almost hope that she is. At any rate she is lost to me."

An idea leapt to my mind to the effect that she might have run away with somebody else, a thing which often happens in the world. But fortunately I kept it to myself and only said,

"She was nearly lost once before, was she not?"

"Yes, when you saved her. Oh! if only you had been with us, Quatermain, this would never have happened. Listen: About eighteen months ago she had a son, a very beautiful child. She recovered well from the business and we were as happy as two mortals could be, for we loved each other, Quatermain, and God has blessed us in every way; we were so happy that I remember her telling me that our great good fortune made her feel afraid. One day last September when I was out shooting, she drove in a little pony cart we had, with the nurse, and the child but no man, to call on Mrs. Scroope who also had been recently confined. She often went out thus, for the pony was an old animal and quiet as a sheep.

"By some cursed trick of fate it chanced that when they were passing through the little town which you may remember near Ragnall, they met a travelling menagerie that was going to some new encampment. At the head of the procession marched a large bull elephant, which I discovered afterwards was an ill-tempered brute that had already killed a man and should never have been allowed upon the roads. The sight of the pony cart, or perhaps a red cloak which my wife was wearing, as she always liked bright colours, for some unknown reason seems to have infuriated this beast, which trumpeted. The pony becoming frightened wheeled round and overturned the cart right in front of the animal, but apparently without hurting anybody. Then"—here he paused a moment and with an effort continued—"that devil in beast's shape cocked its ears, stretched out its long trunk, dragged the baby from the nurse's arms, whirled it round and threw it high into the air, to fall crushed upon the kerb. It sniffed at the body of the child, feeling it over with the tip of its trunk, as though to make sure that it was dead. Next, once more it trumpeted triumphantly, and without attempting to harm my wife or anybody else, walked quietly past the broken cart and continued its journey, until outside the town it was made fast and shot."

"What an awful story!" I said with a gasp.

"Yes, but there is worse to follow. My poor wife went off her head, with the shock I suppose, for no physical injury could be found upon her. She did not suffer in health or become violent, quite the reverse indeed for her gentleness increased. She just went off her head. For hours at a time she would sit silent and smiling, playing with the stones of that red necklace which those conjurers gave her, or rather counting them, as a nun might do with the beads of her rosary. At times, however, she would talk, but always to the baby, as though it lay before her or she were nursing it. Oh! Quatermain, it was pitiful, pitiful!

"I did everything I could. She was seen by three of the greatest brain-doctors in England, but none of them was able to help. The only hope they gave was that the fit might pass off as suddenly as it had come. They said too that a thorough change of scene would perhaps be beneficial, and suggested Egypt; that was in October. I did not take much to the idea, I don't know why, and personally should not have acceded to it had it not been for a curious circumstance. The last consultation took place in the big drawing-room at Ragnall. When it was over my wife remained with her mother at one end of the room while I and the doctors talked together at the other, as I thought quite out of her earshot. Presently, however, she called to me, saying in a perfectly clear and natural voice:

"'Yes, George, I will go to Egypt. I should like to go to Egypt.' Then she went on playing with the necklace and talking to the imaginary child.

"Again on the following morning as I came into her room to kiss her, she exclaimed,

"'When do we start for Egypt? Let it be soon.'

"With these sayings the doctors were very pleased, declaring that they showed signs of a returning interest in life and begging me not to thwart her wish.

"So I gave way and in the end we went to Egypt together with Lady Longden, who insisted upon accompanying us although she is a wretched sailor. At Cairo a large dahabeeyah that I had hired in advance, manned by an excellent crew and a guard of four soldiers, was awaiting us. In it we started up the Nile. For a month or more all went well; also to my delight my wife seemed now and again to show signs of returning intelligence. Thus she took some interest in the sculptures on the walls of the temples, about which she had been very fond of reading when in health. I remember that only a few days before the—the catastrophe, she pointed out one of them to me, it was of Isis and the infant Horus, saying, 'Look, George, the holy Mother and the holy Child,' and then bowed to it reverently as she might have done to an altar. At length after passing the First Cataract and the Island of Philæ we came to the temple of Abu Simbel, opposite to which our boat was moored. On the following morning we explored the temple at daybreak and saw the sun strike upon the four statues which sit at its farther end, spending the rest of that day studying the colossal figures of Rameses that are carved upon its face and watching some cavalcades of Arabs mounted upon camels travelling along the banks of the Nile.

"My wife was unusually quiet that afternoon. For hour after hour she sat still upon the deck, gazing first at the mouth of the rock-hewn temple and the mighty figures which guard it and then at the surrounding desert. Only once did I hear her speak and then she said, 'Beautiful, beautiful! Now I am at home.' We dined and as there was no moon, went to bed rather early after listening to the Sudanese singers as they sang one of their weird chanties.

"My wife and her mother slept together in the state cabin of the dahabeeyah, which was at the stern of the boat. My cabin, a small one, was on one side of this, and that of the trained nurse on the other. The crew and the guard were forward of the saloon. A gangway was fixed from the side to the shore and over it a sentry stood, or was supposed to stand. During the night a Khamsin wind began to blow, though lightly as was to be expected at this season of the year. I did not hear it for, as a matter of fact, I slept very soundly, as it appears did everyone else upon the dahabeeyah, including the sentry as I suspect.

"The first thing I remember was the appearance of Lady Longden just at daybreak at the doorway of my cabin and the frightened sound of her voice asking if Luna, that is my wife, was with me. Then it transpired that she had left her cabin clad in a fur cloak, evidently some time before, as the bed in which she had been lying was quite cold. Quatermain, we searched everywhere; we searched for four days, but from that hour to this no trace whatever of her has been found."

"Have you any theory?" I asked.

"Yes, or at least all the experts whom we consulted have a theory. It is that she slipped down the saloon in the dark, gained the deck and thence fell or threw herself into the Nile, which of course would have carried her body away. As you may have heard, the Nile is full of bodies. I myself saw two of them during that journey. The Egyptian police and others were so convinced that this was what had happened that, notwithstanding the reward of a thousand pounds which I offered for any valuable information, they could scarcely be persuaded to continue the search."

"You said that a wind was blowing and I understand that the shores are sandy, so I suppose that all footprints would have been filled in?"

He nodded and I went on. "What is your own belief? Do you think she was drowned?"

He countered my query with another of:

"What do *you* think?"

"I? Oh! although I have no right to say so, I don't think at all. I am quite sure that she was *not* drowned; that she is living at this moment."

"Where?"

"As to that you had better inquire of our friends, Harût and Marût," I answered dryly.

"What have you to go on, Quatermain? There is no clue."

"On the contrary I hold that there are a good many clues. The whole English part of the story in which we were concerned, and the threats those mysterious persons uttered are the first and greatest of these clues. The second is the fact that your hiring of the dahabeeyah regardless of expense was known a long time before your arrival in Egypt, for I suppose you did so in your own name, which is not exactly that of Smith or Brown. The third is your wife's sleep-walking propensities, which would have made it quite easy for her to be drawn ashore under some kind of mesmeric influence. The fourth is that you had seen Arabs mounted on camels upon the banks of the Nile. The fifth is the heavy sleep you say held everybody on board that particular night, which suggests to me that your food may have been drugged. The sixth is the apathy displayed by those employed in the search, which suggests to me that some person or persons in authority may have been bribed, as is common in the East, or perhaps frightened with threats of bewitchment. The seventh is that a night was chosen when a wind blew which would obliterate all spoor whether of men or of swiftly travelling camels. These are enough to begin with, though doubtless if I had time to think I could find others. You must remember too that although the journey would be long, this country of the Kendah can doubtless be reached from the Sudan by those who know the road, as well as from southern or eastern Africa."

"Then you think that my wife has been kidnapped by those villains, Harût and Marût?"

"Of course, though villains is a strong term to apply to them. They might be quite honest men according to their peculiar lights, as indeed I expect they are. Remember that they serve a god or a fetish, or rather, as they believe, a god *in* a fetish, who to them doubtless is a very terrible master, especially when, as I understand, that god is threatened by a rival god."

"Why do you say that, Quatermain?"

By way of answer I repeated to him the story which Hans said he had heard from the old woman at Beza, the town of the Mazitu. Lord Ragnall listened with the deepest interest, then said in an agitated voice:

"That is a very strange tale, but has it struck you, Quatermain, that if your suppositions are correct, one of the most terrible circumstances connected with my case is that our child should have chanced to come to its dreadful death through the wickedness of an elephant?"

"That curious coincidence has struck me most forcibly, Lord Ragnall. At the same time I do not see how it can be set down as more than a coincidence, since the elephant which slaughtered your child was certainly not that called Jana. To suppose because there is a war between an elephant-god and a child-god somewhere in the heart of Africa, that therefore another elephant can be so influenced that it kills a child in England, is to my mind out of all reason."

That is what I said to him, as I did not wish to introduce a new horror into an affair that was already horrible enough. But, recollecting that these priests, Harût and Marût, believed the mother of this murdered infant to be none other than the oracle of their worship (though how this chanced passed my comprehension), and therefore the great enemy of the evil elephant-god, I confess that at heart I felt afraid. If any powers of magic, black or white or both, were mixed up with the matter as my experiences in England seemed to suggest, who could say what might be their exact limits? As, however, it has been demonstrated again and again by the learned that no such thing as African magic exists, this line of thought appeared to be too foolish to follow. So passing it by I asked Lord Ragnall to continue.

"For over a month," he went on, "I stopped in Egypt waiting till emissaries who had been sent to the chiefs of various tribes in the Sudan and elsewhere, returned with the news that nothing whatsoever had been seen of a white woman travelling in the company of natives, nor had they heard of any such woman being sold as a slave. Also through the Khedive, on whom I was able to bring influence to bear by help of the British Government, I caused many harems in Egypt to be visited, entirely without result. After this, leaving the inquiry in the hands of the British Consul and a firm of French lawyers, although in truth all hope had gone, I returned to England whither I had already sent Lady Longden, broken-hearted, for it occurred to me as possible that my wife might have drifted or been taken thither. But here, too, there was no trace of her or of anybody who could possibly answer to her description. So at last I came to the conclusion that her bones must lie somewhere at the bottom of the Nile, and gave way to despair."

"Always a foolish thing to do," I remarked.

"You will say so indeed when you hear the end, Quatermain. My bereavement and the sleeplessness which it caused prayed upon me so much, for now that the child was dead my wife was everything to me, that, I will tell you the truth, my brain became affected and like Job I cursed God in my heart and determined to die. Indeed I should have died by my own hand, had it not been for Savage. I had procured the laudanum and loaded the pistol with which I proposed to shoot myself immediately after it was swallowed so that there might be no mistake. One night only a couple of months or so ago, Quatermain, I sat in my study at Ragnall, with the doors locked as I thought, writing a few final letters before I did the deed. The last of them was just finished about twelve when hearing a noise, I looked up and saw Savage standing before me. I asked him angrily how he came there (I suppose he must have had another key to one of the other doors) and what he wanted. Ignoring the first part of the question he replied:

"'My lord, I have been thinking over our trouble'—he was with us in Egypt—'I have been thinking so much that it has got a hold of my sleep. To-night as you said you did not want me any more and I was tired, I went to bed early and had a dream. I dreamed that we were once more in the shrubbery, as happened some years ago, and that the little African gent who shot like a book, was showing us the traces of those two black men, just as he did when they tried to steal her ladyship. Then in my dream I seemed to go back to bed and that beastly snake which we found lying under the parcel in the road seemed to follow me. When I had got to sleep again, all in the dream, there it was standing on its tail at the end of the bed, hissing till it woke me. Then it spoke in good English and not in African as might have been expected.

"'"Savage," it said, "get up and dress yourself and go at once and tell his lordship to travel to Natal and find Mr. Allan Quatermain" (you may remember that was the African gentleman's name, my lord, which, with so many coming and going in this great house, I had quite forgotten, until I had the dream). "Find Mr. Allan Quatermain," that slimy reptile went on, opening and shutting its mouth for all the world like a Christian making a speech, "for he will have something to tell him as to that which has made a hole in his heart that is now filled with the seven devils. Be quick, Savage, and don't stop to put on your shirt or your tie"—I have not, my lord, as you may see. "He is shut up in the study, but you know how to get into it. If he will not listen to you let him look round the study and he will see something which will tell him that this is a true dream."

"'Then the snake vanished, seeming to wriggle down the left bottom bed-post, and I woke up in a cold sweat, my lord, and did what it had told me.'

"Those were his very words, Quatermain, for I wrote them down afterwards while they were fresh in my memory, and you see here they are in my pocket-book.

"Well, I answered him, rather brusquely I am afraid, for a crazed man who is about to leave the world under such circumstances does not show at his best when disturbed almost in the very act, to the edge of which long agony has brought him. I told him that all his dream of snakes seemed ridiculous, which obviously it was, and was about to send him away, when it occurred to me that the suggestion it conveyed that I should put myself in communication with you was not ridiculous in view of the part you had already played in the story."

"Very far from ridiculous," I interpolated.

"To tell the truth," went on Lord Ragnall, "I had already thought of doing the same thing, but somehow beneath the pressure of my imminent grief the idea was squeezed out of my mind, perhaps because you were so far away and I did not know if I could find you even if I tried. Pausing for a moment before I dismissed Savage, I rose from the desk at which I was writing and began to walk up and down the room thinking what I would do. I am not certain if you saw it when you were at Ragnall, but it is a large room, fifty feet long or so though not very broad. It has two fireplaces, in both of which fires were burning on this night, and it was lit by four standing lamps besides that upon my desk. Now between these fireplaces, in a kind of niche in the wall, and a little in the shadow because none of the lamps was exactly opposite to it, hung a portrait of my wife which I had caused to be painted by a fashionable artist when first we became engaged."

"I remember it," I said. "Or rather, I remember its existence. I did not see it because a curtain hung over the picture, which Savage told me you did not wish to be looked at by anybody but yourself. At the time I remarked to him, or rather to myself, that to veil the likeness of a living woman in such a way seemed to me rather an ill-omened thing to do, though why I should have thought it so I do not quite know."

"You are quite right, Quatermain. I had that foolish fancy, a lover's freak, I suppose. When we married the curtain was removed although the brass rod on which it hung was left by some oversight. On my return to England after my loss, however, I found that I could not bear to look upon this lifeless likeness of one who had been taken from me so cruelly, and I caused it to be replaced. I did more. In order that it might not be disturbed by some dusting housemaid, I myself made it fast with three or four tin-tacks which I remember I drove through the velvet stuff into the panelling, using a fireiron as a hammer. At the time I thought it a good job although by accident I struck the nail of the third finger of my left hand so hard that it came off. Look, it has not quite finished growing again," and he showed the finger on which the new nail was still in process of formation.

"Well, as I walked up and down the room some impulse caused me to look towards the picture. To my astonishment I saw that it was no longer veiled, although to the best of my belief the curtain had been drawn over it as lately as that afternoon; indeed I could have sworn that this was so. I called to Savage to bring the lamp that stood upon my table, and by its light made an examination. The curtain was drawn back, very tidily, being fastened in its place clear of the little alcove by means of a thin brass chain. Also along one edge of it, that which I had nailed to the panelling, the tin-tacks were still in their places; that is, three of them were, the fourth I found afterwards upon the floor.

"'She looks beautiful, doesn't she, my lord,' said Savage, 'and please God so we shall still find her somewhere in the world.'

"I did not answer him, or even remark upon the withdrawal of the curtain, as to which indeed I never made an inquiry. I suppose that it was done by some zealous servant while I was pretending to eat my dinner—there were one or two new ones in the house whose names and appearance I did not know. What impressed itself upon my mind was that the face which I had never expected to see again on the earth, even in a picture, was once more given to my eyes, it mattered not how. This, in my excited state, for laudanum waiting to be swallowed and a pistol at full cock for firing do not induce calmness in a man already almost mad, at any rate until they have fulfilled their offices, did in truth appear to me to be something of the nature of a sign such as that spoken of in Savage's idiotic dream, which I was to find if 'I looked round the study.'

"'Savage,' I said, 'I don't think much of your dreams about snakes that talk to you, but I do think that it might be well to see Mr. Quatermain. To-day is Sunday and I believe that the African mail sails on Friday. Go to town early to-morrow and book passages.'

"Also I told him to see various gunsmiths and bid them send down a selection of rifles and other weapons for me to choose from, as I did not know whither we might wander in Africa, and to make further necessary arrangements. All of these things he did, and—here we are."

"Yes," I answered reflectively, "here you are. What is more, here is your luggage of which there seems to be enough for a regiment," and I pointed to a Scotch cart piled up with baggage and followed by a long line of Kafirs carrying sundry packages upon their heads that, marshalled by Savage, had halted at my gate.

VIII

The Start

That evening when the baggage had been disposed of and locked up in my little stable and arrangements were made for the delivery of some cases containing tinned foods, etc., which had proved too heavy for the Scotch cart, Lord Ragnall and I continued our conversation. First, however, we unpacked the guns and checked the ammunition, of which there was a large supply, with more to follow.

A beautiful battery they were of all sorts from elephant guns down, the most costly and best finished that money could buy at the time. It made me shiver to think what the bill for them must have been, while their appearance when they were put together and stood in a long line against the wall of my sitting-room, moved old Hans to a kind of ecstasy. For a long while he contemplated them, patting the stocks one after the other and giving to each a name as though they were all alive, then exclaimed:

"With such weapons as these the Baas could kill the devil himself. Still, let the Baas bring Intombi with him"—a favourite old rifle of mine and a mere toy in size, that had however done me good service in the past, as those who have read what I have written in "Marie" and "The Holy Flower" may remember. "For, Baas, after all, the wife of one's youth often proves more to be trusted than the fine young ones a man buys in his age. Also one knows all her faults, but who can say how many there may be hidden up in new women however beautifully they are tattooed?" and he pointed to the elaborate engraving upon the guns.

I translated this speech to Lord Ragnall. It made him laugh, at which I was glad for up till then I had not seen him even smile. I should add that in addition to these sporting weapons there were no fewer than fifty military rifles of the best make, they were large-bore Sniders that had just then been put upon the market, and with them, packed in tin cases, a great quantity of ammunition. Although the regulations were not so strict then as they are now, I met with a great deal of difficulty in getting all this armament through the Customs. Lord Ragnall however had letters from the Colonial Office to such authorities as ruled in Natal, and on our giving a joint undertaking that they were for defensive purposes only in unexplored territory and not for sale, they were allowed through. Fortunate did it prove for us in after days that this matter was arranged.

That night before we went to bed I narrated to Lord Ragnall all the history of our search for the Holy Flower, which he seemed to find very entertaining. Also I told him of my adventures, to me far more terrible, as chairman of the Bona Fide Gold Mine and of their melancholy end.

"The lesson of which is," he remarked when I had finished, "that because a man is master of one trade, it does not follow that he is master of another. You are, I should judge, one of the finest shots in the world, you are also a great hunter and explorer. But when it comes to companies, Quatermain—! Still," he went on, "I ought to be grateful to that Bona Fide Gold Mine, since I gather that had it not been for it and for your rascally friend, Mr. Jacob, I should not have found you here."

"No," I answered, "it is probable that you would not, as by this time I might have been far in the interior where a man cannot be traced and letters do not reach him."

Then he made a few pointed inquiries about the affairs of the mine, noting my answers down in his pocket-book. I thought this odd but concluded that he wished to verify my statements before entering into a close companionship with me, since for aught he knew I might be the largest liar in the world and a swindler to boot. So I said nothing, even when I heard through a roundabout channel on the morrow that he had sought an interview with the late secretary of the defunct company.

A few days later, for I may as well finish with this matter at once, the astonishing object of these inquiries was made clear to me. One morning I found upon my table a whole pile of correspondence, at the sight of which I groaned, feeling sure that it must come from duns and be connected with that infernal mine. Curiosity and a desire to face the worst, however, led me to open the first letter which as it happened proved to be from that very shareholder who had proposed a vote of confidence in me at the winding-up meeting. By the time that it was finished my eyes were swimming and really I felt quite faint. It ran:

"Honoured Sir,—I knew that I was putting my money on the right horse when I said the other day that you were one of the straightest that ever ran. Well, I have got the cheque sent me by the lawyer on your account, being payment in full for every farthing I invested in the Bona Fide Gold Mine, and I can only say that it is uncommonly useful, for that business had pretty well cleaned me out. God bless you, Mr. Quatermain."

I opened another letter, and another, and another. They were all to the same effect. Bewildered I went on to the stoep, where I found Hans with an epistle in his hand which he requested me to be good enough to read. I read it. It was from a well-known firm of local lawyers and said:

"On behalf of Allan Quatermain, Esq., we beg to enclose a draft for the sum of £650, being the value of the interest in the Bona Fide Gold Company, Limited (in liquidation), which stands in your name on the books of the company. Please sign enclosed receipt and return same to us."

Yes, and there was the draft for £650 sterling!

I explained the matter to Hans, or rather I translated the document, adding:

"You see you have got your money back again. But Hans, I never sent it; I don't know where it comes from."

"Is it money, Baas?" asked Hans, surveying the draft with suspicion. "It looks very much like the other bit of paper for which I paid money."

Again I explained, reiterating that I knew nothing of the transaction.

"Well, Baas," he said, "if you did not send it someone did—perhaps your father the reverend Predikant, who sees that you are in trouble and wishes to wash your name white again. Meanwhile, Baas, please put that bit of paper in your pocket-book and keep it for me, for otherwise I might be tempted to buy square-face with it."

"No," I answered, "you can now buy your land back, or some other land, and there will be no need for you to come with me to the country of the Kendah."

Hans thought a moment and then very deliberately began to tear up the draft; indeed I was only just in time to save it from destruction.

"If the Baas is going to turn me off because of this paper," he said, "I will make it small and eat it."

"You silly old fool," I said as I possessed myself of the cheque.

Then the conversation was interrupted, for who should appear but Sammy, my old cook, who began in his pompous language:

"The perfect rectitude of your conduct, Mr. Quatermain, moves me to the deepest gratitude, though indeed I wish that I had put something into the food of the knave Jacob who beguiled us all, that would have caused him internal pangs of a severe if not of a dangerous order. My holding in the gold mine was not extensive, but the unpaid bill of the said Jacob and his friends—"

Here I cut him short and fled, since I saw yet another shareholder galloping to the gate, and behind him two more in a spider. First I took refuge in my room, my idea being to put away that pile of letters. In so doing I observed that there was one still unopened. Half mechanically I took it from the envelope and glanced at its contents. They were word for word identical with those of that addressed to "Mr. Hans, Hottentot," only my name was at the bottom of it instead of that of Hans and the cheque was for £1,500, the amount I had paid for the shares I held in the venture.

Feeling as though my brain were in a melting-pot, I departed from the house into a patch of native bush that in those days still grew upon the slope of the hill behind. Here I sat myself down, as I had often done before when there was a knotty point to be considered, aimlessly watching a lovely emerald cuckoo flashing, a jewel of light, from tree to tree, while I turned all this fairy-godmother business over in my mind.

Of course it soon became clear to me. Lord Ragnall in this case was the little old lady with the wand, the touch of which could convert worthless share certificates into bank-notes of their face value. I remembered now that his wealth was said to be phenomenal and after all the cash capital of the company was quite small. But the question was—could I accept his bounty?

I returned to the house where the first person whom I met was Lord Ragnall himself, just arrived from some interview about the fifty Snider rifles, which were still in bond. I told him solemnly that I wished to speak to him, whereon he remarked in a cheerful voice,

"Advance, friend, and all's well!"

I don't know that I need set out the details of the interview. He waited till I had got through my halting speech of mingled gratitude and expostulation, then remarked:

"My friend, if you will allow me to call you so, it is quite true that I have done this because I wished to do it. But it is equally true that to me it is a small thing—to be frank, scarcely a month's income; what I have saved travelling on that ship to Natal would pay for it all. Also I have weighed my own interest in the matter, for I am anxious that you should start upon this hazardous journey of ours up country with a mind absolutely free from self-reproach or any money care, for thus you will be able to do me better service. Therefore I beg that you will say no more of the episode. I have only one thing to add, namely that I have myself bought up at par value a few of the debentures. The price of them will pay the lawyers and the liquidation fees; moreover they give me a status as a shareholder which will enable me to sue Mr. Jacob for his fraud, to which business I have already issued instructions. For please understand that I have not paid off any shares still standing in his name or in those of his friends."

Here I may add that nothing ever came of this action, for the lawyers found themselves unable to serve any writ upon that elusive person, Mr. Jacob, who by then had probably adopted the name of some other patriarch.

"Please put it all down as a rich man's whim," he concluded.

"I can't call that a whim which has returned £1,500 odd to my pocket that I had lost upon a gamble, Lord Ragnall."

"Do you remember, Quatermain, how you won £250 upon a gamble at my place and what you did with it, which sum probably represented to you twenty or fifty times what it would to me? Also if that argument does not appeal to you, may I remark that I do not expect you to give me your services as a professional hunter and guide for nothing."

"Ah!" I answered, fixing on this point and ignoring the rest, "now we come to business. If I may look upon this amount as salary, a very handsome salary by the way, paid in advance, you taking the risks of my dying or becoming incapacitated before it is earned, I will say no more of the matter. If not I must refuse to accept what is an unearned gift."

"I confess, Quatermain, that I did not regard it in that light, though I might have been willing to call it a retaining fee. However, do not let us wrangle about money any more. We can always settle our accounts when the bill is added up, if ever we reach so far. Now let us come to more important details."

So we fell to discussing the scheme, route and details of our proposed journey. Expenditure being practically no object, there were several plans open to us. We might sail up the coast and go by Kilwa, as I had done on the search for the Holy Flower, or we might retrace the line of our retreat from the Mazitu country which ran through Zululand. Again, we might advance by whatever road we selected with a small army of drilled and disciplined retainers, trusting to force to break a way through to the Kendah. Or we might go practically unaccompanied, relying on our native wit and good fortune to attain our ends. Each of these alternatives had so much to recommend it and yet presented so many difficulties, that after long hours of discussion, for this talk was renewed again and again, I found it quite impossible to decide upon any one of them, especially as in the end Lord Ragnall always left the choice with its heavy responsibilities to me.

At length in despair I opened the window and whistled twice on a certain low note. A minute later Hans shuffled in, shaking the wet off the new corduroy clothes which he had bought upon the strength of his return to affluence, for it was raining outside, and squatted himself down upon the floor at a little distance. In the shadow of the table which cut off the light from the hanging lamp he looked, I remember, exactly like an enormous and antique toad. I threw him a piece of tobacco which he thrust into his corn-cob pipe and lit with a match.

"The Baas called me," he said when it was drawing to his satisfaction, "what does Baas want of Hans?"

"Light in darkness!" I replied, playing on his native name, and proceeded to set out the whole case to him.

He listened without a word, then asked for a small glass of gin, which I gave him doubtfully. Having swallowed this at a gulp as though it were water, he delivered himself briefly to this effect:

"I think the Baas will do well not to go to Kilwa, since it means waiting for a ship, or hiring one; also there may be more slave-traders there by now who will bear him no love because of a lesson he taught them a while ago. On the other hand the road through Zululand is open, though it be long, and there the name of Macumazana is one well known. I think also that the Baas would do well not to take too many men, who make marching slow, only a wagon or two and some drivers which might be sent back when they can go no farther. From Zululand messengers can be dispatched to the Mazitu, who love you, and Bausi or whoever is king there to-day will order bearers to meet us on the road, until which time we can hire other bearers in Zululand. The old woman at Beza-Town told me, moreover, as you will remember, that the Kendah are a very great people who live by themselves and will allow none to enter their land, which is bordered by deserts. Therefore no force that you could take with you and feed upon a road without water would be strong enough to knock down their gates like an elephant, and it seems better that you should try to creep through them like a wise snake, although they appear to be shut in your face. Perhaps also they will not be shut since did you not say that two of their great doctors promised to meet you and guide you through them?"

"Yes," I interrupted, "I dare say it will be easier to get in than to get out of Kendahland."

"Last of all, Baas, if you take many men armed with guns, the black part of the Kendah people of whom I told you will perhaps think you come to make war, whatever the white Kendah may say, and kill us all, whereas if we be but a few perchance they will let us pass in peace. I think that is all, Baas. Let the Baas and the Lord Igeza forgive me if my words are foolish."

Here I should explain that "Igeza" was the name which the natives had given to Lord Ragnall because of his appearance. The word means a handsome person in the Zulu tongue. Savage they called "Bena," I don't know why. "Bena" in Zulu means to push out the breast and it may be that the name was a round-about allusion to the proud appearance of the dignified Savage, or possibly it had some other recondite signification. At any rate Lord Ragnall, Hans and myself knew the splendid Savage thenceforward by the homely appellation of Beans. His master said it suited him very well because he was so green.

"The advice seems wise, Hans. Go now. No, no more gin," I answered.

As a matter of fact careful consideration convinced us it was so wise that we acted on it down to the last detail.

So it came about that one fine afternoon about a fortnight later, for hurry as we would our preparations took a little time, we trekked for Zululand over the sandy roads that ran from the outskirts of Durban. Our baggage and stores were stowed in two half-tented wagons, very good wagons since everything we had with us was the best that money could buy, the after-part of which served us as sleeping-places at night. Hans sat on the *voor-kisse* or driving-seat of one of the wagons; Lord Ragnall, Savage and I were mounted upon "salted" horses, that is, horses which had recovered from and were therefore supposed to be proof against the dreadful sickness, valuable and docile animals which were trained to shooting.

At our start a little contretemps occurred. To my amazement I saw Savage, who insisted upon continuing to wear his funereal upper servant's cut-away coat, engaged with grim determination in mounting his steed from the wrong side. He got into the saddle somehow, but there was worse to follow. The horse, astonished at such treatment, bolted a little way, Savage sawing at its mouth. Lord Ragnall and I cantered after it past the wagons, fearing disaster. All of a sudden it swerved violently and Savage flew into the air, landing heavily in a sitting posture.

"Poor Beans!" exclaimed Lord Ragnall as we sped forward. "I expect there is an end of his journeyings."

To our surprise, however, we saw him leap from the ground with the most marvellous agility and begin to dance about slapping at his posterior parts and shouting,

"Take it off! Kill it!"

A few seconds later we discovered the reason. The horse had shied at a sleeping puff adder which was curled up in the sand of that little frequented road, and on this puff adder Savage had descended with so much force, for he weighed thirteen stone, that the creature was squashed quite flat and never stirred again. This, however, he did not notice in his agitation, being convinced indeed that it was hanging to him behind like a bulldog.

"Snakes! my lord," he exclaimed, when at last after careful search we demonstrated to him that the adder had died before it could come into action.

"I hate 'em, my lord, and they haunts" (he said 'aunts) "me. If ever I get out of this I'll go and live in Ireland, my lord, where they say there ain't none. But it isn't likely that I shall," he added mournfully, "for the omen is horrid."

"On the contrary," I answered, "it is splendid, for you have killed the snake and not the snake you. 'The dog it was that died,' Savage."

After this the Kafirs gave Savage a second very long name which meant "He-who-sits-down-on-snakes-and-makes-them-flat." Having remounted him on his horse, which was standing patiently a few yards away, at length we got off. I lingered a minute behind the others to give some directions to my old Griqua gardener, Jack, who snivelled at parting with me, and to take a last look at my little home. Alack! I feared it might be the last indeed, knowing as I did that this was a dangerous enterprise upon which I found myself embarked, I who had vowed that I would be done with danger.

With a lump in my throat I turned from the contemplation of that peaceful dwelling and happy garden in which each tree and plant was dear to me, and waving a good-bye to Jack, cantered on to where Ragnall was waiting for me.

"I am afraid this is rather a sad hour for you, who are leaving your little boy and your home," he said gently, "to face unknown perils."

"Not so sad as others I have passed," I answered, "and perils are my daily bread in every sense of the word. Moreover, whatever it is for me it is for you also."

"No, Quatermain. For me it is an hour of hope; a faint hope, I admit, but the only one left, for the letters I got last night from Egypt and England report that no clue whatsoever has been found, and indeed that the search for any has been abandoned. Yes, I follow the last star left in my sky and if it sets I hope that I may set also, at any rate to this world. Therefore I am happier than I have been for months, thanks to you," and he stretched out his hand, which I shook.

It was a token of friendship and mutual confidence which I am glad to say nothing that happened afterwards ever disturbed for a moment.

IX

The Meeting in the Desert

Now I do not propose to describe all our journey to Kendahland, or at any rate the first part thereof. It was interesting enough in its way and we met with a few hunting adventures, also some others. But there is so much to tell of what happened to us after we reached the place that I have not the time, even if I had the inclination to set all these matters down. Let it be sufficient, then, to say that although owing to political events the country happened to be rather disturbed at the time, we trekked through Zululand without any great difficulty. For here my name was a power in the land and all parties united to help me. Thence, too, I managed to dispatch three messengers, half-bred border men, lean fellows and swift of foot, forward to the king of the Mazitu, as Hans had suggested that I should do, advising him that his old friends, Macumazana, Watcher-by-Night, and the yellow man who was named Light-in-Darkness and Lord-of-the-Fire, were about to visit him again.

As I knew we could not take the wagons beyond a certain point where there was a river called the Luba, unfordable by anything on wheels, I requested him, moreover, to send a hundred bearers with whatever escort might be necessary, to meet us on the banks of that river at a spot which was known to both of us. These words the messengers promised to deliver for a fee of five head of cattle apiece, to be paid on their return, or to their families if they died on the road, which cattle we purchased and left in charge of a chief, who was their kinsman. As it happened two of the poor fellows did die, one of them of cold in a swamp through which they took a short cut, and the other at the teeth of a hungry lion. The third, however, won through and delivered the message.

After resting for a fortnight in the northern parts of Zululand, to give time to our wayworn oxen to get some flesh on their bones in the warm bushveld where grass was plentiful even in the dry season, we trekked forward by a route known to Hans and myself. Indeed it was the same which we had followed on our journey from Mazituland after our expedition in search for the Holy Flower.

We took with us a small army of Zulu bearers. This, although they were difficult to feed in a country where no corn could be bought, proved fortunate in the end, since so many of our cattle died from tsetse bite that we were obliged to abandon one of the wagons, which meant that the goods it contained must be carried by men. At length we reached the banks of the river, and camped there one night by three tall peaks of rock which the natives called "The Three Doctors," where I had instructed the messengers to tell the Mazitu to meet us. For four days we remained here, since rains in the interior had made the river quite impassable. Every morning I climbed the tallest of the "Doctors" and with my glasses looked over its broad yellow flood, searching the wide, bush-clad land beyond in the hope of discovering the Mazitu advancing to meet us. Not a man was to be seen, however, and on the fourth evening, as the river had now become fordable, we determined that we would cross on the morrow, leaving the remaining wagon, which it was impossible to drag over its rocky bottom, to be taken back to Natal by our drivers.

Here a difficulty arose. No promise of reward would induce any of our Zulu bearers even to wet their feet in the waters of this River Luba, which for some reason that I could not extract from them they declared to be *tagati*, that is, bewitched, to people of their blood. When I pointed out that three Zulus had already undertaken to cross it, they answered that those men were half-breeds, so that for them it was only half bewitched, but they thought that even so one or more of them would pay the penalty of death for this rash crime.

It chanced that this happened, for, as I have said, two of the poor fellows did die, though not, I think, owing to the magical properties of the waters of the Luba. This is how African superstitions are kept alive. Sooner or later some saying of the sort fulfils itself and then the instance is remembered and handed down for generations, while other instances in which nothing out of the common has occurred are not heeded, or are forgotten.

This decision on the part of those stupid Zulus put us in an awkward fix, since it was impossible for us to carry over all our baggage and ammunition without help. Therefore glad was I when before dawn on the fifth morning the nocturnal Hans crept into the wagon, in the after part of which Ragnall and I were sleeping, and informed us that he heard men's voices on the farther side of the river, though how he could hear anything above that roar of water passed my comprehension.

At the first break of dawn again we climbed the tallest of the "Doctor" rocks and stared into the mist. At length it rolled away and there on the farther side of the river I saw quite a hundred men who by their dress and spears I knew to be Mazitu. They saw me also and raising a cheer, dashed into the water, groups of them holding each other round the middle to prevent their being swept away. Thereupon our silly Zulus seized their spears and formed up upon the bank. I slid down the steep side of the "Great Doctor" and ran forward, calling out that these were friends who came.

"Friends or foes," answered their captain sullenly, "it is a pity that we should walk so far and not have a fight with those Mazitu dogs."

Well, I drove them off to a distance, not knowing what might happen if the two peoples met, and then went down to the bank. By now the Mazitu were near, and to my delight at the head of them I perceived no other than my old friend, their chief general, Babemba, a one-eyed man with whom Hans and I had shared many adventures. Through the water he plunged with great bounds and reaching the shore, greeted me literally with rapture.

"O Macumazana," he said, "little did I hope that ever again I should look upon your face. Welcome to you, a thousand welcomes, and to you too, Light-in-Darkness, Lord-of-the-Fire, Cunning-one whose wit saved us in the battle of the Gate. But where is Dogeetah, where is Wazeela, and where are the Mother and the Child of the Flower?"

"Far away across the Black Water, Babemba," I answered. "But here are two others in place of them," and I introduced him to Ragnall and Savage by their native names of Igeza and Bena.

He contemplated them for a moment, then said:

"This," pointing to Ragnall, "is a great lord, but this," pointing to Savage, who was much the better dressed of the two, "is a cock of the ashpit arrayed in an eagle's feathers," a remark I did not translate, but one which caused Hans to snigger vacuously.

While we breakfasted on food prepared by the "Cock of the Ashpit," who amongst many other merits had that of being an excellent cook, I heard all the news. Bausi the king was dead but had been succeeded by one of his sons, also named Bausi, whom I remembered. Beza-Town had been rebuilt after the great fire that destroyed the slavers, and much more strongly fortified than before. Of the slavers themselves nothing more had been seen, or of the Pongo either, though the Mazitu declared that their ghosts, or those of their victims, still haunted the island in the lake. That was all, except the ill tidings as to two of our messengers which the third, who had returned with the Mazitu, reported to us.

After breakfast I addressed and sent away our Zulus, each with a handsome present from the trade goods, giving into their charge the remaining wagon and our servants, none of whom, somewhat to my relief, wished to accompany us farther. They sang their song of good-bye, saluted and departed over the rise, still looking hungrily behind them at the Mazitu, and we were very pleased to see the last of them without bloodshed or trouble.

When we had watched the white tilt of the wagon vanish, we set to work to get ourselves and our goods across the river. This we accomplished safely, for the Mazitu worked for us like friends and not as do hired men. On the farther bank, however, it took us two full days so to divide up the loads that the bearers could carry them without being overladen.

At length all was arranged and we started. Of the month's trek that followed there is nothing to tell, except that we completed it without notable accidents and at last reached the new Beza-Town, which much resembled the old, where we were accorded a great public reception. Bausi II himself headed the procession which met us outside the south gate on that very mound which we had occupied in the great fight, where the bones of the gallant Mavovo and my other hunters lay buried. Almost did it seem to me as though I could hear their deep voices joining in the shouts of welcome.

That night, while the Mazitu feasted in our honour, we held an *indaba* in the big new guest house with Bausi II, a pleasant-faced young man, and old Babemba. The king asked us how long we meant to stay at Beza-Town, intimating his hope that the visit would be prolonged. I replied, but a few days, as we were travelling far to the north to find a people called the Kendah whom we wished to see, and hoped that he would give us bearers to carry our goods as far as the confines of their country. At the name of Kendah a look of astonishment appeared upon their faces and Babemba said:

"Has madness seized you, Macumazana, that you would attempt this thing? Oh surely you must be mad."

"You thought us mad, Babemba, when we crossed the lake to Rica Town, yet we came back safely."

"True, Macumazana, but compared to the Kendah the Pongo were but as the smallest star before the face of the sun."

"What do you know of them then?" I asked. "But stay—before you answer, I will speak what I know," and I repeated what I had learned from Hans, who confirmed my words, and from Harût and Marût, leaving out, however, any mention of their dealings with Lady Ragnall.

"It is all true," said Babemba when I had finished, "for that old woman of whom Light-in-the-Darkness speaks, was one of the wives of my uncle and I knew her well. Hearken! These Kendah are a terrible nation and countless in number and of all the people the fiercest. Their king is called Simba, which means Lion. He who rules is always called Simba, and has been so called for hundreds of years. He is of the Black Kendah whose god is the elephant Jana, but as Light-in-Darkness has said, there are also the White Kendah who are Arab men, the priests and traders of the people. The Kendah will allow no stranger within their doors; if one comes they kill him by torment, or blind him and turn him out into the desert which surrounds their country, there to die. These things the old woman who married my uncle told me, as she told them to Light-in-Darkness, also I have heard them from others, and what she did not tell me, that the White Kendah are great breeders of the beasts called camels which they sell to the Arabs of the north. Go not near them, for if you pass the desert the Black Kendah will kill you; and if you escape these, then their king, Simba, will kill you; and if you escape him, then their god Jana will kill you; and if you escape him, then their white priests will kill you with their magic. Oh! long before you look upon the faces of those priests you will be dead many times over."

"Then why did they ask me to visit them, Babemba?"

"I know not, Macumazana, but perhaps because they wished to make an offering of you to the god Jana, whom no spear can harm; no, nor even your bullets that pierce a tree."

"I am willing to make trial of that matter," I answered confidently, "and any way we must go to see these things for ourselves."

"Yes," echoed Ragnall, "we must certainly go," while even Savage, for I had been translating to them all this while, nodded his head although he looked as though he would much rather stay behind.

"Ask him if there are any snakes there, sir," he said, and foolishly enough I put the question to give me time to think of other things.

"Yes, O Bena. Yes, O Cock of the Ashpit," replied Babemba. "My uncle's Kendar wife told me that one of the guardians of the shrine of the White Kendah is such a snake as was never seen elsewhere in the world."

"Then say to him, sir," said Savage, when I had translated almost automatically, "that shrine ain't a church where *I* shall go to say my prayers."

Alas! poor Savage little knew the future and its gifts.

Then we came to the question of bearers. The end of it was that after some hesitation Bausi II, because of his great affection for us, promised to provide us with these upon our solemnly undertaking to dismiss them at the borders of the desert, "so that they might escape our doom," as he remarked cheerfully.

Four days later we started, accompanied by about one hundred and twenty picked men under the command of old Babemba himself, who, he explained, wished to be the last to see us alive in the world. This was depressing, but other circumstances connected with our start were calculated to weigh even more upon my spirit. Thus the night before we left Hans arrived and asked me to "write a paper" for him. I inquired what he wanted me to put in the paper. He replied that as he was going to his death and had property, namely the £650 that had been left in a bank to his credit, he desired to make a "white man's will" to be left in the charge of Babemba. The only provision of the said will was that I was to inherit his property, if I lived. If I died, which, he added, "of course you must, Baas, like the rest of us," it was to be devoted to furnishing poor black people in hospital with something comforting to drink instead of the "cow's water" that was given to them there. Needless to say I turned him out at once, and that testamentary deposition remained unrecorded. Indeed it was unnecessary, since, as I reminded him, on my advice he had already made a will before we left Durban, a circumstance that he had quite forgotten.

The second event, which occurred about an hour before our departure, was, that hearing a mighty wailing in the market-place where once Hans and I had been tied to stakes to be shot to death with arrows, I went out to see what was the matter. At the gateway I was greeted by the sight of about a hundred old women plastered all over with ashes, engaged in howling their loudest in a melancholy unison. Behind these stood the entire population of Beza-Town, who chanted a kind of chorus.

"What the devil are they doing?" I asked of Hans.

"Singing our death-song, Baas," he replied stolidly, "as they say that where we are going no one will take the trouble to do so, and it is not right that great lords should die and the heavens above remain uninformed that they are coming."

"That's cheerful," I remarked, and wheeling round, asked Ragnall straight out if he wished to persevere in this business, for to tell the truth my nerve was shaken.

"I must," he answered simply, "but there is no reason why you and Hans should, or Savage either for the matter of that."

"Oh! I'm going where you go," I said, "and where I go Hans will go. Savage must speak for himself."

This he did and to the same effect, being a very honest and faithful man. It was the more to his credit since, as he informed me in private, he did not enjoy African adventure and often dreamed at nights of his comfortable room at Ragnall whence he superintended the social activities of that great establishment.

So we departed and marched for the matter of a month or more through every kind of country. After we had passed the head of the great lake wherein lay the island, if it really was an island, where the Pongo used to dwell (one clear morning through my glasses I discerned the mountain top that marked the former residence of the Mother of the Flower, and by contrast it made me feel quite homesick), we struck up north, following a route known to Babemba and our guides. After this we steered by the stars through a land with very few inhabitants, timid and nondescript folk who dwelt in scattered villages and scarcely understood the art of cultivating the soil, even in its most primitive form.

A hundred miles or so farther on these villages ceased and thenceforward we only encountered some nomads, little bushmen who lived on game which they shot with poisoned arrows. Once they attacked us and killed two of the Mazitu with those horrid arrows, against the venom of which no remedy that we had in our medicine chest proved of any avail. On this occasion Savage exhibited his courage if not his discretion, for rushing out of our thorn fence, after missing a bushmen with both barrels at a distance of five yards—he was, I think, the worst shot I ever saw—he seized the little viper with his hands and dragged him back to camp. How Savage escaped with his life I do not know, for one poisoned arrow went through his hat and stuck in his hair and another just grazed his leg without drawing blood.

This valorous deed was of great service to us, since we were able through Hans, who knew something of the bushmen's language, to explain to our prisoner that if we were shot at again he would be hung.

This information he contrived to shout, or rather to squeak and grunt, to his amiable tribe, of which it appeared he was a kind of chief, with the result that we were no more molested. Later, when we were clear of the bushmen country, we let him depart, which he did with great rapidity.

By degrees the land grew more and more barren and utterly devoid of inhabitants, till at last it merged into desert. At the edge of this desert which rolled away without apparent limit we came, however, to a kind of oasis where there was a strong and beautiful spring of water that formed a stream which soon lost itself in the surrounding sand. As we could go no farther, for even if we had wished to do so, and were able to find water there, the Mazitu refused to accompany us into the desert, not knowing what else to do, we camped in the oasis and waited.

As it happened, the place was a kind of hunter's paradise, since every kind of game, large and small, came to the water to drink at night, and in the daytime browsed upon the saltish grass that at this season of the year grew plentifully upon the edge of the wilderness.

Amongst other creatures there were elephants in plenty that travelled hither out of the bushlands we had passed, or sometimes emerged from the desert itself, suggesting that beyond this waste there lay fertile country. So numerous were these great beasts indeed that for my part I hoped earnestly that it would prove impossible for us to continue our journey, since I saw that in a few months I could collect an enormous amount of ivory, enough to make me comparatively rich, if only I were able to get it away. As it was we only killed a few of them, ten in all to be accurate, that we might send back the tusks as presents to Bausi II. To slaughter the poor animals uselessly was cruel, especially as being unaccustomed to the sight of man, they were as easy to approach as cows. Even Savage slew one—by carefully aiming at another five paces to its left.

For the rest we lived on the fat of the land and, as meat was necessary to us, had as much sport as we could desire among the various antelope.

For fourteen days or so this went on, till at length we grew thoroughly tired of the business, as did the Mazitu, who were so gorged with flesh that they began to desire vegetable food. Twice we rode as far into the desert as we dared, for our horses remained to us and had grown fresh again after the rest, but only to return without information. The place was just a vast wilderness strewn with brown stones beautifully polished by the wind-driven sand of ages, and quite devoid of water.

After our second trip, on which we suffered severely from thirst, we held a consultation. Old Babemba said that he could keep his men no longer, even for us, as they insisted upon returning home, and inquired what we meant to do and why we sat here "like a stone." I answered that we were waiting for some of the Kendah who had bid me to shoot game hereabouts until they arrived to be our guides. He remarked that the Kendah to the best of his belief lived in a country that was still hundreds of miles away and that, as they did not know of our presence, any communication across the desert being impossible, our proceedings seemed to be foolish.

I retorted that I was not quite so sure of this, since the Kendah seemed to have remarkable ways of acquiring information.

"Then, Macumazana, I fear that you will have to wait by yourselves until you discover which of us is right," he said stolidly.

Turning to Ragnall, I asked him what he would do, pointing out that to journey into the desert meant death, especially as we did not know whither we were going, and that to return alone, without the stores which we must abandon, through the country of the bushmen to Mazituland, would also be a risky proceeding. However, it was for him to decide.

Now he grew much perturbed. Taking me apart again he dwelt earnestly upon his secret reasons for wishing to visit these Kendah, with which of course I was already acquainted, as indeed was Savage.

"I desire to stay here," he ended.

"Which means that we must all stay, Ragnall, since Savage will not desert you. Nor will Hans desert me although he thinks us mad. He points out that I came to seek ivory and here about is ivory in plenty for the trouble of taking."

"I might remain alone, Quatermain—" he began, but I looked at him in such a way that he never finished the sentence.

Ultimately we came to a compromise. Babemba, on behalf of the Mazitu, agreed to wait three more days. If nothing happened during that period we on our part agreed to return with them to a stretch of well-watered bush about fifty miles behind us, which we knew swarmed with elephants, that by now were growing shy of approaching our oasis where there was so much noise and shooting. There we would kill as much ivory as we could carry, an operation in which they were willing to assist for the fun of it, and then go back with them to Mazituland.

The three days went by and with every hour that passed my spirits rose, as did those of Savage and Hans, while Lord Ragnall became more and more depressed. The third afternoon was devoted to a jubilant packing of loads, for in accordance with the terms of our bargain we were to start backwards on our spoor at dawn upon the morrow. Most happily did I lay myself down to sleep in my little bough shelter that night, feeling that at last I was rid of an uncommonly awkward adventure. If I thought that we could do any good by staying on, it would have been another matter. But as I was certain that there was no earthly chance of our finding among the Kendah—if ever we reached them—the lady who had tumbled in the Nile in Egypt, well, I was glad that Providence had been so good as to make it impossible for us to commit suicide by thirst in a desert, or otherwise. For, notwithstanding my former reasonings to the contrary, I was now convinced that this was what had happened to poor Ragnall's wife.

That, however, was just what Providence had not done. In the middle of the night, to be precise, at exactly two in the morning, I was awakened by Hans, who slept at the back of my shanty, into which he had crept through a hole in the faggots, exclaiming in a frightened voice,

"Open your eyes and look, Baas. There are two *spooks* waiting to see you outside, Baas."

Very cautiously I lifted myself a little and stared out into the moonlight. There, seated about five paces from the open end of the hut were the "spooks" sure enough, two white-robed figures squatting silent and immovable on the ground. At first I was frightened. Then I bethought me of thieves and felt for my Colt pistol under the rug that served me as a pillow. As I got hold of the handle, however, a deep voice said:

"Is it your custom, O Macumazana, Watcher-by-Night, to receive guests with bullets?"

Now thought I to myself, who is there in the world who could see a man catch hold of the handle of a pistol in the recesses of a dark place and under a blanket at night, except the owner of that voice which I seemed to remember hearing in a certain drawing-room in England?

"Yes, Harût," I answered with an unconcerned yawn, "when the guests come in such a doubtful fashion and in the middle of the night. But as you are here at last, will you be so good as to tell us why you have kept us waiting all this time? Is that your way of fulfilling an engagement?"

"O Lord Macumazana," answered Harût, for of course it was he, in quite a perturbed tone, "I offer to you our humble apologies. The truth is that when we heard of your arrival at Beza-Town we started, or tried to start, from hundreds of miles away to keep our tryst with you here as we promised we would do. But we are mortal, Macumazana, and accidents intervened. Thus, when we had ascertained the weight of your baggage, camels had to be collected to carry it, which were grazing at a distance. Also it was necessary to send forward to dig out a certain well in the desert where they must drink. Hence the delay. Still, you will admit that we have arrived in time, five, or at any rate four hours before the rising of that sun which was to light you on your homeward way."

"Yes, you have, O Prophets, or O Liars, whichever you may be," I exclaimed with pardonable exasperation, for really their knowledge of my private affairs, however obtained, was enough to anger a saint. "So as you are here at last, come in and have a drink, for whether you are men or devils, you must be cold out there in the damp."

In they came accordingly, and, not being Mohammedans, partook of a tot of square-face from a bottle which I kept locked in a box to put Hans beyond the reach of temptation.

"To your health, Harût and Marût," I said, drinking a little out of the pannikin and giving the rest to Hans, who gulped the fiery liquor down with a smack of his lips. For I will admit that I joined in this unholy midnight potation to gain time for thought and to steady my nerve.

"To your health, O Lord Macumazana," the pair answered as they swallowed their tots, which I had made pretty stiff, and set down their pannikins in front of them with as much reverence as though these had been holy vessels.

"Now," I said, throwing a blanket over my shoulders, for the air was chilly, "now let us talk," and taking the lantern which Hans had thoughtfully lighted, I held it up and contemplated them.

There they were, Harût and Marût without doubt, to all appearance totally unchanged since some years before I had seen them at Ragnall in England. "What are you doing here?" I asked in a kind of fiery indignation inspired by my intense curiosity. "How did you get out of England after you had tried to steal away the lady to whom you sent the necklace? What did you do with that lady after you had beguiled her from the boat at Abu-Simbel? In the name of your Holy Child, or of Shaitan of the Mohammedans, or of Set of the Egyptians, answer me,

H. RIDER HAGGARD,

lest I should make an end of both of you, which I can do here without any questions being asked," and I whipped out my pistol.

"Pardon us," said Harût with a grave smile, "but if you were to do as you say, Lord Macumazana, many questions would be asked which *you* might find it hard to answer. So be pleased to put that death-dealer back into its place, and to tell us before we reply to you, what you know of Set of the Egyptians."

"As much or as little as you do," I replied.

Both bowed as though this information were of the most satisfactory order. Then Harût went on: "In reply to your requests, O Macumazana, we left England by a steamboat and in due course after long journeyings we reached our own country. We do not understand your allusions to a place called Abu-Simbel on the Nile, whence, never having been there, we have taken no lady. Indeed, we never meant to take that lady to whom we sent a necklace in England. We only meant to ask certain questions of her, as she had the gift of vision, when you appeared and interrupted us. What should we want with white ladies, who have already far too many of our own?"

"I don't know," I replied, "but I do know that you are the biggest liars I ever met."

At these words, which some might have thought insulting, Harût and Marût bowed again as though to acknowledge a great compliment. Then Harût said:

"Let us leave the question of ladies and come to matters that have to do with men. You are here as we told you that you would be at a time when you did not believe us, and we here to meet *you*, as we told you that we would be. How we knew that you were coming and how we came do not matter at all. Believe what you will. Are you ready to start with us, O Lord Macumazana, that you may bring to its death the wicked elephant Jana which ravages our land, and receive the great reward of ivory? If so, your camel waits."

"One camel cannot carry four men," I answered, avoiding the question.

"In courage and skill you are more than many men, O Macumazana, yet in body you are but one and not four."

"If you think that I am going with you alone, you are much mistaken, Harût and Marût," I exclaimed. "Here with me is my servant without whom I do not stir," and I pointed to Hans, whom they contemplated gravely. "Also there is the Lord Ragnall, who in this land is named

Igeza, and his servant who here is named Bena, the man out of whom you drew snakes in the room in England. They also must accompany us."

At this news the impassive countenances of Harût and Marût showed, I thought, some signs of disturbance. They muttered together in an unknown tongue. Then Harût said:

"Our secret land is open to you alone, O Macumazana, for one purpose only—to kill the elephant Jana, for which deed we promise you a great reward. We do not wish to see the others there."

"Then you can kill your own elephant, Harût and Marût, for not one step do I go with you. Why should I when there is as much ivory here as I want, to be had for the shooting?"

"How if we take you, O Macumazana?"

"How if I kill you both, O Harût and Marût? Fools, here are many brave men at my command, and if you or any with you want fighting it shall be given you in plenty. Hans, bid the Mazitu stand to their arms and summon Igeza and Bena."

"Stay, Lord," said Harût, "and put down that weapon," for once more I had produced the pistol. "We would not begin our fellowship by shedding blood, though we are safer from you than you think. Your companions shall accompany you to the land of the Kendah, but let them know that they do so at their own risk. Learn that it is revealed to us that if they go in there some of them will pass out again as spirits but not as men."

"Do you mean that you will murder them?"

"No. We mean that yonder are some stronger than us or any men, who will take their lives in sacrifice. Not yours, Macumazana, for that, it is decreed, is safe, but those of two of the others, which two we do not know."

"Indeed, Harût and Marût, and how am I to be sure that any of us are safe, or that you do not but trick us to your country, there to kill us with treachery and steal our goods?"

"Because we swear it by the oath that may not be broken; we swear it by the Heavenly Child," both of them exclaimed solemnly, speaking with one voice and bowing till their foreheads almost touched the ground.

I shrugged my shoulders and laughed a little.

"You do not believe us," went on Harût, "who have not heard what happens to those who break this oath. Come now and see something. Within five paces of your hut is a tall ant-heap upon which doubtless you have been accustomed to stand and overlook the desert." (This was true, but how did they guess it, I wondered.) "Go climb that ant-heap once more."

Perhaps it was rash, but my curiosity led me to accept this invitation. Out I went, followed by Hans with a loaded double-barrelled rifle, and scrambled up the ant-heap which, as it was twenty feet high and there were no trees just here, commanded a very fine view of the desert beyond.

"Look to the north," said Harût from its foot.

I looked, and there in the bright moonlight five or six hundred yards away, ranged rank by rank upon a slope of sand and along the crest of the ridge beyond, I saw quite two hundred kneeling camels, and by each camel a tall, white-robed figure who held in his hand a long lance to the shaft of which, not far beneath the blade, was attached a little flag. For a while I stared to make sure that I was not the victim of an illusion or a mirage. Then when I had satisfied myself that these were indeed men and camels I descended from the ant-heap.

"You will admit, Macumazana," said Harût politely, "that if we had meant you any ill, with such a force it would have been easy for us to take a sleeping camp at night. But these men come here to be your escort, not to kill or enslave you or yours. And, Macumazana, we have sworn to you the oath that may not be broken. Now we go to our people. In the morning, after you have eaten, we will return again unarmed and alone."

Then like shadows they slipped away.

X

Charge!

Ten minutes later the truth was known and every man in the camp was up and armed. At first there were some signs of panic, but these with the help of Babemba we managed to control, setting the men to make the best preparations for defence that circumstances would allow, and thus occupying their minds. For from the first we saw that, except for the three of us who had horses, escape was impossible. That great camel corps could catch us within a mile.

Leaving old Babemba in charge of his soldiers, we three white men and Hans held a council at which I repeated every word that had passed between Harût and Marût and myself, including their absolute denial of their having had anything to do with the disappearance of Lady Ragnall on the Nile.

"Now," I asked, "what is to be done? My fate is sealed, since for purposes of their own, of which probably we know nothing, these people intend to take me with them to their country, as indeed they are justified in doing, since I have been fool enough to keep a kind of assignation with them here. But they don't want anybody else. Therefore there is nothing to prevent you Ragnall, and you Savage, and you Hans, from returning with the Mazitu."

"Oh! Baas," said Hans, who could understand English well enough although he seldom spoke it, "why are you always bothering me with such *praatjes*?"—(that is, chatter). "Whatever you do I will do, and I don't care what you do, except for your own sake, Baas. If I am going to die, let me die; it doesn't at all matter how, since I must go soon and make report to your reverend father, the Predikant. And now, Baas, I have been awake all night, for I heard those camels coming a long while before the two spook men appeared, and as I have never heard camels before, could not make out what they were, for they don't walk like giraffes. So I am going to sleep, Baas, there in the sun. When you have settled things, you can wake me up and give me your orders," and he suited the action to the word, for when I glanced at him again he was, or appeared to be, slumbering, just like a dog at its master's feet.

I looked at Ragnall in interrogation.

"I am going on," he said briefly.

"Despite the denial of these men of any complicity in your wife's fate?" I asked. "If their words are true, what have you to gain by this journey, Ragnall?"

"An interesting experience while it lasts; that is all. Like Hans there, if what they say *is* true, my future is a matter of complete indifference to me. But I do not believe a word of what they say. Something tells me that they know a great deal which they do not choose to repeat—about my wife I mean. That is why they are so anxious that I should not accompany you."

"You must judge for yourself," I answered doubtfully, "and I hope to Heaven that you are judging right. Now, Savage, what have you decided? Remember before you reply that these uncanny fellows declare that if we four go, two of us will never return. It seems impossible that they can read the future, still, without doubt, they *are* most uncanny."

"Sir," said Savage, "I will take my chance. Before I left England his lordship made a provision for my old mother and my widowed sister and her children, and I have none other dependent upon me. Moreover, I won't return alone with those Mazitu to become a barbarian, for how could I find my way back to the coast without anyone to guide me? So I'll go on and leave the rest to God."

"Which is just what we have all got to do," I remarked. "Well, as that is settled, let us send for Babemba and tell him."

This we did accordingly. The old fellow received the news with more resignation than I had anticipated. Fixing his one eye upon me, he said:

"Macumazana, these words are what I expected from you. Had any other man spoken them I should have declared that he was quite mad. But I remember that I said this when you determined to visit the Pongo, and that you came back from their country safe and sound, having done wonderful things there, and that it was the Pongo who suffered, not you. So I believe it will be again, so far as you are concerned, Macumazana, for I think that some devil goes with you who looks after his own. For the others I do not know. They must settle the matter with their own devils, or with those of the Kendah people. Now farewell, Macumazana, for it comes to me that we shall meet no more. Well, that happens to all at last, and it is good to have known you who are so great in your own way. Often I shall think of you as you will think of me, and hope that in a country beyond that of the Kendah I may hear from your lips all that has befallen you on this and other journeys. Now I go to withdraw my men before these white-robed Arabs come on their strange beasts to seize you, lest they should take us also and there should be a fight in which we, being the fewer, must die. The loads are all in order ready to be laden on their strange beasts. If they declare that the horses cannot cross the desert, leave them loose and we will catch them and take them home with us, and since they are male and female, breed young ones from them which shall be yours when you send for them, or Bausi the king's if you never send. Nay, I want no more presents who have the gun and the powder and the bullets you gave me, and the tusks of ivory for Bausi the king, and what is best of all, the memory of you and of your courage and wisdom. May these and the gods you worship befriend you. From yonder hill we will watch till we see that you have gone. Farewell," and waiting for no answer, he departed with the tears running from his solitary eye.

Ten minutes later the Mazitu bearers had also saluted us and gone, leaving us seated in that deserted camp surrounded by our baggage, and so far as I was concerned, feeling most lonely. Another ten minutes went by which we occupied in packing our personal belongings. Then Hans, who was now washing out the coffee kettle at a little distance, looked up and said:

"Here come the spook-men, Baas, the whole regiment of them." We ran and looked. It was true. Marshalled in orderly squadrons, the camels with their riders were sweeping towards us, and a fine sight the beasts made with their swaying necks and long, lurching gait. About fifty yards away they halted just where the stream from our spring entered the desert, and there proceeded to water the camels, twenty of them at a time. Two men, however, in whom I recognized Harût and Marût, walked forward and presently were standing before us, bowing obsequiously.

"Good morning, Lord," said Harût to Ragnall in his broken English. "So you come with Macumazana to call at our poor house, as we call at your fine one in England. You think we got the beautiful lady you marry, she we give old necklace. That is not so. No white lady ever in Kendahland. We hear story from Macumazana and believe that lady drowned in Nile, for you 'member she walk much in her sleep. We very sorry for you, but gods know their business. They leave when they will leave, and take when they will take. You find her again some day more beautiful still and with her soul come back."

Here I looked at him sharply. I had told him nothing about Lady Ragnall having lost her wits. How then did he know of the matter? Still

I thought it best to hold my peace. I think that Harût saw he had made some mistake, for leaving the subject of Lady Ragnall, he went on:

"You very welcome, O Lord, but it right tell you this most dangerous journey, since elephant Jana not like strangers, and," he continued slowly, "think no elephant like your blood, and all elephants brothers. What one hate rest hate everywhere in world. See it in your face that you already suffer great hurt from elephant, you or someone near you. Also some of Kendah very fierce people and love fighting, and p'raps there war in the land while you there, and in war people get killed."

"Very good, my friend," said Ragnall, "I am prepared to take my chance of these things. Either we all go to your country together, as Macumazana has explained to you, or none of us go."

"We understand. That is our bargain and we no break word," replied Harût.

Then he turned his benevolent gaze upon Savage, and said: "So you come too, Mr. Bena. That your name here, eh? Well, you learn lot things in Kendahland, about snakes and all rest."

Here the jovial-looking Marût whispered something into the ear of his companion, smiling all over his face and showing his white teeth as he did so. "Oh!" went on Harût, "my brother tells me you meet one snake already, down in country called Natal, but sit on him so hard, that he grow quite flat and no bite."

"Who told him that?" gasped Savage.

"Oh! forget. Think Macumazana. No? Then p'raps you tell him in sleep, for people talk much in sleep, you know, and some other people got good ears and hear long way. Or p'raps little joke Harût. You 'member, he first-rate conjurer. P'raps he send that snake. No trouble if know how. Well, we show you much better snake Kendahland. But you no sit on *him*, Mr. Bena."

To me, I know not why, there was something horrible in all this jocosity, something that gave me the creeps as always does the sight of a cat playing with a mouse. I felt even then that it foreshadowed terrible things. How *could* these men know the details of occurrences at which they were not present and of which no one had told them? Did that strange "tobacco" of theirs really give them some clairvoyant power, I wondered, or had they other secret methods of obtaining news? I glanced at poor Savage and perceived that he too felt as I did, for he had turned quite pale beneath his tan. Even Hans was affected, for he whispered to me in Dutch: "These are not men; these are devils, Baas, and this journey of ours is one into hell."

Only Ragnall sat stern, silent, and apparently quite unmoved. Indeed there was something almost sphinx-like about the set and expression of his handsome face. Moreover, I felt sure that Harût and Marût recognized the man's strength and determination and that he was one with whom they must reckon seriously. Beneath all their smiles and courtesies I could read this knowledge in their eyes; also that it was causing them grave anxiety. It was as though they knew that here was one against whom their power had no avail, whose fate was the master of their fate. In a sense Harût admitted this to me, for suddenly he looked up and said in a changed voice and in Bantu:

"You are a good reader of hearts, O Macumazana, almost as good as I am. But remember that there is One Who writes upon the book of the heart, Who is the Lord of us who do but read, and that what He writes, that will befall, strive as we may, for in His hands is the future."

"Quite so," I replied coolly, "and that is why I am going with you to Kendahland and fear you not at all."

"So it is and so let it be," he answered. "And now, Lords, are you ready to start? For long is the road and who knows what awaits us ere we see its end?"

"Yes," I replied, "long is the road of life and who knows what awaits us ere we see its end—and after?"

Three hours later I halted the splendid white riding-camel upon which I was mounted, and looked back from the crest of a wave of the desert. There far behind us on the horizon, by the help of my glasses, I could make out the site of the camp we had left and even the tall ant-hill whence I had gazed in the moonlight at our mysterious escort which seemed to have sprung from the desert as though by magic.

This was the manner of our march: A mile or so ahead of us went a picket of eight or ten men mounted on the swiftest beasts, doubtless to give warning of any danger. Next, three or four hundred yards away, followed a body of about fifty Kendah, travelling in a double line, and behind these the baggage men, mounted like everyone else, and leading behind them strings of camels laden with water, provisions, tents of skin and all our goods, including the fifty rifles and the ammunition that Ragnall had brought from England. Then came we three white men and Hans, each of us riding as swift and fine a camel as Africa can breed. On our right at a distance of about half a mile, and also on our left, travelled other bodies of the Kendah of the same numerical strength as that ahead, while the rear was brought up by the remainder of the company who drove a number of spare camels.

Thus we journeyed in the centre of a square whence any escape would have been impossible, for I forgot to say that our keepers Harût and Marût rode exactly behind us, at such a distance that we could call to them if we wished.

At first I found this method of travelling very tiring, as does everyone who is quite unaccustomed to camel-back. Indeed the swing and the jolt of the swift creature beneath me seemed to wrench my bones asunder to such an extent that at the beginning I had once or twice to be lifted from the saddle when, after hours of torture, at length we camped for the night. Poor Savage suffered even more than I did, for the motion reduced him to a kind of jelly. Ragnall, however, who I think had ridden camels before, felt little inconvenience, and the same may be said of Hans, who rode in all sorts of positions, sometimes sideways like a lady, and at others kneeling on the saddle like a monkey on a barrel-organ. Also, being very light and tough as rimpis, the swaying motion did not seem to affect him.

By degrees all these troubles left us to such an extent that I could cover my fifty miles a day, more or less, without even feeling tired. Indeed I grew to like the life in that pure and sparkling desert air, perhaps because it was so restful. Day after day we journeyed on across the endless, sandy plain, watching the sun rise, watching it grow high, watching it sink again. Night after night we ate our simple food with appetite and slept beneath the glittering stars till the new dawn broke in glory from the bosom of the immeasurable East.

We spoke but little during all this time. It was as though the silence of the wilderness had got hold of us and sealed our lips. Or perhaps each of us was occupied with his own thoughts. At any rate I know that for my part I seemed to live in a kind of dreamland, thinking of the past, reflecting much upon the innumerable problems of this passing show called life, but not paying much heed to the future. What did the future matter to me, who did not know whether I should have a share of it even for another month, or week, or day, surrounded as I was by the shadow of death? No, I troubled little as to any earthly future, although I admit that in this oasis of calm I reflected upon that state where past, present and future will all be one; also that those reflections, which were in their essence a kind of unshaped prayer, brought much calm to my spirit.

With the regiment of escort we had practically no communication; I think that they had been forbidden to talk to us. They were a very silent set of men, finely-made, capable persons, of an Arab type, light rather than dark in colour, who seemed for the most part to communicate with each other by signs or in low-muttered words. Evidently they looked upon Harût and Marût with great veneration, for any order which either of these brethren gave, if they were brethren, was obeyed without dispute or delay. Thus, when I happened to mention that I had lost a pocket-knife at one of our camping-places two days' journey back, three of them, much against my wish, were ordered to return to look for it, and did so, making no question. Eight days later they rejoined us much exhausted and having lost a camel, but with the knife, which they handed to me with a low bow; and I confess that I felt ashamed to take the thing.

Nor did we exchange many further confidences with Harût and Marût. Up to the time of our arrival at the boundaries of the Kendah country, our only talk with them was of the incidents of travel, of where we should camp, of how far it might be to the next water, for water-holes or old wells existed in this desert, of such birds as we saw, and so forth. As to other and more important matters a kind of truce seemed to prevail. Still, I observed that they were always studying us, and especially Lord Ragnall, who rode on day after day, self-absorbed and staring straight in front of him as though he looked at something we could not see.

Thus we covered hundreds of miles, not less than five hundred at the least, reckoning our progress at only thirty miles a day, including stoppages. For occasionally we stopped at the water-holes or small oases, where the camels drank and rested. Indeed, these were so conveniently arranged that I came to the conclusion that once there must have been some established route running across these wastelands to the south, of which the traditional knowledge remained with the Kendah people. If so, it had not been used for generations, for save those of one or two that had died on the outward march, we saw no skeletons of camels or other beasts, or indeed any sign of man. The place was an absolute wilderness where nothing lived except a few small mammals at the oases and the birds that passed over it in the air on their way to more fertile regions. Of these, by the way, I saw many that are known both to Europe and Africa, especially ducks and cranes; also storks that, for aught I can say, may have come from far-off, homely Holland.

At last the character of the country began to change. Grass appeared on its lower-lying stretches, then bushes, then occasional trees and among the trees a few buck. Halting the caravan I crept out and shot two of these buck with a right and left, a feat that caused our grave escort to stare in a fashion which showed me that they had never seen anything of the sort done before.

That night, while we were eating the venison with relish, since it was the first fresh meat that we had tasted for many a day, I observed that the disposition of our camp was different from its common form. Thus it was smaller and placed on an eminence. Also the camels were not allowed to graze where they would as usual, but were kept within a limited area while their riders were arranged in groups outside of them. Further, the stores were piled near our tents, in the centre, with guards set over them. I asked Harût and Marût, who were sharing our meal, the reason of these alterations.

"It is because we are on the borders of the Kendah country," answered old Harût. "Four days' more march will bring us there, Macumazana."

"Then why should you take precautions against your own people? Surely they will welcome you."

"With spears perhaps. Macumazana, learn that the Kendah are not one but two people. As you may have heard before, we are the White Kendah, but there are also Black Kendah who outnumber us many times over, though in the beginning we from the north conquered them, or so says our history. The White Kendah have their own territory; but as there is no other road, to reach it we must pass through that of the Black Kendah, where it is always possible that we may be attacked, especially as we bring strangers into the land."

"How is it then that the Black Kendah allow you to live at all, Harût, if they are so much the more numerous?"

"Because of fear, Macumazana. They fear our wisdom and the decrees of the Heavenly Child spoken through the mouth of its oracle, which, if it is offended, can bring a curse upon them. Still, if they find us outside our borders they may kill us, if they can, as we may kill them if we find them within our borders."

"Indeed, Harût. Then it looks to me as though there were a war breeding between you."

"A war is breeding, Macumazana, the last great war in which either the White Kendah or the Black Kendah must perish. Or perhaps both will die together. Maybe that is the real reason why we have asked you to be our guest, Macumazana," and with their usual courteous bows, both of them rose and departed before I could reply.

"You see how it stands," I said to Ragnall. "We have been brought here to fight for our friends, Harût, Marût and Co., against their rebellious subjects, or rather the king who reigns jointly with them."

"It looks like it," he replied quietly, "but doubtless we shall find out the truth in time and meanwhile speculation is no good. Do you go to bed, Quatermain, I will watch till midnight and then wake you."

That night passed in safety. Next day we marched before the dawn, passing through country that grew continually better watered and more fertile, though it was still open plain but sloping upwards ever more steeply. On this plain I saw herds of antelopes and what in the distance looked like cattle, but no human being. Before evening we camped where there was good water and plenty of food for the camels.

While the camp was being set Harût came and invited us to follow him to the outposts, whence he said we should see a view. We walked with him, a matter of not more than a quarter of a mile to the head of that rise up which we had been travelling all day, and thence perceived one of the most glorious prospects on which my eyes have fallen in all great Africa. From where we stood the land sloped steeply for a matter of ten or fifteen miles, till finally the fall ended in a vast plain like to the bottom of a gigantic saucer, that I presume in some far time of the world's history was once an enormous lake. A river ran east and west across this plain and into it fell tributaries. Far beyond this river the contours of the country rose again till, many, many miles away, there appeared a solitary hill, tumulus-shaped, which seemed to be covered with bush.

Beyond and surrounding this hill was more plain which with the aid of my powerful glasses was, we could see, bordered at last by a range of great mountains, looking like a blue line pencilled across the northern distance. To the east and west the plain seemed to be illimitable. Obviously its soil was of a most fertile character and supported numbers of inhabitants, for everywhere we could see their kraals or villages.

Much of it to the west, however, was covered with dense forest with, to all appearance, a clearing in its midst.

"Behold the land of the Kendah," said Harût. "On this side of the River Tava live the Black Kendah, on the farther side, the White Kendah."

"And what is that hill?"

"That is the Holy Mount, the Home of the Heavenly Child, where no man may set foot"—here he looked at us meaningly—"save the priests of the Child."

"What happens to him if he does?" I asked.

"He dies, my Lord Macumazana."

"Then it is guarded, Harût?"

"It is guarded, not with mortal weapons, Macumazana, but by the spirits that watch over the Child."

As he would say no more on this interesting matter, I asked him as to the numbers of the Kendah people, to which he replied that the Black Kendah might number twenty thousand men of arm-bearing age, but the White Kendah not more than two thousand.

"Then no wonder you want spirits to guard your Heavenly Child," I remarked, "since the Black Kendah are your foes and with you warriors are few."

At this moment our conversation was interrupted by the arrival of a picket on a camel, who reported something to Harût which appeared to disturb him. I asked him what was the matter.

"That is the matter," he said, pointing to a man mounted on a rough pony who just then appeared from behind some bushes about half a mile away, galloping down the slope towards the plain. "He is one of the scouts of Simba, King of the Black Kendah, and he goes to Simba's town in yonder forest to make report of our arrival. Return to camp, Macumazana, and eat, for we must march with the rising of the moon."

As soon as the moon rose we marched accordingly, although the camels, many of which were much worn with the long journey, scarcely had been given time to fill themselves and none to rest. All night we marched down the long slope, only halting for half an hour before daylight to eat something and rearrange the loads on the baggage beasts, which now, I noticed, were guarded with extra care. When we were starting again Marût came to us and remarked with his usual smile, on behalf of his brother Harût, who was otherwise engaged, that it might be well if we had our guns ready, since we were entering the land of the elephant Jana and "who knew but that we might meet him?"

"Or his worshippers on two legs," I suggested, to which his only reply was a nod.

So we got our repeating rifles, some of the first that were ever made, serviceable but rather complicated weapons that fired five cartridges. Hans, however, with my permission, armed himself with the little Purdey piece that was named "Intombi," the singe-barrelled, muzzle-loading gun which had done me so much service in earlier days, and even on my last journey to Pongoland. He said that he was accustomed to it and did not understand these new-fangled breechloaders, also that it was "lucky." I consented as I did not think that it made much difference with what kind of rifle Hans was provided. As a marksman he had this peculiarity: up to a hundred yards or so he was an excellent shot, but beyond that distance no good at all.

A quarter of an hour later, as the dawn was breaking, we passed through a kind of *nek* of rough stones bordering the flat land, and emerged into a compact body on to the edge of the grassy plain. Here the word was given to halt for a reason that became clear to me so soon as I was out of the rocks. For there, marching rapidly, not half a mile away, were some five hundred white-robed men. A large proportion of these were mounted, the best being foot-soldiers, of whom more were running up every minute, appearing out of bush that grew upon the hill-side, apparently to dispute our passage. These people, who were black-faced with fuzzy hair upon which they wore no head-dress, all seemed to be armed with spears.

Presently from out of the mass of them two horsemen dashed forward, one of whom bore a white flag in token that they came to parley. Our advance guard allowed them to pass and they galloped on, dodging in and out between the camels with wonderful skill till at length they came to where we were with Harût and Marût, and pulling up their horses so sharply that the animals almost sat down on their haunches, saluted by raising their spears. They were very fine-looking fellows, perfectly black in colour with a negroid cast of countenance and long frizzled hair which hung down on to their shoulders. Their clothing was light, consisting of hide riding breeches that resembled bathing drawers, sandals, and an arrangement of triple chains which seemed to be made of some silvery metal that hung from their necks across the breast and back. Their arms consisted of a long lance similar to that carried by the White Kendah, and a straight, cross-handled sword suspended from a belt. This, as I ascertained afterwards, was the regulation cavalry equipment among these people. The footmen carried a shorter spear, a round leather shield, two throwing javelins or assegais, and a curved knife with a horn handle.

"Greeting, Prophets of the Child!" cried one of them. "We are messengers from the god Jana who speaks through the mouth of Simba the King."

"Say on, worshippers of the devil Jana. What word has Simba the King for us?" answered Harût.

"The word of war, Prophet. What do you beyond your southern boundary of the Tava river in the territory of the Black Kendah, that was sealed to them by pact after the battle of a hundred years ago? Is not all the land to the north as far as the mountains and beyond the mountains enough for you? Simba the King let you go out, hoping that the desert would swallow you, but return you shall not."

"That we shall know presently," replied Harût in a suave voice. "It depends upon whether the Heavenly Child or the devil Jana is the more powerful in the land. Still, as we would avoid bloodshed if we may, we desire to explain to you, messengers of King Simba, that we are here upon a peaceful errand. It was necessary that we should convey the white lords to make an offering to the Child, and this was the only road by which we could lead them to the Holy Mount, since they come from the south. Through the forests and the swamps that lie to the east and west camels cannot travel."

"And what is the offering that the white men would make to the Child, Prophet? Oh! we know well, for like you we have our magic. The offering that they must make is the blood of Jana our god, which you have brought them here to kill with their strange weapons, as though any weapon could prevail against Jana the god. Now, give to us these white men that we may offer them to the god, and perchance Simba the King will let you go through."

"Why?" asked Harût, "seeing that you declare that the white men cannot harm Jana, to whom indeed they wish no harm. To surrender them to you that they may be torn to pieces by the devil Jana would be to break the law of hospitality, for they are our guests. Now return to Simba the King, and say to Simba that if he lifts a spear against us the threefold curse of the Child shall fall upon him and upon you his people: The curse of Heaven by storm or by drought. The curse of famine. The curse of war. I the prophet have spoken. Depart."

Watching, I could see that this ultimatum delivered by Harût in a most impressive voice, and seconded as it was by the sudden and simultaneous lifting of the spears of all our escort that were within hearing, produced a considerable effect upon the messengers. Their faces grew afraid and they shrank a little. Evidently the "threefold curse of the Child" suggested calamities which they dreaded. Making no answer, they wheeled their horses about and galloped back to the force that was gathering below as swiftly as they had come.

"We must fight, my Lord Macumazana," said Harût, "and if we would live, conquer, as I know that we shall do."

Then he issued some orders, of which the result was that the caravan adopted a wedge-shaped formation like to that of a great flock of wildfowl on the wing. Harût stationed himself almost at the apex of the triangle. I with Hans and Marût were about the centre of the line, while Ragnall and Savage were placed opposite to us in the right line, the whole width of the wedge being between us. The baggage camels and their leaders occupied the middle space between the lines and were followed by a small rear-guard.

At first we white men were inclined to protest at this separation, but when Marût explained to us that its object was to give confidence to the two divisions of the force and also to minimize the risk of destruction or capture of all three of us, of course we had nothing more to say. So we just shook hands, and with as much assurance as we could command wished each other well through the job.

Then we parted, poor Savage looking very limp indeed, for this was his first experience of war. Ragnall, however, who came of an old fighting stock, seemed to be happy as a king. I who had known so many battles, was the reverse of happy, for inconveniently enough there flashed into my mind at this juncture the dying words of the Zulu captain and seer, Mavovo, which foretold that I too should fall far away in war; and I wondered whether this were the occasion that had been present to his foreseeing mind.

Only Hans seemed quite unconcerned. Indeed I noted that he took the opportunity of the halt to fill and light his large corn-cob pipe, a bit of bravado in the face of Providence for which I could have kicked him had he not been perched in his usual monkey fashion on the top of a very tall camel. The act, however, excited the admiration of the Kendah, for I heard one of them call to the others:

"Look! He is not a monkey after all, but a man—more of a man than his master."

The arrangements were soon made. Within a quarter of an hour of the departure of the messengers Harût, after bowing thrice towards the Holy Mountain, rose in his stirrups and shaking a long spear above his head, shouted a single word:

"Charge!"

XI

Allan is Captured

The ride that followed was really quite exhilarating. The camels, notwithstanding their long journey, seemed to have caught some of the enthusiasm of the war-horse as described in the Book of Job; indeed I had no idea that they could travel at such a rate. On we swung down the slope, keeping excellent order, the forest of tall spears shining and the little lancer-like pennons fluttering on the breeze in a very gallant way. In silence we went save for the thudding of the hoofs of the camels and an occasional squeal of anger as some rider drove his lance handle into their ribs. Not until we actually joined battle did a single man open his lips. Then, it is true, there went up one simultaneous and mighty roar of:

"The Child! Death to Jana! The Child! The Child!"

But this happened a few minutes later.

As we drew near the enemy I saw that they had massed their footmen in a dense body, six or eight lines thick. There they stood to receive the impact of our charge, or rather they did not all stand, for the first two ranks were kneeling with long spears stretched out in front of them. I imagine that their appearance must have greatly resembled that of the Greek phalanx, or that of the Swiss prepared to receive cavalry in the Middle Ages. On either side of this formidable body, which by now must have numbered four or five hundred men, and at a distance perhaps of a quarter of a mile from them, were gathered the horsemen of the Black Kendah, divided into two bodies of nearly equal strength, say about a hundred horse in each body.

As we approached, our triangle curved a little, no doubt under the direction of Harût. A minute or so later I saw the reason. It was that we might strike the foot-soldiers not full in front but at an angle. It was an admirable manoeuvre, for when presently we did strike, we caught them swiftly on the flank and crumpled them up. My word! we went through those fellows like a knife through butter; they had as much chance against the rush of our camels as a brown-paper screen has against a typhoon. Over they rolled in heaps while the White Kendah spitted them with their lances.

"The Child is top dog! My money on the Child," reflected I in irreverent ecstasy. But that exultation was premature, for those Black Kendah were by no means all dead. Presently I saw that scores of them had appeared among the camels, which they were engaged in stabbing, or trying to stab, in the stomach with their spears. Also I had forgotten the horsemen. As our charge slackened owing to the complication in front, these arrived on our flanks like two thunderbolts. We faced about and did our best to meet the onslaught, of which the net result was that both our left and right lines were pierced through about fifty yards behind the baggage camels. Luckily for us the very impetuosity of the Black Kendah rush deprived it of most of the fruits of victory, since the two squadrons, being unable to check their horses, ended by charging into each other and becoming mixed in inextricable confusion. Then, I do not know who gave the order, we wheeled our camels in and fell upon them, a struggling, stationary mass, with the result that many of them were speared, or overthrown and trampled.

"I have said we, but that is not quite correct, at any rate so far as Marût, Hans, I and about fifteen camelmen were concerned. How it happened I could not tell in that dust and confusion, but we were cut off from the main body and presently found ourselves fighting desperately in a group at which Black Kendah horsemen were charging again and again. We made the best stand we could. By degrees the bewildered camels sank under the repeated spear-thrusts of the enemy, all except one, oddly enough that ridden by Hans, which by some strange chance was never touched. The rest of us were thrown or tumbled off the camels and continued the fight from behind their struggling bodies."

That is where I came in. Up to this time I had not fired a single shot, partly because I do not like missing, which it is so easy to do from the back of a swaying camel, and still more for the reason that I had not the slightest desire to kill any of these savage men unless I was obliged to do so in self-defence. Now, however, the thing was different, as I was fighting for my life. Leaning against my camel, which was dying and beating its head upon the ground, groaning horribly the while, I emptied the five cartridges of the repeater into those Black Kendah, pausing between each shot to take aim, with the result that presently five riderless horses were galloping loose about the veld.

The effect was electrical, since our attackers had never seen anything of the kind before. For a while they all drew off, which gave me time to reload. Then they came on again and I repeated the process. For a second time they retreated and after consultation which lasted for a minute or more, made a third attack. Once more I saluted them to the best of my ability, though on this occasion only three men and a horse fell. The fifth shot was a clean miss because they came on in such a scattered formation that I had to turn from side to side to fire.

Now at last the game was up, for the simple reason that I had no more cartridges save two in my double-barrelled pistol. It may be asked why. The answer is, want of foresight. Too many cartridges in one's pocket are apt to chafe on camel-back and so is a belt full of them. In those days also the engagements were few in which a man fired over fifteen. I had forty or fifty more in a bag, which bag Savage with his usual politeness had taken and hung upon his saddle without saying a word to me. At the beginning of the action I found this out, but could not then get them from him as he was separated from me. Hans, always careless in small matters, was really to blame as he ought to have seen that I had the cartridges, or at any rate to have carried them himself. In short, it was one of those accidents that will happen. There is nothing more to be said.

After a still longer consultation our enemies advanced on us for the fourth time, but very slowly. Meanwhile I had been taking stock of the position. The camel corps, or what was left of it, oblivious of our plight which the dust of conflict had hidden from them, was travelling on to the north, more or less victorious. That is to say, it had cut its way through the Black Kendah and was escaping unpursued, huddled up in a mob with the baggage animals safe in its centre. The Black Kendah themselves were engaged in killing our wounded and succouring their own; also in collecting the bodies of the dead. In short, quite unintentionally, we were deserted. Probably, if anybody thought about us at all in the turmoil of desperate battle, they concluded that we were among the slain.

Marût came up to me, unhurt, still smiling and waving a bloody spear.

"Lord Macumazana," he said, "the end is at hand. The Child has saved the others, or most of them, but us it has abandoned. Now what will you do? Kill yourself, or if that does not please you, suffer me to kill you? Or shoot on until you must surrender?"

"I have nothing to shoot with any more," I answered. "But if we surrender, what will happen to us?"

"We shall be taken to Simba's town and there sacrificed to the devil Jana—I have not time to tell you how. Therefore I propose to kill myself."

"Then I think you are foolish, Marût, since once we are dead, we are dead; but while we are alive it is always possible that we may escape from Jana. If the worst comes to the worst I have a pistol with two bullets in it, one for you and one for me."

"The wisdom of the Child is in you," he replied. "I shall surrender with you, Macumazana, and take my chance."

Then he turned and explained things to his followers, who spoke together for a moment. In the end these took a strange and, to my mind, a very heroic decision. Waiting till the attacking Kendah were quite close to us, with the exception of three men, who either because they lacked courage or for some other reason, stayed with us, they advanced humbly as though to make submission. A number of the Black Kendah dismounted and ran up, I suppose to take them prisoners. The men waited till these were all round them. Then with a yell of "The Child!" they sprang forward, taking the enemy unawares and fighting like demons, inflicted great loss upon them before they fell themselves covered with wounds.

"Brave men indeed!" said Marût approvingly. "Well, now they are all at peace with the Child, where doubtless we shall find them ere long."

I nodded but answered nothing. To tell the truth, I was too much engaged in nursing the remains of my own courage to enter into conversation about that of other people.

This fierce and cunning stratagem of desperate men which had cost their enemies so dear, seemed to infuriate the Black Kendah.

At us came the whole mob of them—we were but six now—roaring "Jana! Jana!" and led by a grey-beard who, to judge from the number of silver chains upon his breast and his other trappings, seemed to be a great man among them. When they were about fifty yards away and I was preparing for the worst, a shot rang out from above and behind me. At the same instant Greybeard threw his arms wide and letting fall the spear he held, pitched from his horse, evidently stone dead. I glanced back and saw Hans, the corn-cob pipe still in his mouth and the little rifle, "Intombi," still at his shoulder. He had fired from the back of the camel, I think for the first time that day, and whether by chance or through good marksmanship, I do not know, had killed this man.

His sudden and unexpected end seemed to fill the Black Kendah with grief and dismay. Halting in their charge they gathered round him, while a fierce-looking middle-aged man, also adorned with much barbaric finery, dismounted to examine him.

"That is Simba the King," said Marût, "and the slain one is his uncle, Goru, the great general who brought him up from a babe."

"Then I wish I had another cartridge left for the nephew," I began and stopped, for Hans was speaking to me.

"Good-bye, Baas," he said, "I must go, for I cannot load 'Intombi' on the back of this beast. If you meet your reverend father the Predikant before I do, tell him to make a nice place ready for me among the fires."

Then before I could get out an answer, Hans dragged his camel round; as I have said, it was quite uninjured. Urging it to a shambling gallop with blows of the rifle stock, he departed at a great rate, not towards the home of the Child but up the hill into a brake of giant grass mingled with thorn trees that grew quite close at hand. Here with startling suddenness both he and the camel vanished away.

If the Black Kendah saw him go, of which I am doubtful, for they all seemed to be lost in consultation round their king and the dead general, Goru, they made no attempt to follow him. Another possibility is that they thought he was trying to lead them into some snare or ambush.

I do not know what they thought because I never heard them mention Hans or the matter of his disappearance, if indeed they ever realized that there was such a person. Curiously enough in the case of men who had just shown themselves so brave, this last accident of the decease of Goru coming on the top of all their other casualties, seemed to take the courage out of them. It was as though they had come to the conclusion that we with our guns were something more than mortal.

For several minutes they debated in evident hesitation. At last from out of their array rode a single man, in whom I recognized one of the envoys who had met us in the morning, carrying in his hand a white flag as he had done before. Thereon I laid down my rifle in token that I would not fire at him, which indeed I could not do having nothing to fire. Seeing this he came to within a few yards and halting, addressed Marût.

"O second Prophet of the Child," he said, "these are the words of Simba the King: Your god has been too strong for us to-day, though in a day to come it may be otherwise. I thought I had you in a pit; that you were the bucks and I the hunter. But, though with loss, you have escaped out of the pit," and the speaker glanced towards our retreating force which was now but a cloud of dust in the far distance, "while I the hunter have been gored by your horns," and again he glanced at the dead that were scattered about the plain. "The noblest of the buck, the white bull of the herd," and he looked at me, who in any other circumstances would have felt complimented, "and you, O Prophet Marût, and one or two others, besides those that I have slain, are however still in the pit and your horn is a magic horn," here he pointed to my rifle, "which pierces from afar and kills dead all by whom it is touched."

"So I caught those gentry well in the middle," thought I to myself, "and with soft-nosed bullets!"

"Therefore I, Simba the King, make you an offer. Yield yourselves and I swear that no spear shall be driven through your hearts and no knife come near your throats. You shall only be taken to my town and there be fed on the best and kept as prisoners, till once more there is peace between the Black Kendah and the White. If you refuse, then I will ring you round and perhaps in the dark rush on you and kill you all. Or perhaps I will watch you from day to day till you, who have no water, die of thirst in the heat of the sun. These are my words to which nothing may be added and from which nothing shall be taken away."

Having finished this speech he rode back a few yards out of earshot, and waited.

"What will you answer, Lord Macumazana?" asked Marût.

I replied by another question. "Is there any chance of our being rescued by your people?"

He shook his head. "None. What we have seen to-day is but a small part of the army of the Black Kendah, one regiment of foot and one of horse, that are always ready. By to-morrow thousands will be gathered, many more than we can hope to deal with in the open and still less in their strongholds, also Harût will believe that we are dead. Unless the Child saves us we shall be left to our fate."

"Then it seems that we are indeed in a pit, as that black brute of a king puts it, Marût, and if he does what he says and rushes us at sundown, everyone of us will be killed. Also I am thirsty already and there is nothing to drink. But will this king keep his word? There are other ways of dying besides by steel."

"I think that he will keep his word, but as that messenger said, he will not add to his word. Choose now, for see, they are beginning to hedge us round."

"What do you say, men?" I asked of the three who had remained with us.

"We say, Lord, that we are in the hands of the Child, though we wish now that we had died with our brothers," answered their spokesman fatalistically.

So after Marût and I had consulted together for a little as to the form of his reply, he beckoned to the messenger and said:

"We accept the offer of Simba, although it would be easy for this lord to kill him now where he stands, namely, to yield ourselves as prisoners on his oath that no harm shall come to us. For know that if harm does come, the vengeance will be terrible. Now in proof of his good faith, let Simba draw near and drink the cup of peace with us, for we thirst."

"Not so," said the messenger, "for then that white lord might kill him with his tube. Give me the tube and Simba shall come."

"Take it," I said magnanimously, handing him the rifle, which he received in a very gingerly fashion. After all, I reflected, there is nothing much more useless than a rifle without ammunition.

Off he went holding the weapon at arm's length, and presently Simba himself, accompanied by some of his men, one of whom carried a skin of water and another a large cup hollowed from an elephant's tusk, rode up to us. This Simba was a fine and rather terrifying person with a large moustache and a chin shaved except for a little tuft of hair which he wore at its point like an Italian. His eyes were big and dark, frank-looking, yet now and again with sinister expression in the corners of them. He was not nearly so black as most of his followers; probably in bygone generations his blood had been crossed with that of the White Kendah. He wore his hair long without any head-dress, held in place by a band of gold which I suppose represented a crown. On his forehead was a large white scar, probably received in some battle. Such was his appearance.

He looked at me with great curiosity, and I have often wondered since what kind of an impression I produced upon him. My hat had fallen off, or I had knocked it off when I fired my last cartridge into his people, and forgotten to replace it, and my intractable hair, which was longer than usual, had not been recently brushed. My worn Norfolk jacket was dyed with blood from a wounded or dying man who had tumbled against me in the scrimmage when the cavalry charged us, and my right leg and boot were stained in a similar fashion from having rubbed against my camel where a spear had entered it. Altogether I must have appeared a most disreputable object.

Some indication of his opinion was given, however, in a remark, which of course I pretended not to understand, that I overheard him make to one of his officers:

"Truly," he said, "we must not always look to the strong for strength. And yet this little white porcupine is strength itself, for see how much damage he has wrought us. Also consider his eyes that appear to pierce everything. Jana himself might fear those eyes. Well, time that grinds the rocks will tell us all."

All of this I caught perfectly, my ears being very sharp, although he thought that he spoke out of my hearing, for after spending a month in their company I understood the Kendah dialect of Bantu very well.

Having delivered himself thus he rode nearer and said:

"You, Prophet Marût, my enemy, have heard the terms of me, Simba the King, and have accepted them. Therefore discuss them no more. What I have promised I will keep. What I have given I give, neither greater nor less by the weight of a hair."

"So be it, O King," answered Marût with his usual smile, which nothing ever seemed to disturb. "Only remember that if those terms are broken either in the letter or in the spirit, especially the spirit" (that is the best rendering I can give of his word), "the manifold curses of the Child will fall upon you and yours. Yes, though you kill us all by treachery, still those curses will fall."

"May Jana take the Child and all who worship it," exclaimed the king with evident irritation.

"In the end, O King, Jana will take the Child and its followers—or the Child will take Jana and his followers. Which of these things must happen is known to the Child alone, and perchance to its prophets. Meanwhile, for every one of those of the Child I think that three of the followers of Jana, or more, lie dead upon this field. Also the caravan is now out of your reach with two of the white lords and many of such tubes which deal death, like that which we have surrendered to you. Therefore because we are helpless, do not think that the Child is helpless. Jana must have been asleep, O King, or you would have set your trap better."

I thought that this coolly insolent speech would have produced some outburst, but in fact it seemed to have an opposite effect. Making no reply to it, Simba said almost humbly:

"I come to drink the cup of peace with you and the white lord, O Prophet. Afterwards we can talk. Give me water, slave."

Then a man filled the great ivory cup with water from the skin he carried. Simba took it and having sprinkled a little upon the ground, I suppose as an offering, drank from the cup, doubtless to show that it was not poisoned. Watching carefully, I made sure that he swallowed what he drank by studying the motions of his throat. Then he handed the cup with a bow to Marût, who with a still deeper bow passed it to me. Being absolutely parched I absorbed about a pint of it, and feeling a new man, passed the horn to Marût, who swallowed the rest. Then it was filled again for our three White Kendah, the King first tasting the water as before, after which Marût and I had a second pull.

When at length our thirst was satisfied, horses were brought to us, serviceable and docile little beasts with sheepskins for saddles and loops of hide for stirrups. On these we mounted and for the next three hours rode across the plain, surrounded by a strong escort and with an armed Black Kendah running on each side of our horses and holding in his hand a thong attached to the ring of the bridle, no doubt to prevent any attempt to escape.

Our road ran past but not through some villages whence we saw many women and children staring at us, and through beautiful crops of mealies and other sorts of grain that in this country were now just ripening. The luxuriant appearance of these crops suggested that the rains must have been plentiful and the season all that could be desired. From some of the villages by the track arose a miserable sound of wailing. Evidently their inhabitants had already heard that certain of their menkind had fallen in that morning's fight.

At the end of the third hour we began to enter the great forest which I had seen when first we looked down on Kendahland. It was filled with splendid trees, most of them quite strange to me, but perhaps because of the denseness of their overshadowing crowns there was comparatively no undergrowth. The general effect of the place was very gloomy, since little light could pass through the interlacing foliage of the tops of those mighty trees.

Towards evening we came to a clearing in this forest, it may have been four or five miles in diameter, but whether it was natural or artificial I am not sure. I think, however, that it was probably the former for two reasons: the hollow nature of the ground, which lay a good many feet lower than the surrounding forest, and the wonderful fertility of the soil, which suggested that it had once been deposited upon an old lake bottom. Never did I see such crops as those that grew upon that clearing; they were magnificent.

Wending our way along the road that ran through the tall corn, for here every inch was cultivated, we came suddenly upon the capital of the Black Kendah, which was known as Simba Town. It was a large place, somewhat different from any other African settlement with which I am acquainted, inasmuch as it was not only stockaded but completely surrounded by a broad artificial moat filled with water from a stream that ran through the centre of the town, over which moat there were four timber bridges placed at the cardinal points of the compass. These bridges were strong enough to bear horses or stock, but so made that in the event of attack they could be destroyed in a few minutes.

Riding through the eastern gate, a stout timber structure on the farther side of the corresponding bridge, where the king was received with salutes by an armed guard, we entered one of the main streets of the town which ran from north to south and from east to west. It was broad and on either side of it were the dwellings of the inhabitants set close together because the space within the stockade was limited. These were not huts but square buildings of mud with flat roofs of some kind of cement. Evidently they were built upon the model of Oriental and North African houses of which some debased tradition remained with these people. Thus a stairway or ladder ran from the interior to the roof of each house, whereon its inhabitants were accustomed, as I discovered afterwards, to sleep during a good part of the year, also to eat in the cool of the day. Many of them were gathered there now to watch us pass, men, women, and children, all except the little ones decently clothed in long garments of various colours, the women for the most part in white and the men in a kind of bluish linen.

I saw at once that they had already heard of the fight and of the considerable losses which their people had sustained, for their reception of us prisoners was most unfriendly. Indeed the men shook their fists at us, the women screamed out curses, while the children stuck out their tongues in token of derision or defiance. Most of these demonstrations, however, were directed at Marût and his followers, who only smiled indifferently. At me they stared in wonder not unmixed with fear.

A quarter of a mile or so from the gate we came to an inner enclosure, that answered to the South African cattle kraal, surrounded by a dry ditch and a timber palisade outside of which was planted a green fence of some shrub with long white thorns. Here we passed through more gates, to find ourselves in an oval space, perhaps five acres in extent. Evidently this served as a market ground, but all around it were open sheds where hundreds of horses were stabled. No cattle seemed to be kept there, except a few that with sheep and goats were driven in every day for slaughter purposes at a shambles at the north end, from the great stock kraals built beyond the forest to the south, where they were safe from possible raiding by the White Kendah.

A tall reed fence cut off the southern end of this marketplace, outside of which we were ordered to dismount. Passing through yet another gate we found within the fence a large hut or house built on the same model as the others in the town, which Marût whispered to me was that of the king. Behind it were smaller houses in which lived his queen and women, good-looking females, who advanced to meet him with obsequious bows. To the right and left were two more buildings of about equal size, one of which was occupied by the royal guard and the other was the guest-house whither we were conducted.

It proved to be a comfortable dwelling about thirty feet square but containing only one room, with various huts behind it that served for cooking and other purposes. In one of these the three camelmen were placed. Immediately on our arrival food was brought to us, a lamb or kid roasted whole upon a wooden platter, and some green mealie-cobs boiled upon another platter; also water to drink and wash with in earthenware jars of sun-dried clay.

I ate heartily, for I was starving. Then, as it was useless to attempt precautions against murder, without any talk to my fellow prisoner, for which we were both too tired, I threw myself down on a mattress stuffed with corn husks in a corner of the hut, drew a skin rug over me and, having commended myself to the protection of the Power above, fell fast asleep.

H. RIDER HAGGARD

XII

The First Curse

The next thing I remember was feeling upon my face the sunlight that poured through a window-place which was protected by immovable wooden bars. For a while I lay still, reflecting as memory returned to me upon all the events of the previous day and upon my present unhappy position. Here I was a prisoner in the hands of a horde of fierce savages who had every reason to hate me, for though this was done in self-defence, had I not killed a number of their people against whom personally I had no quarrel? It was true that their king had promised me safety, but what reliance could be put upon the word of such a man? Unless something occurred to save me, without doubt my days were numbered. In this way or in that I should be murdered, which served me right for ever entering upon such a business.

The only satisfactory point in the story was that, for the present at any rate, Ragnall and Savage had escaped, though doubtless sooner or later fate would overtake them also. I was sure that they had escaped, since two of the camelmen with us had informed Marût that they saw them swept away surrounded by our people and quite unharmed. Now they would be grieving over my death, since none survived who could tell them of our capture, unless the Black Kendah chose to do so, which was not likely. I wondered what course they would take when Ragnall found that his quest was vain, as of course must happen. Try to get out of the country, I suppose, as I prayed they might succeed in doing, though this was most improbable.

Then there was Hans. He of course would attempt to retrace our road across the desert, if he had got clear away. Having a good camel, a rifle and some ammunition, it was just possible that he might win through, as he never forgot a path which he had once travelled, though probably in a week's time a few bones upon the desert would be all that remained of him. Well, as he had suggested, perhaps we should soon be talking the event over in some far sphere with my father—and others. Poor old Hans!

I opened my eyes and looked about me. The first thing I noticed was that my double-barrelled pistol, which I had placed at full cock beside me before I went to sleep, was gone, also my large clasp-knife. This discovery did not tend to raise my spirits, since I was now quite weaponless. Then I observed Marût seated on the floor of the hut staring straight in front of him, and noted that at length even he had ceased to smile, but that his lips were moving as though he were engaged in prayer or meditation.

"Marût," I said, "someone has been in this place while we were asleep and stolen my pistol and knife."

"Yes, Lord," he answered, "and my knife also. I saw them come in the middle of the night, two men who walked softly as cats, and searched everything."

"Then why did you not wake me?"

"What would have been the use, Lord? If we had caught hold of the men, they would have called out and we should have been murdered at once. It was best to let them take the things, which after all are of no good to us here."

"The pistol might have been of some good," I replied significantly.

"Yes," he said, nodding, "but at the worst death is easy to find."

"Do you think, Marût, that we could manage to let Harût and the others know our plight? That smoke which I breathed in England, for instance, seemed to show me far-off things—if we could get any of it."

"The smoke was nothing, Lord, but some harmless burning powder which clouded your mind for a minute, and enabled you to see the thoughts that were in *our* minds. *We* drew the pictures at which you looked. Also here there is none."

"Oh!" I said, "the old trick of suggestion; just what I imagined. Then there's an end of that, and as the others will think that we are dead and we cannot communicate with them, we have no hope except in ourselves."

"Or the Child," suggested Marût gently.

"Look here!" I said with irritation. "After you have just told me that your smoke vision was a mere conjurer's trick, how do you expect me to believe in your blessed Child? Who is the Child? What is the Child, and—this is more important—what can it do? As your throat is going to be cut shortly you may as well tell me the truth."

"Lord Macumazana, I will. Who and what the Child is I cannot say because I do not know. But it has been our god for thousands of years, and we believe that our remote forefathers brought it with them when they were driven out of Egypt at some time unknown. We have writings concerning it done up in little rolls, but as we cannot read them they are of no use to us. It has an hereditary priesthood, of which Harût my uncle, for he is my uncle, is the head. We believe that the Child is God, or rather a symbol in which God dwells, and that it can save us in this world and the next, for we hold that man is an immortal spirit. We believe also that through its Oracle—a priestess who is called Guardian of the Child—it can declare the future and bring blessings or curses upon men, especially upon our enemies. When the Oracle dies we are helpless since the Child has no 'mouth' and our enemies prevail against us. This happened a long while ago, and the last Oracle having declared before her death that her successor was to be found in England, my uncle and I travelled thither disguised as conjurers and made search for many years. We thought that we had found the new Oracle in the lady who married the Lord Igeza, because of that mark of the new moon upon her neck. After our return to Africa, however, for as I have spoken of this matter I may as well tell you all," here he stared me full in the eyes and spoke in a clear metallic voice which somehow no longer convinced me, "we found that we had made a mistake, for the real Oracle, a mere girl, was discovered among our own people, and has now been for two years installed in her office. Without doubt the last Guardian of the Child was wandering in her mind when she told us that story before her death as to a woman in England, a country of which she had heard through Arabs. That is all."

"Thank you," I replied, feeling that it would be useless to show any suspicion of his story. "Now will you be so good as to tell me who and what is the god, or the elephant Jana, whom you have brought me here to kill? Is the elephant a god, or is the god an elephant? In either case what has it to do with the Child?"

"Lord, Jana among us Kendah represents the evil in the world, as the Child represents the good. Jana is he whom the Mohammedans call Shaitan and the Christians call Satan, and our forefathers, the old Egyptians, called Set."

"Ah!" thought I to myself, "now we have got it. Horus the Divine Child, and Set the evil monster, with whom it strives everlastingly."

"Always," went on Marût, "there has been war between the Child and Jana, that is, between Good and Evil, and we know that in the end one of them must conquer the other."

"The whole world has known that from the beginning," I interrupted. "But who and what is this Jana?"

"Among the Black Kendah, Lord, Jana is an elephant, or at any rate his symbol is an elephant, a very terrible beast to which sacrifices are made, that kills all who do not worship him if he chances to meet them. He lives farther on in the forest yonder, and the Black Kendah make use of him in war, for the devil in him obeys their priests."

"Indeed, and is this elephant always the same?"

"I cannot tell you, but for many generations it has been the same, for it is known by its size and by the fact that one of its tusks is twisted downwards."

"Well," I remarked, "all this proves nothing, since elephants certainly live for at least two hundred years, and perhaps much longer. Also, after they become 'rogues' they acquire every kind of wicked and unnatural habit, as to which I could tell you lots of stories. Have you seen this elephant?"

"No, Macumazana," he answered with a shiver. "If I had seen it should I have been alive to-day? Yet I fear I am fated to see it ere long, not alone," and again he shivered, looking at me in a very suggestive manner.

At this moment our conversation was interrupted by the arrival of two Black Kendahs who brought us our breakfast of porridge and a boiled fowl, and stood there while we ate it. For my part I was not sorry, as I had learned all I wanted to know of the theological opinions and practice of the land, and had come to the conclusion that the terrible devil-god of the Black Kendah was merely a rogue elephant of unusual size and ferocity, which under other circumstances it would have given me the greatest pleasure to try to shoot.

When we had finished eating, that is soon, for neither of our appetites was good that morning, we walked out of the house into the surrounding compound and visited the camelmen in their hut. Here we found them squatted on the ground looking very depressed indeed. When I asked them what was the matter they replied, "Nothing," except that they were men about to die and life was pleasant. Also they had wives and children whom they would never see again.

Having tried to cheer them up to the best of my ability, which I fear I did without conviction, for in my heart I agreed with their view of the case, we returned to the guest-house and mounted the stair which led to the flat roof. Hence we saw that some curious ceremony was in progress in the centre of the market-place. At that distance we could not make out the details, for I forgot to say that my glasses had been stolen with the pistol and knife, probably because they were supposed to be lethal weapons or instruments of magic.

A rough altar had been erected, on which a fire burned. Behind it the king, Simba, was seated on a stool with various councillors about him. In front of the altar was a stout wooden table, on which lay what looked like the body of a goat or a sheep. A fantastically dressed man, assisted by other men, appeared to be engaged in inspecting the inside of this animal with, we gathered, unsatisfactory results, for presently he raised his arms and uttered a loud wail. Then the creature's viscera were removed from it and thrown upon the fire, while the rest of the carcass was carried off.

I asked Marût what he thought they were doing. He replied dejectedly:

"Consulting their Oracle; perhaps as to whether we should live or die, Macumazana."

Just then the priest in the strange, feathered attire approached the king, carrying some small object in his hand. I wondered what it could be, till the sound of a report reached my ears and I saw the man begin to jump round upon one leg, holding the other with both his hands at the knee and howling loudly.

"Ah!" I said, "that pistol was full cocked, and the bullet got him in the foot."

Simba shouted out something, whereon a man picked up the pistol and threw it into the fire, round which the others gathered to watch it burn.

"You wait," I said to Marût, and as I spoke the words the inevitable happened.

Off went the other barrel of the pistol, which hopped out of the fire with the recoil like a living thing. But as it happened one of the assistant priests was standing in front of the mouth of that barrel, and he also hopped once, but never again, for the heavy bullet struck him somewhere in the body and killed him. Now there was consternation. Everyone ran away, leaving the dead man lying on the ground. Simba led the rout and the head-priest brought up the rear, skipping along upon one leg.

Having observed these events, which filled me with an unholy joy, we descended into the house again as there was nothing more to see, also because it occurred to me that our presence on the roof, watching their discomfiture, might irritate these savages. About ten minutes later the gate of the fence round the guest-house was thrown open, and through it came four men carrying on a stretcher the body of the priest whom the bullet had killed, which they laid down in front of our door. Then followed the king with an armed guard, and after him the befeathered diviner with his foot bound up, who supported himself upon the shoulders of two of his colleagues. This man, I now perceived, wore a hideous mask, from which projected two tusks in imitation of those of an elephant. Also there were others, as many as the space would hold.

The king called to us to come out of the house, which, having no choice, we did. One glance at him showed me that the man was frantic with fear, or rage, or both.

"Look upon your work, magicians!" he said in a terrible voice, pointing first to the dead priest, then to the diviner's wounded foot.

"It is no work of ours, King Simba," answered Marût. "It is your own work. You stole the magic weapon of the white lord and made it angry, so that it has revenged itself upon you."

"It is true," said Simba, "that the tube has killed one of those who took it away from you and wounded the other" (here was luck indeed). "But it was you who ordered it to do so, magicians. Now, hark! Yesterday I promised you safety, that no spear should pierce your hearts and no knife come near your throats, and drank the cup of peace with you. But you have broken the pact, working us more harm, and therefore it no longer holds, since there are many other ways in which men can die. Listen again! This is my decree. By your magic you have taken away the life of one of my servants and hurt another of my servants, destroying the middle toe of his left foot. If within three days you do not give back the life to him who seems to be dead, and give back the toe to him who seems to be hurt, as you well can do, then you shall join those whom you have slain in the land of death, how I will not tell you."

Now when I heard this amazing sentence I gasped within myself, but thinking it better to keep up my rôle of understanding nothing of their talk, I preserved an immovable countenance and left Marût to answer. This, to his credit be it recorded, he did with his customary pleasant smile.

"O King," he said, "who can bring the dead back to life? Not even the Child itself, at any rate in this world, for there is no way."

"Then, Prophet of the Child, you had better find a way, or, I repeat, I send you to join them," he shouted, rolling his eyes.

"What did my brother, the great Prophet, promise to you but yesterday, O King, if you harmed us?" asked Marût. "Was it not that the three great curses should fall upon your people? Learn now that if so much as one of us is murdered by you, these things shall swiftly come to pass. I, Marût, who am also a Prophet of the Child, have said it."

Now Simba seemed to go quite mad, so mad that I thought all was over. He waved his spear and danced about in front of us, till the silver chains clanked upon his breast. He vituperated the Child and its worshippers, who, he declared, had worked evil on the Black Kendah for generations. He appealed to his god Jana to avenge these evils, "to pierce the Child with his tusks, to tear it with his trunk, and to trample it with his feet," all of which the wounded diviner ably seconded through his horrid mask.

There we stood before him, I leaning against the wall of the house with an air of studied nonchalance mingled with mild interest, at least that is what I meant to do, and Marût smiling sweetly and staring at the heavens. Whilst I was wondering what exact portion of my frame was destined to become acquainted with that spear, of a sudden Simba gave it up. Turning to his followers, he bade them dig a hole in the corner of our little enclosure and set the dead man in it, "with his head out so that he may breathe," an order which they promptly executed.

Then he issued a command that we should be well fed and tended, and remarking that if the departed was not alive and healthy on the third morning from that day, we should hear from him again, he and his company stalked off, except those men who were occupied with the interment.

Soon this was finished also. There sat the deceased buried to the neck with his face looking towards the house, a most disagreeable sight. Presently, however, matters were improved in this respect by one of the sextons fetching a large earthenware pot and several smaller pots full of food and water. The latter they set round the head, I suppose for the sustenance of the body beneath, and then placed the big vessel inverted over all, "to keep the sun off our sleeping brother," as I heard one say to the other.

This pot looked innocent enough when all was done, like one of those that gardeners in England put over forced rhubarb, no more. And yet, such is the strength of the imagination, I think that on the whole I should have preferred the object underneath naked and unadorned. For instance, I have forgotten to say that the heads of those of the White

Kendah who had fallen in the fight had been set up on poles in front of Simba's house. They were unpleasant to contemplate, but to my mind not so unpleasant as that pot.

As a matter of fact, this precaution against injury from the sun to the late diviner proved unnecessary, since by some strange chance from that moment the sun ceased to shine. Quite suddenly clouds arose which gradually covered the whole sky and the weather began to turn very cold, unprecedentedly so, Marût informed me, for the time of year, which, it will be remembered, in this country was the season just before harvest. Obviously the Black Kendah thought so also, since from our seats on the roof, whither we had retreated to be as far as possible from the pot, we saw them gathered in the market-place, staring at the sky and talking to each other.

The day passed without any further event, except the arrival of our meals, for which we had no great appetite. The night came, earlier than usual because of the clouds, and we fell asleep, or rather into a series of dozes. Once I thought that I heard someone stirring in the huts behind us, but as it was followed by silence I took no more notice. At length the light broke very slowly, for now the clouds were denser than ever. Shivering with the cold, Marût and I made a visit to the camel-drivers, who were not allowed to enter our house. On going into their hut we saw to our horror that only two of them remained, seated stonily upon the floor. We asked where the third was. They replied they did not know. In the middle of the night, they said, men had crept in, who seized, bound and gagged him, then dragged him away. As there was nothing to be said or done, we returned to breakfast filled with horrid fears.

Nothing happened that day except that some priests arrived, lifted the earthenware pot, examined their departed colleague, who by now had become an unencouraging spectacle, removed old dishes of food, arranged more about him, and went off. Also the clouds grew thicker and thicker, and the air more and more chilly, till, had we been in any northern latitude, I should have said that snow was pending. From our perch on the roof-top I observed the population of Simba Town discussing the weather with ever-increasing eagerness; also that the people who were going out to work in the fields wore mats over their shoulders.

Once more darkness came, and this night, notwithstanding the cold, we spent wrapped in rugs, on the roof of the house. It had occurred to us that kidnapping would be less easy there, as we could make some sort of a fight at the head of the stairway, or, if the worst came to the worst, dive from the parapet and break our necks. We kept watch turn and turn about. During my watch about midnight I heard a noise going on in the hut behind us; scuffling and a stifled cry which turned my blood cold. About an hour later a fire was lighted in the centre of the market-place where the sheep had been sacrificed, and by the flare of it I could see people moving. But what they did I could not see, which was perhaps as well.

Next morning only one of the camelmen was left. This remaining man was now almost crazy with fear, and could give no clear account of what had happened to his companion.

The poor fellow implored us to take him away to our house, as he feared to be left alone with "the black devils." We tried to do so, but armed guards appeared mysteriously and thrust him back into his own hut.

This day was an exact repetition of the others. The same inspection of the deceased and renewal of his food; the same cold, clouded sky, the same agitated conferences in the market-place.

For the third time darkness fell upon us in that horrible place. Once more we took refuge on the roof, but this night neither of us slept. We were too cold, too physically miserable, and too filled with mental apprehensions. All nature seemed to be big with impending disaster. The sky appeared to be sinking down upon the earth. The moon was hidden, yet a faint and lurid light shone now in one quarter of the horizon, now in another. There was no wind, but the air moaned audibly. It was as though the end of the world were near as, I reflected, probably might be the case so far as we were concerned. Never, perhaps, have I felt so spiritually terrified as I was during the dreadful inaction of that night. Even if I had known that I was going to be executed at dawn, I think that by comparison I should have been light-hearted. But the worst part of the business was that I knew nothing. I was like a man forced to walk through dense darkness among precipices, quite unable to guess when my journey would end in space, but enduring all the agonies of death at every step.

About midnight again we heard that scuffle and stifled cry in the hut behind us.

"He's gone," I whispered to Marût, wiping the cold sweat from my brow.

"Yes," answered Marût, "and very soon we shall follow him, Macumazana."

I wished that his face were visible so that I could see if he still smiled when he uttered those words.

An hour or so later the usual fire appeared in the marketplace, round which the usual figures flitted dimly. The sight of them fascinated me, although I did not want to look, fearing what I might see. Luckily, however, we were too far off to discern anything at night.

While these unholy ceremonies were in progress the climax came, that is so far as the weather was concerned. Of a sudden a great gale sprang up, a gale of icy wind such as in Southern Africa sometimes precedes a thunderstorm. It blew for half an hour or more, then lulled. Now lightning flashed across the heavens, and by the glare of it we perceived that all the population of Simba Town seemed to be gathered in the market-place. At least there were some thousands of them, talking, gesticulating, pointing at the sky.

A few minutes later there came a great crash of thunder, of which it was impossible to locate the sound, for it rolled from everywhere. Then suddenly something hard struck the roof by my side and rebounded, to be followed next moment by a blow upon my shoulder which nearly knocked me flat, although I was well protected by the skin rugs.

"Down the stair!" I called. "They are stoning us," and suited the action to the word.

Ten seconds later we were both in the room, crouched in its farther corner, for the stones or whatever they were seemed to be following us. I struck a match, of which fortunately I had some, together with my pipe and a good pocketful of tobacco—my only solace in those days—and, as it burned up, saw first that blood was running down Marût's face, and secondly, that these stones were great lumps of ice, some of them weighing several ounces, which hopped about the floor like live things.

"Hailstorm!" remarked Marût with his accustomed smile.

"Hell storm!" I replied, "for whoever saw hail like that before?"

Then the match burnt out and conversation came to an end for the reason that we could no longer hear each other speak. The hail came down with a perpetual, rattling roar, that in its sum was one of the most terrible sounds to which I ever listened. And yet above it I thought that I could catch another, still more terrible, the wail of hundreds of people in agony. After the first few minutes I began to be afraid that the roof would be battered in, or that the walls would crumble beneath this perpetual fire of the musketry of heaven. But the cement was good and the place well built.

So it came about that the house stood the tempest, which had it been roofed with tiles or galvanized iron I am sure it would never have done, since the lumps of ice must have shattered one and pierced the other like paper. Indeed I have seen this happen in a bad hailstorm in Natal which killed my best horse. But even that hail was as snowflakes compared to this.

I suppose that this natural phenomenon continued for about twenty minutes, not more, during ten of which it was at its worst. Then by degrees it ceased, the sky cleared and the moon shone out beautifully. We climbed to the roof again and looked. It was several inches deep in jagged ice, while the market-place and all the country round appeared in the bright moonlight to be buried beneath a veil of snow.

Very rapidly, as the normal temperature of that warm land reasserted itself, this snow or rather hail melted, causing a flood of water which, where there was any fall, began to rush away with a gurgling sound. Also we heard other sounds, such as that from the galloping hoofs of many of the horses which had broken loose from their wrecked stables at the north end of the market-place, where in great number they had been killed by the falling roofs or had kicked each other to death, and a wild universal wail that rose from every quarter of the big town, in which quantities of the worst-built houses had collapsed. Further, lying here and there about the market-place we could see scores of dark shapes that we knew to be those of men, women and children, whom those sharp missiles hurled from heaven had caught before they could escape and slain or wounded almost to death. For it will be remembered that perhaps not fewer than two thousand people were gathered on this market-place, attending the horrid midnight sacrifice and discussing the unnatural weather when the storm burst upon them suddenly as an avalanche.

"The Child is small, yet its strength is great. Behold the first curse!" said Marût solemnly.

I stared at him, but as he chose to believe that a very unusual hailstorm was a visitation from heaven I did not think it worth while arguing the point. Only I wondered if he really did believe this. Then I remembered that such an event was said to have afflicted the old Egyptians in the hour of their pride because they would not "let the people go." Well, these blackguardedly Black Kendah were certainly worse than the Egyptians can ever have been; also they would not let *us* go. It was not wonderful therefore that Marût should be the victim of phantasies on the matter.

Not until the following morning did we come to understand the full extent of the calamity which had overtaken the Black Kendah. I think I have said that their crops this year were magnificent and just ripening to harvest. From our roof on previous days we could see a great area of them stretching to the edge of the forest. When the sun rose that morning this area had vanished, and the ground was covered with a carpet of green pulp. Also the forest itself appeared suddenly to have experienced the full effects of a northern winter. Not a leaf was left upon the trees, which stood their pointing their naked boughs to heaven.

No one who had not seen it could imagine the devastating fury of that storm. For example, the head of the diviner who was buried in the court-yard awaiting resurrection through our magic was, it may be recalled, covered with a stout earthenware pot. Now that pot had shattered into sherds and the head beneath was nothing but bits of broken bone which it would have been impossible for the very best magic to reconstruct to the likeness of a human being.

Calamity indeed stalked naked through the land.

XIII

JANA

No breakfast was brought to us that morning, probably for the reason that there was none to bring. This did not matter, however, seeing that plenty of food accumulated from supper and other meals stood in a corner of the house practically untouched. So we ate what we could and then paid our usual visit to the hut in which the camelmen had been confined. I say had been, for now it was quite empty, the last poor fellow having vanished away like his companions.

The sight of this vacuum filled me with a kind of fury.

"They have all been murdered!" I said to Marût.

"No," he replied with gentle accuracy. "They have been sacrificed to Jana. What we have seen on the market-place at night was the rite of their sacrifice. Now it will be our turn, Lord Macumazana."

"Well," I exclaimed, "I hope these devils are satisfied with Jana's answer to their accursed offerings, and if they try their fiendish pranks on us—"

"Doubtless there will be another answer. But, Lord, the question is, will that help us?"

Dumb with impotent rage I returned to the house, where presently the remains of the reed gate opened. Through it appeared Simba the King, the diviner with the injured foot walking upon crutches, and others of whom the most were more or less wounded, presumably by the hailstones. Then it was that in my wrath I put off the pretence of not understanding their language and went for them before they could utter a single word.

"Where are our servants, you murderers?" I asked, shaking my fist at them. "Have you sacrificed them to your devil-god? If so, behold the fruits of sacrifice!" and I swept my arm towards the country beyond. "Where are your crops?" I went on. "Tell me on what you will live this winter?" (At these words they quailed. In their imagination already they saw famine stalking towards them.) "Why do you keep us here? Is it that you wait for a worse thing to befall you? Why do you visit us here now?" and I paused, gasping with indignation.

"We came to look whether you had brought back to life that doctor whom you killed with your magic, white man," answered the king heavily.

I stepped to the corner of the court-yard and, drawing aside a mat that I had thrown there, showed them what lay beneath.

"Look then," I said, "and be sure that if you do not let us go, as yonder thing is, so shall all of you be before another moon has been born and died. Such is the life we shall give to evil men like you."

Now they grew positively terrified.

"Lord," said Simba, for the first time addressing me by a title of respect, "your magic is too strong for us. Great misfortune has fallen upon our land. Hundreds of people are dead, killed by the ice-stones that you have called down. Our harvest is ruined, and there is but little corn left in the storepits now when we looked to gather the new grain. Messengers come in from the outlying land telling us that nearly all the sheep and goats and very many of the cattle are slain. Soon we shall starve."

"As you deserve to starve," I answered. "Now—will you let us go?"

Simba stared at me doubtfully, then began to whisper into the ear of the lamed diviner. I could not catch what they said, so I watched their faces. That of the diviner whose head I was glad to see had been cut by a hailstone so that both ends of him were now injured, told me a good deal. His mask had been ugly, but now that it was off the countenance beneath was far uglier. Of a negroid type, pendulous-lipped, sensuous and loose-eyed, he was indeed a hideous fellow, yet very cunning and cruel-looking, as men of his class are apt to be. Humbled as he was for the moment, I felt sure that he was still plotting evil against us, somewhat against the will of his master. The issue showed that I was right. At length Simba spoke, saying:

"We had intended, Lord, to keep you and the priest of the Child here as hostages against mischief that might be worked on us by the followers of the Child, who have always been our bitter enemies and done us much undeserved wrong, although on our part we have faithfully kept the pact concluded in the days of our grandfathers. It seems, however, that fate, or your magic, is too strong for us, and therefore I have determined to let you go. To-night at sundown we will set you on the road which leads to the ford of the River Tava, which divides our territory from that of the White Kendah, and you may depart where you will, since our wish is that never again may we see your ill-omened faces."

At this intelligence my heart leapt in joy that was altogether premature. But, preserving my indignant air, I exclaimed:

"To-night! Why to-night? Why not at once? It is hard for us to cross unknown rivers in the dark."

"The water is low, Lord, and the ford easy. Moreover, if you started now you would reach it in the dark; whereas if you start at sundown, you will reach it in the morning. Lastly, we cannot conduct you hence until we have buried our dead."

Then, without giving me time to answer, he turned and left the place, followed by the others. Only at the gateway the diviner wheeled round on his crutches and glared at us both, muttering something with his thick lips; probably it was curses.

"At any rate they are going to set us free," I said to Marût, not without exultation, when they had all vanished.

"Yes, Lord," he replied, "but *where* are they going to set us free? The demon Jana lives in the forests and the swamps by the banks of the Tava River, and it is said that he ravages at night."

I did not pursue the subject, but reflected to myself cheerfully that this mystic rogue-elephant was a long way off and might be circumvented, whereas that altar of sacrifice was extremely near and very difficult to avoid.

Never did a thief with a rich booty in view, or a wooer having an assignation with his lady, wait for sundown more eagerly than I did that day. Hour after hour I sat upon the house-top, watching the Black Kendah carrying off the dead killed by the hailstones and generally trying to repair the damage done by the terrific tempest. Watching the sun also as it climbed down the cloudless sky, and literally counting the minutes till it should reach the horizon, although I knew well that it would have been wiser after such a night to prepare for our journey by lying down to sleep.

At length the great orb began to sink in majesty behind the tattered western forest, and, punctual to the minute, Simba, with a mounted escort of some twenty men and two led horses, appeared at our gate. As our preparations, which consisted only of Marût stuffing such food as was available into the breast of his robe, were already made, we walked out of that accursed guest-house and, at a sign from the king, mounted the horses. Riding across the empty market-place and past the spot where the rough stone altar still stood with charred bones protruding from the ashes of its extinguished fire—were they those of our friends the camel-drivers? I wondered—we entered the north street of the town.

Here, standing at the doors of their houses, were many of the inhabitants who had gathered to watch us pass. Never did I see hate more savage than was written on those faces as they shook their fists at us and muttered curses not loud but deep.

No wonder! for they were all ruined, poor folk, with nothing to look forward to but starvation until long months hence the harvest came again for those who would live to gather it. Also they were convinced that we, the white magician and the prophet of their enemy the Child, had brought this disaster on them. Had it not been for the escort I believe they would have fallen on us and torn us to pieces. Considering them I understood for the first time how disagreeable real unpopularity *can be*. But when I saw the actual condition of the fruitful gardens without in the waning daylight, I confess that I was moved to some sympathy with their owners. It was appalling. Not a handful of grain was there left to gather, for the corn had been not only "laid" but literally cut to ribbons by the hail.

After running for some miles through the cultivated land the road entered the forest. Here it was dark as pitch, so dark that I wondered how our guides found their way. In that blackness dreadful apprehensions seized me, for I became convinced that we had been brought here to be murdered. Every minute I expected to feel a knife-thrust in my back. I thought of digging my heels into the horse's sides and trying to gallop off anywhere, but abandoned the idea, first because I could not desert Marût, of whom I had lost touch in the gloom, and secondly because I was hemmed in by the escort. For the same reason I did not try to slip from the horse and glide away into the forest. There was nothing to be done save to go on and await the end.

It came at last some hours later. We were out of the forest now, and there was the moon rising, past her full but still very bright. Her light showed me that we were on a wild moorland, swampy, with scattered trees growing here and there, across which what seemed to be a game track ran down hill. That was all I could make out. Here the escort halted, and Simba the King said in a sullen voice:

"Dismount and go your ways, evil spirits, for we travel no farther across this place which is haunted. Follow the track and it will lead you to a lake. Pass the lake and by morning you will come to the river beyond which lies the country of your friends. May its waters swallow you if you reach them. For learn, there is one who watches on this road whom few care to meet."

As he finished speaking men sprang at us and, pulling us from the horses, thrust us out of their company. Then they turned and in another minute were lost in the darkness, leaving us alone.

"What now, friend Marût?" I asked.

"Now, Lord, all we can do is to go forward, for if we stay here Simba and his people will return and kill us at the daylight. One of them said so to me."

"Then, 'come on, Macduff,'" I exclaimed, stepping out briskly, and though he had never read Shakespeare, Marût understood and followed.

"What did Simba mean about 'one on the road whom few care to meet'?" I asked over my shoulder when we had done half a mile or so.

"I think he meant the elephant Jana," replied Marût with a groan.

"Then I hope Jana isn't at home. Cheer up, Marût. The chances are that we shall never meet a single elephant in this big place."

"Yet many elephants have been here, Lord," and he pointed to the ground. "It is said that they come to die by the waters of the lake and this is one of the roads they follow on their death journey, a road that no other living thing dare travel."

"Oh!" I exclaimed. "Then after all that was a true dream I had in the house in England."

"Yes, Lord, because my brother Harût once lost his way out hunting when he was young and saw what his mind showed you in the dream, and what we shall see presently, if we live to come so far."

I made no reply, both because what he said was either true or false, which I should ascertain presently, and because I was engaged in searching the ground with my eyes. He was right; many elephants had travelled this path—one quite recently. I, a hunter of those brutes, could not be deceived on this point. Once or twice also I thought that I caught sight of the outline of some tall creature moving silently through the scattered thorns a couple of hundred yards or so to our right. It might have been an elephant or a giraffe, or perhaps nothing but a shadow, so I said nothing. As I heard no noise I was inclined to believe the latter explanation. In any case, what was the good of speaking? Unarmed and solitary amidst unknown dangers, our position was desperate, and as Marût's nerve was already giving out, to emphasize its horrors to him would be mere foolishness.

On we trudged for another two hours, during which time the only living thing that I saw was a large owl which sailed round our heads as though to look at us, and then flew away ahead.

This owl, Marût informed me, was one of "Jana's spies" that kept him advised of all that was passing in his territory. I muttered "Bosh" and tramped on. Still I was glad that we saw no more of the owl, for in certain circumstances such dark fears are catching.

We reached the top of a rise, and there beneath us lay the most desolate scene that ever I have seen. At least it would have been the most desolate if I did not chance to have looked on it before, in the drawing-room of Ragnall Castle! There was no doubt about it. Below was the black, melancholy lake, a large sheet of water surrounded by reeds. Around, but at a considerable distance, appeared the tropical forest. To the east of the lake stretched a stony plain. At the time I could make out no more because of the uncertain light and the distance, for we had still over a mile to go before we reached the edge of the lake.

The aspect of the place filled me with tremblings, both because of its utter uncanniness and because of the inexplicable truth that I had seen it before. Most people will have experienced this kind of moral shock when on going to some new land they recognize a locality as being quite familiar to them in all its details. Or it may be the rooms of a house hitherto unvisited by them. Or it may be a conversation of which, when it begins, they already foreknow the sequence and the end, because in some dim state, when or how who can say, they have taken part in that talk with those same speakers. If this be so even in cheerful surroundings and among our friends or acquaintances, it is easy to imagine how much greater was the shock to me, a traveller on such a journey and in such a night.

I shrank from approaching the shores of this lake, remembering that as yet all the vision was not unrolled. I looked about me. If we went to the left we should either strike the water, or if we followed its edge, still bearing to the left, must ultimately reach the forest, where probably we should be lost. I looked to the right. The ground was strewn with boulders, among which grew thorns and rank grass, impracticable for men on foot at night. I looked behind me, meditating retreat, and there, some hundreds of yards away behind low, scrubby mimosas mixed with aloe-like plants, I saw something brown toss up and disappear again that might very well have been the trunk of an elephant. Then, animated by the courage of despair and a desire to know the worst, I began to descend the elephant track towards the lake almost at a run.

Ten minutes or so more brought us to the eastern head of the lake, where the reeds whispered in the breath of the night wind like things alive. As I expected, it proved to be a bare, open space where nothing seemed to grow. Yes, and all about me were the decaying remains of elephants, hundreds of them, some with their bones covered in moss, that may have lain here for generations, and others more newly dead. They were all old beasts as I could tell by the tusks, whether male or female. Indeed about me within a radius of a quarter of a mile lay enough ivory to make a man very rich for life, since although discoloured, much of it seemed to have kept quite sound, like human teeth in a mummy case. The sight gave me a new zest for life. If only I could manage to survive and carry off that ivory! I would. In this way or in that I swore that I would! Who could possibly die with so much ivory to be had for the taking? Not that old hunter, Allan Quatermain.

Then I forgot about the ivory, for there in front of me, just where it should be, just as I had seen it in the dream-picture, was the bull elephant dying, a thin and ancient brute that had lived its long life to the last hour. It searched about as though to find a convenient resting-place, and when this was discovered, stood over it, swaying to and fro for a full minute. Then it lifted its trunk and trumpeted shrilly thrice, singing its swan-song, after which it sank slowly to its knees, its trunk outstretched and the points of its worn tusks resting on the ground. Evidently it was dead.

I let my eyes travel on, and behold! about fifty yards beyond the dead bull was a mound of hard rock. I watched it with gasping expectation and—yes, on the top of the mound something slowly materialized. Although I knew what it must be well enough, for a while I could not see quite clearly because there were certain little clouds about and one of them had floated over the face of the moon. It passed, and before me, perhaps a hundred and forty paces away, outlined clearly against the sky, I perceived the devilish elephant of my vision.

Oh! what a brute was that! In bulk and height it appeared to be half as big again as any of its tribe which I had known in all my life's experience. It was enormous, unearthly; a survivor perhaps of some ancient species that lived before the Flood, or at least a very giant of its kind. Its grey-black sides were scarred as though with fighting. One of its huge tusks, much worn at the end, for evidently it was very old, gleamed white in the moonlight. The other was broken off about halfway down its length. When perfect it had been malformed, for it curved downwards and not upwards, also rather out to the right.

There stood this mammoth, this leviathan, this *monstrum horrendum, informe, ingens*, as I remember my old father used to call a certain gigantic and misshapen bull that we had on the Station, flapping a pair of ears that looked like the sides of a Kafir hut, and waving a trunk as big as a weaver's beam—whatever a weaver's beam may be—an appalling and a petrifying sight.

I squatted behind the skeleton of an elephant which happened to be handy and well covered with moss and ferns and watched the beast, fascinated, wishing that I had a large-bore rifle in my hand. What became of Marût I do not exactly know, but I think that he lay down on the ground.

During the minute or so that followed I reflected a good deal, as we do in times of emergency, often after a useless sort of a fashion. For instance, I wondered why the brute appeared thus upon yonder mound, and the thought suggested itself to me that it was summoned thither from some neighbouring lair by the trumpet call of the dying elephant. It occurred to me even that it was a kind of king of the elephants, to which they felt bound to report themselves, as it were, in the hour of their decease. Certainly what followed gave some credence to my fantastical notion which, if there were anything in it, might account for this great graveyard at that particular spot.

After standing for a while in the attitude that I have described, testing the air with its trunk, Jana, for I will call him so, lumbered down the mound and advanced straight to where the elephant that I had thought to be dead was kneeling. As a matter of fact it was not quite dead, for when Jana arrived it lifted its trunk and curled it round that of Jana as though in affectionate greeting, then let it fall to the ground again. Thereon Jana did what I had seen it do in my dream or vision at Ragnall, namely, attacked it, knocking it over on to its side, where it lay motionless; quite dead this time.

Now I remembered that the vision was not accurate after all, since in it I had seen Jana destroy a woman and a child, who on the present occasion were wanting. Since then I have thought that this was because Harût, clairvoyantly or telepathically, had conveyed to me, as indeed Marût declared, a scene which he had witnessed similar to that which I was witnessing, but not identical in its incidents. Thus it happened, perhaps, that while the act of the woman and the child was omitted, in our case there was another act of the play to follow of which I had received no inkling in my Ragnall experience. Indeed, if I had received it, I should not have been there that night, for no inducement on earth would have brought me to Kendahland.

This was the act. Jana, having prodded his dead brother to his satisfaction, whether from viciousness or to put it out of pain, I cannot say, stood over the carcass in an attitude of grief or pious meditation. At this time, I should mention, the wind, which had been rustling the hail-stripped reeds at the lake border, had died away almost, but not completely; that is to say, only a very faint gust blew now and again, which, with a hunter's instinct, I observed with satisfaction drew *from* the direction of Jana towards ourselves. This I knew, because it struck on my forehead, which was wet with perspiration, and cooled the skin.

Presently, however, by a cursed spite of fate, one of these gusts—a very little one—came from some quarter behind us, for I felt it in my back hair, that was as damp as the rest of me. Just then I was glancing to my right, where it seemed to me that out of the corner of my eye I had caught sight of something passing among the stones at a distance of a hundred yards or so, possibly the shadow of a cloud or another elephant. At the time I did not ascertain which it was, since a faint rattle from Jana's trunk reconcentrated all my faculties on him in a painfully vivid fashion.

I looked to see that all the contemplation had departed from his attitude, now as alert as that of a fox-terrier which imagines he has seen a rat. His vast ears were cocked, his huge bulk trembled, his enormous trunk sniffed the air.

"Great Heavens!" thought I to myself, "he has winded us!" Then I took such consolation as I could from the fact that the next gust once more struck upon my forehead, for I hoped he would conclude that he had made a mistake.

Not a bit of it! Jana as far too old a bird—or beast—to make any mistake. He grunted, got himself going like a luggage train, and with great deliberation walked towards us, smelling at the ground, smelling at the air, smelling to the right, to the left, and even towards heaven above, as though he expected that thence might fall upon him vengeance for his many sins. A dozen times as he came did I cover him with an imaginary rifle, marking the exact spots where I might have hoped to send a bullet to his vitals, in a kind of automatic fashion, for all my real brain was contemplating my own approaching end.

I wondered how it would happen. Would he drive that great tusk through me, would he throw me into the air, or would he kneel upon my poor little body, and avenge the deaths of his kin that had fallen at my hands? Marût was speaking in a rattling whisper:

"His priests have told Jana to kill us; we are about to die," he said. "Before I die I want to say that the lady, the wife of the lord—"

"Silence!" I hissed. "He will hear you," for at that instant I took not the slightest interest in any lady on the earth. Fiercely I glared at Marût and noted even then how pitiful was his countenance. There was no smile there now. All its jovial roundness had vanished. It had sunk in; it was blue and ghastly with large, protruding eyes, like to that of a man who had been three days dead.

I was right—Jana *had* heard. Low as the whisper was, through that intense silence it had penetrated to his almost preternatural senses. Forward he came at a run for twenty paces or more with his trunk held straight out in front of him. Then he halted again, perhaps the length of a cricket pitch away, and smelt as before.

The sight was too much for Marût. He sprang up and ran for his life towards the lake, purposing, I suppose, to take refuge in the water. Oh! how he ran. After him went Jana like a railway engine—express this time—trumpeting as he charged. Marût reached the lake, which was quite close, about ten yards ahead, and plunging into it with a bound, began to swim.

Now, I thought, he may get away if the crocodiles don't have him, for that devil will scarcely take to the water. But this was just where I made a mistake, for with a mighty splash in went Jana too. Also he was the better swimmer. Marût soon saw this and swung round to the shore, by which manoeuvre he gained a little as he could turn quicker than Jana.

Back they came, Jana just behind Marût, striking at him with his great trunk. They landed, Marût flew a few yards ahead doubling in and out among the rocks like a hare and, to my horror, making for where I lay, whether by accident or in a mad hope of obtaining protection, I do not know.

It may be asked why I had not taken the opportunity to run also in the opposite direction. There are several answers. The first was that there seemed to be nowhere to run; the second, that I felt sure, if I did run, I should trip up over the skeletons of those elephants or the stones; the third, that I did not think of it at once; the fourth, that Jana had not yet seen me, and I had no craving to introduce myself to him personally; and the fifth and greatest, that I was so paralysed with fear that I did not feel as though I could lift myself from the ground. Everything about me seemed to be dead, except my powers of observation, which were painfully alive.

Of a sudden Marût gave up. Less than a stone's throw from me he wheeled round and, facing Jana, hurled at him some fearful and concentrated curse, of which all that I could distinguish were the words: "The Child!"

Oddly enough it seemed to have an effect upon the furious rogue, which halted in its rush and, putting its four feet together, slid a few paces nearer and stood still. It was just as though the beast had understood the words and were considering them. If so, their effect was to rouse him to perfect madness. He screamed terribly; he lashed his sides with his trunk; his red and wicked eyes rolled; foam flew from the cavern of his open mouth; he danced upon his great feet, a sort of hideous Scottish reel. Then he charged!

I shut my eyes for a moment. When I opened them again it was to see poor Marût higher in the air than ever he flew before. I thought that he would never come down, but he did at last with an awesome thud. Jana went to him and very gently, now that he was dead, picked him up in his trunk. I prayed that he might carry him away to some hiding-place and leave me in peace. But not so. With slow and stately strides, rocking the deceased Marût up and down in his trunk, as a nurse might rock a baby, he marched on to the very stone where I lay, behind which I suppose he had seen or smelt me all the time.

For quite a long while, it seemed more than a century, he stood over me, studying me as though I interested him very much, the water of the lake trickling in a refreshing stream from his great ears on to my back. Had it not been for that water I think I should have fainted, but as it was I did the next best thing—pretended to be dead. Perhaps this monster would scorn to touch a dead man. Watching out of the corner of my eye, I saw him lift one vast paw that was the size of an arm-chair and hold it over me.

Now good-bye to the world, thought I. Then the foot descended as a steam-hammer does, but also as a steam-hammer sometimes does when used to crack nuts, stopped as it touched my back, and presently came to earth again alongside of me, perhaps because Jana thought the foothold dangerous. At any rate, he took another and better way. Depositing the remains of Marût with the most tender care beside me, as though the nurse were putting the child to bed, he unwound his yards of trunk and began to feel me all over with its tip, commencing at the back of my neck. Oh! the sensation of that clammy, wriggling tip upon my spinal column!

Down it went till it reached the seat of my trousers. There it pinched, presumably to ascertain whether or no I were malingering, a most agonizing pinch like to that of a pair of blacksmith's tongs. So sharp was it that, although I did not stir, who was aware that the slightest movement meant death, it tore a piece out of the stout cloth of my breeches, to say nothing of a portion of the skin beneath. This seemed to astonish the beast, for it lifted the tip of its trunk and shifted its head, as though to examine the fragment by the light of the moon.

Now indeed all was over, for when it saw blood upon that cloth—! I put up one short, piteous prayer to Heaven to save me from this terrible end, and lo, it was answered!

For just as Jana, the results of the inspection being unsatisfactory, was cocking his ears and making ready to slay me, there rang out the short, sharp report of a rifle fired within a few yards. Glancing up at the instant, I saw blood spurt from the monster's left eye, where evidently the bullet had found a home.

He felt at his eye with his trunk; then, uttering a scream of pain, wheeled round and rushed away.

XIV

THE CHASE

I suppose that I swooned for a minute or two. At any rate I remember a long and very curious dream, such a dream as is evolved by a patient under laughing gas, that is very clear and vivid at the time but immediately afterwards slips from the mind's grasp as water does from the clenched hand. It was something to the effect that all those hundreds of skeleton elephants rose and marshalled themselves before me, making obeisance to me by bending their bony knees, because, as I quite understood, I was the only human being that had ever escaped from Jana. Moreover, on the foremost elephant's skull Hans was perched like a mahout, giving words of command, to their serried ranks and explaining to them that it would be very convenient if they would carry their tusks, for which they had no further use, and pile them in a certain place—I forget where—that must be near a good road to facilitate their subsequent transport to a land where they would be made into billiard balls and the backs of ladies' hair-brushes. Next, through the figments of that retreating dream, I heard the undoubted voice of Hans himself, which of course I knew to be absurd as Hans was lost and doubtless dead, saying:

"If you are alive, Baas, please wake up soon, as I have finished reloading Intombi, and it is time to be going. I think I hit Jana in the eye, but so big a beast will soon get over so little a thing as that and look for us, and the bullet from Intombi is too small to kill him, Baas, especially as it is not likely that either of us could hit him in the other eye."

Now I sat up and stared. Yes, there was Hans himself looking just the same as usual, only perhaps rather dirtier, engaged in setting a cap on to the nipple of the little rifle Intombi.

"Hans," I said in a hollow voice, "why the devil are you here?"

"To save you from the devil, of course, Baas," he replied aptly. Then, resting the gun against the stone, the old fellow knelt down by my side and, throwing his arms around me, began to blubber over me, exclaiming:

"Just in time, Baas! Only just in time, for as usual Hans made a mess of things and judged badly—I'll tell you afterwards. Still, just in time, thanks be to your reverend father, the Predikant. Oh! if he had delayed me for one more minute you would have been as flat as my nose, Baas. Now come quickly. I've got the camel tied up there, and he can carry two, being fat and strong after four days' rest with plenty to eat. This place is haunted, Baas, and that king of the devils, Jana, will be back after us presently, as soon as he has wiped the blood out of his eye."

I didn't make any remark, having no taste for conversation just then, but only looked at poor Marût, who lay by me as though he was sleeping.

"Oh, Baas," said Hans, "there is no need to trouble about him, for his neck is broken and he's quite dead. Also it is as well," he added cheerfully. "For, as your reverend father doubtless remembered, the camel could never carry three. Moreover, if he stops here, perhaps Jana will come back to play with him instead of following us."

Poor Marût! This was his requiem as sung by Hans.

With a last glance at the unhappy man to whom I had grown attached in a way during our time of joint captivity and trial, I took the arm of the old Hottentot, or rather leant upon his shoulder, for at first I felt too weak to walk by myself, and picked my path with him through the stones and skeletons of elephants across the plateau eastwards, that is, away from the lake. About two hundred yards from the scene of our tragedy was a mound of rock similar to that on which Jana had appeared, but much smaller, behind which we found the camel, kneeling as a well-trained beast of the sort should do and tethered to a stone.

As we went, in brief but sufficient language Hans told me his story. It seemed that after he had shot the Kendah general it came into his cunning, foreseeing mind that he might be of more use to me free than as a companion in captivity, or that if I were killed he might in that case live to bring vengeance on my slayers. So he broke away, as has been described, and hid till nightfall on the hill-side. Then by the light of the moon he tracked us, avoiding the villages, and ultimately found a place of shelter in a kind of cave in the forest near to Simba Town, where no people lived. Here he fed the camel at night, concealing it at dawn in the cave. The days he spent up a tall tree, whence he could watch all that went on in the town beneath, living meanwhile on some food which he carried in a bag tied to the saddle, helped out by green mealies which he stole from a neighbouring field.

Thus he saw most of what passed in the town, including the desolation wrought by the fearful tempest of hail, which, being in their cave, both he and the camel escaped without harm. On the next evening from his post of outlook up the tree, where he had now some difficulty in hiding himself because the hail had stripped off all its leaves, he saw Marût and myself brought from the guest-house and taken away by the escort. Descending and running to the cave, he saddled the camel and started in pursuit, plunging into the forest and hiding there when he perceived that the escort were leaving us.

Here he waited until they had gone by on their return journey. So close did they pass to him that he could overhear their talk, which told him they expected, or rather were sure, that we should be destroyed by the elephant Jana, their devil god, to whom the camelmen had been already sacrificed. After they had departed he remounted and followed us. Here I asked him why he had not overtaken us before we came to the cemetery of elephants, as I presumed he might have done, since he stated that he was close in our rear. This indeed was the case, for it was the head of the camel I saw behind the thorn trees when I looked back, and not the trunk of an elephant as I had supposed.

At the time he would give me no direct answer, except that he grew muddled as he had already suggested, and thought it best to keep in the background and see what happened. Long afterwards, however, he admitted to me that he acted on a presentiment.

"It seemed to me, Baas," he said, "that your reverend father was telling me that I should do best to let you two go on and not show myself, since if I did so we should all three be killed, as one of us must walk whom the other two could not desert. Whereas if I left you as you were, one of you would be killed and the other escape, and that the one to be killed would not be *you*, Baas. All of which came about as the Spirit spoke in my head, for Marût was killed, who did not matter, and—you know the rest, Baas."

To return to Hans' story. He saw us march down to the borders of the lake, and, keeping to our right, took cover behind the knoll of rock, whence he watched also all that followed. When Jana advanced to attack us Hans crept forward in the hope, a very wild one, of crippling him with the little Purdey rifle. Indeed, he was about to fire at the hind leg when Marût made his run for life and plunged into the lake. Then he crawled on to lead me away to the camel, but when he was within a few yards the chase returned our way and Marût was killed.

From that moment he waited for an opportunity to shoot Jana in the only spot where so soft a bullet would, as he knew, have the faintest chance of injuring him vitally—namely, in the eye—for he was sure that its penetration would not be sufficient to reach the vitals through that thick hide and the mass of flesh behind. With an infinite and wonderful patience he waited, knowing that my life or death hung in the balance. While Jana held his foot over me, while he felt me with his trunk, still Hans waited, balancing the arguments for and against firing upon the scales of experience in his clever old mind, and in the end coming to a right and wise conclusion.

At length his chance came, the brute exposed his eye, and by the light of the clear moon Hans, always a very good shot at a distance when it was not necessary to allow for trajectory and wind, let drive and *hit*. The bullet did not get to the brain as he had hoped; it had not strength for that, but it destroyed this left eye and gave Jana such pain that for a while he forgot all about me and everything else except escape.

Such was the Hottentot's tale as I picked it up from his laconic, colourless, Dutch *patois* sentences, then and afterwards; a very wonderful tale I thought. But for him, his fidelity and his bushman's cunning, where should I have found myself before that moon set?

We mounted the camel after I had paused a minute to take a pull from a flask of brandy which remained in the saddlebags. Although he loved strong drink so well Hans had saved it untouched on the mere chance that it might some time be of service to me, his master. The monkey-like Hottentot sat in front and directed the camel, while I accommodated myself as best I could on the sheepskins behind. Luckily they were thick and soft, for Jana's pinch was not exactly that of a lover.

Off we went, picking our way carefully till we reached the elephant track beyond the mound where Jana had appeared, which, in the light of faith, we hoped would lead us to the River Tava. Here we made better progress, but still could not go very fast because of the holes made by the feet of Jana and his company. Soon we had left the cemetery behind us, and lost sight of the lake which I devoutly trusted I might never see again.

Now the track ran upwards from the hollow to a ridge two or three miles away. We reached the crest of this ridge without accident, except that on our road we met another aged elephant, a cow with very poor tusks, travelling to its last resting place, or so I suppose. I don't know which was the more frightened, the sick cow or the camel, for camels hate elephants as horses hate camels until they get used to them. The cow bolted to the right as quickly as it could, which was not very fast, and the camel bolted to the left with such convulsive bounds that we were nearly thrown off its back. However, being an equable brute, it soon recovered its balance, and we got back to the track beyond the cow.

From the top of the rise we saw that before us lay a sandy plain lightly clothed in grass, and, to our joy, about ten miles away at the foot of a very gentle slope, the moonlight gleamed upon the waters of a broad river. It was not easy to make out, but it was there, we were both sure it was there; we could not mistake the wavering, silver flash. On we went for another quarter of a mile, when something caused me to turn round on the sheepskin and look back.

Oh Heavens! At the very top of the rise, clearly outlined against the sky, stood Jana himself with his trunk lifted. Next instant he trumpeted, a furious, rattling challenge of rage and defiance.

"Allemagte! Baas," said Hans, "the old devil is coming to look for his lost eye, and has seen us with that which remains. He has been travelling on our spoor."

"Forward!" I answered, bringing my heels into the camel's ribs.

Then the race began. The camel was a very good camel, one of the real running breed; also, as Hans said, it was comparatively fresh, and may, moreover, have been aware that it was near to the plains where it had been bred. Lastly, the going was now excellent, soft to its spongy feet but not too deep in sand, nor were there any rocks over which it could fall. It went off like the wind, making nothing of our united weights which did not come to more than two hundred pounds, or a half of what it could carry with ease, being perhaps urged to its top speed by the knowledge that the elephant was behind. For mile after mile we rushed down the plain. But we did not go alone, for Jana came after us like a cruiser after a gunboat. Moreover, swiftly as we travelled, he travelled just a little swifter, gaining say a few yards in every hundred. For the last mile before we came to the river bank, half an hour later perhaps, though it seemed to be a week, he was not more than fifty paces to our rear. I glanced back at him, and in the light of the moon, which was growing low, he bore a strange resemblance to a mud cottage with broken chimneys (which were his ears flapping on each side of him), and the yard pump projecting from the upper window.

"We shall beat him now, Hans," I said looking at the broad river which was now close at hand.

"Yes, Baas," answered Hans doubtfully and in jerks. "This is very good camel, Baas. He runs so fast that I have no inside left, I suppose because he smells his wife over that river, to say nothing of death behind him. But, Baas, I am not sure; that devil Jana is still faster than the camel, and he wants to settle for his lost eye, which makes him lively. Also I see stones ahead, which are bad for camels. Then there is the river, and I don't know if camels can swim, but Jana can as Marût learned. Do you think, Baas, that you could manage to sting him up with a bullet in his knee or that great trunk of his, just to give him something to think about besides ourselves?"

Thus he prattled on, I believe to occupy my mind and his own, till at length, growing impatient, I replied:

"Be silent, donkey. Can I shoot an elephant backwards over my shoulder with a rifle meant for springbuck? Hit the camel! Hit it hard!"

Alas! Hans was right! There *were* stones at the verge of the river, which doubtless it had washed out in periods of past flood, and presently we were among them. Now a camel, so good on sand that is its native heath, is a worthless brute among stones, over which it slips and flounders. But to Jana these appeared to offer little or no obstacle. At any rate he came over them almost if not quite as fast as before. By the time that we reached the brink of the water he was not more than ten yards behind. I could even see the blood running down from the socket of his ruined eye.

Moreover, at the sight of the foaming but shallow torrent, the camel, a creature unaccustomed to water, pulled up in a mulish kind of way and for a moment refused to stir. Luckily at this instant Jana let off one of his archangel kind of trumpetings which started our beast again, since it was more afraid of elephants than it was of water.

In we went and were presently floundering among the loose stones at the bottom of the river, which was nowhere over four feet deep, with Jana splashing after us not more than five yards behind. I twisted myself round and fired at him with the rifle. Whether I hit him or no I could not say, but he stopped for a few seconds, perhaps because he remembered the effect of a similar explosion upon his eye, which gave us a trifling start. Then he came on again in his steam-engine fashion.

When we were about in the middle of the river the inevitable happened. The camel fell, pitching us over its head into the stream. Still clinging to the rifle I picked myself up and began half to swim half to wade towards the farther shore, catching hold of Hans with my free hand. In a moment Jana was on to that camel. He gored it with his tusks, he trampled it with his feet, he got it round the neck with his trunk, dragging nearly the whole bulk of it out of the water. Then he set to work to pound it down into the mud and stones at the bottom of the river with such a persistent thoroughness, that he gave us time to reach the other bank and climb up a stout tree which grew there, a sloping, flat-topped kind of tree that was fortunately easy to ascend, at least for a man. Here we sat gasping, perhaps about thirty feet above the ground level, and waited.

Presently Jana, having finished with the camel, followed us, and without any difficulty located us in that tree. He walked all round it considering the situation. Then he wound his huge trunk about the bole of the tree and, putting out his strength, tried to pull it over. It was an anxious moment, but this particular child of the forest had not grown there for some hundreds of years, withstanding all the shocks of wind, weather and water, in order to be laid low by an elephant, however enormous. It shook a little—no more. Abandoning this attempt as futile, Jana next began to try to dig it up by driving his tusk under its roots. Here, too, he failed because they grew among stones which evidently jarred him.

Ceasing from these agricultural efforts with a deep rumble of rage, he adopted yet a third expedient. Rearing his huge bulk into the air he brought down his forefeet with all the tremendous weight of his great body behind them on to the sloping trunk of the tree just below where the branches sprang, perhaps twelve or thirteen feet above the ground. The shock was so heavy that for a moment I thought the tree would be uprooted or snapped in two. Thank Heaven! it held, but the vibration was such that Hans and I were nearly shaken out of the upper branches, like autumn apples from a bough. Indeed, I think I should have gone had not the monkey-like Hans, who had toes to cling with as well as fingers, gripped me by the collar.

Thrice did Jana repeat this manoeuvre, and at the third onslaught I saw to my horror that the roots were loosening. I heard some of them snap, and a crack appeared in the ground not far from the bole. Fortunately Jana never noted these symptoms, for abandoning a plan which he considered unavailing, he stood for a while swaying his trunk and lost in gentle thought.

"Hans," I whispered, "load the rifle quick! I can get him in the spine or the other eye."

"Wet powder won't go off, Baas," groaned Hans. "The water got to it in the river."

"No," I answered, "and it is all your fault for making me shoot at him when I could take no aim."

"It would have been just the same, Baas, for the rifle went under water also when we fell from the camel, and the cap would have been damp, and perhaps the powder too. Also the shot made Jana stop for a moment."

This was true, but it was maddening to be obliged to sit there with an empty gun, when if I had but one charge, or even my pistol, I was sure that I could have blinded or crippled this satanic pachyderm.

A few minutes later Jana played his last card. Coming quite close to the trunk of the tree he reared himself up as before, but this time stretched out his forelegs so that these and his body were supported on the broad bole. Then he elongated his trunk and with it began to break off boughs which grew between us and him.

"I don't think he can reach us," I said doubtfully to Hans, "that is, unless he brings a stone to stand on."

"Oh! Baas, pray be silent," answered Hans, "or he will understand and fetch one."

Although the idea seemed absurd, on the whole I thought it well to take the hint, for who knew how much this experienced beast did or did not understand? Then, as we could go no higher, we wriggled as far as we dared along our boughs and waited.

Presently Jana, having finished his clearing operations, began to lengthen his trunk to its full measure. Literally, it seemed to expand like a telescope or an indiarubber ring. Out it came, foot after foot, till its snapping tip was waving within a few inches of us, just short of my foot and Han's head, or rather felt hat. One final stretch and he reached the hat, which he removed with a flourish and thrust into the red cavern of his mouth. As it appeared no more I suppose he ate it. This loss of his hat moved Hans to fury. Hurling horrible curses at Jana he drew his butcher's knife and made ready.

Once more the sinuous brown trunk elongated itself. Evidently Jana had got a better hold with his hind legs this time, or perhaps had actually wriggled himself a few inches up the tree. At any rate I saw to my dismay that there was every prospect of my making a second acquaintance with that snapping tip. The end of the trunk was lying along my bough like a huge brown snake and creeping up, up, up.

"He'll get us," I muttered.

Hans said nothing but leaned forward a little, holding on with his left hand. Next instant in the light of the rising sun I saw a knife flash,

H. RIDER HAGGARD

saw also that the point of it had been driven through the lower lip of Jana's trunk, pinning it to the bough like a butterfly to a board.

My word! what a commotion ensued! Up the trunk came a scream which nearly blew me away. Then Jana, with a wriggling motion, tried to unnail himself as gently as possible, for it was clear that the knife point hurt him, but could not do so because Hans still held the handle and had driven the blade deep into the wood. Lastly he dragged himself downwards with such energy that something had to go, that something being the skin and muscle of the lower lip, which was cut clean through, leaving the knife erect in the bough.

Over he went backwards, a most imperial cropper. Then he picked himself up, thrust the tip of his trunk into his mouth, sucked it as one does a cut finger, and finally, roaring in defeated rage, fled into the river, which he waded, and back upon his tracks towards his own home. Yes, off he went, Hans screaming curses and demands that he should restore his hat to him, and very seldom in all my life have I seen a sight that I thought more beautiful than that of his whisking tail.

"Now, Baas," chuckled Hans, "the old devil has got a sore nose as well as a sore eye by which to remember us. And, Baas, I think we had better be going before he has time to think and comes back with a long stick to knock us out of this tree."

So we went, in double-quick time I can assure you, or at any rate as fast as my stiff limbs and general condition would allow. Fortunately we had now no doubt as to our direction, since standing up through the mists of dawn with the sunbeams resting on its forest-clad crest, we could clearly see the strange, tumulus-shaped hill which the White Kendah called the Holy Mount, the Home of the Child. It appeared to be about twenty miles away, but in reality was a good deal farther, for when we had walked for several hours it seemed almost as distant as ever.

In truth that was a dreadful trudge. Not only was I exhausted with all the terrors I had passed and our long midnight flight, but the wound where Jana had pinched out a portion of my frame, inflamed by the riding, had now grown stiff and intolerably sore, so that every step gave me pain which sometimes culminated in agony. Moreover, it was no use giving in, foodless as we were, for Marût had carried the provisions, and with the chance of Jana returning to look us up. So I stuck to it and said nothing.

For the first ten miles the country seemed uninhabited; doubtless it was too near the borders of the Black Kendah to be popular as a place of residence. After this we saw herds of cattle and a few camels, apparently untended; perhaps their guards were hidden away in the long grass. Then we came to some fields of mealies that were, I noticed, quite untouched by the hailstorm, which, it would seem, had confined its attentions to the land of the Black Kendah. Of these we ate thankfully enough. A little farther on we perceived huts perched on an inaccessible place in a kloof. Also their inhabitants perceived us, for they ran away as though in a great fright.

Still we did not try to approach the huts, not knowing how we should be received. After my sojourn in Simba Town I had become possessed of a love of life in the open.

For another two hours I limped forward with pain and grief—by now I was leaning on Hans' shoulder—up an endless, uncultivated rise clothed with euphorbias and fern-like cycads. At length we reached its top and found ourselves within a rifle shot of a fenced native village. I suppose that its inhabitants had been warned of our coming by runners from the huts I have mentioned. At any rate the moment we appeared the men, to the number of thirty or more, poured out of the south gate armed with spears and other weapons and proceeded to ring us round and behave in a very threatening manner. I noticed at once that, although most of them were comparatively light in colour, some of these men partook of the negro characteristics of the Black Kendah from whom we had escaped, to such an extent indeed that this blood was clearly predominant in them. Still, it was also clear that they were deadly foes of this people, for when I shouted out to them that we were the friends of Harût and those who worshipped the Child, they yelled back that we were liars. No friends of the Child, they said, came from the country of the Black Kendah, who worshipped the devil Jana. I tried to explain that least of all men in the world did we worship Jana, who had been hunting us for hours, but they would not listen.

"You are spies of Simba's, the smell of Jana is upon you" (this may have been true enough), they yelled, adding: "We will kill you, white-faced goat. We will kill you, little yellow monkey, for none who are not enemies come here from the land of the Black Kendah."

"Kill us then," I answered, "and bring the curse of the Child upon you. Bring famine, bring hail, bring war!"

These words were, I think, well chosen; at any rate they induced a pause in their murderous intentions. For a while they hesitated, all talking together at once. At last the advocates of violence appeared to get the upper hand, and once more a number of the men began to dance about us, waving their spears and crying out that we must die who came from the Black Kendah.

I sat down upon the ground, for I was so exhausted that at the time I did not greatly care whether I died or lived, while Hans drew his knife and stood over me, cursing them as he had cursed at Jana. By slow degrees they drew nearer and nearer. I watched them with a kind of idle curiosity, believing that the moment when they came within actual spear-thrust would be our last, but, as I have said, not greatly caring because of my mental and physical exhaustion.

I had already closed my eyes that I might not see the flash of the falling steel, when an exclamation from Hans caused me to open them again. Following the line of the knife with which he pointed, I perceived a troop of men on camels emerging from the gates of the village at full speed. In front of these, his white garments fluttering on the wind, rode a bearded and dignified person in whom I recognized Harût, Harût himself, waving a spear and shouting as he came. Our assailants heard and saw him also, then flung down their weapons as though in dismay either at his appearance or his words, which I could not catch. Harût guided his rushing camel straight at the man who I presume was their leader, and struck at him with his spear, as though in fury, wounding him in the shoulder and causing him to fall to the ground. As he struck he called out:

"Dog! Would you harm the guests of the Child?"

Then I heard no more because I fainted away.

XV

THE DWELLER IN THE CAVE

After this it seemed to me that I dreamed a long and very troubled dream concerning all sorts of curious things which I cannot remember. At last I opened my eyes and observed that I lay on a low bed raised about three inches above the floor, in an Eastern-looking room, large and cool. It had window-places in it but no windows, only grass mats hung upon a rod which, I noted inconsequently, worked on a rough, wooden hinge, or rather pin, that enabled the curtain to be turned back against the wall.

Through one of these window-places I saw at a little distance the slope of the forest-covered hill, which reminded me of something to do with a child—for the life of me I could not remember what. As I lay wondering over the matter I heard a shuffling step which I recognized, and, turning, saw Hans twiddling a new hat made of straw in his fingers.

"Hans," I said, "where did you get that new hat?"

"They gave it me here, Baas," he answered. "The Baas will remember that the devil Jana ate the other."

Then I did remember more or less, while Hans continued to twiddle the hat. I begged him to put it on his head because it fidgeted me, and then inquired where we were.

"In the Town of the Child, Baas, where they carried you after you had seemed to die down yonder. A very nice town, where there is plenty to eat, though, having been asleep for three days, you have had nothing except a little milk and soup, which was poured down your throat with a spoon whenever you seemed to half wake up for a while."

"I was tired and wanted a long rest, Hans, and now I feel hungry. Tell me, are the lord and Bena here also, or were they killed after all?"

"Yes, Baas, they are safe enough, and so are all our goods. They were both with Harût when he saved us down by the village yonder, but you went to sleep and did not see them. They have been nursing you ever since, Baas."

Just then Savage himself entered, carrying some soup upon a wooden tray and looking almost as smart as he used to do at Ragnall Castle.

"Good day, sir," he said in his best professional manner. "Very glad to see you back with us, sir, and getting well, I trust, especially after we had given you and Mr. Hans up as dead."

I thanked him and drank the soup, asking him to cook me something more substantial as I was starving, which he departed to do. Then I sent Hans to find Lord Ragnall, who it appeared was out walking in the town. No sooner had they gone than Harût entered looking more dignified than ever and, bowing gravely, seated himself upon the mat in the Eastern fashion.

"Some strong spirit must go with you, Lord Macumazana," he said, "that you should live today, after we were sure that you had been slain."

"That's where you made a mistake. Your magic was not of much service to you there, friend Harût."

"Yet my magic, as you call it, though I have none, was of some service after all, Macumazana. As it chanced I had no opportunity of breathing in the wisdom of the Child for two days from the hour of our arrival here, because I was hurt on the knee in the fight and so weary that I could not travel up the mountain and seek light from the eyes of the Child. On the third day, however, I went and the Oracle told me all. Then I descended swiftly, gathered men and reached those fools in time to keep you from harm. They have paid for what they did, Lord."

"I am sorry, Harût, for they knew no better; and, Harût, although I saved myself, or rather Hans saved me, we have left your brother behind, and with him the others."

"I know. Jana was too strong for them; you and your servant alone could prevail against him."

"Not so, Harût. He prevailed against us; all we could do was to injure his eye and the tip of his trunk and escape from him."

"Which is more than any others have done for many generations, Lord. But doubtless as the beginning was, so shall the end be. Jana, I think, is near his death and through you."

"I don't know," I repeated. "Who and what is Jana?"

"Have I not told you that he is an evil spirit who inhabits the body of a huge elephant?"

"Yes, and so did Marût; but I think that he is just a huge elephant with a very bad temper of his own. Still, whatever he is, he will take some killing, and I don't want to meet him again by that horrible lake."

"Then you will meet him elsewhere, Lord. For if you do not go to look for Jana, Jana will come to look for you who have hurt him so sorely. Remember that henceforth, wherever you go in all this land, it may happen that you will meet Jana."

"Do you mean to say that the brute comes into the territory of the White Kendah?"

"Yes, Macumazana, at times he comes, or a spirit wearing his shape comes; I know not which. What I do know is that twice in my life I myself have seen him upon the Holy Mount, though how he came or how he went none can tell."

"Why was he wandering there, Harût?"

"Who can say, Lord? Tell me why evil wanders through the world and I will answer your question. Only I repeat—let those who have harmed Jana beware of Jana."

"And let Jana beware of me if I can meet him with a decent gun in my hand, for I have a score to settle with the beast. Now, Harût, there is another matter. Just before he was killed Marût, your brother, began to tell me something about the wife of the Lord Ragnall. I had no time to listen to the end of his words, though I thought he said that she was upon yonder Holy Mount. Did I hear alright?"

Instantly Harût's face became like that of a stone idol, impenetrable, impassive.

"Either you misunderstood, Lord," he answered, "or my brother raved in his fear. Wherever she may be, that beautiful lady is not upon the Holy Mount, unless there is another Holy Mount in the Land of Death. Moreover, Lord, as we are speaking of this matter, let me tell you the forest upon that Mount must be trodden by none save the priest of the Child. If others set foot there they die, for it is watched by a guardian more terrible even than Jana, nor is he the only one. Ask me nothing of that guardian, for I will not answer, and, above all, if you or your comrades value life, let them not seek to look upon him."

Understanding that it was quite useless to pursue this subject farther at the moment, I turned to another, remarking that the hailstorm which had smitten the country of the Black Kendah was the worst that I had ever experienced.

"Yes," answered Harût, "so I have learned. That was the first of the curses which the Child, through my mouth, promised to Simba and his people if they molested us upon our road. The second, you will remember, was famine, which for them is near at hand, seeing that they have little corn in store and none left to gather, and that most of their cattle are dead of the hail."

"If they have no corn while, as I noted, you have plenty which the storm spared, will not they, who are many in number but near to starving, attack you and take your corn, Harût?"

"Certainly they will do so, Lord, and then will fall the third curse, the curse of war. All this was foreseen long ago, Macumazana, and you are here to help us in that war. Among your goods you have many guns and much powder and lead. You shall teach our people how to use those guns, that with them we may destroy the Black Kendah."

"I think not," I replied quietly. "I came here to kill a certain elephant, and to receive payment for my service in ivory, not to fight the Black Kendah, of whom I have already seen enough. Moreover, the guns are not my property but that of the Lord Ragnall, who perhaps will ask his own price for the use of them."

"And the Lord Ragnall, who came here against our will, is, as it chances, our property and we may ask your own price for his life. Now, farewell for a while, since you, who are still sick and weak, have talked enough. Only before I go, as your friend and that of those with you, I will add one word. If you would continue to look upon the sun, let none of you try to set foot in the forest upon the Holy Mount. Wander where you will upon its southern slopes, but strive not to pass the wall of rock which rings the forest round."

Then he rose, bowed gravely and departed, leaving me full of reflections.

Shortly afterwards Savage and Hans returned, bringing me some meat which the former had cooked in an admirable fashion. I ate of it heartily, and just as they were carrying off the remains of the meal Ragnall himself arrived. Our greeting was very warm, as might be expected in the case of two comrades who never thought to speak to each other again on this side of the grave. As I had supposed, he was certain that Hans and I had been cut off and killed by the Black Kendah, as, after we were missed, some of the camelmen asserted that they had actually seen us fall. So he went on, or rather was carried on by the rush of the camels, grieving, since, it being impossible to attempt to recover our bodies or even to return, that was the only thing to do, and in due course reached the Town of the Child without further accident. Here they rested and mourned for us, till some days later Harût suddenly announced that we still lived, though how he knew this they could not ascertain. Then they sallied out and found us, as has been told, in great danger from the ignorant villagers who, until we appeared, had not even heard of our existence.

I asked what they had done and what information they had obtained since their arrival at this place. His answer was: Nothing and none worth mentioning. The town appeared to be a small one of not much over two thousand inhabitants, all of whom were engaged in agricultural pursuits and in camel-breeding. The herds of camels, however, they gathered, for the most part were kept at outlying settlements on the farther side of the cone-shaped mountain. As they were unable to talk the language the only person from whom they could gain knowledge was Harût, who spoke to them in his broken English and told them much what he had told me, namely that the upper mountain was a sacred place that might only be visited by the priests, since any uninitiated person who set foot there came to a bad end. They had not seen any of these priests in the town, where no form of worship appeared to be practised, but they had observed men driving small numbers of sheep or goats up the flanks of the mountain towards the forest.

Of what went on upon this mountain and who lived there they remained in complete ignorance. It was a case of stalemate. Harût would not tell them anything nor could they learn anything for themselves. He added in a depressed way that the whole business seemed very hopeless, and that he had begun to doubt whether there was any tidings of his lost wife to be gained among the Kendah, White or Black.

Now I repeated to him Marût's dying words, of which most unhappily I had never heard the end. These seemed to give him new life since they showed that tidings there was of some sort, if only it could be extracted. But how might this be done? How, how?

For a whole week things went on thus. During this time I recovered my strength completely, except in one particular which reduced me to helplessness. The place on my thigh where Jana had pinched out a bit of the skin healed up well enough, but the inflammation struck inwards to the nerve of my left leg, where once I had been injured by a lion, with the result that whenever I tried to move I was tortured by pains of a sciatic nature. So I was obliged to lie still and to content myself with being carried on the bed into a little garden which surrounded the mud-built and white-washed house that had been allotted to us as a dwelling-place.

There I lay hour after hour, staring at the Holy Mount which began to spring from the plain within a few hundred yards of the scattered township. For a mile or so its slopes were bare except for grass on which sheep and goats were grazed, and a few scattered trees. Studying the place through glasses I observed that these slopes were crowned by a vertical precipice of what looked like lava rock, which seemed to surround the whole mountain and must have been quite a hundred feet high. Beyond this precipice, which to all appearance was of an unclimbable nature, began a dense forest of large trees, cedars I thought, clothing it to the very top, that is so far as I could see.

One day when I was considering the place, Harût entered the garden suddenly and caught me in the act.

"The House of the god is beautiful," he said, "is it not?"

"Very," I answered, "and of a strange formation. But how do those who dwell on it climb that precipice?"

"It cannot be climbed," he answered, "but there is a road which I am about to travel who go to worship the Child. Yet I have told you, Macumazana, that any strangers who seek to walk that road find death. If they do not believe me, let them try," he added meaningly.

Then, after many inquiries about my health, he informed me that news had reached him to the effect that the Black Kendah were mad at the loss of their crops which the hail had destroyed and because of the near prospect of starvation.

"Then soon they will be wishing to reap yours with spears," I said.

"That is so. Therefore, my Lord Macumazana, get well quickly that you may be able to scare away these crows with guns, for in fourteen days the harvest should begin upon our uplands. Farewell and have no fears, for during my absence my people will feed and watch you and on the third night I shall return again."

After Harût's departure a deep depression fell upon all of us. Even Hans was depressed, while Savage became like a man under sentence of execution at a near but uncertain date. I tried to cheer him up and asked him what was the matter.

"I don't know, Mr. Quatermain," he answered, "but the fact is this is a 'ateful and un'oly 'ole" (in his agitation he quite lost grip of his h's, which was always weak), "and I am sure that it is the last I shall ever see, except one."

"Well, Savage," I said jokingly, "at any rate there don't seem to be any snakes here."

"No, Mr. Quatermain. That is, I haven't met any, but they crawl about me all night, and whenever I see that prophet man he talks of them to me. Yes, he talks of them and nothing else with a sort of cold look in his eyes that makes my back creep. I wish it was over, I do, who shall never see old England again," and he went away, I think to hide his very painful and evident emotion.

That evening Hans returned from an expedition on which I had sent him with instructions to try to get round the mountain and report what was on its other side. It had been a complete failure, as after he had gone a few miles men appeared who ordered him back. They were so threatening in their demeanour that had it not been for the little rifle, Intombi, which he carried under pretence of shooting buck, a weapon that they regarded with great awe, they would, he thought, have killed him. He added that he had been quite unsuccessful in his efforts to collect any news of value from man, woman or child, all of whom, although very polite, appeared to have orders to tell him nothing, concluding with the remark that he considered the White Kendah bigger devils than the Black Kendah, inasmuch as they were more clever.

SHORTLY AFTER THIS ABORTIVE ATTEMPT we debated our position with earnestness and came to a certain conclusion, of which I will speak in its place.

If I remember right it was on this same night of our debate, after Harût's return from the mountain, that the first incident of interest happened. There were two rooms in our house divided by a partition which ran almost up to the roof. In the left-hand room slept Ragnall and Savage, and in that to the right Hans and I. Just at the breaking of dawn I was awakened by hearing some agitated conversation between Savage and his master. A minute later they both entered my sleeping place, and I saw in the faint light that Ragnall looked very disturbed and Savage very frightened.

"What's the matter?" I asked.

"We have seen my wife," answered Ragnall.

I stared at him and he went on:

"Savage woke me by saying that there was someone in the room. I sat up and looked and, as I live, Quatermain, standing gazing at me in such a position that the light of dawn from the window-place fell upon her, was my wife."

"How was she dressed?" I asked at once.

"In a kind of white robe cut rather low, with her hair loose hanging to her waist, but carefully combed and held outspread by what appeared to be a bent piece of ivory about a foot and a half long, to which it was fastened by a thread of gold."

"Is that all?"

"No. Upon her breast was that necklace of red stones with the little image hanging from its centre which those rascals gave her and she always wore."

"Anything more?"

"Yes. In her arms she carried what looked like a veiled child. It was so still that I think it must have been dead."

"Well. What happened?"

"I was so overcome I could not speak, and she stood gazing at me with wide-opened eyes, looking more beautiful than I can tell you. She never stirred, and her lips never moved—that I will swear. And yet both of us heard her say, very low but quite clearly: 'The mountain, George! Don't desert me. Seek me on the mountain, my dear, my husband.'"

"Well, what next?"

"I sprang up and she was gone. That's all."

"Now tell me what *you* saw and heard, Savage."

"What his lordship saw and heard, Mr. Quatermain, neither more nor less. Except that I was awake, having had one of my bad dreams about snakes, and saw her come through the door."

"Through the door! Was it open then?"

"No, sir, it was shut and bolted. She just came through it as if it wasn't there. Then I called to his lordship after she had been looking at him for half a minute or so, for I couldn't speak at first. There's one more thing, or rather two. On her head was a little cap that looked as though it had been made from the skin of a bird, with a gold snake rising up in front, which snake was the first thing I caught sight of, as of course it would be, sir. Also the dress she wore was so thin that through it I could see her shape and the sandals on her feet, which were fastened at the instep with studs of gold."

"I saw no feather cap or snake," said Ragnall.

"Then that's the oddest part of the whole business," I remarked. "Go back to your room, both of you, and if you see anything more, call me. I want to think things over."

They went, in a bewildered sort of fashion, and I called Hans and spoke with him in a whisper, repeating to him the little that he had not understood of our talk, for as I have said, although he never spoke it, Hans knew a great deal of English.

"Now, Hans," I said to him, "what is the use of you? You are no better than a fraud. You pretend to be the best watchdog in Africa, and yet a woman comes into this house under your nose and in the grey of the morning, and you do not see her. Where is your reputation, Hans?"

The old fellow grew almost speechless with indignation, then he spluttered his answer:

"It was not a woman, Baas, but a spook. Who am I that I should be expected to catch spooks as though they were thieves or rats? As it happens I was wide awake half an hour before the dawn and lay with my eyes fixed upon that door, which I bolted myself last night. It never opened, Baas; moreover, since this talk began I have been to look at it. During the night a spider has made its web from door-post to door-post, and that web is unbroken. If you do not believe me, come and see for yourself. Yet they say the woman came through the doorway and therefore through the spider's web. Oh! Baas, what is the use of wasting thought upon the ways of spooks which, like the wind, come and go as they will, especially in this haunted land from which, as we have all agreed, we should do well to get away."

I went and examined the door for myself, for by now my sciatica, or whatever it may have been, was so much better that I could walk a little. What Hans said was true. There was the spider's web with the spider sitting in the middle. Also some of the threads of the web were fixed from post to post, so that it was impossible that the door could have been opened or, if opened, that anyone could have passed through the doorway without breaking them. Therefore, unless the woman came through one of the little window-places, which was almost incredible as they were high above the ground, or dropped from the smoke-hole in the roof, or had been shut into the place when the door was closed on the previous night, I could not see how she had arrived there. And if any one of these incredible suppositions was correct, then how did she get out again with two men watching her?

There were only two solutions to the problem—namely, that the whole occurrence was hallucination, or that, in fact, Ragnall and Savage had seen something unnatural and uncanny. If the latter were correct I only wished that I had shared the experience, as I have always longed to see a ghost. A real, indisputable ghost would be a great support to our doubting minds, that is if we *knew* its owner to be dead.

But—this was another thought—if by any chance Lady Ragnall were still alive and a prisoner upon that mountain, what they had seen was no ghost, but a shadow or *simulacrum* of a living person projected consciously or unconsciously by that person for some unknown purpose. What could the purpose be? As it chanced the answer was not difficult, and to it the words she was reported to have uttered gave a cue. Only a few hours ago, just before we turned in indeed, as I have said, we had been discussing matters. What I have not said is that in the end we arrived at the conclusion that our quest here was wild and useless and that we should do well to try to escape from the place before we became involved in a war of extermination between two branches of an obscure tribe, one of which was quite and the other semi-savage.

Indeed, although Ragnall still hung back a little, it had been arranged that I should try to purchase camels in exchange for guns, unless I could get them for nothing which might be less suspicious, and that we should attempt such an escape under cover of an expedition to kill the elephant Jana.

Supposing such a vision to be possible, then might it not have come, or been sent to deter us from this plan? It would seem so.

Thus reflecting I went to sleep worn out with useless wonderment, and did not wake again till breakfast time. That morning, when we were alone together, Ragnall said to me:

"I have been thinking over what happened, or seemed to happen last night. I am not at all a superstitious man, or one given to vain imaginings, but I am sure that Savage and I really did see and hear the spirit or the shadow of my wife. Her body it could not have been as you will admit, though how she could utter, or seem to utter, audible speech without one is more than I can tell. Also I am sure that she is captive upon yonder mountain and came to call me to rescue her. Under these circumstances I feel that it is my duty, as well as my desire, to give up any idea of leaving the country and try to find out the truth."

"And how will you do that," I asked, "seeing that no one will tell us anything?"

"By going to see for myself."

"It is impossible, Ragnall. I am too lame at present to walk half a mile, much less to climb precipices."

"I know, and that is one of the reasons why I did not suggest that you should accompany me. The other is that there is no object in all of us risking our lives. I wished to face the thing alone, but that good fellow Savage says that he will go where I go, leaving you and Hans here to make further attempts if we do not return. Our plan is to slip out of the town during the night, wearing white dresses like the Kendah, of which I have bought some for tobacco, and make the best of our way up the slope by starlight that is very bright now. When dawn comes we will try to find the road through that precipice, or over it, and for the rest trust to Providence."

Dismayed at this intelligence, I did all I could to dissuade him from such a mad venture, but quite without avail, for never did I know a more determined or more fearless man than Lord Ragnall. He had made up his mind and there was an end of the matter. Afterwards I talked with Savage, pointing out to him all the perils involved in the attempt, but likewise without avail. He was more depressed than usual, apparently on the ground that "having seen the ghost of her ladyship" he was sure he had not long to live. Still, he declared that where his master went he would go, as he preferred to die with him rather than alone.

So I was obliged to give in and with a melancholy heart to do what I could to help in the simple preparations for this crazy undertaking, realizing all the while that the only real help must come from above, since in such a case man was powerless. I should add that after consultation, Ragnall gave up the idea of adopting a Kendah disguise which was certain to be discovered, also of starting at night when the town was guarded.

That very afternoon they went, going out of the town quite openly on the pretext of shooting partridges and small buck on the lower slopes of the mountain, where both were numerous, as Harût had informed us we were quite at liberty to do. The farewell was somewhat sad, especially with Savage, who gave me a letter he had written for his old mother in England, requesting me to post it if ever again I came to a civilized land.

I did my best to put a better spirit in him but without avail. He only wrung my hand warmly, said that it was a pleasure to have known such a "real gentleman" as myself, and expressed a hope that I might get out of this hell and live to a green old age amongst Christians. Then he wiped away a tear with the cuff of his coat, touched his hat in the orthodox fashion and departed. Their outfit, I should add, was very simple: some food in bags, a flask of spirits, two double-barrelled guns that would shoot either shot or ball, a bull's-eye lantern, matches and their pistols.

Hans walked with them a little way and, leaving them outside the town, returned.

"Why do you look so gloomy, Hans?" I asked.

"Because, Baas," he answered, twiddling his hat, "I had grown to be fond of the white man, Bena, who was always very kind to me and did not treat me like dirt as low-born whites are apt to do. Also he cooked well, and now I shall have to do that work which I do not like."

"What do you mean, Hans? The man isn't dead, is he?"

"No, Baas, but soon he will be, for the shadow of death is in his eyes."

"Then how about Lord Ragnall?"

"I saw no shadow in his eyes; I think that he will live, Baas."

I tried to get some explanation of these dark sayings out of the Hottentot, but he would add nothing to his words.

All the following night I lay awake filled with heavy fears which deepened as the hours went on. Just before dawn we heard a knocking on our door and Ragnall's voice whispering to us to open. Hans did so while I lit a candle, of which we had a good supply. As it burned up Ragnall entered, and from his face I saw at once that something terrible had happened. He went to the jar where we kept our water and drank three pannikin-fuls, one after the other. Then without waiting to be asked, he said:

"Savage is dead," and paused a while as though some awful recollection overcame him. "Listen," he went on presently. "We worked up the hillside without firing, although we saw plenty of partridges and one buck, till just as twilight was closing in, we came to the cliff face. Here we perceived a track that ran to the mouth of a narrow cave or tunnel in the lava rock of the precipice, which looked quite unclimbable. While we were wondering what to do, eight or ten white-robed men appeared out of the shadows and seized us before we could make any resistance. After talking together for a little they took away our guns and pistols, with which some of them disappeared. Then their leader, with many bows, indicated that we were at liberty to proceed by pointing first to the mouth of the cave, and next to the top of the precipice, saying something about '*ingane*,' which I believe means a little child, does it not?"

I nodded, and he went on:

"After this they all departed down the hill, smiling in a fashion that disturbed me. We stood for a while irresolute, until it became quite dark. I asked Savage what he thought we had better do, expecting that he would say 'Return to the town.' To my surprise, he answered:

"'Go on, of course, my lord. Don't let those brutes say that we white men daren't walk a step without our guns. Indeed, in any case I mean to go on, even if your lordship won't.'

"Whilst he spoke he took a bull's-eye lantern from his foodbag, which had not been interfered with by the Kendah, and lit it. I stared at him amazed, for the man seemed to be animated by some tremendous purpose. Or rather it was as though a force from without had got hold of his will and were pushing him on to an unknown end. Indeed his next words showed that this was so, for he exclaimed:

"'There is something drawing me into that cave, my lord. It may be death; I think it is death, but whatever it be, go I must. Perhaps you would do well to stop outside till I have seen.'

"I stepped forward to catch hold of the man, who I thought had gone mad, as perhaps was the case. Before I could lay my hands on him he had run rapidly to the mouth of the cave. Of course I followed, but when I reached its entrance the star of light thrown forward by the bull's-eye lantern showed me that he was about eight yards down the tunnel. Then I heard a terrible hissing noise and Savage exclaiming: 'Oh! my God!' twice over. As he spoke the lantern fell from his hand, but did not go out, because, as you know, it is made to burn in any position. I leapt forward and picked it from the ground, and while I was doing so became aware that Savage was running still farther into the depths of the cave. I lifted the lantern above my head and looked.

"This was what I saw: About ten paces from me was Savage with his arms outstretched and dancing—yes, dancing—first to the right and then to the left, with a kind of horrible grace and to the tune of a hideous hissing music. I held the lantern higher and perceived that beyond him, lifted eight or nine feet into the air, nearly to the roof of the tunnel in fact, was the head of the hugest snake of which I have ever heard. It was as broad as the bottom of a wheelbarrow—were it cut off I think it would fill a large wheelbarrow—while the neck upon which it was supported was quite as thick as my middle, and the undulating body behind it, which stretched far away into the darkness, was the size of an eighteen-gallon cask and glittered green and grey, lined and splashed with silver and with gold.

"It hissed and swayed its great head to the right, holding Savage with cold eyes that yet seemed to be on fire, whereon he danced to the right. It hissed again and swayed its head to the left, whereon he danced to the left. Then suddenly it reared its head right to the top of the cave and so remained for a few seconds, whereon Savage stood still, bending a little forward, as though he were bowing to the reptile. Next instant, like a flash it struck, for I saw its white fangs bury themselves in the back of Savage, who with a kind of sigh fell forward on to his face. Then there was a convulsion of those shining folds, followed by a sound as of bones being ground up in a steam-driven mortar.

"I staggered against the wall of the cave and shut my eyes for a moment, for I felt faint. When I opened them again it was to see something flat, misshapen, elongated like a reflection in a spoon, something that had been Savage lying on the floor, and stretched out over it the huge serpent studying me with its steely eyes. Then I ran; I am not ashamed to say I ran out of that horrible hole and far into the night."

"Small blame to you," I said, adding: "Hans, give me some square-face neat." For I felt as queer as though I also had been in that cave with its guardian.

"There is very little more to tell," went on Ragnall after I had drunk the hollands. "I lost my way on the mountain-side and wandered for many hours, till at last I blundered up against one of the outermost houses of the town, after which things were easy. Perhaps I should add that wherever I went on my way down the mountain it seemed to me that I heard people laughing at me in an unnatural kind of voice. That's all."

After this we sat silent for a long while, till at length Hans said in his unmoved tone:

"The light has come, Baas. Shall I blow out the candle, which it is a pity to waste? Also, does the Baas wish me to cook the breakfast, now that the snake devil is making his off Bena, as I hope to make mine off him before all is done. Snakes are very good to eat, Baas, if you know how to dress them in the Hottentot way."

XVI

Hans Steals the Keys

A few hours later some of the White Kendah arrived at the house and very politely delivered to us Ragnall's and poor Savage's guns and pistols, which they said they had found lying in the grass on the mountain-side, and with them the bull's-eye lantern that Ragnall had thrown away in his flight; all of which articles I accepted without comment. That evening also Harût called and, after salutations, asked where Bena was as he did not see him. Then my indignation broke out:

"Oh! white-bearded father of liars," I said, "you know well that he is in the belly of the serpent which lives in the cave of the mountain."

"What, Lord!" exclaimed Harût addressing Ragnall in his peculiar English, "have you been for walk up to hole in hill? Suppose Bena want see big snake. He always very fond of snake, you know, and they very fond of him. You 'member how they come out of his pocket in your house in England? Well, he know all about snake now."

"You villain!" exclaimed Ragnall, "you murderer! I have a mind to kill you where you are."

"Why you choke me, Lord, because snake choke your man? Poor snake, he only want dinner. If you go where lion live, lion kill you. If you go where snake live, snake kill you. I tell you not to. You take no notice. Now I tell you all—go if you wish, no one stop you. Perhaps you kill snake, who knows? Only you no take gun there, please. That not allowed. When you tired of this town, go see snake. Only, 'member that not right way to House of Child. There another way which you never find."

"Look here," said Ragnall, "what is the use of all this foolery? You know very well why we are in your devilish country. It is because I believe you have stolen my wife to make her the priestess of your evil religion whatever it may be, and I want her back."

"All this great mistake," replied Harût blandly. "We no steal beautiful lady you marry because we find she not right priestess. Also Macumazana here not to look for lady but to kill elephant Jana and get pay in ivory like good business man. You, Lord, come with him as friend though we no ask you, that all. Then you try find temple of our god and snake which watch door kill your servant. Why we not kill *you*, eh?"

"Because you are afraid to," answered Ragnall boldly. "Kill me if you can and take the consequences. I am ready."

Harût studied him not without admiration.

"You very brave man," he said, "and we no wish kill you and p'raps after all everything come right in end. Only Child know about that. Also you help us fight Black Kendah by and by. So, Lord, you quite safe unless you big fool and go call on snake in cave. He very hungry snake and soon want more dinner. You hear, Light-in-Darkness, Lord-of-the-Fire," he added suddenly turning on Hans who was squatted near by twiddling his hat with a face that for absolute impassiveness resembled a deal board. "You hear, he very hungry snake, and you make nice tea for him."

Hans rolled his little yellow eyes without even turning his head until they rested on the stately countenance of Harût, and answered in Bantu:

"I hear, Liar-with-the-White-Beard, but what have I to do with this matter? Jana is my enemy who would have killed Macumazana, my master, not your dirty snake. What is the good of this snake of yours? If it were any good, why does it not kill Jana whom you hate? And if it is no good, why do you not take a stick and knock it on the head? If you are afraid I will do so for you if you pay me. That for your snake," and very energetically he spat upon the floor.

"All right," said Harût, still speaking in English, "you go kill snake. Go when you like, no one say no. Then we give you new name. Then we call you Lord-of-the-Snake."

As Hans, who now was engaged in lighting his corn-cob pipe, did not deign to answer these remarks, Harût turned to me and said:

"Lord Macumazana, your leg still bad, eh? Well, I bring you some ointment what make it quite well; it holy ointment come from the Child. We want you get well quick."

Then suddenly he broke into Bantu. "My Lord, war draws near. The Black Kendah are gathering all their strength to attack us and we must have your aid. I go down to the River Tava to see to certain matters, as to the reaping of the outlying crops and other things. Within a week I will be back; then we must talk again, for by that time, if you will use the ointment that I have given you, you will be as well as ever you were in your life. Rub it on your leg, and mix a piece as large as a mealie grain in water and swallow it at night. It is not poison, see," and taking the cover off a little earthenware pot which he produced he scooped from it with his finger some of the contents, which looked like lard, put it on his tongue and swallowed it.

Then he rose and departed with his usual bows.

Here I may state that I used Harût's prescription with the most excellent results. That night I took a dose in water, very nasty it was, and rubbed my leg with the stuff, to find that next morning all pain had left me and that, except for some local weakness, I was practically quite well. I kept the rest of the salve for years, and it proved a perfect specific in cases of sciatica and rheumatism. Now, alas! it is all used and no recipe is available from which it can be made up again.

The next few days passed uneventfully. As soon as I could walk I began to go about the town, which was nothing but a scattered village much resembling those to be seen on the eastern coasts of Africa. Nearly all the men seemed to be away, making preparations for the harvest, I suppose, and as the women shut themselves up in their houses after the Oriental fashion, though the few that I saw about were unveiled and rather good-looking, I did not gather any intelligence worth noting.

To tell the truth I cannot remember being in a more uninteresting place than this little town with its extremely uncommunicative population which, it seemed to me, lived under a shadow of fear that prevented all gaiety. Even the children, of whom there were not many, crept about in a depressed fashion and talked in a low voice. I never saw any of them playing games or heard them shouting and laughing, as young people do in most parts of the world. For the rest we were very well looked after. Plenty of food was provided for us and every thought taken for our comfort. Thus a strong and quiet pony was brought for me to ride because of my lameness. I had only to go out of the house and call and it arrived from somewhere, all ready saddled and bridled, in charge of a lad who appeared to be dumb. At any rate when I spoke to him he would not answer.

Mounted on this pony I took one or two rides along the southern slopes of the mountain on the old pretext of shooting for the pot. Hans accompanied me on these occasions, but was, I noted, very silent and thoughtful, as though he were hunting something up and down his tortuous intelligence. Once we got quite near to the mouth of the cave or tunnel where poor Savage had met his horrid end. As we stood studying it a white-robed man whose head was shaved, which made me think he must be a priest, came up and asked me mockingly why we did not go through the tunnel and see what lay beyond, adding, almost in the words of Harût himself, that none would attempt to interfere with us as the road was open to any who could travel it. By way of answer I only smiled and put him a few questions about a very beautiful breed of goats with long silky hair, some of which he seemed to be engaged in herding. He replied that these goats were sacred, being the food of "one who dwelt in the Mountain who only ate when the moon changed."

When I inquired who this person was he said with his unpleasant smile that I had better go through the tunnel and see for myself, an invitation which I did not accept.

That evening Harût appeared unexpectedly, looking very grave and troubled. He was in a great hurry and only stayed long enough to congratulate me upon the excellent effects of his ointment, since "no man could fight Jana on one leg."

I asked him when the fight with Jana was to come off. He replied:

"Lord, I go up to the Mountain to attend the Feast of the First-fruits, which is held at sunrise on the day of the new moon. After the offering the Oracle will speak and we shall learn when there will be war with Jana, and perchance other things."

"May we not attend this feast, Harût, who are weary of doing nothing here?"

"Certainly," he answered with his grave bow. "That is, if you come unarmed; for to appear before the Child with arms is death. You know the road; it runs through yonder cave and the forest beyond the cave. Take it when you will, Lord."

"Then if we can pass the cave we shall be welcome at the feast?"

"You will be very welcome. None shall hurt you there, going or returning. I swear it by the Child. Oh! Macumazana," he added, smiling a little, "why do you talk folly, who know well that one lives in yonder cave whom none may look upon and love, as Bena learned not long ago? You are thinking that perhaps you might kill this Dweller in the cave with your weapons. Put away that dream, seeing that henceforth those who watch you have orders to see that none of you leave this house carrying so much as a knife. Indeed, unless you promise me that this shall be so you will not be suffered to set foot outside its garden until I return again. Now do you promise?"

I thought a while and, drawing the two others aside out of hearing, asked them their opinion.

Ragnall was at first unwilling to give any such promise, but Hans said:

"Baas, it is better to go free and unhurt without guns and knives than to become a prisoner once, as you were among the Black Kendah. Often there is but a short step between the prison and the grave."

Both Ragnall and I acknowledged the force of this argument and in the end we gave the promise, speaking one by one.

"It is enough," said Harût; "moreover, know, Lord, that among us White Kendah he who breaks an oath is put across the River Tava unarmed to make report thereof to Jana, Father of Lies. Now farewell. If we do not meet at the Feast of the First-fruits on the day of the new moon, whither once more I invite you, we can talk together here after I have heard the voice of the Oracle."

Then he mounted a camel which awaited him outside the gate and departed with an escort of twelve men, also riding camels.

"There is some other road up that mountain, Quatermain," said Ragnall. "A camel could sooner pass through the eye of a needle than through that dreadful cave, even if it were empty."

"Probably," I answered, "but as we don't know where it is and I dare say it lies miles from here, we need not trouble our heads on the matter. The cave is *our* only road, which means that there is *no* road."

That evening at supper we discovered that Hans was missing; also that he had got possession of my keys and broken into a box containing liquor, for there it stood open in the cooking-hut with the keys in the lock.

"He has gone on the drink," I said to Ragnall, "and upon my soul I don't wonder at it; for sixpence I would follow his example."

Then we went to bed. Next morning we breakfasted rather late, since when one has nothing to do there is no object in getting up early. As I was preparing to go to the cook-house to boil some eggs, to our astonishment Hans appeared with a kettle of coffee.

"Hans," I said, "you are a thief."

"Yes, Baas," answered Hans.

"You have been at the gin box and taking that poison."

"Yes, Baas, I have been taking poison. Also I took a walk and all is right now. The Baas must not be angry, for it is very dull doing nothing here. Will the Baases eat porridge as well as eggs?"

As it was no use scolding him I said that we would. Moreover, there was something about his manner which made me suspicious, for really he did not look like a person who has just been very drunk.

After we had finished breakfast he came and squatted down before me. Having lit his pipe he asked suddenly:

"Would the Baases like to walk through that cave to-night? If so, there will be no trouble."

"What do you mean?" I asked, suspecting that he was still drunk.

"I mean, Baas, that the Dweller-in-the-cave is fast asleep."

"How do you know that, Hans?"

"Because I am the nurse who put him to sleep, Baas, though he kicked and cried a great deal. He is asleep; he will wake no more. Baas, I have killed the Father of Serpents."

"Hans," I said, "now I am sure that you are still drunk, although you do not show it outside."

"Hans," added Ragnall, to whom I had translated as much of this as he did not understand, "it is too early in the day to tell good stories. How could you possibly have killed that serpent without a gun—for you took none with you—or with it either for that matter?"

"Will the Baases come and take a walk through the cave?" asked Hans with a snigger.

"Not till I am quite sure that you are sober," I replied; then, remembering certain other events in this worthy's career, added; "Hans, if you do not tell us the story at once I will beat you."

"There isn't much story, Baas," replied Hans between long sucks at his pipe, which had nearly gone out, "because the thing was so easy. The Baas is very clever and so is the Lord Baas, why then can they never see the stones that lie under their noses? It is because their eyes are always fixed upon the mountains between this world and the next. But the poor Hottentot, who looks at the ground to be sure that he does not stumble, ah! he sees the stones. Now, Baas, did you not hear that man in a night shirt with his head shaved say that those goats were food for One who dwelt in the mountain?"

"I did. What of it, Hans?"

"Who would be the One who dwelt in the mountain except the Father of Snakes in the cave, Baas? Ah, now for the first time you see the stone that lay at your feet all the while. And, Baas, did not the bald man add that this One in the mountain was only fed at new and full moon, and is not to-morrow the day of new moon, and therefore would he not be very hungry on the day before new moon, that is, last night?"

"No doubt, Hans; but how can you kill a snake by feeding it?"

"Oh! Baas, you may eat things that make you ill, and so can a snake. Now you will guess the rest, so I had better go to wash the dishes."

"Whether I guess or do not guess," I replied sagely, the latter being the right hypothesis, "the dishes can wait, Hans, since the Lord there has not guessed; so continue."

"Very well, Baas. In one of those boxes are some pounds of stuff which, when mixed with water, is used for preserving skins and skulls."

"You mean the arsenic crystals," I said with a flash of inspiration.

"I don't know what you call them, Baas. At first I thought they were hard sugar and stole some once, when the real sugar was left behind, to put into the coffee—without telling the Baas, because it was my fault that the sugar was left behind."

"Great Heavens!" I exclaimed, "then why aren't we all dead?"

"Because at the last moment, Baas, I thought I would make sure, so I put some of the hard sugar into hot milk and, when it had melted, I gave it to that yellow dog which once bit me in the leg, the one that came from Beza-Town, Baas, that I told you had run away. He was a very greedy dog, Baas, and drank up the milk at once. Then he gave a howl, twisted about, foamed at the mouth and died and I buried him at once. After that I threw some more of the large sugar mixed with mealies to the fowls that we brought with us for cooking. Two cocks and a hen swallowed them by mistake for the corn. Presently they fell on their backs, kicked a little and died. Some of the Mazitu, who were great thieves, stole those dead fowls, Baas. After this, Baas, I thought it best not to use that sugar in the coffee, and later on Bena told me that it was deadly poison. Well, Baas, it came into my mind that if I could make that great snake swallow enough of this poison, he, too, might die.

"So I stole your keys, as I often do, Baas, when I want anything, because you leave them lying about everywhere, and to deceive you first opened one of the boxes that are full of square-face and brandy and left it open, for I wished you to think that I had just gone to get drunk like anybody else. Then I opened another box and got out two one-pound tins of the sugar which kills dogs and fowls. Half a pound of it I melted in boiling water with some real sugar to make the stuff sweet, and put it into a bottle. The rest I tied with string in twelve little packets in the soft paper which is in one of the boxes, and put them in my pocket. Then I went up the hill, Baas, to the place where I saw those goats are kraaled at night behind a reed fence. As I had hoped, no one was watching them because there are no tigers so near this town, and man does not steal the goats that are sacred. I went into the kraal and found a fat young ewe which had a kid. I dragged it out and, taking it behind some stones, I made its leg fast with a bit of cord and poured this stuff out of the bottle all over its skin, rubbing it in well. Then I tied the twelve packets of hard poison-sugar everywhere about its body, making them very fast deep in the long hair so that they could not tumble or rub off.

"After this I untied the goat, led it near to the mouth of the cave and held it there for a time while it kept on bleating for its kid. Next I took it almost up to the cave, wondering how I should drive it in, for I did not wish to enter there myself, Baas. As it happened I need not have troubled about that. When the goat was within five yards of the cave, it stopped bleating, stood still and shivered. Then it began to go forward with little jumps, as though it did not want to go, yet must do so. Also, Baas, I felt as though I wished to go with it. So I lay down and put my heels against a rock, leaving go of the goat.

"For now, Baas, I did not care where that goat went so long as I could keep out of the hole where dwelt the Father of Serpents that had eaten Bena. But it was all right, Baas; the goat knew what it had to do and did it, jumping straight into the cave. As it entered it turned its head and looked at me. I could see its eyes in the starlight, and, Baas, they were dreadful. I think it knew what was coming and did not like it at all. And yet it had to walk on because it could not help it. Just like a man going to the devil, Baas!

"Holding on to the stone I peered after it, for I had heard something stirring in the cave making a soft noise like a white lady's dress upon the floor. There in the blackness I saw two little sparks of fire, which were the eyes of the serpent, Baas. Then I heard a sound of hissing like four big kettles boiling all at once, and a little bleat from the goat. After this there was a noise as of men wrestling, followed by another noise as of bones breaking, and lastly, yet another sucking noise as of a pump that won't draw up the water. Then everything grew nice and quiet and I went some way off, sat down a little to one side of the cave, and waited to see if anything happened.

"It must have been nearly an hour later that something did begin to happen, Baas. It was as though sacks filled with chaff were being beaten against stone walls there in the cave. Ah! thought I to myself, your stomach is beginning to ache, Eater-up-of-Bena, and, as that goat had little horns on its head—to which I tied two of the bags of the poison,

Baas—and, like all snakes, no doubt you have spikes in your throat pointing downwards, you won't be able to get it up again. Then—I expect this was after the poison-sugar had begun to melt nicely in the serpent's stomach, Baas—there was a noise as though a whole company of girls were dancing a war-dance in the cave to a music of hisses.

"And then—oh! then, Baas, of a sudden that Father of Serpents came out. I tell you, Baas, that when I saw him in the bright starlight my hair stood up upon my head, for never has there been such another snake in the whole world. Those that live in trees and eat bucks in Zululand, of whose skins men make waistcoats and slippers, are but babies compared to this one. He came out, yard after yard of him. He wriggled about, he stood upon his tail with his head where the top of a tree might be, he made himself into a ring, he bit at stones and at his own stomach, while I hid behind my rock praying to your reverend father that he might not see me. Then at last he rushed away down the hill, faster than any horse could gallop.

"Now I hoped that he had gone for good and thought of going myself. Still I feared to do so lest I should meet him somewhere, so I made up my mind to wait till daylight. It was as well, Baas, for about half an hour later he came back again. Only now he could not jump, he could only crawl. Never in my life did I see a snake look so sick, Baas. Into the cave he went and lay there hissing. By degrees the hissing grew very faint, till at length they died away altogether. I waited another half-hour, Baas, and then I grew so curious that I thought that I would go to look in the cave.

"I lit the little lantern I had with me and, holding it in one hand and my stick in the other, I crept into the hole. Before I had crawled ten paces I saw something white stretched along the ground. It was the belly of the great snake, Baas, which lay upon its back quite dead.

"I know that it was dead, for I lit three wax matches, setting them to burn upon its tail and it never stirred, as any live snake will do when it feels fire. Then I came home, Baas, feeling very proud because I had outwitted that great-grandfather of all snakes who killed Bena my friend, and had made the way clear for us to walk through the cave.

"That is all the story, Baas. Now I must go to wash those dishes," and without waiting for any comment off he went, leaving us marvelling at his wit, resource and courage.

"What next?" I asked presently.

"Nothing till to-night," answered Ragnall with determination, "when I am going to look at the snake which the noble Hans has killed and whatever lies beyond the cave, as you will remember Harût invited us to do unmolested, if we could."

"Do you think Harût will keep his word, Ragnall?"

"On the whole, yes, and if he doesn't I don't care. Anything is better than sitting here in this suspense."

"I agree as to Harût, because we are too valuable to be killed just now, if for no other reason; also as to the suspense, which is unendurable. Therefore I will walk with you to look at that snake, Ragnall, and so no doubt will Hans. The exercise will do my leg good."

"Do you think it wise?" he asked doubtfully; "in your case, I mean."

"I think it most unwise that we should separate any more. We had better stand or fall altogether; further, we do not seem to have any luck apart."

XVII

The Sanctuary and the Oath

That evening shortly after sundown the three of us started boldly from our house wearing over our clothes the Kendah dresses which Ragnall had bought, and carrying nothing save sticks in our hands, some food and the lantern in our pockets. On the outskirts of the town we were met by certain Kendah, one of whom I knew, for I had often ridden by his side on our march across the desert.

"Have any of you arms upon you, Lord Macumazana?" he asked, looking curiously at us and our white robes.

"None," I answered. "Search us if you will."

"Your word is sufficient," he replied with the grave courtesy of his people. "If you are unarmed we have orders to let you go where you wish however you may be dressed. Yet, Lord," he whispered to me, "I pray you do not enter the cave, since One lives there who strikes and does not miss, One whose kiss is death. I pray it for your own sakes, also for ours who need you."

"We shall not wake him who sleeps in the cave," I answered enigmatically, as we departed rejoicing, for now we had learned that the Kendah did not yet know of the death of the serpent.

An hour's walk up the hill, guided by Hans, brought us to the mouth of the tunnel. To tell the truth I could have wished it had been longer, for as we drew near all sorts of doubts assailed me. What if Hans really had been drinking and invented this story to account for his absence? What if the snake had recovered from a merely temporary indisposition? What if it had a wife and family living in that cave, every one of them thirsting for vengeance?

Well, it was too late to hesitate now, but secretly I hoped that one of the others would prefer to lead the way. We reached the place and listened. It was silent as a tomb. Then that brave fellow Hans lit the lantern and said:

"Do you stop here, Baases, while I go to look. If you hear anything happen to me, you will have time to run away," words that made me feel somewhat ashamed of myself.

However, knowing that he was quick as a weasel and silent as a cat, we let him go. A minute or two later suddenly he reappeared out of the darkness, for he had turned the metal shield over the bull's-eye of the lantern, and even in that light I could see that he was grinning.

"It is all right, Baas," he said. "The Father of Serpents has really gone to that land whither he sent Bena, where no doubt he is now roasting in the fires of hell, and I don't see any others. Come and look at him."

So in we went and there, true enough, upon the floor of the cave lay the huge reptile stone dead and already much swollen. I don't know how long it was, for part of its body was twisted into coils, so I will only say that it was by far the most enormous snake that I have ever seen. It is true that I have heard of such reptiles in different parts of Africa, but hitherto I had always put them down as fabulous creatures transformed into and worshipped as local gods. Also this particular specimen was, I presume, of a new variety, since, according to Ragnall, it both struck like the cobra or the adder, and crushed like the boa-constrictor. It is possible, however, that he was mistaken on this point; I do not know, since I had no time, or indeed inclination, to examine its head for the poison fangs, and when next I passed that way it was gone.

I shall never forget the stench of that cave. It was horrible, which is not to be wondered at seeing that probably this creature had dwelt there for centuries, since these large snakes are said to be as long lived as tortoises, and, being sacred, of course it had never lacked for food. Everywhere lay piles of cast bones, amongst one of which I noticed fragments of a human skull, perhaps that of poor Savage. Also the projecting rocks in the place were covered with great pieces of snake skin, doubtless rubbed off by the reptile when once a year it changed its coat.

For a while we gazed at the loathsome and still glittering creature, then pushed on fearful lest we should stumble upon more of its kind. I suppose that it must have been solitary, a kind of serpent rogue, as Jana was an elephant rogue, for we met none and, if the information which I obtained afterwards may be believed, there was no species at all resembling it in the country. What its origin may have been I never learned. All the Kendah could or would say about it was that it had lived in this hole from the beginning and that Black Kendah prisoners, or malefactors, were sometimes given to it to kill, as White Kendah prisoners were given to Jana.

The cave itself proved to be not very long, perhaps one hundred and fifty feet, no more. It was not an artificial but a natural hollow in the lava rock, which I suppose had once been blown through it by an outburst of steam. Towards the farther end it narrowed so much that I began to fear there might be no exit. In this I was mistaken, however, for at its termination we found a hole just large enough for a man to walk in upright and so difficult to climb through that it became clear to us that certainly this was not the path by which the White Kendah approached their sanctuary.

Scrambling out of this aperture with thankfulness, we found ourselves upon the slope of a kind of huge ditch of lava which ran first downwards for about eighty paces, then up again to the base of the great cone of the inner mountain which was covered with dense forest.

I presume that the whole formation of this peculiar hill was the result of a violent volcanic action in the early ages of the earth. But as I do not understand such matters I will not dilate upon them further than to say that, although comparatively small, it bore a certain resemblance to other extinct volcanoes which I had met with in different parts of Africa.

We climbed down to the bottom of the ditch that from its general appearance might have been dug out by some giant race as a protection to their stronghold, and up its farther side to where the forest began on deep and fertile soil. Why there should have been rich earth here and none in the ditch is more than we could guess, but perhaps the presence of springs of water in this part of the mount may have been a cause. At any rate it was so.

The trees in this forest were huge and of a variety of cedar, but did not grow closely together; also there was practically no undergrowth, perhaps for the reason that their dense, spreading tops shut out the light. As I saw afterwards both trunks and boughs were clothed with long grey moss, which even at midday gave the place a very ghostly appearance. The darkness beneath those trees was intense, literally we could not see an inch before our faces. Yet rather than stand still we struggled on, Hans leading the way, for his instincts were quicker than ours. The steep rise of the ground beneath our feet told us that we were going uphill, as we wished to do, and from time to time I consulted a pocket compass I carried by the light of a match, knowing from previous observations that the top of the Holy Mount lay due north.

Thus for hour after hour we crept up and on, occasionally butting into the trunk of a tree or stumbling over a fallen bough, but meeting with no other adventures or obstacles of a physical kind. Of moral, or rather mental, obstacles there were many, since to all of us the atmosphere of this forest was as that of a haunted house. It may have been the embracing darkness, or the sough of the night wind amongst the boughs and mosses, or the sense of the imminent dangers that we had passed and that still awaited us. Or it may have been unknown horrors connected with this place of which some spiritual essence still survived, for without doubt localities preserve such influences, which can be felt by the sensitive among living things, especially in favouring conditions of fear and gloom. At any rate I never experienced more subtle and yet more penetrating terrors than I did upon that night, and afterwards Ragnall confessed to me that my case was his own. Black as it was I thought that I saw apparitions, among them glaring eyes and that of the elephant Jana standing in front of me with his trunk raised against the bole of a cedar. I could have sworn that I saw him, nor was I reassured when Hans whispered to me below his breath, for here we did not seem to dare to raise our voices:

"Look, Baas. Is it Jana glowing like hot iron who stands yonder?"

"Don't be a fool," I answered. "How can Jana be here and, if he were here, how could we see him in the night?" But as I said the words I remembered Harût had told us that Jana had been met with on the Holy Mount "in the spirit or in the flesh." However this may be, next instant he was gone and we beheld him or his shadow no more. Also we thought that from time to time we heard voices speaking all around us, now here, now there and now in the tree tops above our heads, though what they said we could not catch or understand.

Thus the long night wore away. Our progress was very slow, but guided by occasional glimpses at the compass we never stopped but twice, once when we found ourselves apparently surrounded by tree boles and fallen boughs, and once when we got into swampy ground. Then we took the risk of lighting the lantern, and by its aid picked our way through these difficult places. By degrees the trees grew fewer so that we could see the stars between their tops. This was a help to us as I knew that one of them, which I had carefully noted, shone at this season of the year directly over the cone of the mountain, and we were enabled to steer thereby.

It must have been not more than half an hour before the dawn that Hans, who was leading—we were pushing our way through thick bushes at the time—halted hurriedly, saying:

"Stop, Baas, we are on the edge of a cliff. When I thrust my stick forward it stands on nothing."

Needless to say we pulled up dead and so remained without stirring an inch, for who could say what might be beyond us? Ragnall wished to examine the ground with the lantern. I was about to consent, though doubtfully, when suddenly I heard voices murmuring and through the screen of bushes saw lights moving at a little distance, forty feet or more below us. Then we gave up all idea of making further use of the lantern and crouched still as mice in our bushes, waiting for the dawn.

It came at last. In the east appeared a faint pearly flush that by degrees spread itself over the whole arch of the sky and was welcomed by the barking of monkeys and the call of birds in the depths of the dew-steeped forest. Next a ray from the unrisen sun, a single spear of light shot suddenly across the sky, and as it appeared, from the darkness below us arose a sound of chanting, very low and sweet to hear. It died away and for a little while there was silence broken only by a rustling sound like to that of people taking their seats in a dark theatre. Then a woman began to sing in a beautiful, contralto voice, but in what language I do not know, for I could not catch the words, if these were words and not only musical notes.

I felt Ragnall trembling beside me and in a whisper asked him what was the matter. He answered, also in a whisper:

"I believe that is my wife's voice."

"If so, I beg you to control yourself," I replied.

Now the skies began to flame and the light to pour itself into a misty hollow beneath us like streams of many-coloured gems into a bowl, driving away the shadows. By degrees these vanished; by degrees we saw everything. Beneath us was an amphitheatre, on the southern wall of which we were seated, though it was not a wall but a lava cliff between forty and fifty feet high which served as a wall. The amphitheatre itself, however, almost exactly resembled those of the ancients which I had seen in pictures and Ragnall had visited in Italy, Greece, and Southern France. It was oval in shape and not very large, perhaps the flat space at the bottom may have covered something over an acre, but all round this oval ran tiers of seats cut in the lava of the crater. For without doubt this was the crater of an extinct volcano.

Moreover, in what I will call the arena, stood a temple that in its main outlines, although small, exactly resembled those still to be seen in Egypt. There was the gateway or pylon; there the open outer court with columns round it supporting roofed cloisters, which, as we ascertained afterwards, were used as dwelling-places by the priests. There beyond and connected with the first by a short passage was a second rather smaller court, also open to the sky, and beyond this again, built like all the rest of the temple of lava blocks, a roofed erection measuring about twelve feet square, which I guessed at once must be the sanctuary.

This temple was, as I have said, small, but extremely well proportioned, every detail of it being in the most excellent taste though unornamented by sculpture or painting. I have to add that in front of the sanctuary door stood a large block of lava, which I concluded was an altar, and in front of this a stone seat and a basin, also of stone, supported upon a very low tripod. Further, behind the sanctuary was a square house with window-places.

At the moment of our first sight of this place the courts were empty, but on the benches of the amphitheatre were seated about three hundred persons, male and female, the men to the north and the women to the south. They were all clad in pure white robes, the heads of the men being shaved and those of the women veiled, but leaving the face exposed. Lastly, there were two roadways into the amphitheatre, one running east and one west through tunnels hollowed in the encircling rock of the crater, both of which roads were closed at the mouths of the tunnels by massive wooden double doors, seventeen or eighteen feet in height. From these roadways and their doors we learned two things. First, that the cave where had lived the Father of Serpents was, as I had suspected, not the real approach to the shrine of the Child, but only a blind; and, secondly, that the ceremony we were about to witness was secret and might only be attended by the priestly class or families of this strange tribe.

Scarcely was it full daylight when from the cells of the cloisters round the outer court issued twelve priests headed by Harût himself, who looked very dignified in his white garment, each of whom carried on a wooden platter ears of different kinds of corn. Then from the cells of the southern cloister issued twelve women, or rather girls, for all were young and very comely, who ranged themselves alongside of the men. These also carried wooden platters, and on them blooming flowers.

At a sign they struck up a religious chant and began to walk forward through the passage that led from the first court to the second. Arriving in front of the altar they halted and one by one, first a priest and then a priestess, set down the platters of offerings, piling them above each other into a cone. Next the priests and the priestesses ranged themselves in lines on either side of the altar, and Harût took a platter of corn and a platter of flowers in his hands. These he held first towards that quarter of the sky in which swam the invisible new moon, secondly towards the rising sun, and thirdly towards the doors of the sanctuary, making genuflexions and uttering some chanted prayer, the words of which we could not hear.

A pause followed, that was succeeded by a sudden outburst of song wherein all the audience took part. It was a very sonorous and beautiful song or hymn in some language which I did not understand, divided into four verses, the end of each verse being marked by the bowing of every one of those many singers towards the east, towards the west, and finally towards the altar.

Another pause till suddenly the doors of the sanctuary were thrown wide and from between them issued—the goddess Isis of the Egyptians as I have seen her in pictures! She was wrapped in closely clinging draperies of material so thin that the whiteness of her body could be seen beneath. Her hair was outspread before her, and she wore a head-dress or bonnet of glittering feathers from the front of which rose a little golden snake. In her arms she bore what at that distance seemed to be a naked child. With her came two women, walking a little behind her and supporting her arms, who also wore feather bonnets but without the golden snake, and were clad in tight-fitting, transparent garments.

"My God!" whispered Ragnall, "it is my wife!"

"Then be silent and thank Him that she is alive and well," I answered.

The goddess Isis, or the English lady—in that excitement I did not reck which—stood still while the priests and priestesses and all the audience, who, gathered on the upper benches of the amphitheatre, could see her above the wall of the inner court, raised a thrice-repeated and triumphant cry of welcome. Then Harût and the first priestess lifted respectively an ear of corn and a flower from the two topmost platters and held these first to the lips of the child in her arms and secondly to her lips.

This ceremony concluded, the two attendant women led her round the altar to the stone chair, upon which she seated herself. Next fire was kindled in the bowl on the tripod in front of the chair, how I could not see; but perhaps it was already smouldering there. At any rate it burnt up in a thin blue flame, on to which Harût and the head priestess threw something that caused the flame to turn to smoke. Then Isis, for I prefer to call her so while describing this ceremony, was caused to bend her head forward, so that it was enveloped in the smoke exactly as she and I had done some years before in the drawing-room at Ragnall Castle. Presently the smoke died away and the two attendants with the feathered head-dresses straightened her in the chair where she sat still holding the babe against her breast as she might have done to nurse it, but with her head bent forward like that of a person in a swoon.

Now Harût stepped forward and appeared to speak to the goddess at some length, then fell back again and waited, till in the midst of an intense silence she rose from her seat and, fixing her wide eyes on the heavens, spoke in her turn, for although we heard nothing of what she said, in that clear, morning light we could see her lips moving. For some minutes she spoke, then sat down again upon the chair and remained motionless, staring straight in front of her. Harût advanced again, this time to the front of the altar, and, taking his stand upon a kind of stone step, addressed the priests and priestesses and all the encircling audience in a voice so loud and clear that I could distinguish and understand every word he said.

"The Guardian of the heavenly Child, the Nurse decreed, the appointed Nurturer, She who is the shadow of her that bore the Child, She who in her day bears the symbol of the Child and is consecrated to its service from of old, She whose heart is filled with the wisdom of the Child and who utters the decrees of Heaven, has spoken. Hearken now to the voice of the Oracle uttered in answer to the questions of me, Harût, the head priest of the Eternal Child during my life-days. Thus says the Oracle, the Guardian, the Nurturer, marked like all who went before her with the holy mark of the new moon. She on whom the spirit, flitting from generation to generation, has alighted for a while. 'O people of the White Kendah, worshippers of the Child in this land and descendants of those who for thousands of years worshipped the Child in a more ancient land until the barbarians drove it thence with the remnant that remained. War is upon you, O people of the White Kendah. Jana the evil one; he whose other name is Set, he whose other name is Satan, he who for this while lives in the shape of an elephant, he who is worshipped by the thousands whom once you conquered, and whom still you bridle by my might, comes up against you. The Darkness wars against the Daylight, the Evil wars against the Good. My curse has fallen upon the people of Jana, my hail has smitten them, their corn and their cattle; they have no food to eat. But they are still strong for war and there is food in your land. They come to take your corn; Jana comes to trample your god. The Evil comes to destroy the

Good, the Night to Devour the Day. It is the last of many battles. How shall you conquer, O People of the Child? Not by your own strength, for you are few in number and Jana is very strong. Not by the strength of the Child, for the Child grows weak and old, the days of its dominion are almost done, and its worship is almost outworn. Here alone that worship lingers, but new gods, who are still the old gods, press on to take its place and to lead it to its rest.'

"How then shall you conquer that, when the Child has departed to its own place, a remnant of you may still remain? In one way only—so says the Guardian, the Nurturer of the Child speaking with the voice of the Child; by the help of those whom you have summoned to your aid from far. There were four of them, but one you have suffered to be slain in the maw of the Watcher in the cave. It was an evil deed, O sons and daughters of the Child, for as the Watcher is now dead, so ere long many of you who planned this deed must die who, had it not been for that man's blood, would have lived on a while. Why did you do this thing? That you might keep a secret, the secret of the theft of a woman, that you might continue to act a lie which falls upon your head like a stone from heaven.

"Thus saith the Child: 'Lift no hand against the three who remain, and what they shall ask, that give, for thus alone shall some of you be saved from Jana and those who serve him, even though the Guardian and the Child be taken away and the Child itself returned to its own place.' These are the words of the Oracle uttered at the Feast of the First-fruits, the words that cannot be changed and mayhap its last."

HARÛT CEASED, AND THERE WAS silence while this portentous message sank into the minds of his audience. At length they seemed to understand its ominous nature and from them all there arose a universal, simultaneous groan. As it died away the two attendants dressed as goddesses assisted the personification of the Lady Isis to rise from her seat and, opening the robes upon her breast, pointed to something beneath her throat, doubtless that birthmark shaped like the new moon which made her so sacred in their eyes since she who bore it and she alone could fill her holy office.

All the audience and with them the priests and priestesses bowed before her. She lifted the symbol of the Child, holding it high above her head, whereon once more they bowed with the deepest veneration. Then still holding the effigy aloft, she turned and with her two attendants passed into the sanctuary and doubtless thence by a covered way into the house beyond. At any rate we saw her no more.

As soon as she was gone the congregation, if I may call it so, leaving their seats, swarmed down into the outer court of the temple through its eastern gate, which was now opened. Here the priests proceeded to distribute among them the offerings taken from the altar, giving a grain of corn to each of the men to eat and a flower to each of the women, which flower she kissed and hid in the bosom of her robe. Evidently it was a kind of sacrament.

Ragnall lifted himself a little upon his hands and knees, and I saw that his eyes glowed and his face was very pale.

"What are you going to do?" I asked.

"Demand that those people give me back my wife, whom they have stolen. Don't try to stop me, Quatermain, I mean what I say."

"But, but," I stammered, "they never will and we are but three unarmed men."

Hans lifted up his little yellow face between us.

"Baas," he hissed, "I have a thought. The Lord Baas wishes to get the lady dressed like a bird as to her head and like one for burial as to her body, who is, he says, his wife. But for us to take her from among so many is impossible. Now what did that old witch-doctor Harût declare just now? He declared, speaking for his fetish, that by our help alone the White Kendah can resist the hosts of the Black Kendah and that no harm must be done to us if the White Kendah would continue to live. So it seems, Baas, that we have something to sell which the White Kendah must buy, namely our help against the Black Kendah, for if we will not fight for them, they believe that they cannot conquer their enemies and kill the devil Jana. Well now, supposing that the Baas says that our price is the white woman dressed like a bird, to be delivered over to us when we have defeated the Black Kendah and killed Jana—after which they will have no more use for her. And supposing that the Baas says that if they refuse to pay that price we will burn all our powder and cartridges so that the rifles are no use? Is there not a path to walk on here?"

"Perhaps," I answered. "Something of the sort was working in my mind but I had no time to think it out."

Turning, I explained the idea to Ragnall, adding:

"I pray you not to be rash. If you are, not only may we be killed, which does not so much matter, but it is very probable that even if they spare us they will put an end to your wife rather than suffer one whom they look upon as holy and who is necessary to their faith in its last struggle to be separated from her charge of the Child."

This was a fortunate argument of mine and one which went home.

"To lose her now would be more than I could bear," he muttered.

"Then will you promise to let me try to manage this affair and not to interfere with me and show violence?"

He hesitated a moment and answered:

"Yes, I promise, for you two are cleverer than I am and—I cannot trust my judgment."

"Good," I said, assuming an air of confidence which I did not feel. "Now we will go down to call upon Harût and his friends. I want to have a closer look at that temple."

So behind our screen of bushes we wriggled back a little distance till we knew that the slope of the ground would hide us when we stood up. Then as quickly as we could we made our way eastwards for something over a quarter of a mile and after this turned to the north. As I expected, beyond the ring of the crater we found ourselves on the rising, tree-clad bosom of the mountain and, threading our path through the cedars, came presently to that track or roadway which led to the eastern gate of the amphitheatre. This road we followed unseen until presently the gateway appeared before us. We walked through it without attracting any attention, perhaps because all the people were either talking together, or praying, or perhaps because like themselves we were wrapped in white robes. At the mouth of the tunnel we stopped and I called out in a loud voice:

"The white lords and their servant have come to visit Harût, as he invited them to do. Bring us, we pray you, into the presence of Harût."

Everyone wheeled round and stared at us standing there in the shadow of the gateway tunnel, for the sun behind us was still low. My word, how they did stare! A voice cried:

"Kill them! Kill these strangers who desecrate our temple."

"What!" I answered. "Would you kill those to whom your high-priest has given safe-conduct; those moreover by whose help alone, as your Oracle has just declared, you can hope to slay Jana and destroy his hosts?"

"How do they know that?" shouted another voice. "They are magicians!"

"Yes," I remarked, "all magic does not dwell in the hearts of the White Kendah. If you doubt it, go to look at the Watcher in the Cave whom your Oracle told you is dead. You will find that it did not lie."

As I spoke a man rushed through the gates, his white rob streaming on the wind, shouting as he emerged from the tunnel:

"O Priests and Priestesses of the Child, the ancient serpent is dead. I whose office it is to feed the serpent on the day of the new moon have found him dead in his house."

"You hear," I interpolated calmly. "The Father of Snakes is dead. If you want to know how, I will tell you. We looked on it and it died."

They might have answered that poor Savage also looked on it with the result that *he* died, but luckily it did not occur to them to do so. On the contrary, they just stood still and stared at us like a flock of startled sheep.

Presently the sheep parted and the shepherd in the shape of Harût appeared looking, I reflected, the very picture of Abraham softened by a touch of the melancholia of Job, that is, as I have always imagined those patriarchs. He bowed to us with his usual Oriental courtesy, and we bowed back to him. Hans' bow, I may explain, was of the most peculiar nature, more like a *skulpat*, as the Boers call a land-tortoise, drawing its wrinkled head into its shell and putting it out again than anything else. Then Harût remarked in his peculiar English, which I suppose the White Kendah took for some tongue known only to magicians:

"So you get here, eh? Why you get here, how the devil you get here, eh?"

"We got here because you asked us to do so if we could," I answered, "and we thought it rude not to accept your invitation. For the rest, we came through a cave where you kept a tame snake, an ugly-looking reptile but very harmless to those who know how to deal with snakes and are not afraid of them as poor Bena was. If you can spare the skin I should like to have it to make myself a robe."

Harût looked at me with evident respect, muttering:

"Oh, Macumazana, you what you English call cool, quite cool! Is that all?"

"No," I answered. "Although you did not happen to notice us, we have been present at your church service, and heard and seen everything. For instance, we saw the wife of the lord here whom you stole away in Egypt, her that, being a liar, Harût, you swore you never stole. Also we heard her words after you had made her drunk with your tobacco smoke."

Now for once in his life Harût was, in sporting parlance, knocked out. He looked at us, then turning quite pale, lifted his eyes to heaven and rocked upon his feet as though he were about to fall.

"How you do it? How you do it, eh?" he queried in a weak voice.

"Never you mind how we did it, my friend," I answered loftily. "What we want to know is when you are going to hand over that lady to her husband."

"Not possible," he answered, recovering some of his tone. "First we kill you, first we kill her, she Nurse of the Child. While Child there, she stop there till she die."

"See here," broke in Ragnall. "Either you give me my wife or someone else will die. You will die, Harût. I am a stronger man than you are and unless you promise to give me my wife I will kill you now with this stick and my hands. Do not move or call out if you want to live."

"Lord," answered the old man with some dignity, "I know you can kill me, and if you kill me, I think I say thank you who no wish to live in so much trouble. But what good that, since in one minute then you die too, all of you, and lady she stop here till Black Kendah king take her to wife or she too die?"

"Let us talk," I broke in, treading warningly upon Ragnall's foot. "We have heard your Oracle and we know that you believe its words. It is said that we alone can help you to conquer the Black Kendah. If you will not promise what we ask, we will not help you. We will burn our powder and melt our lead, so that the guns we have cannot speak with Jana and with Simba, and after that we will do other things that I need not tell you. But if you promise what we ask, then we will fight for you against Jana and Simba and teach your men to use the fifty rifles which we have here with us, and by our help you shall conquer. Do you understand?"

He nodded and stroking his long beard, asked:

"What you want us promise, eh?"

"We want you to promise that after Jana is dead and the Black Kendah are driven away, you will give up to us unharmed that lady whom you have stolen. Also that you will bring her and us safely out of your country by the roads you know, and meanwhile that you will let this lord see his wife."

"Not last, no," replied Harût, "that not possible. That bring us all to grave. Also no good, 'cause her mind empty. For rest, you come to other place, sit down and eat while I talk with priests. Be afraid nothing; you quite safe."

"Why should we be afraid? It is you who should be afraid, you who stole the lady and brought Bena to his death. Do you not remember the words of your own Oracle, Harût?"

"Yes, I know words, but how *you* know them *that* I not know," he replied.

Then he issued some orders, as a result of which a guard formed itself about us and conducted us through the crowd and along the passage to the second court of the temple, which was now empty. Here the guard left us but remained at the mouth of the passage, keeping watch. Presently women brought us food and drink, of which Hans and I partook heartily though Ragnall, who was so near to his lost wife and yet so far away, could eat but little. Mingled joy because after these months of arduous search he found her yet alive, and fear lest she should again be taken from him for ever, deprived him of all appetite.

While we ate, priests to the number of about a dozen, who I suppose had been summoned by Harût, were admitted by the guard and, gathering out of earshot of us between the altar and the sanctuary, entered on an earnest discussion with him. Watching their faces I could see that there was a strong difference of opinion between them, about half taking one view on the matter of which they disputed, and half another. At length Harût made some proposition to which they all agreed. Then the door of the sanctuary was opened with a strange sort of key which one of the priests produced, showing a dark interior in which gleamed a white object, I suppose the statue of the Child. Harût and two others entered, the door being closed behind them. About five minutes later they appeared again and others, who listened earnestly and after renewed consultation signified assent by holding up the right hand. Now one of the priests walked to where we were and, bowing, begged us to advance to the altar. This we did, and were stood in a line in front of it, Hans being set in the middle place, while the priests ranged themselves on either side. Next Harût, having once more opened the door of the sanctuary, took his stand a little to the right of it and addressed us, not in English but in his own language, pausing at the end of each sentence that I might translate to Ragnall.

"Lords Macumazana and Igeza, and yellow man who is named Light-in-Darkness," he said, "we, the head priests of the Child, speaking on behalf of the White Kendah people with full authority so to do, have taken counsel together and of the wisdom of the Child as to the demands which you make of us. Those demands are: First, that after you have killed Jana and defeated the Black Kendah we should give over to you the white lady who was born in a far land to fill the office of Guardian of the Child, as is shown by the mark of the new moon upon her breast, but who, because for the second time we could not take her, became the wife of you, the Lord Igeza. Secondly, that we should conduct you and her safely out of our land to some place whence you can return to your own country. Both of these things we will do, because we know from of old that if once Jana is dead we shall have no cause to fear the Black Kendah any more, since we believe that then they will leave their home and go elsewhere, and therefore that we shall no longer need an Oracle to declare to us in what way Heaven will protect us from Jana and from them. Or if another Oracle should become necessary to us, doubtless in due season she will be found. Also we admit that we stole away this lady because we must, although she was the wife of one of you. But if we swear this, you on your part must also swear that you will stay with us till the end of the war, making our cause your cause and, if need be, giving your lives for us in battle. You must swear further that none of you will attempt to see or to take hence that lady who is named Guardian of the Child until we hand her over to you unharmed. If you will not swear these things, then since no blood may be shed in this holy place, here we will ring you round until you die of hunger and of thirst, or if you escape from this temple, then we will fall upon you and put you to death and fight our own battle with Jana as best we may."

"And if we make these promises how are we to know that you will keep yours?" I interrupted.

"Because the oath that we shall give you will be the oath of the Child that may not be broken."

"Then give it," I said, for although I did not altogether like the security, obviously it was the best to be had.

So very solemnly they laid their right hands upon the altar and "in the presence of the Child and the name of the Child and of all the White Kendah people," repeated after Harût a most solemn oath of which I have already given the substance. It called down on their heads a very dreadful doom in this world and the next, should it be broken either in the spirit or the letter; the said oath, however, to be only binding if we, on our part, swore to observe their terms and kept our engagement also in the spirit and the letter.

Then they asked us to fulfil our share of the pact and very considerately drew out of hearing while we discussed the matter; Harût, the only one of them who understood a word of English, retiring behind the sanctuary. At first I had difficulties with Ragnall, who was most unwilling to bind himself in any way. In the end, on my pointing out that nothing less than our lives were involved and probably that of his wife as well, also that no other course was open to us, he gave way, to my great relief.

Hans announced himself ready to swear anything, adding blandly that words mattered nothing, as afterwards we could do whatever seemed best in our own interests, whereon I read him a short moral lecture on the heinousness of perjury, which did not seem to impress him very much.

This matter settled, we called back the priests and informed them of our decision. Harût demanded that we should affirm it "by the Child," which we declined to do, saying that it was our custom to swear only in the name of our own God. Being a liberal-minded man who had travelled, Harût gave way on the point. So I swore first to the effect that I would fight for the White Kendah to the finish in consideration of the promises that they had made to us. I added that I would not attempt either to see or to interfere with the lady here known as the Guardian of the Child until the war was over or even to bring our existence to her knowledge, ending up, "so help me God," as I had done several times when giving evidence in a court of law.

Next Ragnall with a great effort repeated my oath in English, Harût listening carefully to every word and once or twice asking me to explain the exact meaning of some of them.

Lastly Hans, who seemed very bored with the whole affair, swore, also repeating the words after me and finishing on his own account with "so help me the reverend Predikant, the Baas's father," a form that he utterly declined to vary although it involved more explanations. When pressed, indeed, he showed considerable ingenuity by pointing out to the priests that to his mind my poor father stood in exactly the same relation to the Power above us as their Oracle did to the Child. He offered generously, however, to throw in the spirits of his grandfather and grandmother and some extraordinary divinity they worshipped, I think it was a hare, as an additional guarantee of good faith. This proposal the priests accepted gravely, whereon Hans whispered into my ear in Dutch:

"Those fools do not remember that when pressed by dogs the hare often doubles on its own spoor, and that your reverend father will be very pleased if I can play them the same trick with the white lady that they played with the Lord Igeza."

I only looked at him in reply, since the morality of Hans was past argument. It might perhaps be summed up in one sentence: To get the better of his neighbour in his master's service, honestly if possible; if not, by any means that came to his hand down to that of murder. At the bottom of his dark and mysterious heart Hans worshipped only one god, named Love, not of woman or child, but of my humble self. His principles were those of a rather sly but very high-class and exclusive dog, neither better nor worse. Still, when all is said and done, there are lower creatures in the world than high-class dogs. At least so the masters whom they adore are apt to think, especially if their watchfulness and courage have often saved them from death or disaster.

XVIII

The Embassy

The ceremonies were over and the priests, with the exception of Harût and two who remained to attend upon him, vanished, probably to inform the male and female hierophants of their result, and through these the whole people of the White Kendah. Old Harût stared at us for a little while, then said in English, which he always liked to talk when Ragnall was present, perhaps for the sake of practice:

"What you like do now, eh? P'r'aps wish fly back to Town of Child, for suppose this how you come. If so, please take me with you, because that save long ride."

"Oh! no," I answered. "We walked here through that hole where lived the Father of Snakes who died of fear when he saw us, and just mixed with the rest of you in the court of the temple."

"Good lie," said Harût admiringly, "very first-class lie! Wonder how you kill great snake, which we all think never die, for he live there hundred, hundred years; our people find him there when first they come to this country, and make him kind of god. Well, he nasty beast and best dead. I say, you like see Child? If so, come, for you our brothers now, only please take off hat and not speak."

I intimated that we should "like see Child," and led by Harût we entered the little sanctuary which was barely large enough to hold all of us. In a niche of the end wall stood the sacred effigy which Ragnall and I examined with a kind of reverent interest. It proved to be the statue of an infant about two feet high, cut, I imagine, from the base of a single but very large elephant's tusk, so ancient that the yellowish ivory had become rotten and was covered with a multitude of tiny fissures. Indeed, for its appearance I made up my mind that several thousands of years must have passed since the beast died from which this ivory was taken, especially as it had, I presume, always been carefully preserved under cover.

The workmanship of the object was excellent, that of a fine artist who, I should think, had taken some living infant for his model, perhaps a child of the Pharaoh of the day. Here I may say at once that there could be no doubt of its Egyptian origin, since on one side of the head was a single lock of hair, while the fourth finger of the right hand was held before the lips as though to enjoin silence. Both of these peculiarities, it will be remembered, are characteristic of the infant Horus, the child of Osiris and Isis, as portrayed in bronzes and temple carvings. So at least Ragnall, who recently had studied many such effigies in Egypt, informed me later. There was nothing else in the place except an ancient, string-seated chair of ebony, adorned with inlaid ivory patterns; an effigy of a snake in porcelain, showing that serpent worship was in some way mixed up with their religion; and two rolls of papyrus, at least that is what they looked like, which were laid in the niche with the statue. These rolls, to my disappointment, Harût refused to allow us to examine or even to touch.

After we had left the sanctuary I asked Harût when this figure was brought to their land. He replied that it came when they came, at what date he could not tell us as it was so long ago, and that with it came the worship and the ceremonies of their religion.

In answer to further questions he added that this figure, which seemed to be of ivory, contained the spirits which ruled the sun and the moon, and through them the world. This, said Ragnall, was just a piece of Egyptian theology, preserved down to our own times in a remote corner of Africa, doubtless by descendants of dwellers on the Nile who had been driven thence in some national catastrophe, and brought away with them their faith and one of the effigies of their gods. Perhaps they fled at the time of the Persian invasion by Cambyses.

After we had emerged from this deeply interesting shrine, which was locked behind us, Harût led us, not through the passage connecting it with the stone house that we knew was occupied by Ragnall's wife in her capacity as Guardian of the Child, or a latter-day personification of Isis, Lady of the Moon, at which house he cast many longing glances, but back through the two courts and the pylon to the gateway of the temple. Here on the road by which we had entered the place, a fact which we did not mention to him, he paused and addressed us.

"Lords," he said, "now you and the People of the White Kendah are one; your ends are their ends, your fate is their fate, their secrets are your secrets. You, Lord Igeza, work for a reward, namely the person of that lady whom we took from you on the Nile."

"How did you do that?" interrupted Ragnall when I had interpreted.

"Lord, we watched you. We knew when you came to Egypt; we followed you in Egypt, whither we had journeyed on our road to

England once more to seek our Oracles, till the day of our opportunity dawned. Then at night we called her and she obeyed the call, as she must do whose mind we have taken away—ask me not how—and brought her to dwell with us, she who is marked from her birth with the holy sign and wears upon her breast certain charmed stones and a symbol that for thousands of years have adorned the body of the Child and those of its Oracles. Do you remember a company of Arabs whom you saw riding on the banks of the Great River on the day before the night when she was lost to you? We were with that company and on our camels we bore her thence, happy and unharmed to this our land, as I trust, when all is done, we shall bear her back again and you with her."

"I trust so also, for you have wrought me a great wrong," said Ragnall briefly, "perhaps a greater wrong than I know at present, for how came it that my boy was killed by an elephant?"

"Ask that question of Jana and not of me," Harût answered darkly. Then he went on: "You also, Lord Macumazana, work for a reward, the countless store of ivory which your eyes have beheld lying in the burial place of elephants beyond the Tava River. When you have slain Jana who watches the store, and defeated the Black Kendah who serve him, it is yours and we will give you camels to bear it, or some of it, for all cannot be carried, to the sea where it can be taken away in ships. As for the yellow man, I think that he seeks no reward who soon will inherit all things."

"The old witch-doctor means that I am going to die," remarked Hans expectorating reflectively. "Well, Baas, I am quite ready, if only Jana and certain others die first. Indeed I grow too old to fight and travel as I used to do, and therefore shall be glad to pass to some land where I become young again."

"Stuff and rubbish!" I exclaimed, then turned and listened to Harût who, not understanding our Dutch conversation, was speaking once more.

"Lords," he said, "these paths which run east and west are the real approach to the mountain top and the temple, not that which, as I suppose, led you through the cave of the old serpent. The road to the west, which wanders round the base of the hill to a pass in those distant mountains and thence across the deserts to the north, is so easy to stop that by it we need fear no attack. With this eastern road the case is, however, different, as I shall now show you, if you will ride with me."

Then he gave some orders to two attendant priests who departed at a run and presently reappeared at the head of a small train of camels which had been hidden, I know not where. We mounted and, following the road across a flat piece of ground, found that not more than half a mile away was another precipitous ridge of rock which had presumably once formed the lip of an outer crater. This ridge, however, was broken away for a width of two or three hundred yards, perhaps by some outrush of lava, the road running through the centre of the gap on which schanzes had been built here and there for purposes of defence. Looking at these I saw that they were very old and inefficient and asked when they had been erected. Harût replied about a century before when the last war took place with the Black Kendah, who had been finally driven off at this spot, for then the White Kendah were more numerous than at present.

"So Simba knows this road?" I said.

"Yes, Lord, and Jana knows it also, for he fought in that war and still at times visits us here and kills any whom he may meet. Only to the temple he has never dared to come."

Now I wondered whether we had really seen Jana in the forest on the previous night, but coming to the conclusion that it was useless to investigate the matter, made no inquiries, especially as these would have revealed to Harût the route by which we approached the temple. Only I pointed out to him that proper defences should be put up here without delay, that is if they meant to make a stronghold of the mountain.

"We do, Lord," he answered, "since we are not strong enough to attack the Black Kendah in their own country or to meet them in pitched battle on the plain. Here and in no other place must be fought the last fight between Jana and the Child. Therefore it will be your task to build walls cunningly, so that when they come we may defeat Jana and the hosts of the Black Kendah."

"Do you mean that this elephant will accompany Simba and his soldiers, Harût?"

"Without doubt, Lord, since he has always done so from the beginning. Jana is tame to the king and certain priests of the Black Kendah, whose forefathers have fed him for generations, and will obey their orders. Also he can think for himself, being an evil spirit and invulnerable."

"His left eye and the tip of his trunk are not invulnerable," I remarked, "though from what I saw of him I should say there is no doubt about his being able to think for himself. Well, I am glad the brute is coming as I have an account to settle with him."

"As he, Lord, who does not forget, has an account to settle with you and your servant, Light-in-Darkness," commented Harût in an unpleasant and suggestive tone.

Then after we had taken a few measurements and Ragnall, who understands such matters, had drawn a rough sketch of the place in his pocket-book to serve as data for our proposed scheme of fortifications, we pursued our journey back to the town, where we had left all our stores and there were many things to be arranged. It proved to be quite a long ride, down the eastern slope of the mountain which was easy to negotiate, although like the rest of this strange hill it was covered with dense cedar forests that also seemed to me to have defensive possibilities. Reaching its foot at length we were obliged to make a detour by certain winding paths to avoid ground that was too rough for the camels, so that in the end we did not come to our own house in the Town of the Child till about midday.

Glad enough were we to reach it, since all three of us were tired out with our terrible night journey and the anxious emotions that we had undergone. Indeed, after we had eaten we lay down and I rejoiced to see that, notwithstanding the state of mental excitement into which the discovery of his wife had plunged him, Ragnall was the first of us to fall asleep.

About five o'clock we were awakened by a messenger from Harût, who requested our attendance on important business at a kind of meeting-house which stood at a little distance on an open place where the White Kendah bartered produce. Here we found Harût and about twenty of the headmen seated in the shade of a thatched roof, while behind them, at a respectful distance, stood quite a hundred of the White Kendah. Most of these, however, were women and children, for as I have said the greater part of the male population was absent from the town because of the commencement of the harvest.

We were conducted to chairs, or rather stools of honour, and when we two had seated ourselves, Hans taking his stand behind us, Harût rose and informed us that an embassy had arrived from the Black Kendah which was about to be admitted.

Presently they came, five of them, great, truculent-looking fellows of a surprising blackness, unarmed, for they had not been allowed to bring their weapons in to the town, but adorned with the usual silver chains across their breasts to show their rank, and other savage finery. In the man who was their leader I recognized one of those messengers who had accosted us when first we entered their territory on our way from the south, before that fight in which I was taken prisoner. Stepping forward and addressing himself to Harût, he said:

"A while ago, O Prophet of the Child, I, the messenger of the god Jana, speaking through the mouth of Simba the King, gave to you and your brother Marût a certain warning to which you did not listen. Now Jana has Marût, and again I come to warn you, Harût."

"If I remember right," interrupted Harût blandly, "I think that on that occasion two of you delivered the message and that the Child marked one of you upon the brow. If Jana has my brother, say, where is yours?"

"We warned you," went on the messenger, "and you cursed us in the name of the Child."

"Yes," interrupted Harût again, "we cursed you with three curses. The first was the curse of Heaven by storm or drought, which has fallen upon you. The second was the curse of famine, which is falling upon you; and the third was the curse of war, which is yet to fall on you."

"It is of war that we come to speak," replied the messenger, diplomatically avoiding the other two topics which perhaps he found it awkward to discuss.

"That is foolish of you," replied the bland Harût, "seeing that the other day you matched yourselves against us with but small success. Many of you were killed but only a very few of us, and the white lord whom you took captive escaped out of your hands and from the tusks of Jana who, I think, now lacks an eye. If he is a god, how comes it that he lacks an eye and could not kill an unarmed white man?"

"Let Jana answer for himself, as he will do ere long, O Harût. Meanwhile, these are the words of Jana spoken through the mouth of Simba the King: The Child has destroyed my harvest and therefore I demand this of the people of the Child—that they give me three-fourths of their harvest, reaping the same and delivering it on the south bank of the River Tava. That they give me the two white lords to be sacrificed to me. That they give the white lady who is Guardian of the Child to be a wife of Simba the King, and with her a hundred virgins of your people. That the image of the Child be brought to the god Jana in the presence of his priests and Simba the King. These are the demands of Jana spoken through the mouth of Simba the King."

Watching, I saw a thrill of horror shake the forms of Harût and of all those with him as the full meaning of these, to them, most impious requests sank into their minds. But he only asked very quietly:

"And if we refuse the demands, what then?"

"Then," shouted the messenger insolently, "then Jana declares war upon you, the last war of all, war till every one of your men be dead and the Child you worship is burnt to grey ashes with fire. War till your women are taken as slaves and the corn which you refuse is stored in our grain pits and your land is a waste and your name forgotten. Already the hosts of Jana are gathered and the trumpet of Jana calls them to the fight. To-morrow or the next day they advance upon you, and ere the moon is full not one of you will be left to look upon her."

Harût rose, and walking from under the shed, turned his back upon the envoys and stared at the distant line of great mountains which stood out far away against the sky. Out of curiosity I followed him and observed that these mountains were no longer visible. Where they had been was nothing but a line of black and heavy cloud. After looking for a while he returned and addressing the envoys, said quite casually:

"If you will be advised by me, friends, you will ride hard for the river. There is such rain upon the mountains as I have never seen before, and you will be fortunate if you cross it before the flood comes down, the greatest flood that has happened in our day."

This intelligence seemed to disturb the messengers, for they too stepped out of the shed and stared at the mountains, muttering to each other something that I could not understand. Then they returned and with a fine appearance of indifference demanded an immediate answer to their challenge.

"Can you not guess it?" answered Harût. Then changing his tone he drew himself to his full height and thundered out at them: "Get you back to your evil spirit of a god that hides in the shape of a beast of the forest and to his slave who calls himself a king, and say to them: 'Thus speaks the Child to his rebellious servants, the Black Kendah dogs: Swim my river when you can, which will not be yet, and come up against me when you will; for whenever you come I shall be ready for you. You are already dead, O Jana. You are already dead, O Simba the slave. You are scattered and lost, O dogs of the Black Kendah, and the home of such of you as remain shall be far away in a barren land, where you must dig deep for water and live upon the wild game because there little corn will grow.' Now begone, and swiftly, lest you stop here for ever."

So they turned and went, leaving me full of admiration for the histrionic powers of Harût.

I must add, however, that being without doubt a keen observer of the weather conditions of the neighbourhood, he was quite right about the rain upon the mountains, which by the way never extended to the territory of the People of the Child. As we heard afterwards, the flood came down just as the envoys reached the river; indeed, one of them was drowned in attempting its crossing, and for fourteen days after this it remained impassable to an army.

That very evening we began our preparations to meet an attack which was now inevitable. Putting aside the supposed rival powers of the tribal divinities worshipped under the names of the Child and Jana, which, while they added a kind of Homeric interest to the contest, could, we felt, scarcely affect an issue that must be decided with cold steel and other mortal weapons, the position of the White Kendah was serious indeed. As I think I have said, in all they did not number more than about two thousand men between the ages of twenty and fifty-five, or, including lads between fourteen and twenty and old men still able-bodied between fifty-five and seventy, say two thousand seven hundred capable of some sort of martial service. To these might be added something under two thousand women, since among this dwindling folk, oddly enough, from causes that I never ascertained, the males out-numbered the females, which accounted for their marriage customs that were, by comparison with those of most African peoples, monogamous. At any rate only the rich among them had more than one wife, while the poor or otherwise ineligible often had none at all, since inter-marriage with other races and above all with the Black Kendah dwelling beyond the river was so strictly taboo that it was punishable with death or expulsion.

Against this little band the Black Kendah could bring up twenty thousand men, besides boys and aged persons who with the women would probably be left to defend their own country, that is, not less than ten to one. Moreover, all of these enemies would be fighting with the courage of despair, since quite three-fourths of their crops with many of their cattle and sheep had been destroyed by the terrific hail-burst that I have described. Therefore, since no other corn was available in the surrounding land, where they dwelt alone encircled by deserts, either they must capture that of the White Kendah, or suffer terribly from starvation until a year later when another harvest ripened.

The only points I could see in favour of the People of the Child were that they would fight on the vantage ground of their mountain stronghold, a formidable position if properly defended. Also they would have the benefit of the skill and knowledge of Ragnall and myself. Lastly, the enemy must face our rifles. Neither the White nor the Black Kendah, I should say, possessed any guns, except a few antiquated flintlock weapons that the former had captured from some nomadic tribe and kept as curiosities. Why this was the case I do not know, since undoubtedly at times the White Kendah traded in camels and corn with Arabs who wandered as far as the Sudan, or Egypt, nomadic tribes to whom even then firearms were known, although perhaps rarely used by them. But so it was, possibly because of some old law or prejudice which forbade their introduction into the country, or mayhap of the difficulty of procuring powder and lead, or for the reason that they had none to teach them the use of such new-fangled weapons.

Now it will be remembered that, on the chance of their proving useful, Ragnall, in addition to our own sporting rifles, had brought with him to Africa fifty Snider rifles with an ample supply of ammunition, the same that I had trouble in passing through the Customs at Durban, all of which had arrived safely at the Town of the Child. Clearly our first duty was to make the best possible use of this invaluable store. To that end I asked Harût to select seventy-five of the boldest and most intelligent young men among his people, and to hand them over to me and Hans for instruction in musketry. We had only fifty rifles but I drilled seventy-five men, or fifty per cent. more, that some might be ready to replace any who fell.

From dawn to dark each day Hans and I worked at trying to convert these Kendah into sharpshooters. It was no easy task with men, however willing, who till then had never held a gun, especially as I must be very sparing of the ammunition necessary to practice, of which of course our supply was limited. Still we taught them how to take cover, how to fire and to cease from firing at a word of command, also to hold the rifles low and waste no shot. To make marksmen of them was more than I could hope to do under the circumstances.

With the exception of these men nearly the entire male population were working day and night to get in the harvest. This proved a very difficult business, both because some of the crops were scarcely fit and because all the grain had to be carried on camels to be stored in and at the back of the second court of the temple, the only place where it was likely to be safe. Indeed in the end a great deal was left unreaped. Then the herds of cattle and breeding camels which grazed on the farther sides of the Holy Mount must be brought into places of safety, glens in the forest on its slope, and forage stacked to feed them. Also it was necessary to provide scouts to keep watch along the river.

Lastly, the fortifications in the mountain pass required unceasing labour and attention. This was the task of Ragnall, who fortunately in his youth, before he succeeded unexpectedly to the title, was for some years an officer in the Royal Engineers and therefore thoroughly understood that business. Indeed he understood it rather too well, since the result of his somewhat complicated and scientific scheme of defence was a little confusing to the simple native mind. However, with the assistance of all the priests and of all the women and children who were not engaged in provisioning the Mount, he built wall after wall and redoubt after redoubt, if that is the right word, to say nothing of the shelter trenches he dug and many pitfalls, furnished at the bottom with sharp stakes, which he hollowed out wherever the soil could be easily moved, to discomfit a charging enemy.

Indeed, when I saw the amount of work he had concluded in ten days, which was not until I joined him on the mountain, I was quite astonished.

About this time a dispute arose as to whether we should attempt to prevent the Black Kendah from crossing the river which was now running down, a plan that some of the elders favoured. At last the controversy was referred to me as head general and I decided against anything of the sort. It seemed to me that our force was too small, and that if I took the rifle-men a great deal of ammunition might be expended with poor result. Also in the event of any reverse or when we were finally driven back, which must happen, there might be difficulty about remounting the camels, our only means of escape from the horsemen who would possibly gallop us down. Moreover the Tava had several fords, any one of which might be selected by the enemy. So it was arranged that we should make our first and last stand upon the Holy Mount.

On the fourteenth night from new moon our swift camel-scouts who were posted in relays between the Tava and the Mount reported that the Black Kendah were gathered in thousands upon the farther side of the river, where they were engaged in celebrating magical ceremonies. On the fifteenth night the scouts reported that they were crossing the river, about five thousand horsemen and fifteen thousand foot soldiers, and that at the head of them marched the huge god-elephant Jana, on which rode Simba the King and a lame priest (evidently my friend whose foot had been injured by the pistol), who acted as a mahout. This part of the story I confess I did not believe, since it seemed to me impossible that anyone could ride upon that mad rogue, Jana. Yet, as subsequent events showed, it was in fact true. I suppose that in certain hands the beast became tame. Or perhaps it was drugged.

Two nights later, for the Black Kendah advanced but slowly, spreading themselves over the country in order to collect such crops as had not been gathered through lack of time or because they were still unripe, we saw flames and smoke arising from the Town of the Child beneath us, which they had fired. Now we knew that the time of trial had come and until near midnight men, women and children worked feverishly finishing or trying to finish the fortifications and making every preparation in our power.

Our position was that we held a very strong post, that is, strong against an enemy unprovided with big guns or even firearms, which, as all other possible approaches had been blocked, was only assailable by direct frontal attack from the east. In the pass we had three main lines of defence, one arranged behind the other and separated by distances of a few hundred yards. Our last refuge was furnished by the walls of the temple itself, in the rear of which were camped the whole White Kendah tribe, save a few hundred who were employed in watching the herds of camels and stock in almost inaccessible positions on the northern slopes of the Mount.

There were perhaps five thousand people of both sexes and every age gathered in this camp, which was so well provided with food and water that it could have stood a siege of several months. If, however, our defences should be carried there was no possibility of escape, since we learned from our scouts that the Black Kendah, who by tradition and through spies were well acquainted with every feature of the country, had detached a party of several thousand men to watch the western road and the slopes of the mountain, in case we should try to break out by that route. The only one remaining, that which ran through the cave of the serpent, we had taken the precaution of blocking up with great stones, lest through it our flank should be turned.

In short, we were rats in a trap and where we were there we must either conquer or die—unless indeed we chose to surrender, which for most of us would mean a fate worse than death.

XIX

ALLAN QUATERMAIN MISSES

I had made my last round of the little corps that I facetiously named "The Sharpshooters," though to tell the truth at shooting they were anything but sharp, and seen that each man was in his place behind a wall with a reserve man squatted at the rear of every pair of them, waiting to take his rifle if either of these should fall. Also I had made sure that all of them had twenty rounds of ammunition in their skin pouches. More I would not serve out, fearing lest in excitement or in panic they might fire away to the last cartridge uselessly, as before now even disciplined white troops have been known to do. Therefore I had arranged that certain old men of standing who could be trusted should wait in a place of comparative safety behind the line, carrying all our reserve ammunition, which amounted, allowing for what had been expended in practice, to nearly sixty rounds per rifle. This they were instructed to deliver from their wallets to the firing line in small lots when they saw that it was necessary and not before.

It was, I admit, an arrangement apt to miscarry in the heat of desperate battle, but I could think of none better, since it was absolutely necessary that no shot should be wasted.

After a few words of exhortation and caution to the natives who acted as sergeants to the corps, I returned to a bough shelter that had been built for us behind a rock to get a few hours' sleep, if that were possible, before the fight began.

Here I found Ragnall, who had just come in from his inspection. This was of a much more extensive nature than my own, since it involved going round some furlongs of the rough walls and trenches that he had prepared with so much thought and care, and seeing that the various companies of the White Kendah were ready to play their part in the defence of them.

He was tired and rather excited, too much so to sleep at once. So we talked a little while, first about the prospects of the morrow's battle, as to which we were, to say the least of it, dubious, and afterwards of other things. I asked him if during his stay in this place, while I was below at the town or later, he had heard or seen anything of his wife.

"Nothing," he answered. "These priests never speak of her, and if they did Harût is the only one of them that I can really understand. Moreover, I have kept my word strictly and, even when I had occasion to see to the blocking of the western road, made a circuit on the mountain-top in order to avoid the neighbourhood of that house where I suppose she lives Oh! Quatermain, my friend, my case is a hard one, as you would think if the woman you loved with your whole heart were shut up within a few hundred yards of you and no communication with her possible after all this time of separation and agony. What makes it worse is, as I gathered from what Harût said the other day, that she is still out of her mind."

"That has some consolations," I replied, "since the mindless do not suffer. But if such is the case, how do you account for what you and poor Savage saw that night in the Town of the Child? It was not altogether a phantasy, for the dress you described was the same we saw her wearing at the Feast of the First-fruits."

"I don't know what to make of it, Quatermain, except that many strange things happen in the world which we mock at as insults to our limited intelligence because we cannot understand them." (Very soon I was to have another proof of this remark.) "But what are you driving at? You are keeping something back."

"Only this, Ragnall. If your wife were utterly mad I cannot conceive how it came about that she searched you out and spoke to you even in a vision—for the thing was not an individual dream since both you and Savage saw her. Nor did she actually visit you in the flesh, as the door never opened and the spider's web across it was not broken. So it comes to this: either some part of her is not mad but can still exercise sufficient will to project itself upon your senses, or she is dead and her disembodied spirit did this thing. Now we know that she is not dead, for we have seen her and Harût has confessed as much. Therefore I maintain that, whatever may be her temporary state, she must still be fundamentally of a reasonable mind, as she is of a natural body. For instance, she may only be hypnotized, in which case the spell will break one day."

"Thank you for that thought, old fellow. It never occurred to me and it gives me new hope. Now listen! If I should come to grief in this business, which is very likely, and you should survive, you will do your best to get her home; will you not? Here is a codicil to my will which I drew up after that night of dream, duly witnessed by Savage and Hans.

It leaves to you whatever sums may be necessary in this connexion and something over for yourself. Take it, it is best in your keeping, especially as if you should be killed it has no value."

"Of course I will do my best," I answered as I put away the paper in my pocket. "And now don't let us take any more thought of being killed, which may prevent us from getting the sleep we want. I don't mean to be killed if I can help it. I mean to give those beggars, the Black Kendah, such a doing as they never had before, and then start for the coast with you and Lady Ragnall, as, God willing, we shall do. Good night."

After this I slept like a top for some hours, as I believe Ragnall did also. When I awoke, which happened suddenly and completely, the first thing that I saw was Hans seated at the entrance to my little shelter smoking his corn-cob pipe, and nursing the single-barrelled rifle, Intombi, on his knee. I asked him what the time was, to which he replied that it lacked two hours to dawn. Then I asked him why he had not been sleeping. He replied that he had been asleep and dreamed a dream. Idly enough I inquired what dream, to which he replied:

"Rather a strange one, Baas, for a man who is about to go into battle. I dreamed that I was in a large place that was full of quiet. It was light there, but I could not see any sun or moon, and the air was very soft and tasted like food and drink, so much so, Baas, that if anyone had offered me a cup quite full of the best 'Cape smoke' I should have told him to take it away. Then, Baas, suddenly I saw your reverend father, the Predikant, standing beside me and looking just as he used to look, only younger and stronger and very happy, and so of course knew at once that I was dead and in hell. Only I wondered where the fire that does not go out might be, for I could not see it. Presently your reverend father said to me: 'Good day, Hans. So you have come here at last. Now tell me, how has it gone with my son, the Baas Allan? Have you looked after him as I told you to do?'

"I answered: 'I have looked after him as well as I could, O reverend sir. Little enough have I done; still, not once or twice or three times only have I offered up my life for him as was my duty, and yet we both have lived.' And that I might be sure he heard the best of me, as was but natural, I told him the times, Baas, making a big story out of small things, although all the while I could see that he knew exactly just where I began to lie and just where I stopped from lying. Still he did not scold me, Baas; indeed, when I had finished, he said:

"'Well done, O good and faithful servant,' words that I think I have heard him use before when he was alive, Baas, and used to preach to us for such a long time on Sunday afternoons. Then he asked: 'And how goes it with Baas Allan, my son, now, Hans?' to which I replied:

"'The Baas Allan is going to fight a very great battle in which he may well fall, and if I could feel sorry here, which I can't, I should weep, O reverend sir, because I have died before that battle began and therefore cannot stand at his side in the battle and be killed for him as a servant should for his master!'

"'You will stand at his side in the battle,' said your reverend father, 'and those things which you desire you will do, as it is fitting that you should. And afterwards, Hans, you will make report to me of how the battle went and of what honour my son has won therein. Moreover, know this, Hans, that though while you live in the world you seem to see many other things, they are but dreams, since in all the world there is but one real thing, and its name is Love, which if it be but strong enough, the stars themselves must obey, for it is the king of every one of them, and all who dwell in them worship it day and night under many names for ever and for ever, Amen.'

"What he meant by that I am sure I don't know, Baas, seeing that I have never thought much of women, at least not for many years since my last old vrouw went and drank herself to death after lying in her sleep on the baby which I loved much better than I did her, Baas.

"Well, before I could ask him, or about hell either, he was gone like a whiff of smoke from a rifle mouth in a strong wind."

Hans paused, puffed at his pipe, spat upon the ground in his usual reflective way and asked:

"Is the Baas tired of the dream or would he like to hear the rest?"

"I should like to hear the rest," I said in a low voice, for I was strangely moved.

"Well, Baas, while I was standing in that place which was so full of quiet, turning my hat in my hands and wondering what work they would set me to there among the devils, I looked up. There I saw coming towards me two very beautiful women, Baas, who had their arms round each other's necks. They were dressed in white, with the little hard things that are found in shells hanging about them, and bright stones in their hair. And as they came, Baas, wherever they set a foot flowers sprang up, very pretty flowers, so that all their path across the quiet place was marked with flowers. Birds too sang as they passed, at least I think they were birds though I could not see them."

"What were they like, Hans?" I whispered.

"One of them, Baas, the taller I did not know. But the other I knew well enough; it was she whose name is holy, not to be mentioned. Yet I must mention that name; it was the Missie Marie herself as last we saw her alive many, many years ago, only grown a hundred times more beautiful."*

Now I groaned, and Hans went on:

"The two White Ones came up to me, and stood looking at me with eyes that were more soft than those of bucks. Then the Missie Marie said to the other: 'This is Hans of whom I have so often told you, O Star.'"

Here I groaned again, for how did this Hottentot know that name, or rather its sweet rendering?

"Then she who was called Star asked, 'How goes it with one who is the heart of all three of us, O Hans?' Yes, Baas, those Shining Ones joined *me*, the dirty little Hottentot in my old clothes and smelling of tobacco, with themselves when they spoke of you, for I knew they were speaking of you, Baas, which made me think I must be drunk, even there in the quiet place. So I told them all that I had told your reverend father, and a very great deal more, for they seemed never to be tired of listening. And once, when I mentioned that sometimes, while pretending to be asleep, I had heard you praying aloud at night for the Missie Marie who died for you, and for another who had been your wife whose name I did not remember but who had also died, they both cried a little, Baas. Their tears shone like crystals and smelt like that stuff in a little glass tube which Harût said that he brought from some far land when he put a drop or two on your handkerchief, after you were faint from the pain in your leg at the house yonder. Or perhaps it was the flowers that smelt, for where the tears fell there sprang up white lilies shaped like two babes' hands held together in prayer."

Hearing this, I hid my face in my hands lest Hans should see human tears unscented with attar of roses, and bade him continue.

"Baas, the White One who was called Star, asked me of your son, the young Baas Harry, and I told her that when last I had seen him he was strong and well and would make a bigger man than you were, whereat

---

* See the book called *Marie* by H. Rider Haggard.

she sighed and shook her head. Then the Missie Marie said: 'Tell the Baas, Hans, that I also have a child which he will see one day, but it is not a son.'

"After this they, too, said something about Love, but what it was I cannot remember, since even as I repeat this dream to you it is beginning to slip away from me fast as a swallow skimming the water. Their last words, however, I do remember. They were: 'Say to the Baas that we who never met in life, but who here are as twin sisters, wait and count the years and count the months and count the days and count the hours and count the minutes and count the seconds until once more he shall hear our voices calling to him across the night.' That's what they say, Baas. Then they were gone and only the flowers remained to show that they had been standing there.

"Now I set off to bring you the message and travelled a very long way at a great rate; if Jana himself had been after me I could not have gone more fast. At last I got out of that quiet place and among mountains where there were dark kloofs, and there in the kloofs I heard Zulu impis singing their war-song; yes, they sang the *ingoma* or something very like it. Now suddenly in the pass of the mountains along which I sped, there appeared before me a very beautiful woman whose skin shone like the best copper coffee kettle after I have polished it, Baas. She was dressed in a leopard-like moocha and wore on her shoulders a fur kaross, and about her neck a circlet of blue beads, and from her hair there rose one crane's feather tall as a walking-stick, and in her hand she held a little spear. No flowers sprang beneath her feet when she walked towards me and no birds sang, only the air was filled with the sound of a royal salute which rolled among the mountains like the roar of thunder, and her eyes flashed like summer lightning."

Now I let my hands fall and stared at him, for well I knew what was coming.

"'Stand, yellow man!' she said, 'and give me the royal salute.'

"So I gave her the *Bayéte*, though who she might be I did not know, since I did not think it wise to stay to ask her if it were hers of right, although I should have liked to do so. Then she said: 'The Old Man on the plain yonder and those two pale White Ones have talked to you of their love for your master, the Lord Macumazana. I tell you, little Yellow Dog, that they do not know what love can be. There is more love for him in my eyes alone than they have in all that makes them fair. Say it to the Lord Macumazana that, as I know well, he goes down to battle and that the Lady Mameena will be with him in the battle as, though he saw her not, she has been with him in other battles, and will be with him till the River of Time has run over the edge of the world and is lost beyond the sun. Let him remember this when Jana rushes on and death is very near to him to-day, and let him look—for then perchance he shall see me. Begone now, Yellow Dog, to the heels of your master, and play your part well in the battle, for of what you do or leave undone you shall give account to me. Say that Mameena sends her greetings to the Lord Macumazana and that she adds this, that when the Old Man and the White ones told you that Love is the secret blood of the worlds which makes them to be they did not lie. Love reigns and I, Mameena, am its priestess, and the heart of Macumazana is my holy house.'

"Then, Baas, I tumbled off a precipice and woke up here; and, Baas, as we may not light a fire I have kept some coffee hot for you buried in warm ashes," and without another word he went to fetch that coffee, leaving me shaken and amazed.

For what kind of a dream was it which revealed to an old Hottentot all these mysteries and hidden things about persons whom he had never seen and of whom I had never spoken to him? My father and my wife Marie might be explained, for with these he had been mixed up, but how about Stella and above all Mameena, although of course it was possible that he had heard of the latter, who made some stir in her time? But to hit her off as he had done in all her pride, splendour, and dominion of desire!

Well, that was his story which, perhaps fortunately, I lacked time to analyse or brood upon, since there was much in it calculated to unnerve a man just entering the crisis of a desperate fray. Indeed a minute or so later, as I was swallowing the last of the coffee, messengers arrived about some business, I forget what, sent by Ragnall I think, who had risen before I woke. I turned to give the pannikin to Hans, but he had vanished in his snake-like fashion, so I threw it down upon the ground and devoted my mind to the question raised in Ragnall's message.

Next minute scouts came in who had been watching the camp of the Black Kendah all night.

These were sleeping not more than half a mile away, in an open place on the slope of the hill with pickets thrown out round them, intending to advance upon us, it was said, as soon as the sun rose, since because of their number they feared lest to march at night should throw them into confusion and, in case of their falling into an ambush, bring about a disaster. Such at least was the story of two spies whom our people had captured.

There had been some question as to whether we should not attempt a night attack upon their camp, of which I was rather in favour. After full debate, however, the idea had been abandoned, owing to the fewness of our numbers, the dislike which the White Kendah shared with the Black of attempting to operate in the dark, and the well chosen position of our enemy, whom it would be impossible to rush before we were discovered by their outposts. What I hoped in my heart was that they might try to rush us, notwithstanding the story of the two captured spies, and in the gloom, after the moon had sunk low and before the dawn came, become entangled in our pitfalls and outlying entrenchments, where we should be able to destroy a great number of them. Only on the previous afternoon that cunning old fellow, Hans, had pointed out to me how advantageous such an event would be to our cause and, while agreeing with him, I suggested that probably the Black Kendah knew this as well as we did, as the prisoners had told us.

Yet that very thing happened, and through Hans himself. Thus: Old Harût had come to me just one hour before the dawn to inform me that all our people were awake and at their stations, and to make some last arrangements as to the course of the defence, also about our final concentration behind the last line of walls and in the first court of the temple, if we should be driven from the outer entrenchments. He was telling me that the Oracle of the Child had uttered words at the ceremony that night which he and all the priests considered were of the most favourable import, news to which I listened with some impatience, feeling as I did that this business had passed out of the range of the Child and its Oracle. As he spoke, suddenly through the silence that precedes the dawn, there floated to our ears the unmistakable sound of a rifle. Yes, a rifle shot, half a mile or so away, followed by the roaring murmur of a great camp unexpectedly alarmed at night.

"Who can have fired that?" I asked. "The Black Kendah have no guns."

He replied that he did not know, unless some of my fifty men had left their posts.

While we were investigating the matter, scouts rushed in with the intelligence that the Black Kendah, thinking apparently that they were being attacked, had broken camp and were advancing towards us. We passed a warning all down the lines and stood to arms. Five minutes later, as I stood listening to that approaching roar, filled with every kind of fear and melancholy foreboding such as the hour and the occasion might well have evoked, through the gloom, which was dense, the moon being hidden behind the hill, I thought I caught sight of something running towards me like a crouching man. I lifted my rifle to fire but, reflecting that it might be no more than a hyena and fearing to provoke a fusilade from my half-trained company, did not do so.

Next instant I was glad indeed, for immediately on the other side of the wall behind which I was standing I heard a well-known voice gasp out:

"Don't shoot, Baas, it is I."

"What have you been doing, Hans?" I said as he scrambled over the wall to my side, limping a little as I fancied.

"Baas," he puffed, "I have been paying the Black Kendah a visit. I crept down between their stupid outposts, who are as blind in the dark as a bat in daytime, hoping to find Jana and put a bullet into his leg or trunk. I didn't find him, Baas, although I heard him. But one of their captains stood up in front of a watchfire, giving a good shot. My bullet found *him*, Baas, for he tumbled back into the fire making the sparks fly this way and that. Then I ran and, as you see, got here quite safely."

"Why did you play that fool's trick?" I asked, "seeing that it ought to have cost you your life?"

"I shall die just when I have to die, not before, Baas," he replied in the intervals of reloading the little rifle. "Also it was the trick of a wise man, not of a fool, seeing that it has made the Black Kendah think that we were attacking them and caused them to hurry on to attack *us* in the dark over ground that they do not know. Listen to them coming!"

As he spoke a roar of sound told us that the great charge had swept round a turn there was in the pass and was heading towards us up the straight. Ivory horns brayed, captains shouted orders, the very mountains shook beneath the beating of thousands of feet of men and horses, while in one great yell that echoed from the cliffs and forests went up the battle-cry of "*Jana! Jana!*"—a mixed tumult of noise which contrasted very strangely with the utter silence in our ranks.

"They will be among the pitfalls presently," sniggered Hans, shifting his weight nervously from one leg on to the other. "Hark! they are going into them."

It was true. Screams of fear and pain told me that the front ranks had begun to fall, horse and foot together, into the cunningly devised snares of which with so much labour we had dug many, concealing them with earth spread over thin wickerwork, or rather interlaced boughs. Into them went the forerunners, to be pierced by the sharp, fire-hardened stakes set at the bottom of each pit. Vainly did those who were near enough to understand their danger call to the ranks behind to stop. They could not or would not comprehend, and had no room to extend their front. Forward surged the human torrent, thrusting all in front of it to death by wounds or suffocation in those deadly holes, till one by one they were filled level with the ground by struggling men and horses, over whom the army still rushed on.

How many perished there I do not know, but after the battle was over we found scarcely a pit that was not crowded to the brim with dead. Truly this device of Ragnall's, for if I had conceived the idea, which was unfamiliar to the Kendah, it was he who had carried it out in so masterly a fashion, had served us well.

Still the enemy surged on, since the pits were only large enough to hold a tithe of them, till at length, horsemen and footmen mixed up together in inextricable confusion, their mighty mass became faintly visible quite close to us, a blacker blot upon the gloom.

Then my turn came. When they were not more than fifty yards away from the first wall, I shouted an order to my riflemen to fire, aiming low, and set the example by loosing both barrels of an elephant gun at the thickest of the mob. At that distance even the most inexperienced shots could not miss such a mark, especially as those bullets that went high struck among the oncoming troops behind, or caught the horsemen lifted above their fellows. Indeed, of the first few rounds I do not think that one was wasted, while often single balls killed or injured several men.

The result was instantaneous. The Black Kendah who, be it remembered, were totally unaccustomed to the effects of rifle fire and imagined that we only possessed two or three guns in all, stopped their advance as though paralyzed. For a few seconds there was silence, except for the intermittent crackle of the rifles as my men loaded and fired. Next came the cries of the smitten men and horses that were falling everywhere, and then—the unmistakable sound of a stampede.

"They have gone. That was too warm for them, Baas," chuckled Hans exultingly.

"Yes," I answered, when I had at length succeeded in stopping the firing, "but I expect they will come back with the light. Still, that trick of yours has cost them dear, Hans."

By degrees the dawn began to break. It was, I remember, a particularly beautiful dawn, resembling a gigantic and vivid rose opening in the east, or a cup of brightness from which many coloured wines were poured all athwart the firmament. Very peaceful also, for not a breath of wind was stirring. But what a scene the first rays of the sun revealed upon that narrow stretch of pass in front of us. Everywhere the pitfalls and trenches were filled with still surging heaps of men and horses, while all about lay dead and wounded men, the red harvest of our rifle fire. It was dreadful to contrast the heavenly peace above and the hellish horror beneath.

We took count and found that up to this moment we had not lost a single man, one only having been slightly wounded by a thrown spear. As is common among semi-savages, this fact filled the White Kendah with an undue exultation. Thinking that as the beginning was so the end must be, they cheered and shouted, shaking each other's hands, then fell to eating the food which the women brought them with appetite, chattering incessantly, although as a general rule they were very silent people. Even the grave Harût, who arrived full of congratulations, seemed as high-spirited as a boy, till I reminded him that the real battle had not yet commenced.

The Black Kendah had fallen into a trap and lost some of their number, that was all, which was fortunate for us but could scarcely affect the issue of the struggle, since they had many thousands left. Ragnall, who had come up from his lines, agreed with me. As he said, these people were fighting for life as well as honour, seeing that most of the corn which they needed for their sustenance was stored in great heaps either in or to the rear of the temple behind us. Therefore they must come on until they won or were destroyed. How with our small force could we hope to destroy this multitude? That was the problem which weighed upon our hearts.

About a quarter of an hour later two spies that we had set upon the top of the precipitous cliffs, whence they had a good view of the pass beyond the bend, came scrambling down the rocks like monkeys by a route that was known to them. These boys, for they were no more, reported that the Black Kendah were reforming their army beyond the bend of the pass, and that the cavalry were dismounting and sending their horses to the rear, evidently because they found them useless in such a place. A little later solitary men appeared from behind the bend, carrying bundles of long sticks to each of which was attached a piece of white cloth, a proceeding that excited my curiosity.

Soon its object became apparent. Swiftly these men, of whom in the end there may have been thirty or forty, ran to and fro, testing the ground with spears in search for pitfalls. I think they only found a very few that had not been broken into, but in front of these and also of those that were already full of men and horses they set up the flags as a warning that they should be avoided in the advance. Also they removed a number of their wounded.

We had great difficulty in restraining the White Kendah from rushing out to attack them, which of course would only have led us into a trap in our turn, since they would have fled and conducted their pursuers into the arms of the enemy. Nor would I allow my riflemen to fire, as the result must have been many misses and a great waste of ammunition which ere long would be badly wanted. I, however, did shoot two or three, then gave it up as the remainder took no notice whatever.

When they had thoroughly explored the ground they retired until, a little later, the Black Kendah army began to appear, marching in serried regiments and excellent order round the bend, till perhaps eight or ten thousand of them were visible, a very fierce and awe-inspiring *impi*. Their front ranks halted between three and four hundred yards away, which I thought farther off than it was advisable to open fire on them with Snider rifles held by unskilled troops. Then came a pause, which at length was broken by the blowing of horns and a sound of exultant shouting beyond the turn of the pass.

Now from round this turn appeared the strangest sight that I think my eyes had ever seen. Yes, there came the huge elephant, Jana, at a slow, shambling trot. On his back and head were two men in whom, with my glasses, I recognized the lame priest whom I already knew too well and Simba, the king of the Black Kendah, himself, gorgeously apparelled and waving a long spear, seated in a kind of wooden chair. Round the brute's neck were a number of bright metal chains, twelve in all, and each of these chains was held by a spearman who ran alongside, six on one side and six on the other. Lastly, ingeniously fastened to the end of his trunk were three other chains to which were attached spiked knobs of metal.

On he came as docilely as any Indian elephant used for carrying teak logs, passing through the centre of the host up a wide lane which had been left, I suppose for his convenience, and intelligently avoiding the pitfalls filled with dead. I thought that he would stop among the first ranks. But not so. Slackening his pace to a walk he marched forwards towards our fortifications. Now, of course, I saw my chance and made sure that my double-barrelled elephant rifle was ready and that Hans held a second rifle, also double-barrelled and of similar calibre, full-cocked in such a position that I could snatch it from him in a moment.

"I am going to kill that elephant," I said. "Let no one else fire. Stand still and you shall see the god Jana die."

Still the enormous beast floundered forward; up to that moment I had never realized how truly huge it was, not even when it stood over me in the moonlight about to crush me with its foot. Of this I am sure, that none to equal it ever lived in Africa, at least in any times of which I have knowledge.

"Fire, Baas," whispered Hans, "it is near enough."

But like the Frenchman and the cock pheasant, I determined to wait until it stopped, wishing to finish it with a single ball, if only for the prestige of the thing.

At length it did stop and, opening its cavern of a mouth, lifted its great trunk and trumpeted, while Simba, standing up in his chair, began to shout out some command to us to surrender to the god Jana, "the Invincible, the Invulnerable."

"I will show you if you are invulnerable, my boy," said I to myself, glancing round to make sure that Hans had the second rifle ready and catching sight of Ragnall and Harût and all the White Kendah standing up in their trenches, breathlessly awaiting the end, as were the Black Kendah a few hundred yards away. Never could there have been a fairer shot and one more certain to result in a fatal wound. The brute's head was up and its mouth was open. All I had to do was to send a hard-tipped bullet crashing through the palate to the brain behind. It was so easy that I would have made a bet that I could have finished him with one hand tied behind me.

I lifted the heavy rifle. I got the sights dead on to a certain spot at the back of that red cave. I pressed the trigger; the charge boomed—and nothing happened! I heard no bullet strike and Jana did not even take the trouble to close his mouth.

An exclamation of "O-oh!" went up from the watchers. Before it had died away the second bullet followed the first, with the same result or rather lack of result, and another louder "O-oh!" arose. Then Jana tranquilly shut his mouth, having finished trumpeting, and as though to give me a still better target, turned broadside on and stood quite still.

With an inward curse I snatched the second rifle and aiming behind the ear at a spot which long experience told me covered the heart let drive again, first one barrel and then the other.

Jana never stirred. No bullet thudded. No mark of blood appeared upon his hide. The horrible thought overcame me that I, Allan Quatermain, I the famous shot, the renowned elephant-hunter, had four times missed this haystack of a brute from a distance of forty yards. So great was my shame that I think I almost fainted. Through a kind of mist I heard various exclamations:

"Great Heavens!" said Ragnall.

"*Allemagte!*" remarked Hans.

"The Child help us!" muttered Harût.

All the rest of them stared at me as though I were a freak or a lunatic. Then somebody laughed nervously, and immediately everybody began to laugh. Even the distant army of the Black Kendah became convulsed with roars of unholy merriment and I, Allan Quatermain, was the centre of all this mockery, till I felt as though I were going mad. Suddenly the laughter ceased and once more Simba the King began to roar out something about "Jana the Invincible and Invulnerable," to which the White Kendah replied with cries of "Magic" and "Bewitched! Bewitched!"

"Yes," yelled Simba, "no bullet can touch Jana the god, not even those of the white lord who was brought from far to kill him."

Hans leaped on to the top of the wall, where he danced up and down like an intoxicated monkey, and screamed:

"Then where is Jana's left eye? Did not my bullet put it out like a lamp? If Jana is invulnerable, why did my bullet put out his left eye?"

Hans ceased from dancing on the wall and steadying himself, lifted the little rifle Intombi, shouting:

"Let us see whether after all this beast is a god or an elephant."

Then he touched the trigger, and simultaneously with the report, I heard the bullet clap and saw blood appear on Jana's hide just by the very spot over the heart at which I had aimed without result. Of course, the soft ball driven from a small-bore rifle with a light charge of powder was far too weak to penetrate to the vitals. Probably it did not do much more than pierce through the skin and an inch or two of flesh behind it.

Still, its effects upon this "invulnerable" god were of a marked order. He whipped round; he lifted his trunk and screamed with rage and pain. Then off he lumbered back towards his own people, at such a pace that the attendants who held the chains on either side of him were thrown over and forced to leave go of him, while the king and the priest upon his back could only retain their seats by clinging to the chair and the rope about his neck.

The result was satisfactory so far as the dispelling of magical illusions went, but it left me in a worse position than before, since it now became evident that what had protected Jana from my bullets was nothing more supernatural than my own lack of skill. Oh! never in my life did I drink of such a cup of humiliation as it was my lot to drain to the dregs in this most unhappy hour. Almost did I hope that I might be killed at once.

And yet, and yet, how was it possible that with all my skill I should have missed this towering mountain of flesh four times in succession. The question is one to which I have never discovered any answer, especially as Hans hit it easily enough, which at the time I wished heartily he had not done, since his success only served to emphasize my miserable failure. Fortunately, just then a diversion occurred which freed my unhappy self from further public attention. With a shout and a roar the great army of the Black Kendah woke into life.

The advance had begun.

XX

ALLAN WEEPS

On they came, slowly and steadily, preceded by a cloud of skirmishers—a thousand or more of these—who kept as open an order as the narrow ground would allow and carried, each of them, a bundle of throwing spears arranged in loops or sockets at the back of the shield. When these men were about a hundred yards away we opened fire and killed a great number of them, also some of the marshalled troops behind. But this did not stop them in the least, for what could fifty rifles do against a horde of brave barbarians who, it seemed, had no fear of death? Presently their spears were falling among us and a few casualties began to occur, not many, because of the protecting wall, but still some. Again and again we loaded and fired, sweeping away those in front of us, but always others came to take their places. Finally at some word of command these light skirmishers vanished, except whose who were dead or wounded, taking shelter behind the advancing regiments which now were within fifty yards of us.

Then, after a momentary pause another command was shouted out and the first regiment charged in three solid ranks. We fired a volley point blank into them and, as it was hopeless for fifty men to withstand such an onslaught, bolted during the temporary confusion that ensued, taking refuge, as it had been arranged that we should do, at a point of vantage farther down the line of fortifications, whence we maintained our galling fire.

Now it was that the main body of the White Kendah came into action under the leadership of Ragnall and Harût. The enemy scrambled over the first wall, which we had just vacated, to find themselves in a network of other walls held by our spearmen in a narrow place where numbers gave no great advantage.

Here the fighting was terrible and the loss of the attackers great, for always as they carried one entrenchment they found another a few yards in front of them, out of which the defenders could only be driven at much cost of life.

Two hours or more the battle went on thus. In spite of the desperate resistance which we offered, the multitude of the Black Kendah, who I must say fought magnificently, stormed wall after wall, leaving hundreds of dead and wounded to mark their difficult progress. Meanwhile I and my riflemen rained bullets on them from certain positions which we had selected beforehand, until at length our ammunition began to run low.

At half-past eight in the morning we were driven back over the open ground to our last entrenchment, a very strong one just outside of the eastern gate of the temple which, it will be remembered, was set in a tunnel pierced through the natural lava rock. Thrice did the Black Kendah come on and thrice we beat them off, till the ditch in front of the wall was almost full of fallen. As fast as they climbed to the top of it the White Kendah thrust them through with their long spears, or we shot them with our rifles, the nature of the ground being such that only a direct frontal attack was possible.

In the end they drew back sullenly, having, as we hoped, given up the assault. As it turned out, this was not so. They were only resting and waiting for the arrival of their reserve. It came up shouting and singing a war-song, two thousand strong or more, and presently once more they charged like a flood of water. We beat them back. They reformed and charged a second time and we beat them back.

Then they took another counsel. Standing among the dead and dying at the base of the wall, which was built of loose stones and earth, where we could not easily get at them because of the showers of spears which were rained at anyone who showed himself, they began to undermine it, levering out the bottom stones with stakes and battering them with poles.

In five minutes a breach appeared, through which they poured tumultuously. It was hopeless to withstand that onslaught of so vast a number. Fighting desperately, we were driven down the tunnel and through the doors that were opened to us, into the first court of the temple. By furious efforts we managed to close these doors and block them with stones and earth. But this did not avail us long, for, bringing brushwood and dry grass, they built a fire against them that soon caught the thick cedar wood of which they were made.

While they burned we consulted together. Further retreat seemed impossible, since the second court of the temple, save for a narrow passage, was filled with corn which allowed no room for fighting, while behind it were gathered all the women and children, more than two thousand of them. Here, or nowhere, we must make our stand and conquer or die. Up to this time, compared with what which we had inflicted upon the Black Kendah, of whom a couple of thousand or more had fallen, our loss was comparatively slight, say two hundred killed and as many more wounded. Most of such of the latter as could not walk we had managed to carry into the first court of the temple, laying them close against the cloister walls, whence they watched us in a grisly ring.

This left us about sixteen hundred able-bodied men or many more than we could employ with effect in that narrow place. Therefore we determined to act upon a plan which we had already designed in case such an emergency as ours should arise. About three hundred and fifty of the best men were to remain to defend the temple till all were slain. The rest, to the number of over a thousand, were to withdraw through the second court and the gates beyond to the camp of the women and children. These they were to conduct by secret paths that were known to them to where the camels were kraaled, and mounting as many as possible of them on the camels to fly whither they could. Our hope was that the victorious Black Kendah would be too exhausted to follow them across the plain to the distant mountains. It was a dreadful determination, but we had no choice.

"What of my wife?" Ragnall asked hoarsely.

"While the temple stands she must remain in the temple," replied Harût. "But when all is lost, if I have fallen, do you, White Lord, go to the sanctuary with those who remain and take her and the Ivory Child and flee after the others. Only I lay this charge on you under pain of the curse of Heaven, that you do not suffer the Ivory Child to fall into the hands of the Black Kendah. First must you burn it with fire or grind it to dust with stones. Moreover, I give this command to all in case of the priests in charge of it should fail me, that they set flame to the brushwood that is built up with the stacks of corn, so that, after all, those of our enemies who escape may die of famine."

Instantly and without murmuring, for never did I see more perfect discipline than that which prevailed among these poor people, the orders given by Harût, who in addition to his office as head priest was a kind of president of what was in fact a republic, were put in the way of execution. Company by company the men appointed to escort the women and children departed through the gateway of the second court, each company turning in the gateway to salute us who remained, by raising their spears, till all were gone. Then we, the three hundred and fifty who were left, marshalled ourselves as the Greeks may have done in the Pass of Thermopylæ.

First stood I and my riflemen, to whom all the remaining ammunition was served out; it amounted to eight rounds per man. Then, ranged across the court in four lines, came the spearmen armed with lances and swords under the immediate command of Harût. Behind these, near the gate of the second court so that at the last they might attempt the rescue of the priestess, were fifty picked men, captained by Ragnall, who, I forgot to say, was wounded in two places, though not badly, having received a spear thrust in the left shoulder and a sword cut to the left thigh during his desperate defence of the entrenchment.

By the time that all was ready and every man had been given to drink from the great jars of water which stood along the walls, the massive wooden doors began to burn through, though this did not happen for quite half an hour after the enemy had begun to attempt to fire them. They fell at length beneath the battering of poles, leaving only the mound of earth and stones which we had piled up in the gateway after the closing of the doors. This the Black Kendah, who had raked out the burning embers, set themselves to dig away with hands and sticks and spears, a task that was made very difficult to them by about a score of our people who stabbed at them with their long lances or dashed them down with stones, killing and disabling many. But always the dead and wounded were dragged off while others took their places, so that at last the gateway was practically cleared. Then I called back the spearmen who passed into the ranks behind us, and made ready to play my part.

I had not long to wait. With a rush and a roar a great company of the Black Kendah charged the gateway. Just as they began to emerge into the court I gave the word to fire, sending fifty Snider bullets tearing into them from a distance of a few yards. They fell in a heap; they fell like corn before the scythe, not a man won through. Quickly we reloaded and waited for the next rush. In due course it came and the dreadful scene repeated itself. Now the gateway and the tunnel beyond were so choked with fallen men that the enemy must drag these out before they could charge any more. It was done under the fire of myself, Hans and a few picked shots—somehow it was done.

Once more they charged, and once more were mown down. So it went on till our last cartridge was spent, for never did I see more magnificent courage than was shown by those Black Kendah in the face of terrific loss. Then my people threw aside their useless rifles and arming themselves with spears and swords fell back to rest, leaving Harût and his company to take their place. For half an hour or more raged that awful struggle, since the spot being so narrow, charge as they would, the Black Kendah could not win through the spears of despairing warriors defending their lives and the sanctuary of their god. Nor, the encircling cliffs being so sheer, could they get round any other way.

At length the enemy drew back as though defeated, giving us time to drag aside our dead and wounded and drink more water, for the heat in the place was now overwhelming. We hoped against hope that they had given up the attack. But this was far from the case; they were but making a new plan.

Suddenly in the gateway there appeared the huge bulk of the elephant Jana, rushing forward at speed and being urged on by men who pricked it with spears behind. It swept through the defenders as though they were but dry grass, battering those in front of it with its great trunk from which swung the iron balls that crushed all on whom they fell, and paying no more heed to the lance thrusts than it might have done to the bites of gnats. On it came, trumpeting and trampling, and after it in a flood flowed the Black Kendah, upon whom our spearmen flung themselves from either side.

At the time I, followed by Hans, was just returning from speaking with Ragnall at the gate of the second court. A little before I had retired exhausted from the fierce and fearful fighting, whereon he took my place and repelled several of the Black Kendah charges, including the last. In this fray he received a further injury, a knock on the head from a stick or stone which stunned him for a few minutes, whereon some of our people had carried him off and set him on the ground with his back against one of the pillars of the second gate. Being told that he was hurt I ran to see what was the matter. Finding to my joy that it was nothing very serious, I was hurrying to the front again when I looked up and saw that devil Jana charging straight towards me, the throng of armed men parting on each side of him, as rough water does before the leaping prow of a storm-driven ship.

To tell the truth, although I was never fond of unnecessary risks, I rejoiced at the sight. Not even all the excitement of that hideous and prolonged battle had obliterated from my mind the burning sense of shame at the exhibition which I had made of myself by missing this beast with four barrels at forty yards.

Now, thought I to myself with a kind of exultant thrill, now, Jana, I will wipe out both my disgrace and you. This time there shall be no mistake, or if there is, let it be my last.

On thundered Jana, whirling the iron balls among the soldiers, who fled to right and left leaving a clear path between me and him. To make quite sure of things, for I was trembling a little with fatigue and somewhat sick from the continuous sight of bloodshed, I knelt down upon my right knee, using the other as a prop for my left elbow, and since I could not make certain of a head shot because of the continual whirling of the huge trunk, got the sight of my big-game rifle dead on to the beast where the throat joins the chest. I hoped that the heavy conical bullet would either pierce through to the spine or cut one of the large arteries in the neck, or at least that the tremendous shock of its impact would bring him down.

At about twenty paces I fired and hit—not Jana but the lame priest who was fulfilling the office of mahout, perched upon his shoulders many feet above the point at which I had aimed. Yes! I hit him in the head, which was shattered like an eggshell, so that he fell lifeless to the ground.

In perfect desperation again I aimed, and fired when Jana was not more than thirty feet away. This time the bullet must have gone wide to the left, for I saw a chip fly from the end of the animal's broken and deformed tusk, which stuck out in that direction several feet clear of its side.

Then I gave up all hope. There was no time to gain my feet and escape; indeed I did not wish to do so, who felt that there are some failures which can only be absolved by death. I just knelt there, waiting for the end.

In an instant the giant creature was almost over me. I remember looking up at it and thinking in a queer sort of a way—perhaps it was some ancestral memory—that I was a little ape-like child about to be slain by a primordial elephant, thrice as big as any that now inhabit the earth. Then something appeared to happen which I only repeat to show how at such moments absurd and impossible things seem real to us.

The reader may remember the strange dream which Hans had related to me that morning.

One incident of this phantasy was that he had met the spirit of the Zulu lady Mameena, whom I knew in bygone years, and that she bade him tell me she would be with me in the battle and that I was to look for her when death drew near to me and "Jana thundered on," for then perchance I should see her.

Well, no doubt in some lightning flash of thought the memory of these words occurred to me at this juncture, with the ridiculous result that my subjective intelligence, if that is the right term, actually created the scene which they described. As clearly, or perhaps more clearly than ever I saw anything else in my life, I appeared to behold the beautiful Mameena in her fur cloak and her blue beads, standing between Jana and myself with her arms folded upon her breast and looking exactly as she did in the tremendous moment of her death before King Panda. I even noted how the faint breeze stirred a loose end of her outspread hair and how the sunlight caught a particular point of a copper bangle on her upper arm.

So she stood, or rather seemed to stand, quite still; and as it happened, at that moment the giant Jana, either because something had frightened him, or perhaps owing to the shock of my bullet striking on his tusk having jarred the brain, suddenly pulled up, sliding along a little with all his four feet together, till I thought he was going to sit down like a performing elephant. Then it appeared to me as though Mameena turned round very slowly, bent towards me, whispering something which I could not hear although her lips moved, looked at me sweetly with those wonderful eyes of hers and vanished away.

A fraction of a second later all this vision had gone and something that was no vision took its place. Jana had recovered himself and was at me again with open mouth and lifted trunk. I heard a Dutch curse and saw a little yellow form; saw Hans, for it was he, thrust the barrels of my second elephant rifle almost into that red cave of a mouth, which however they could not reach, and fire, first one barrel, then the other.

Another moment, and the mighty trunk had wrapped itself about Hans and hurled him through the air to fall on to his head and arms thirty or forty feet away.

Jana staggered as though he too were about to fall; recovered himself, swerved to the right, perhaps to follow Hans, stumbled on a few paces, missing me altogether, then again came to a standstill. I wriggled myself round and, seated on the pavement of the court, watched what followed, and glad am I that I was able to do so, for never shall I behold such another scene.

First I saw Ragnall run up with a rifle and fire two barrels at the brute's head, of which he took no notice whatsoever. Then I saw his wife, who in this land was known as the Guardian of the Child, issuing from the portals of the second court, dressed in her goddess robes, wearing the cap of bird's feathers, attended by the two priestesses also dressed as goddesses, as we had seen her on the morning of sacrifice, and holding in front of her the statue of the Ivory Child.

On she came quite quietly, her wide, empty eyes fixed upon Jana. As she advanced the monster seemed to grow uneasy. Turning his head, he lifted his trunk and thrust it along his back until it gripped the ankle of the King Simba, who all this while was seated there in his chair making no movement.

With a slow, steady pull he dragged Simba from the chair so that he fell upon the ground near his left foreleg. Next very composedly he wound his trunk about the body of the helpless man, whose horrified eyes I can see to this day, and began to whirl him round and round in the air, gently at first but with a motion that grew ever more rapid, until the bright chains on the victim's breast flashed in the sunlight like a silver wheel. Then he hurled him to the ground, where the poor king lay a mere shattered pulp that had been human.

Now the priestess was standing in front of the beast-god, apparently quite without fear, though her two attendants had fallen back. Ragnall sprang forward as though to drag her away, but a dozen men leapt on to him and held him fast, either to save his life or for some secret reason of their own which I never learned.

Jana looked down at her and she looked up at Jana. Then he screamed furiously and, shooting out his trunk, snatched the Ivory Child from her hands, whirled it round as he had whirled Simba, and at last dashed it to the stone pavement as he had dashed Simba, so that its substance, grown brittle on the passage of the ages, shattered into ten thousand fragments.

At this sight a great groan went up from the men of the White Kendah, the women dressed as goddesses shrieked and tore their robes, and Harût, who stood near, fell down in a fit or faint.

Once more Jana screamed. Then slowly he knelt down, beat his trunk and the clattering metal balls upon the ground thrice, as though he were making obeisance to the beautiful priestess who stood before him, shivered throughout his mighty bulk, and rolled over—dead!

THE FIGHTING CEASED. THE BLACK Kendah, who all this while had been pressing into the court of the temple, saw and stood stupefied.

It was as though in the presence of events to them so pregnant and terrible men could no longer lift their swords in war.

A voice called: "The god is dead! The king is dead! Jana has slain Simba and has himself been slain! Shattered is the Child; spilt is the blood of Jana! Fly, People of the Black Kendah; fly, for the gods are dead and your land is a land of ghosts!"

From every side was this wail echoed: "Fly, People of the Black Kendah, for the gods are dead!"

They turned; they sped away like shadows, carrying their wounded with them, nor did any attempt to stay them. Thirty minutes later, save for some desperately hurt or dying men, not one of them was left in the temple or the pass beyond. They had all gone, leaving none but the dead behind them.

The fight was finished! The fight that had seemed lost was won!

I DRAGGED MYSELF FROM THE ground. As I gained my tottering feet, for now that all was over I felt as if I were made of running water, I saw the men who held Ragnall loose their grip of him. He sprang to where his wife was and stood before her as though confused, much as Jana had stood, Jana against whose head he rested, his left hand holding to the brute's gigantic tusk, for I think that he also was weak with toil, terror, loss of blood and emotion.

"Luna," he gasped, "Luna!"

Leaning on the shoulder of a Kendah man, I drew nearer to see what passed between them, for my curiosity overcame my faintness. For quite a long while she stared at him, till suddenly her eyes began to change. It was as though a soul were arising in their emptiness as the moon arises in the quiet evening sky, giving them light and life. At length she spoke in a slow, hesitating voice, the tones of which I remembered well enough, saying:

"Oh! George, that dreadful brute," and she pointed to the dead elephant, "has killed our baby. Look at it! Look at it! We must be everything to each other now, dear, as we were before it came—unless God sends us another."

Then she burst into a flood of weeping and fell into his arms, after which I turned away. So, to their honour be it said, did the Kendah, leaving the pair alone behind the bulk of dead Jana.

Here I may state two things: first, that Lady Ragnall, whose bodily health had remained perfect throughout, entirely recovered her reason from that moment. It was as though on the shattering of the Ivory Child some spell had been lifted off her. What this spell may have been I am quite unable to explain, but I presume that in a dim and unknown way she connected this effigy with her own lost infant and that while she held and tended it her intellect remained in abeyance. If so, she must also have connected its destruction with the death of her own child which, strangely enough, it will be remembered, was likewise killed by an elephant. The first death that occurred in her presence took away her reason, the second seeming death, which also occurred in her presence, brought it back again!

Secondly, from the moment of the destruction of her boy in the streets of the English country town to that of the shattering of the Ivory Child in Central Africa her memory was an utter blank, with one exception. This exception was a dream which a few days later she narrated to Ragnall in my presence. That dream was that she had seen him and Savage sleeping together in a native house one night. In view of a certain incident recorded in this history I leave the reader to draw his own conclusions as to this curious incident. I have none to offer, or if I have I prefer to keep them to myself.

Leaving Ragnall and his wife, I staggered off to look for Hans and found him lying senseless near the north wall of the temple. Evidently he was beyond human help, for Jana seemed to have crushed most of his ribs in his iron trunk. We carried him to one of the priest's cells and there I watched him till the end, which came at sundown.

Before he died he became quite conscious and talked with me a good deal.

"Don't grieve about missing Jana, Baas," he said, "for it wasn't you who missed him but some devil that turned your bullets. You see, Baas, he was bewitched against you white men. When you look at him closely you will find that the Lord Igeza missed him also" (strange as it may seem, this proved to be the case), "and when you managed to hit the tip of his tusk with the last ball the magic was wearing off him, that's all. But, Baas, those Black Kendah wizards forgot to bewitch him against the little yellow man, of whom they took no account. So I hit him sure enough every time I fired at him, and I hope he liked the taste of my bullets in that great mouth of his. He knew who had sent them there very well. That's why he left you alone and made for me, as I had hoped he would. Oh! Baas, I die happy, quite happy since I have killed Jana and he caught me and not you, me who was nearly finished anyhow.

For, Baas, though I didn't say anything about it, a thrown spear struck my groin when I went down among the Black Kendah this morning. It was only a small cut, which bled little, but as the fighting went on something gave way and my inside began to come through it, though I tied it up with a bit of cloth, which of course means death in a day or two." (Subsequent examination showed me that Hans's story of this wound was perfectly true. He could not have lived for very long.)

"Baas," he went on after a pause, "no doubt I shall meet that Zulu lady Mameena to-night. Tell me, is she really entitled to the royal salute? Because if not, when I am as much a spook as she is I will not give it to her again. She never gave me my titles, which are good ones in their way, so why should I give her the *Bayéte*, unless it is hers by right of blood, although I am only a little 'yellow dog' as she chose to call me?"

As this ridiculous point seemed to weigh upon his mind I told him that Mameena was not even of royal blood and in nowise entitled to the salute of kings.

"Ah!" he said with a feeble grin, "then now I shall know how to deal with her, especially as she cannot pretend that I did not play my part in the battle, as she bade me do. Did you see anything of her when Jana charged, Baas, because I thought I did?"

"I seemed to see something, but no doubt it was only a fancy."

"A fancy? Explain to me, Baas, where truths end and fancies begin and whether what we think are fancies are not sometimes the real truths. Once or twice I have thought so of late, Baas."

I could not answer this riddle, so instead I gave him some water which he asked for, and he continued:

"Baas, have you any messages for the two Shining ones, for her whose name is holy and her sister, and for the child of her whose name is holy, the Missie Marie, and for your reverend father, the Predikant? If so, tell it quickly before my head grows too empty to hold the words."

I will confess, however foolish it may seem, that I gave him certain messages, but what they were I shall not write down. Let them remain secret between me and him. Yes, between me and him and perhaps those to whom they were to be delivered. For after all, in his own words, who can know exactly where fancies end and truth begin, and whether at times fancies are not the veritable truths in this universal mystery of which the individual life of each of us is so small a part?

Hans repeated what I had spoken to him word for word, as a native does, repeated it twice over, after which he said he knew it by heart and remained silent for a long while. Then he asked me to lift him up in the doorway of the cell so that he might look at the sun setting for the last time, "for, Baas," he added, "I think I am going far beyond the sun."

He stared at it for a while, remarking that from the look of the sky there should be fine weather coming, "which will be good for your journey towards the Black Water, Baas, with all that ivory to carry."

I answered that perhaps I should never get the ivory from the graveyard of the elephants, as the Black Kendah might prevent this.

"No, no, Baas," he replied, "now that Jana is dead the Black Kendah will go away. I know it, I know it!"

Then he wandered for a space, speaking of sundry adventures we had shared together, till quite before the last indeed, when his mind returned to him.

"Baas," he said, "did not the captain Mavovo name me Light-in-Darkness, and is not that my name? When you too enter the Darkness, look for that Light; it will be shining very close to you."

He only spoke once more. His words were:

"Baas, I understand now what your reverend father, the Predikant, meant when he spoke to me about Love last night. It had nothing to do with women, Baas, at least not much. It was something a great deal bigger, Baas, something as big as what I feel for you!"

Then Hans died with a smile on his wrinkled face.

I wept!

XXI

Homewards

There is not much more to write of this expedition, or if that statement be not strictly true, not much more that I wish to write, though I have no doubt that Ragnall, if he had a mind that way, could make a good and valuable book concerning many matters on which, confining myself to the history of our adventure, I have scarcely touched. All the affinities between this Central African Worship of the Heavenly Child and its Guardian and that of Horus and Isis in Egypt from which it was undoubtedly descended, for instance. Also the part which the great serpent played therein, as it may be seen playing a part in every tomb upon the Nile, and indeed plays a part in our own and other religions. Further, our journey across the desert to the Red Sea was very interesting, but I am tired of describing journeys—and of making them.

The truth is that after the death of Hans, like to Queen Sheba when she had surveyed the wonders of Solomon's court, there was no more spirit in me. For quite a long while I did not seem to care at all what happened to me or to anybody else. We buried him in a place of honour, exactly where he shot Jana before the gateway of the second court, and when the earth was thrown over his little yellow face I felt as though half my past had departed with him into that hole. Poor drunken old Hans, where in the world shall I find such another man as you were? Where in the world shall I find so much love as filled the cup of that strange heart of yours?

I dare say it is a form of selfishness, but what every man desires is something that cares for him *alone*, which is just why we are so fond of dogs. Now Hans was a dog with a human brain and he cared for me alone. Often our vanity makes us think that this has happened to some of us in the instance of one or more women. But honest and quiet reflection may well cause us to doubt the truth of such supposings. The woman who as we believed adored us solely has probably in the course of her career adored others, or at any rate other things.

To take but one instance, that of Mameena, the Zulu lady whom Hans thought he saw in the Shades. She, I believe, did me the honour to be very fond of me, but I am convinced that she was fonder still of her ambition. Now Hans never cared for any living creature, or for any human hope or object, as he cared for me. There was no man or woman whom he would not have cheated, or even murdered for my sake. There was no earthly advantage, down to that of life itself, that he would not, and in the end did not forgo for my sake; witness the case of his little fortune which he invested in my rotten gold mine and thought nothing of losing—for my sake.

That is love *in excelsis*, and the man who has succeeded in inspiring it in any creature, even in a low, bibulous, old Hottentot, may feel proud indeed. At least I am proud and as the years go by the pride increases, as the hope grows that somewhere in the quiet of that great plain which he saw in his dream, I may find the light of Hans's love burning like a beacon in the darkness, as he promised I should do, and that it may guide and warm my shivering, new-born soul before I dare the adventure of the Infinite.

Meanwhile, since the sublime and the ridiculous are so very near akin, I often wonder how he and Mameena settled that question of her right to the royal salute. Perhaps I shall learn one day—indeed already I have had a hint of it. If so, even in the blaze of a new and universal Truth, I am certain that their stories will differ wildly.

HANS WAS QUITE RIGHT ABOUT the Black Kendah. They cleared out, probably in search of food, where I do not know and I do not care, though whether this were a temporary or permanent move on their part remains, and so far as I am concerned is likely to remain, veiled in obscurity. They were great blackguards, though extraordinarily fine soldiers, and what became of them is a matter of complete indifference to me. One thing is certain, however, a very large percentage of them never migrated at all, for something over three thousand of their bodies did our people have to bury in the pass and about the temple, a purpose for which all the pits and trenches we had dug came in very useful. Our loss, by the way, was five hundred and three, including those who died of wounds. It was a great fight and, except for those who perished in the pitfalls during the first rush, all practically hand to hand.

Jana we interred where he fell because we could not move him, within a few feet of the body of his slayer Hans. I have always regretted that I did not take the exact measurements of this brute, as I believe the record elephant of the world, but I had no time to do so and no rule or tape at hand. I only saw him for a minute on the following morning, just as he was being tumbled into a huge hole, together with the remains of his master, Simba the King. I found, however, that the sole wounds upon him, save some cuts and scratches from spears, were those inflicted by Hans—namely, the loss of one eye, the puncture through the skin over the heart made when he shot at him for the second time with the little rifle Intombi, and two neat holes at the back of the mouth through which the bullets from the elephant gun had driven upwards to the base of the brain, causing his death from hæmorrhage on that organ.

I asked the White Kendah to give me his two enormous tusks, unequalled, I suppose, in size and weight in Africa, although one was deformed and broken. But they refused. These, I presume, they wished to keep, together with the chains off his breast and trunk, as mementoes of their victory over the god of their foes. At any rate they hewed the former out with axes and removed the latter before tumbling the carcass into the grave. From the worn-down state of the teeth I concluded that this beast must have been extraordinarily old, how old it is impossible to say.

That is all I have to tell of Jana. May he rest in peace, which certainly he will not do if Hans dwells anywhere in his neighbourhood, in the region which the old boy used to call that of the "fires that do not go out." Because of my horrible failure in connection with this beast, the very memory of which humiliates me, I do not like to think of it more than I can help.

For the rest the White Kendah kept faith with us in every particular. In a curious and semi-religious ceremony, at which I was not present, Lady Ragnall was absolved from her high office of Guardian or Nurse to a god whereof the symbol no longer existed, though I believe that the priests collected the tiny fragments of ivory, or as many of them as could be found, and preserved them in a jar in the sanctuary. After this had been done women stripped the Nurse of her hallowed robes, of the ancient origin of which, by the way, I believe that none of them, except perhaps Harût, had any idea, any more than they knew that the Child represented the Egyptian Horus and his lady Guardian the moon-goddess Isis. Then, dressed in some native garments, she was handed over to Ragnall and thenceforth treated as a stranger-guest, like ourselves, being allowed, however, to live with her husband in the same house that she had occupied during all the period of her strange captivity. Here they abode together, lost in the mutual bliss of this wonderful reunion to which they had attained through so much bodily and spiritual darkness and misery, until a month or so later we started upon our journey across the mountains and the great desert that lay beyond them.

Only once did I find any real opportunity of private conversation with Lady Ragnall.

This happened after her husband had recovered from the hurts he received in the battle, on an occasion when he was obliged to separate from her for a day in order to attend to some matter in the Town of the Child. I think it had to do with the rifles used in the battle, which he had presented to the White Kendah. So, leaving me to look after her, he went, unwillingly enough, who seemed to hate losing sight of his wife even for an hour.

I took her for a walk in the wood, to that very point indeed on the lip of the crater whence we had watched her play her part as priestess at the Feast of the First-fruits. After we had stood there a while we went down among the great cedars, trying to retrace the last part of our march through the darkness of that anxious night, whereof now for the first time I told her all the story.

Growing tired of scrambling among the fallen boughs, at length Lady Ragnall sat down and said:

"Do you know, Mr. Quatermain, these are the first words we have really had since that party at Ragnall before I was married, when, as you may have forgotten, you took me in to dinner."

I replied that there was nothing I recollected much more clearly, which was both true and the right thing to say, or so I supposed.

"Well," she said slowly, "you see that after all there was something in those fancies of mine which at the time you thought would best be dealt with by a doctor—about Africa and the rest, I mean."

"Yes, Lady Ragnall, though of course we should always remember that coincidence accounts for many things. In any case they are done with now."

"Not quite, Mr. Quatermain, even as you mean, since we have still a long way to go. Also in another sense I believe that they are but begun."

"I do not understand, Lady Ragnall."

"Nor do I, but listen. You know that of anything which happened during those months I have no memory at all, except of that one dream when I seemed to see George and Savage in the hut. I remember my baby being killed by that horrible circus elephant, just as the Ivory Child was killed or rather destroyed by Jana, which I suppose is another of your coincidences, Mr. Quatermain. After that I remember nothing until I woke up and saw George standing in front of me covered with blood, and you, and Jana dead, and the rest."

"Because during that time your mind was gone, Lady Ragnall."

"Yes, but where had it gone? I tell you, Mr. Quatermain, that although I remember nothing of what was passing about me then, I do remember a great deal of what seemed to be passing either long ago or in some time to come, though I have said nothing of it to George, as I hope you will not either. It might upset him."

"What do you remember?" I asked.

"That's the trouble; I can't tell you. What was once very clear to me has for the most part become vague and formless. When my mind tries to grasp it, it slips away. It was another life to this, quite a different life; and there was a great story in it of which I think what we have been going through is either a sequel or a prologue. I see, or saw, cities and temples with people moving about them, George and you among them, also that old priest, Harût. You will laugh, but my recollection is that you stood in some relationship to me, either that of father or brother."

"Or perhaps a cousin," I suggested.

"Or perhaps a cousin," she repeated, smiling, "or a great friend; at any rate something very intimate. As for George, I don't know what he was, or Harût either. But the odd thing is that little yellow man, Hans, whom I only saw once living for a few minutes that I can remember, comes more clearly back to my mind than any of you. He was a dwarf, much stouter than when I saw him the other day, but very like. I recall him curiously dressed with feathers and holding an ivory rod, seated upon a stool at the feet of a great personage—a king, I think. The king asked him questions, and everyone listened to his answers. That is all, except that the scenes seemed to be flooded with sunlight."

"Which is more than this place is. I think we had better be moving, Lady Ragnall, or you will catch a chill under these damp cedars."

I said this because I did not wish to pursue the conversation. I considered it too exciting under all her circumstances, especially as I perceived that mystical look gathering on her face and in her beautiful eyes, which I remembered noting before she was married.

She read my thoughts and answered with a laugh:

"Yes, it is damp; but you know I am very strong and damp will not hurt me. For the rest you need not be afraid, Mr. Quatermain. I did not lose my mind. It was taken from me by some power and sent to live elsewhere. Now it has been given back and I do not think it will be taken again in that way."

"Of course it won't," I exclaimed confidently. "Whoever dreamed of such a thing?"

"*You* did," she answered, looking me in the eyes. "Now before we go I want to say one more thing. Harût and the head priestess have made me a present. They have given me a box full of that herb they called tobacco, but of which I have discovered the real name is Taduki. It is the same that they burned in the bowl when you and I saw visions at Ragnall Castle, which visions, Mr. Quatermain, by another of your coincidences, have since been translated into facts."

"I know. We saw you breathe that smoke again as priestess when you uttered the prophecy as Oracle of the Child at the Feast of the First-fruits. But what are you going to do with this stuff, Lady Ragnall? I think you have had enough of visions just at present."

"So do I, though to tell you the truth I like them. I am going to keep it and do nothing—as yet. Still, I want you always to remember one thing—don't laugh at me"—here again she looked me in the eyes—"that there is a time coming, some way off I think, when I and you—no one else, Mr. Quatermain—will breathe that smoke again together and see strange things."

"No, no!" I replied, "I have given up tobacco of the Kendah variety; it is too strong for me."

"Yes, yes!" she said, "for something that is stronger than the Kendah tobacco will make you do it—when I wish."

"Did Harût tell you that, Lady Ragnall?"

"I don't know," she answered confusedly. "I think the Ivory Child told me; it used to talk to me often. You know that Child isn't really destroyed. Like my reason that seemed to be lost, it has only gone backwards or forwards where you and I shall see it again. You and I and no others—unless it be the little yellow man. I repeat that I do not know when that will be. Perhaps it is written in those rolls of papyrus, which they have given me also, because they said they belonged to me who am 'the first priestess and the last.' They told me, however, or perhaps," she added, passing her hand across her forehead, "it was the Child who told me, that I was not to attempt to read them or have them read, until after a great change in my life. What the change will be I do not know."

"And had better not inquire, Lady Ragnall, since in this world most changes are for the worse."

"I agree, and shall not inquire. Now I have spoken to you like this because I felt that I must do so. Also I want to thank you for all you have done for me and George. Probably we shall not talk in such a way again; as I am situated the opportunity will be lacking, even if the wish is present. So once more I thank you from my heart. Until we meet again—I mean really meet—good-bye," and she held her right hand to me in such a fashion that I knew she meant me to kiss it.

This I did very reverently and we walked back to the temple almost in silence.

THAT MONTH OF REST, OR rather the last three weeks of it, since for the first few days after the battle I was quite prostrate, I occupied in various ways, amongst others in a journey with Harût to Simba Town. This we made after our spies had assured us that the Black Kendah were really gone somewhere to the south-west, in which direction fertile and unoccupied lands were said to exist about three hundred miles away. It was with very strange feelings that I retraced our road and looked once more upon that wind-bent tree still scored with the marks of Jana's huge tusk, in the boughs of which Hans and I had taken refuge from the monster's fury. Crossing the river, quite low now, I travelled up the slope down which we raced for our lives and came to the melancholy lake and the cemetery of dead elephants.

Here all was unchanged. There was the little mount worn by his feet, on which Jana was wont to stand. There were the rocks behind which I had tried to hide, and near to them some crushed human bones which I knew to be those of the unfortunate Marût. These we buried with due reverence on the spot where he had fallen, I meanwhile thanking God that my own bones were not being interred at their side, as but for Hans would have been the case—if they were ever interred at all. All about lay the skeletons of dead elephants, and from among these we collected as much of the best ivory as we could carry, namely about fifty camel loads. Of course there was much more, but a great deal of the stuff had been exposed for so long to sun and weather that it was almost worthless.

Having sent this ivory back to the Town of the Child, which was being rebuilt after a fashion, we went on to Simba Town through the forest, dispatching pickets ahead of us to search and make sure that it was empty. Empty it was indeed; never did I see such a place of desolation.

The Black Kendah had left it just as it stood, except for a pile of corpses which lay around and over the altar in the market-place, where the three poor camelmen were sacrificed to Jana, doubtless those of wounded men who had died during or after the retreat. The doors of the houses stood open, many domestic articles, such as great jars resembling that which had been set over the head of the dead man whom we were commanded to restore life, and other furniture lay about because they could not be carried away. So did a great quantity of spears and various weapons of war, whose owners being killed would never want them again. Except a few starved dogs and jackals no living creature remained in the town. It was in its own way as waste and even more impressive than the graveyard of elephants by the lonely lake.

"The curse of the Child worked well," said Harût to me grimly. "First, the storm; the hunger; then the battle; and now the misery of flight and ruin."

"It seems so," I answered. "Yet that curse, like others, came back to roost, for if Jana is dead and his people fled, where are the Child and many of its people? What will you do without your god, Harût?"

"Repent us of our sins and wait till the Heavens send us another, as doubtless they will in their own season," he replied very sadly.

I wonder whether they ever did and, if so, what form that new divinity put on.

I slept, or rather did not sleep, that night in the same guest-house in which Marût and I had been imprisoned during our dreadful days of fear, reconstructing in my mind every event connected with them. Once more I saw the fires of sacrifice flaring upon the altar and heard the roar of the dancing hail that proclaimed the ruin of the Black Kendah as loudly as the trumpet of a destroying angel. Very glad was I when the morning came at length and, having looked my last upon Simba Town, I crossed the moats and set out homewards through the forest whereof the stripped boughs also spoke of death, though in the spring these would grow green again.

Ten days later we started from the Holy Mount, a caravan of about a hundred camels, of which fifty were laden with the ivory and the rest ridden by our escort under the command of Harût and our three selves. But there was an evil fate upon this ivory, as on everything else that had to do with Jana. Some weeks later in the desert a great sandstorm overtook us in which we barely escaped with our lives. At the height of the storm the ivory-laden camels broke loose, flying before it. Probably they fell and were buried beneath the sand; at any rate of the fifty we only recovered ten.

Ragnall wished to pay me the value of the remaining loads, which ran into thousands of pounds, but I would not take the money, saying it was outside our bargain. Sometimes since then I have thought that I was foolish, especially when on glancing at that codicil to his will in after days, the same which he had given me before the battle, I found that he had set me down for a legacy of £10,000. But in such matters every man must follow his own instinct.

The White Kendah, an unemotional people especially now when they were mourning for their lost god and their dead, watched us go without any demonstration of affection, or even of farewell. Only those priestesses who had attended upon the person of Lady Ragnall while she played a divine part among them wept when they parted from her, and uttered prayers that they might meet her again "in the presence of the Child."

The pass through the great mountains proved hard to climb, as the foothold for the camels was bad. But we managed it at last, most of the way on foot, pausing a little while on their crest to look our last for ever at the land which we had left, where the Mount of the Child was still dimly visible. Then we descended their farther slope and entered the northern desert.

Day after day and week after week we travelled across that endless desert by a way known to Harût on which water could be found, the only living things in all its vastness, meeting with no accidents save that of the sandstorm in which the ivory was lost. I was much alone during that time, since Harût spoke little and Ragnall and his wife were wrapped up in each other.

At length, months later, we struck a little port on the Red Sea, of which I forget the Arab name, a place as hot as the infernal regions. Shortly afterwards, by great good luck, two trading vessels put in for water, one bound for Aden, in which I embarked en route for Natal, and the other for the port of Suez, whence Ragnall and his wife could travel overland to Alexandria.

Our parting was so hurried at the last, as is often the way after long fellowship, that beyond mutual thanks and good wishes we said little to one another. I can see them now standing with their arms about each other watching me disappear. Concerning their future there is so much to tell that of it I shall say nothing; at any rate here and now, except that Lady Ragnall was right. We did not part for the last time.

As I shook old Harût's hand in farewell he told me that he was going on to Egypt, and I asked him why.

"Perchance to look for another god, Lord Macumazana," he answered gravely, "whom now there is no Jana to destroy. We may speak of that matter if we should meet again."

Such are some of the things that I remember about this journey, but to tell truth I paid little attention to them and many others.

For oh! my heart was sore because of Hans.

bookfinity & MINT EDITIONS

Enjoy more of your favorite classics with Bookfinity,
a new search and discovery experience for readers.
With Bookfinity, you can discover more vintage
literature for your collection, find your Reader Type,
track books you've read or want to read,
and add reviews to your favorite books.
Visit www.bookfinity.com, and click on
Take the Quiz to get started.

Don't forget to follow us
@bookfinityofficial and @mint_editions

CPSIA information can be obtained
at www.ICGtesting.com
Printed in the USA
JSHW010016170822
29340JS00005B/3

9 781513 277677